Blood on the Ground

Blood on the Ground

Paul Usiskin

Blood on the Ground / Paul Usiskin

Contact: melekhshaul66@gmail.com

ISBN 978-1537788036

For my Stephi (1950-2016)
My first star in the sky
Always with me.
Love you and let you go?
Never.

There are too many people to thank for the long gestation of this first Dov Chizzik saga. I apologize to those I may have left out. Amongst those I recall who helped and encouraged me, are Ahmad Khalidi, Richard Velleman, Dalia Fadila, Rosemary Hollis, Mohammad Darawashe, Lana Tatour, Lana from Arabba, Matt Fry, David Solomons, Anshel Pfeffer, Beni and Tali Carmi, Liam Erskine, and by no means least Tammi and Lawrence Levene.

There are bound to be errors in a book with this complex backdrop, and I accept full responsibility for them. After all, though based on fact, this is a work of fiction; it contains, as Aristotle preferred, more "probable impossibilities" than "possible improbabilities" and thus enabled me to take a few liberties. But sometimes, the paradoxes of this particular backdrop create fiction out of reality without an author trying too hard.

Chapter 1
September 1996

For Dov it was a city built on sand. It shouldn't stand. But it did. The sun hadn't consumed it. The sea hadn't engulfed it. He marveled at the magic of its survival. It laughed. It cried. It danced. It crawled. It was blind and deaf and dumb. It breathed. It choked. It mourned. It was a city of all seasons, this City of Spring, Tel Aviv. On a hill time had obliterated. It flourished out of desert sands where long ago, cornfields swayed in sea breezes. It was a young city for an old people. Ever sprawling. Its summer humidity suffocated everyone and itself. In winter the rains mixed with angry ocean waters trying to drench fine promenades. Behind its doors all manner of human behavior went on. It was Sodom and Gomorrah. Together.

Dov hated it and loved it. He knew its desires and its rejections. Sometimes what he knew scared him. Yet the first glimpse after he'd been away always brought tears to his eyes and a smile to his lips. It was his city. They were his people.

At passport control, his anonymity only lasted until the girl in the glass booth waved him through, smiling at his familiar face, Dov Chizzik, Super Cop.

He would walk on through the arrivals hall, and out through the waiting mob, defender of their morality, protector of their laws, their order. Part of them, but apart from them, on into a normal day.

He'd begun all those years ago, sharp and sure, certain of his vocation, ready to serve, ignoring his doubts. The last brick in his delusion was gently pulled away with the words of his boss, Commander Yigal Shalit. "You're promoted and transferred. It's a special sex crimes unit, TPI."

Murder investigations were clean. TPI wasn't just dirty. It reeked.

The scale of the sex industry bewildered him. It was the relentless 24/7 of it. He'd always been detached from death in the countless murder cases he'd solved. Sex he did too, and liked and enjoyed it. And so did everyone else in the city. Rich and poor, replete or starving, low-lit in cool silk sheets, on refuse-pocked sands, on leather couches, against derelict walls, all races, all ages. It was as if the city was an infinite insatiate beast.

"Why Vice?" he'd asked. "It's the pits." And then, "Why me?"

"This is Vice, but not as you know it," Shalit's smile was like a whore's come-on. "It's a new unit. You'll head it. Because the Commissioner says so."

"What's TPI stand for?"

"TPI – Techno-Pornography-Investigations. And it's final. You're heading it and there's no point appealing to your rabbi in the Justice Ministry."

"TPI. Sounds like a despatch company or a computer program."

Shalit removed his glasses and stared absently at their unblemished lenses. "There's an epidemic of video pornography. It's linked to women trafficking. We have to act."

"How big's the unit?"

"Two."

"And administrative support?"

"You'll use what we've got."

"We're going all out for it then."

"Nothing new. You know how we are, no budget increases, too many criminals."

Dov's daily fare had been murderers in all shapes and sizes. Now he would protect citizens from a different form of violation, pornography.

The zipless feckless fuck; it was all just a fuck. It came in many forms, or didn't come at all. The oldest profession in the world, now on industrial proportions, was alive and well in the city on the hill of spring.

"Who do I answer to?"

"Good question. And the answer is, me."

"You? TPI? Two men and a dog?"

"Dog? No budget for one." No smile. "We're short staffed. Why are you complaining? This is a promotion and more pay. We're now the same rank. But I'm your line manager and I'll always have the last word."

"Even if it's for a unit of two and shared admin? Who's my number two?"

"Aviel Weiss. You've worked with him before and we see him as an up and coming Detective Sergeant, bright, almost as bright as you."

"Welcome to the Israel Police Force."

They chorused the well worn comeback, "You're welcome to it!"

That was how Shalit recalled it, a firm but friendly discussion about a sideways promotion. Every policeman knew it took Samsonian efforts to erase the taint of Vice, once you worked it. Shalit hoped it would seal Dov's fate. He didn't like smartass heroes with degrees. Police work was all about relentless tough shit, degrees and medals could never replace it. He smiled at Dov in false congratulation. That was Shalit's recollection of their chat. It wasn't Dov's.

Dov Chizzik was thirty-eight at the time of his TPI appointment. He was five eleven with only a hint of paunch. Face on he was handsome, classical sculpted nose, good chin, eyes the color of bitter chocolate set well apart, conspicuous in a crowd, an unhelpful characteristic for a policeman. He looked more like an academic than an investigator, with slowly greying black hair, often tousled as his workday progressed. His wife Liora said he was growing old gracefully, and despite her mockery he loved her still. Or thought he did.

TPI brought him right up to a red line that he'd never confronted, the thick bloody line in the landscape of conscience. His introduction to video pornography hooked him immediately. He sat in front of the TV screen in his desk and watched. And watched. Soon, it was his phallus plunging in and out of a long lithe blonde in black stockings, whilst her crimson haired girlfriend licked them both. He had questions, trying to ignore his erection. Who were the women in those scenes? Where were they from? Who filmed them? Who paid? Why did the men always come outside the women?

"How was your day sweetheart?" Liora would ask, in his first TPI weeks, as they got in between the sheets and she reached for him the way she always had.

"It was fine, just fine," he'd reply, after they'd made love, but Liora wondered what had infused his new voraciousness.

He told her little; he'd always précised the details of his murder investigations. Was that early hypocrisy raising its nose above the line? No, he told himself, just protecting her. Of his TPI day he restricted himself to generalities.

Dov was born between wars, after the 1956 Suez campaign and before the 1967 Six Days War. His high school days were ordinary and happy, despite the constant threat of more wars. He was a well-adjusted only child from Ramat Gan, a northeast suburb, then not yet lost in the burgeoning Tel Aviv metropolis. He was good at sports, Hebrew and English literature, and Math and Biology. His father Dan was an ambitious bank clerk. His grandfather Dudik had been a right wing underground fighter. Fighters like him in the nationalist underground movements claimed they'd forced the British out of Palestine.

Dudik entered banking and was a natural business man. He found many from the nationalists' ranks drawn to making money after the 1948 War of Independence, reticent to publicly discuss their past, dreaming of the time when they could. His connections and influence helped smooth Dan's rise to district bank branch manager.

Dan imagined that Dov's school romance with Liora Livnat would secure Dov a career. So when he realized that her father Efi Livnat had been in the underground, he offered preferential terms to Efi's expanding foundry business. Then Dan moved house onto the Livnat's street in Ramat Gan.

Efi was tough, barking at workers, suppliers and contractors alike. He was as reliable as he was fierce but credit lines were essential. He had graduated from running a small collection of underground weapons making workshops through the late 1930s and 40s to producing everything from gun mounts to diesel engines for the IDF.

The mothers, Vikki Livnat and Hava Chizzik behaved like pious Victorians about their children's growing relationship but they were unable to stop their love struck children from seeing each other.

Dov loved everything about Liora. She was his height, slim, with shoulder length fair hair, intense blue eyes, and unswervingly loyal to him. She also loved him like crazy, but didn't make a fuss about it. Despite their families' growing wealth they were just a normal pair of youngsters, hanging out with the rest.

Nine o'clock on a Friday night they all gathered in the main square. The boys sat on the railings making sucking whistling noises as the girls flaunted themselves. Gershon and Gilad were classmates and became Dov's lifelong friends. Gershon was pale, gangly, quiet, a bit of a hanger on, and Gilad was a short, stocky, extrovert, but bright and straight. Gilad made the boys' noises, Gershon grinned nervously but did and said nothing. They envied Dov and Liora.

Dov would often sit in the school library reading histories of great Zionists. There were two Chizziks in the books, Dov told Liora proudly, "One died in a Bedouin raid in 1920. She was only two years older than me. The other was briefly military governor of Yafo after '48."

"Destined for greatness then, are you?" Liora teased.

He had ambition, for what he wasn't clear, but greatness he didn't understand.

***

The big gun's shattering crash, firing up at the Beaufort Castle, had no impact on Dov. As commander he was immune. It was the second day of the 1978 Litani Operation. The Litani River was the stated limit of Israel's incursion into south Lebanon. It was a full-scale response to what became known as the Coastal Road Massacre in which South Lebanon-based Palestinian terrorists hijacked two buses and began driving down the main road to Tel Aviv, shooting at everyone. Thirty-seven Israelis were killed, including thirteen children, and seventy-six were wounded.

The Israel Defense Forces occupied southern Lebanon up to the Litani and the Beaufort looked out over their lines and deep into the Galilee. This was Israel's fifth war, it's first in Lebanon, a limited-aim operation but with a large IDF ground force. Dov couldn't see the point. The IDF's commandos had time and again proved themselves the best, carrying out precision strikes against selected PLO terrorist targets inside Lebanon, and always with a limited loss of Israeli life.

According to his history teacher, "Israel is in a constant state of embattlement brought about by almost permanent isolation." Dov identified with that. He was convinced that 'They' always wanted to destroy Israel. 'They' were the amorphous Arabs from the surrounding Arab countries. The Arabs of Israel were 'They' also.

Dov studied Zionism which promoted the return of the Jewish people to the land from which they had originated, Eretz Israel, the Land of Israel. 'They', the Palestinians, became the latest in a long line of "our haters and potential destroyers", according to his teacher; the Jews, in Palestinian eyes, emerged as the 'They' who "wanted our land at any cost."

The version of Israel's War of Independence in 1948 that Dov knew was that the Arab armies of all the surrounding countries attacked the nascent Jewish state on behalf of their Palestinian Arab brothers and sisters. But the Jews defeated those armies as well as the few fighting Palestinians who were ill lead and poorly trained, in almost two bloody years of war. Some Palestinians 'chose' to remain in Israel after 1948. The rest fled. To Dov that the Palestinians of Israel became a minority in the land where they were once the majority was irrelevant. There was no equivalence between Shoah, the Holocaust, and Nakba, as the Palestinians called their 1948 tragedy. They were Arabs and they lost. They were not to be trusted even with begrudgingly granted Israeli citizenship. Dov believed the popular rhetoric that Israeli Palestinians enjoyed a better standard of living than in the Arab countries.

He was only nine when Israel won the 1967 Six-Day War. He remembered the fevered conversations between his parents as Egypt expelled all UN forces from the Sinai desert, filled it with their own forces and stopped shipping going to Eilat, Israel's southern port. IDF reserve units, including Dov's father's, were called up and then stood down as tension rose and waned. On the morning of 5th June the world awoke to the news of Israel's victorious pre-emptive air strikes against the air forces of Egypt, Syria and Jordan. After six days of fighting Israel held Jordan's West Bank of the river Jordan, Egypt's Sinai desert and the Gaza Strip and Syria's Golan Heights. Israel had arrived on the world stage and Israelis celebrated unlimited power and became occupiers. They relaxed and stretched out for the first time since 1948. Dov went sightseeing with his parents in Sinai, and shopping in East Jerusalem and Bethlehem.

The Palestinians in the Bank and the Strip exchanged Jordanian and Egyptian occupiers for Israel. They would never be granted Israeli citizenship. That would involve annexation and a responsibility too far. The Palestine Liberation Organization carried out cross-border terror attacks, the IDF responded with reprisal raids, and the teenage

Dov, like most Israelis, wondered why Israel continued to allow the Palestinian Israelis to remain in Israel.

Dov loved poetry and liked W H Auden's, "September 1 1939" and the lines, "Those to whom evil is done, Do evil in return." He thought he understood it until his teacher asked whether he appreciated that this might apply to the Jews of Israel, to whom the evil of the Shoah was done, and who might be doing evil to the occupied Palestinians. He rejected that and never read Auden again.

Dov's self-propelled gun had been in constant action since the start of the operation in a slowly warming mid-March. The crew functioned, as they were trained, like human extensions of a machine.

Gilad was his number two. They'd been called up and sent to the artillery corps together. "We need more shells and charges for a covering barrage," he reminded Dov. They'd done numerous live fire exercises, but this was their third combat shoot, the first and second had been the previous day.

Gilad reported "ready". He was sweating profusely in their claustrophobic turret. "This'll be tricky," he said. Tricky meant avoiding hitting their own forces, advancing up the Beaufort's near vertical slopes.

"Yeah," Dov agreed. "What can we do? We have to shift the terrorists."

"I'd rather be down here than with the boys going up." Gilad said. Dov couldn't disagree.

For reasons he later put down to the smoke of war, Dov's gun got separated from the rest of their unit as they began moving down to the coast. Radio contact became sporadic. Dov decided to scout ahead in his jeep, leaving orders to camouflage the gun.

Intelligence notes on his map indicated that the village twenty kilometers north-west of the Beaufort was a terrorist enclave, but since his unit's bombardment, there'd been no return of fire from the village. Dov wanted to pinpoint what he was actually firing at and find the rest of his unit.

The VW microbus stood in the middle of a road, leading straight into the village, slewed across as if it had swerved. There were figures inside, in Dov's binoculars, but there was something peculiar about them. He approached the microbus on foot, his weapon loaded.

The smell was overwhelming, a sweet rotting meat stench. Dov got within ten feet and was able to see five dead people in the vehicle. The rear seat passengers caught his attention, two adults and a child. The rear door was left open. Close up, he saw that a shell had gone straight through the window, decapitating the adults. The blast had killed the child. The driver and the front seat passenger were fused together in the fire that had consumed the cabin. The shell's entry and exit holes indicated that the shot had come from the direction Dov had just driven. Had his gun done that?

Nothing else registered with him. He was not a smoker but he found cigarettes under his seat and smoked all the way back.

"There wasn't anyone around," he said. "There was this nothing."

"What do you mean?" Gilad asked.

"It was empty. You could see down the street. No movement, no people, like in derelict towns in westerns. All that was missing was the tumble weed."

Gilad nodded at the image.

Minutes later the radio spontaneously crackled back into life with coordinates for their unit's location.

Dov was rotated through South Lebanon for the rest of the year. His conscription ended in August 1979 and he and Liora began tentatively discussing plans for marriage.

Chapter 2
June 1982

At the beginning, twenty four year old Dov was enthusiastic about "Arik's War", officially, "Operation Peace in the Galilee", ending the PLO's rocketing of Israel's northern border towns, and the state within a state that the Palestinian terrorists had made of South Lebanon. It was personal for Defense Minister Sharon. He'd never made Chief of Staff. His career was littered with questionable tactics, high IDF losses, and wars with the General Staff. This war with the PLO in Lebanon was to be proof that they'd all been very wrong about him. Arik Sharon knew what he was doing, his troops believed, and they loved and trusted him.

Since the Litani Operation four years before, Dov had been promoted to Captain in the reserves and had done extra training on the latest self-propelled artillery weapon. It had taken him away from his Psychology Masters degree. He didn't complain. The PLO needed to learn once and for all that they could not attack Israel with impunity.

Dov learned Napoleon's maxim, "God fights on the side with the best artillery". His men felt as if God was with them; they were the best. Once again Dov witnessed chaos created by the contrast between the reality of rocky terrain and what the map suggested. And as if the Beaufort Castle was unfinished business, the Golani infantry brigade's reconnaissance commandos had been tasked with assaulting it. It was to be a daylight operation and every conceivable scenario had been considered and practiced. As the first day of the war wore on, his gun, planned to support the commandos, made painful progress once it had forded the Litani River, along crowded steep rough roads that were more like tracks. With nightfall Dov in his jeep overheard confused radio traffic including an order that the Beaufort attack should be delayed.

By then the IDF's advance north into Lebanon had by-passed the Beaufort. Dov's big gun was part of the IDF's main thrust north, deep into Lebanon. The US-made artillery piece was designed to 'shoot n' scoot', but the topography made scooting impossible. Dov was in the rear of the advance and still within range of the Beaufort. More radio traffic told Dov that the commandos had begun their operation and Dov could hear heavy machine gun fire and occasionally see their twinkle high above. There didn't seem to be any covering artillery fire for the commandos and at first Dov was tempted to provide it. But as it grew dark, his muzzle flashes would be a give away and his shells risked friendly fire on the commandos.

First casualty reports from the Beaufort operation crackled in his headset. He managed to get coordinates, and ordered his crew to prepare to fire illumination flares over the Beaufort to assist the commandos. He gave the shoot order. The gun rocked the ground. Gilad saw Dov looking triumphant. That couldn't be the impassive, methodical Dov Chizzik. He dismissed the image, watched the next shell loaded onto the cradle, waited until it was up in the breach, counted, then CRASH! The shock wave made the earth tremble again. Gilad didn't notice it.

A two-man terrorist Rocket Propelled Grenade unit crept down from the Beaufort to disrupt the flare fire.

Dov, still in his jeep next to his gun, radioed Golani for an update. Doron, a Golani major, came back with, “Those terrorist machine guns’re murdering our boys!”

Dov answered, “I can’t shoot at the sources of fire, how do I know which are theirs and which are ours?”

Doron said, “I know. Go on with the flares, you’re really helping us.”

Dov’s gun fired again.

An RPG, fired in the direction of the big gun’s last flash, gave no warning of its arrival. At the end of its range it exploded. Two shards hit Dov, in the side of his neck and his shoulder. The blast knocked him out of the jeep. He was concussed and bleeding profusely. When Gilad found him, Dov still held the disconnected handset to his ear. “Nu?” he whispered, thinking he was still speaking to Doron.

Seventeen commandos survived thanks to Dov. Six were killed. But out of his many layers of battle memory came that order to delay the commando assault.

In hospital Dov watched Prime Minister Begin on TV with Sharon at the captured Beaufort. Begin with a rare smile said, “How fresh the mountain air is .” Dov didn’t share his glee.

He didn’t want to be in a hospital bed. He wanted to be back in action, anything to quell his disquiet.

He had time to reflect about Liora. They had talked more about plans to marry during their European trip, agreeing to wait until after they’d completed their army conscription service. Of the many memories that came to him during his recuperation was their visit to the Bergen Belsen concentration camp site.

There were no birds. Somehow it seemed to Dov that they knew. This was a place of inhumanity. Liora photographed Dov. He was standing in the middle of the vast uneven grassy area dotted with plaques memorializing individual victims, bounded by burial mounds covered with huge monoliths, massive cement rectangles, each with the impossible numbers of unnamed dead who lay beneath. In the photograph he wore a kippa on his head and he was reciting the Kaddish, the mourner's prayer.

He was a child of the straight line from the Shoah to the creation of Israel. But the photo, combined with his memories of his combat experiences in Lebanon, left him uneasy.

His father Dan appeared at his bedside, accompanied by a wooden plank of a Colonel, to tell him Arik was coming to give him a medal. "Another Chizzik in the history books, what do you think?"

"Arik? Medal? What for?" Dov asked.

The plank muttered, "Distinguished Service of course."

"Ariel Sharon?" Dov's head was spinning. "What did I do?" He croaked. "Distinguished Service is for heroes."

Liora came in as the plank was speaking.

The plank spoke again. "The citation says you displayed courage under fire. You saved comrades' lives at Beaufort."

"Greatness Dov?" Liora said with a little smile. He shook his head in disagreement.

Somehow everyone managed to be there – the Chizziks, the Livnats, Gilad - when Ariel Sharon, Defense Minister, strode in, stomach first, crocodile smile and twitching nose next. Dov didn't join the spontaneous applause.

He was one of only four Distinguished Service medal recipients for Peace in the Galilee. Sharon had been brief. "We're all proud of what you did. Good." After Sharon left, Dov said he was tired. He stared at the medal, the dull silver circle, Roman style sword and olive branch and dark blue ribbon. He closed the box and handed it to Liora. "Look after it for me."

Two months later, they watched a grim Ariel Sharon on TV in silent valedictory, walking past an honor guard at the Defense Ministry in Tel Aviv. Operation Peace In Galilee had gone on and on with the IDF bombarding Beirut night and day for weeks, live war coverage watched on the world's televisions. Then came the Sabra and Shatilla massacres in the south Beirut Palestinian refugee camps, carried out by Lebanese Christian militia. Israel's Commission of Inquiry into the massacres concluded that as Arik Sharon was at the top of the command chain and had given no orders for the IDF to intercede, he bore personal responsibility for what took place in the camps. The Commission recommended Sharon's dismissal.

An internal IDF investigation into the Beaufort commando operation revealed that an order canceling it never reached the Golani commandos, but was inconclusive about why that happened or if the Beaufort was a valuable target. Dov wondered whether the Begin-Sharon photo-op was worth the cost in life.

"Where'd you put that medal?" he asked Liora, sitting in the living room of the little garden apartment they were living in together, days after learning of the IDF investigation's results. She got it for him and he went to their old clothes cupboard and shoved the medal box to the back of the shelf.

Dov and Efi Livnat sat in Efi's rumpus room. Efi had summoned him after he was released from hospital. Efi raised a tumbler of bourbon whiskey, "It's more refined than Scotch," he insisted and in his captain of industry no nonsense bass said, "Dov, you will marry Liora. She will continue as my PA and later as a manager at Livnat Industries. You will be my new sales director." He gestured grandly, "Good salary, excellent prospects, my deputy in five years, my successor in… we'll see. You'll work hard. All I want in return is my daughter's happiness and lots of grandchildren," and he gave one of his booming infectious laughs. "Nu?"

Dov wasn't infected. "I love Liora. I'll make her happy, and please God you'll have grandchildren. For the rest, I've decided. I'm going into the police service as soon as I finish my Masters." He toasted his father-in-law-to-be with Le-Khayim, To Life.

"Fine Dov. Service to the nation. Admirable. But why's a bright Jewish boy like you choosing the police force as a career?"

It was a test of wills. Dov was sure Efi was disconcerted at not having a war hero on the company letterhead.

"Efi, it's my vocation."

"Ah," said Efi slowly, and sipped some more bourbon, and Dov imagined him thinking, "Vocation? What can you say to that?"

Chapter 3
1987-1992

"The Yahud steal everything, Ya'ani, I mean, our land, our history. They will not steal our bread. You tell Yossi the price I agreed last month for his pita order is fixed," Adnan Abdul Karim shouted to his daughter, pulling the lid off the oven, dropping pita bread dough one by one inside. Aisha was always amazed that he never burned himself.

She was unsure of Yossi's reaction. The Abdul Karim bakery inside the Damascus Gate of the Old City of Jerusalem and Shai's Steak House, on Ben Yehuda Street in Jewish West Jerusalem had been supplier and customer for twenty years.

At the Steak House, just over a mile from the bakery, Yossi's father Nissim, the Yahudi, the Jew Adnan had known best, shook his head. "That Adnan. Balls like rocks. His pitot are the best. But we have to cut our costs even if we have to find another bakery. Do you want to go talk to him?"

"After the lunchtime rush." Yossi wanted to see Aisha, see the hint of the smile in her eyes reminding him of their passion these past months. He'd find a compromise on the pita prices. But their love was complicated. They were only a fast walk apart, but they might have been at opposite poles.

They found secret places in the forests and hills outside the city to be together. Yossi was big and tough but soft on the inside, at least with her, and petite Aisha liked the certainty he carried and ignored how uncouth he could be. In their moments of love neither had thought of consequences. She didn't know how Yossi would deal with her secret, growing inside her.

Nissim Shai was born in Baghdad, from a family of restaurateurs. They'd had to leave one of the oldest Jewish communities in the world, begun when Iraq was Babylon. On the birth of Israel there were virtual pogroms and the Shais arrived with nothing. Even though the Steak House was little more than a glorified greasy spoon, Nissim always wore a suit to work.

Nissim and Adnan shared much. They were both from major Middle Eastern cities. They were old school, upholders of faith, family and tradition, touched by their experience of each other's peoples. Theirs was a relationship of convenience, born out of the necessity of one staple, bread.

Nissim had discovered the bakery days after the 1967 war. Israel walked tall after that and when the family restaurant had run out of pita and their Jewish baker let them down, Nissim marched triumphantly through the Damascus Gate, following the unique smell of baking bread.

Adnan sensed the Yahudi watching him at work. He was surprised when in perfect Arabic Nissim asked for thirty pitot. Adnan pulled them fresh from the oven and filled a large paper bag with them. Habit kicked in and they haggled over the price, shook hands, and Adnan added a fresh sesame loaf, spices in a twist of newspaper and a quail's egg. "For the journey home," he said, and Nissim promised to come back.

Yossi was not like his father. When Adnan told him he couldn't lower his price, Yossi hectored him, "Why not? We've been good customers for years and sent you loads of others." Aisha appeared and Yossi quietened. Adnan noted that, then delivered an ancient put down. "Tell your father he shouldn't send a boy to do a man's job."

"Go fuck your mother! I know how to deal with a scummy Arab like you. We don't need you!"

Aisha was horrified. "Don't talk to my father like that," she hissed. It was no good. Yossi's macho was bruised. "Don't interfere Aisha. Just keep out of this."

That familiarity alerted Adnan. "Get out of here, now! Tell your father to find another baker, but it won't be anyone in East Jerusalem. I'll make sure of that."

Yossi hesitated and another look passed between him and Aisha.

He never saw her again.

Adnan decided to act. He quickly found a suitable match for Aisha. She couldn't tell her father the truth, but in the end when her belly began to swell, she too acted. She ran away.

Her last contact with Yossi was a desperate phone call, her only communication with him since the scene with her father. The Steakiyah's chef answered the phone and shouted, "It's some girl. She wants only you Yossi." Yossi took the receiver and stretched its wire outside. Aisha blurted out that she was pregnant and running away. She said, "I love you," then hung up.

***

One day in 1992, a shepherd claiming to have been searching for an errant sheep, reported an ossuary in a cave in the lower Galilee. The inscription suggested it might contain the bones of a disciple of Jesus.

As a war hero with a Psychology Masters, Dov had been fast tracked and made Detective Inspector in three years. Yigal Shalit may have resented Dov's career trajectory, but other investigators of Dov's age welcomed someone who could add a little luster to the force's shabby name. Dov got on with his first big investigation, enjoying the independence his star status gave him. He was keen to prove himself. Liora didn't voice her misgivings about what she saw as Dov dumbing himself down. She thought with her guidance he could climb out of the rut of investigations into the hierarchy and thence to public life. The False Disciple Case as it was originally called attracted local and international media attention and Liora enjoyed the vicarious limelight.

The ossuary was examined at the Division of Identification and Forensic Science labs at the National HQ. Shalit pulled together a panel of archaeological experts, though Dov appealed to him to keep them all away from him so he could progress the investigation rather than referee institutional rivalries. They were predictable, between the privately funded Rockefeller Archaeological Museum in East Jerusalem, the Israel Antiquities Authority and the Ministry of National Infrastructures: Geological Survey.

"I'm loaning you Aviel Weiss, he can be the crowbar to prise these august institutions apart,' Shalit growled with typical bombast. "Put him to work, he'll gnaw his way through them."

There were two characteristics about Aviel that Dov recalled from their first meeting before he became a Super Cop: he was over six feet tall, and he had, as Shalit had intimated, two pronounced front teeth, giving his face a badger-like appearance. To Dov's pleasant surprise, Aviel had proved to be efficient, intuitive and capable of handling even the most intractable situations. Now he managed the warring archaeologists' egos without bruising them. Dov was very polite in rejecting any interview requests from the international and local media and Aviel adopted his boss's attitude.

The first breakthrough was with the patina of the ossuary, the ostensible product of a constant process over centuries. Experts had learned that patinae came from the rock from which ancient caves were hewn, their surfaces incrementally dissolved by water seeping naturally from the earth above. The DIFS lab analysis of this patina's composition revealed that it was recent and the material used to create it bore no relation to the natural conditions of the cave. The faux patina consisted of a carbonate, a mineral composed of calcium, magnesium and other elements in various crystal forms. It appeared to have been ground, spread over the surface and fired in an oven. There were odd specks of flour lodged in some of the letters of the inscription.

Forensic identification of the bones and cause of death of the skeleton in the ossuary was slow. Dov decided to visit the cave in the Galilee and question the shepherd who found the ossuary. On the drive he reviewed what he needed. His cool analytical exterior was like a new suit he wasn't quite used to and it belied his self-doubts. This wasn't his first case; he'd investigated several murders, one or two high profile. But he knew he'd bluffed his way through them even though his bluffs were more productive than the work of more experienced officers. He remembered being a barmitzvah boy, rehearsing his Torah portion until he knew it by heart but clueless as to its significance. So with the issues for which he wanted answers now; his instincts told him that nothing was what it seemed

This was a multi-layered case, with Arab suspects involved, and that made him nervous. Dan Chizzik always quoted grandpa Dudik's "Sei a Mensch", be a good human being, behave with respect and integrity, whatever the circumstances. Any Arab suspect had to be treated the same as Jewish suspects.

At Misgav police station, in the lower Galilee, he met deputy station chief, Superintendent Gil Reiss. "This shouldn't be too complicated. Arabs snitching on each other is always good for us, no? OK, we'll help you any way we can," he said shaking Dov's hand with a grip that threatened to break fingers. Reiss was like a combat officer planning an attack: the cave was a target, the shepherd a national security threat and the ossuary a booby-trap waiting to go off. Reiss did not relax his large frame when he briefed Dov. When he asked for a jeep and a driver, the Superintendent nodded vaguely, with the look of a driven man on the edge of sanity. Dov thanked him and left, pleased to be away from him.

The road ran along a spine of steep hills which the driver said were the Rams Horns Hills. Legend had it that a German pilot in the First World War had named them after flying over their curves. The landscape either side was stunning, in stark contrast to the urban jungle Dov was used to. The police jeep swung off the road onto a steeply descending track, where a valley of patchwork colors stretched away towards the far distant coast.

The driver parked and asked Dov to follow him. The cave was a few hundred meters walk through undergrowth. In the driver's flashlight beam the cave was dry with a sharp right kink masking a further chamber protected from heavy weather. It had signs and smells of human and animal use. Dov determined that bringing the ossuary here had demanded a four-wheel drive vehicle and at least three men.

The shepherd was in an interrogation room when Dov returned to the police station. Reiss said the suspect had been under observation.

The shepherd asked if he could smoke. Dov said, “of course” and the man’s weathered face gleamed briefly in the light of the match. He inhaled, exhaled, relaxed a little and spoke. A while ago, a villager came and gave him a handful of money, more than he’d ever seen, in return for following instructions he would be given. He’d receive more money if he did as he was told.

“Who was the man?” The shepherd hesitated. “You want to leave here quickly don’t you?” Dov asked. “Once you tell me, I’ll make sure the police keep an eye on him so he won’t harm you.” The shepherd squinted through smoke, unconvinced. “You can keep the money,” Dov promised.

“I saw him once more. He came and told me to telephone a number in Al Quds, Jerusalem”, he made it sound like a far away place, “and tell them I found the burial box.” The shepherd described this man and said his name was Mohammad, and that he worked for the Sheikh.

Reiss agreed to release the shepherd and then drove Dov to a kibbutz where a holiday chalet had been booked for him. On the way he said they’d found the owner of the cave and were holding him overnight until Dov questioned him.

“Holding him overnight?” Dov said. “What for?”

“Until you question him,” Reiss replied.

“Why not arrange for me to see him at his home? He’s not a suspect is he?”

“It’s his cave that ossuary was found in. How could he not know? Anyway that’s how I deal with these Arabs. They have to know who’s boss. See you in the morning.”

After breakfast, Reiss drove Dov to meet the Mukhtar, the head of the village, known as the Sheikh. Why he wasn’t being taken straight to quiz the cave owner he decided not to ask. They drove through a big village, out across open countryside, flanked by the hills Dov had driven along the previous afternoon. Approaching the next village Dov was struck by how like a continuous junkyard the outskirts appeared, nothing like the villages he'd seen in Lebanon.

The Mukhtar's house was large and dominated a small square. The living room was furnished in dark wood and heavy furniture, with lurid paintings of men on horses and camels, and a black and white photo possibly of the Mukhtar's father, erect in a dark suit and a fez.

The Mukhtar and another man exited his office. He was like the man in the photo, same pear shaped face, smartly dressed, his greying black hair recently cut. He gave Dov an appraising look then introduced himself as Sheikh Adwan. The other man told Dov he was Dr Basil Khoury, a lecturer at Haifa University. Khoury ignored Reiss.

"Two police officers Adwan? What have you been up to?" Khoury said impishly. He was a pirate of a man, a redhead of wide physique, small blue eyes, fleshy lips, big toothy smile at his own innuendo.

"We'd like to speak to Mohammad your driver," Dov told the Sheikh, who turned to Reiss annoyed. "Why didn't you say it was Mohammad you wanted to see? What's this about?" Reiss said nothing so Dov explained.

Adwan produced a cell phone and barked "M'hammad!" into it.

Mohammad appeared moments later, burly, obsequious. Adwan protested that none of his minions were mixed up in anything illegal, then said curtly, "Question him at the police station, if you don't mind. I've another meeting. You can always call me if you need me."

Mohammad was handcuffed and placed in the rear of Reiss's vehicle and they drove back to the police station where he was put in a cell. Then Reiss insisted on taking

Dov out for lunch. "I hope you like local food. There's this restaurant that serves lamb in tehina with pine nuts to die for." Again Dov wanted to remonstrate about the delay in questioning two suspects kept in the cells, but could see he'd get nowhere. The lamb was as good as Reiss said.

Mohammad was stoic in the face of Dov's questions.

"You're wrong if you think silence helps," he told him. "You're an accomplice to a possible murder."

"I didn't…"

"That means a long time in prison."

"All I did was…"

"Something like ten years."

"It was a member of family…"

"Yes?"

"A cousin on my mother's side from Jerusalem called asking for urgent help."

"Who was this cousin?"

"Nasir. He's a Muallim."

"What's that?"

"A master."

A long time before, he told Dov, Nasir had called him with an offer of several hundred dollars for an urgent job. Mohammad had gone to Jerusalem that night with a 4 x 4 vehicle and a couple of men he could trust to take a heavy box back to the Galilee and hide it in a cave. It wasn't difficult. Mohammad told Dov the cave he chose belonged to a farmer called Ibrahim. Then a few weeks ago Nasir called again and told him to pay the shepherd to call the Rockefeller Museum.

"I never knew what was in the box. It was heavy," Mohammad said.

The second suspect, Ibrahim al Batuf, was wiry, medium build with sunken cheeks and hard eyes. Typical Arab of the land, Dov thought, then analyzed that thought; was he being prejudiced? He couldn't decide. Reiss had told him that Ibrahim had no criminal record, but that there was an old family feud with the Sheikh, and in all likelihood the choice of his cave was part of the feud to implicate him. Where Mohammad had practiced impassivity, Ibrahim's eyes, as black as tar, exuded anger.

Reiss offered to interpret. "I know their language, it's part of knowing your enemy, no?" Ibrahim said he didn't know his cave had been used. It was one of several on land he owned. He didn't rent it out, but allowed shepherds and their flocks to use it. No one had told him about a box in the cave. Dov instinctively sensed that this was an honest man. He told him he was free to go. Reiss looked disappointed and then stunned when Dov requested a car to take Ibrahim home. "No!" Ibrahim barked, hurrying out. At the entrance Dov found a younger version of Ibrahim. He wasn't a farmer, and was gregarious where Ibrahim was taciturn. "I'm Rashid, Ibrahim's youngest brother," he said cheerily shaking Dov's hand.

Dov watched as Ibrahim walked out and immediately erupted at Rashid. He observed the brothers' body language, and guessed that Ibrahim was angry he had brought the woman and the girl with him, and assumed they were Ibrahim's wife and daughter, whose name, Lana, Dov overheard. The only Lana he knew was the actress Lana Turner, who he'd seen in the original of The Postman Always Rings Twice, tamer by far than the 1981 version. This Lana, a girl with curly hair rushed to Ibrahim who hugged and soothed her, as his wife smiled nervously. They stood just inside the cone of the entrance light and Dov could see the woman's relief mixed with an urgency to leave this place. The girl stared back at him through the rear window. It was a look that said, "You wronged my father."

Nasir the Master drove his silver BMW to the Jerusalem HQ enjoying the attention of the media waiting for him. Tall, almost patrician, expensively dressed, loquacious prior to the interrogation, he became restrained as it progressed. He projected successful businessman, and not at all the avaricious faker of ancient relics that he really was.

"Why reveal the ossuary now?" Dov asked.

"It was time," Nasir smiled. "Lot's of press outside." He said nothing of his inner thoughts and dreams. He believed he could fool anyone, especially the Israel Police Force. He planned to do what a few other 'professionals' had done, capitalize on their experiences and retire on the proceeds from a foreign, preferably American, TV documentary and a book, to be called "The Great Master."

"Where did the 'disciple's' remains come from?" Nasir gave him an it's-for-me-to-know-and-you-to-find-out look. Dov let him go with the warning not to leave Jerusalem, there would be more questions. Dov watched as Nasir gave a Pasha's grin to the press outside but made no comment.

Dov re-read the analyses of the ossuary and its contents: the 'disciple's' remains were no more than sixty years old; the limestone construction dated from the Roman period and was probably authentic; traces of flour on the lid might have come from an aging technique; the inscription on the lid had been done with modern tools.

He called the lab about the flour. Masha the chief analyst admitted sheepishly that the team had no logical explanation for it; chalk was often employed for aging, but they had found none, so they concluded by default that that was what the flour was for. Dov asked if they'd found flour traces elsewhere and Masha went quiet and then said no. Dov told her to take another look, and examine the ossuary base.

The ossuary was under brilliant lights on a pallet when Dov came into the basement lab. Masha and a technician began carefully up-ending the limestone box. As it tilted something shifted inside. Masha stopped in mid-tilt. Dov asked whether she'd X-rayed the ossuary when it first arrived. She hadn't, limestone couldn't be X-rayed, she said, implying that he should have known.

When the ossuary was rested on its side, sample scrapings were taken from the base. Dov asked for a section to be cut out of it. Masha asked the technician how long that would take and when he said it could be a couple of hours, to Dov she said, "well what did you expect?" The tungsten carbide electric saw made a racket and sparks flew. When a cavity had been made, it took great self-control for Dov not to reach inside but he let Masha pull out a burnt femur and then several more burnt bones. Dov asked for a flashlight and in its beam saw what looked like a grubby white plastic sheet lining the concealed compartment. After enlarging the cavity the lining was removed and Masha recognized it as an old plastic-sheathed lead radiographer's apron.

What they'd discovered was that the ossuary had a false base concealing a narrow compartment, the apron a crude attempt to deflect X-rays from the contents, burned human bones and two skulls, one normal size and one smaller. Masha sighed, "Whoever did this with the apron thought he was being very clever. He was stupid. He should have wrapped the bones in paper and used more to fill the compartment to stop the bones rattling."

Initial forensic analysis detailed the bones as those of a young female about nineteen years old and a baby of a month old.

The case was renamed "The Woman And The Baby In The Box."

Nasir was recalled for interview and shown the lab photos. His attempt at inscrutability earned him an arrest pending further inquiries.

The flour analysis showed up locally grown wheat, from a family flour-mill near Ramallah serving bakeries in Nablus, Sheikh Jarrah near the HQ, and inside the Damascus Gate of the Old City.

Dov waited as Adnan Abdul Karim pulled steaming fresh pitot from his oven. His mouth watered at the smell. He asked when Adnan had last seen his daughter Aisha. Adnan stood still for a moment at the first mention of her name in so long. He said, "She was in a cave."

In the interrogation room he continued, "I had arranged a marriage for her. She was very beautiful, my Aisha…" He broke down. "She disappeared. I went out of my mind. There's loads of caves all over Jerusalem so I started searching in them. I don't know what made me do that. I imagined where she and he would go…"

"He?" Asked Dov.

"Yossi Shai, Nissim's son, a customer for years. I thought they were… so I tried to find a good match for her from our people."

"And you found her in a cave?"

"Yes."

"How long had she been there?"

"I don't know, some weeks. How she looked after the baby in a cave…"

"What baby?"

"She had a baby boy, the Yahudi's son, she told me."

"What did you do when you found them?"

"You don't know what this meant. It was such a dishonor. She was just a girl, not married and she gave herself to a

Yahudi! A Yahudi!" His hands rose either side of his body, gesturing at the impossible situation.

"What happened?"

"I could not allow the stain on our honor to remain. I had to remove it."

"You killed them both? Your daughter and your grandson?"

"She knew. My beloved little Aisha knew. She didn't even plead. She just lay down on the ground and I put a blanket over her face and pressed hard until she was no longer alive and then I did the same with the baby."

The baker was pale and silent for long moments, holding back tears, the torment of the past surging through him.

Dov asked what he did next. "I packed the bodies in the trunk of my car and drove here."

"I had to make them disappear. I had to." Obsessed with eradicating what had defiled his family name, he'd heated his biggest oven. But it was incapable of reaching the 1400-1600 degrees Fahrenheit for cremating bodies. What remained after several hours was indescribable. When questions were asked about the smell, Adnan told neighbors that he'd been asked to roast a goat that hadn't been properly skinned.

In sheer desperation he called his cousin Nasir who took pity on the almost incoherent Adnan. He instructed, "leave the big oven on, say you had to burn out whatever was left of the goat, apologize to customers for the inconvenience, it would only be for a day. I'll arrange the disposal of the contents."

No one asked about Aisha. Family honor was rumored to be behind her absence. In the minds of many, Adnan earned respect.

Dov sat opposite Adnan. The man who had murdered his daughter and her baby looked peaceful. Peaceful? Dov thought. Peace? How do we get to live with people who do this? He banished the question, it was personal, not for here.

The Shai by the Sea beach bar in Tel Aviv was where Dov found Yossi. He was grotesque, obese, with ear studs and nose rings, completely bald in a tank top and Bermuda shorts that were too small on him.

When Dov introduced himself, Yossi Shai shouted, "Tikvah, it's that cop who phoned. Take over," and his scrawny smooth headed female partner with more earrings than ears, slid from a room behind the bar.

"What's all this about?" Yossi asked in a tone suggesting he talked with the police regularly.

"Aisha Abdul Karim," Dov said, "Adnan's missing daughter."

Yossi opened his mouth to say "who?" and then closed it again and said, "What about her?"

Dov said, "She was murdered". Yossi moved his bulk to the end of the bar. He was genuinely shocked and he didn't stop his tears trickling down his cheeks. He'd never forgotten Aisha's eyes. He said, "I knew her a long time ago."

Dov told him that she'd had a child and the child was dead too. Yossi looked sadder and emptier. He shared his last memory of Aisha with Dov. "She called me," he said looking down at the bar counter, running his finger absently through some beer spill, "weeks after her father stopped supplying us. He and I had a row. She said she was pregnant and running away." His finger stopped. "What could I do? Marry an Araboosh? I got married a year later and came down here."

"Children?" Dov asked, ignoring the "dirty Arab" epithet for the girl Yossi had once loved.

"No," Yossi said looking away, knowing that the question demanded more than his incomplete summary of his life. He said, "It turned out the wife couldn't, but I never let on that I was pretty sure I could. She left me anyway." He glanced over dejectedly at Tikvah who was just out of earshot chatting to a customer and added, "and she can't have kids either." He looked up at Dov, "I'd have loved kids." Then still looking at Tikvah he said, "I loved her, Aisha." Tikvah smiled back uncertainly, not able to hear his words. Then Yossi said, "That Adnan. What balls."

"Why do you say that?" Dov asked.

"Obvious. He must have guessed about Aisha and me and when she fell pregnant, it became an honor thing. If I'd had a daughter who some Araboosh made pregnant, I'd have done the same. Wouldn't you?"

Dov the investigator glanced at Dov the man in the driving mirror on the way back to Jerusalem. The face in the driving mirror looked frostily back and said, "It isn't my job to understand these people or judge them." But Yossi Shai's question, its inherent racism, demanded a response. So Dov the investigator told the man in the mirror that killing Aisha was murder, and murder was a crime. And Dov the man said, "That isn't really it, is it"? There was little comfort in the façade of his superiority over Yossi Shai.

Adnan Abdul Karim maintained a dignified silence as his lawyer confirmed to Dov his confession. Adnan was sentenced to life.

Nasir was found guilty of being an accessory to murder, and grave robbery. He admitted organizing the theft of a body from the Jewish cemetery on the Mount of Olives and was sentenced to ten years. There was no TV documentary or book offer.

His cousin Mohammad got a six months suspended sentence thanks to the Mukhtar's intervention which suggested a deal with Reiss.

An elderly but spry Nissim Shai offered Dov Turkish coffee in his new elegant restaurant on the site of the old Steak House.

"I knew something was up with Yossi and Aisha. She was a bomba – a stunner. I don't blame my son. But once Adnan worked it out, that was the end."

Dov sipped the coffee. It was good, with more than a hint of cardamom, bitter.

Weeks later Dov received a request from Nissim Shai, asking if he would help him get to visit Adnan in prison. He made the arrangements.

Chapter 4
1984-1992

Lana al Batuf was a difficult schoolgirl, but one of the brightest. She had a dimpled smile she gave sparingly and black curly hair she hated. She became rebellious and school exacerbated that; this was not a place for a girl like her. No one loved and spoiled her as at home and she resented the discipline. Lana would only do what Lana wanted to do.

She was a hill village child from the Galilee. In the air she breathed the Nakba was always there, talked about with bitterness by her parents and their friends and family as if it had happened yesterday instead of over four decades before. When she got older Lana dutifully venerated the Nakba's memory, but yearned to live without its sadness.

Most of the villagers had remained after 1948, when Israel won its war of independence and the Jewish state emerged. Few Palestinians imagined that outcome and many left Palestine during the war either by choice or Israeli urging.

The Nakba defined who Palestinian Israelis were. At school Lana learned about the Native American dispossession of their land and sympathized. She learned too that before the Nakba the Palestinian community was a million and half strong. After it they were divided into three - the West Bank

Palestinians under Jordanian control, the Gazan Palestinians under Egypt and those Palestinians who stayed in Israel and became Israeli citizens, the mostly Muslim minority. After the 1967 war, the Palestinians suffered another body blow; they called it the Naksa, the set back. The West Bank and Gazan Palestinians came under Israeli occupation. They were not granted Israeli citizenship. They became progressively alienated and resentful of their occupiers.

Lana knew that her people had suffered loss and were divided amongst themselves by the occupation. Palestinian Israelis felt guilt at having fared better than their occupied brothers and sisters and constrained in their reactions to Palestinian terrorism. Of course they wanted someone to stand up to Israel, but they didn't understand, and many denied, the Shoah. But, along with the subsequent wars, Israelis became resolute, suppressed their fears, and gave the Palestinians no quarter.

At school Lana knew the cliques were uncertain about her. She flitted from one to another, not always welcome. She did not show her frustration at her isolation but determined to do something about it.

She decided to have a special friend share a table in class. Ghazaleh was the daughter of neighbors. They played together during the holidays with Rania, another girl on her street. As the new term approached, Lana asked Ghazaleh, "Will you sit at my table?" Ghazaleh agreed. On the first morning Lana rushed in and guarded the empty seat at her table. But Ghazaleh walked right past her and sat with Rania. She could hear them sniggering.

She found retribution in the playground. Ghazaleh was not as fleet footed as her name, gazelle, suggested. Playing tag one day, Lana repeatedly beat her to the safe space, chalked off near the school doors. Lana was never tagged or 'it', but Ghazaleh constantly was. Lana's deftness won her acceptance by three cliques.

For Lana the land and the trees symbolized the past. The land which her father owned, its olive groves and the many fields of different fruit and vegetable crops, mute witnesses to her first self-awareness and events that changed her, would always be with her.

Of the people who dominated her childhood, her father Ibrahim and her mother Khadija were the most influential.

Lana would walk up the hill from home to the girls' village school. Each morning she'd stop at the crest and wave to her father. She would hear his voice, almost a cry, which reached her heart, "be a good girl Lana." And she would always shout, "of course I will Daddy."

There was something of a feline goddess about Khadija, a nobility suggested by the upward slant of her honey colored eyes above high caramel hued cheeks, a mouth turned down a little at the edges that smiled widely especially around her children. Her signal to them that enough was enough was when her lips narrowed, her head lifted and her eyes fixed on them.

Despite Ibrahim's natural taciturnity, Khadija returned his silent passion for her with open affection. He had learned not to be embarrassed by it. She had given him two sons and Lana. He cherished those blissful moments with his baby daughter sleeping on his chest, her breathing as gentle as butterfly wings.

Lana was the only one in her home with a bookcase, "my little library" of Arabic, Palestinian and English literature, and astronomy. She owed these interests to Mrs al-Taj the headmistress who saw in her a combination of willfulness and tenacity. Given the right motivation Lana could blossom. Since university Mrs al-Taj had devised her own method of teaching English. She designed it to be self-motivational; students would learn English and also develop self-confidence. Mrs al-Taj took pains to teach Lana to pronounce the letter P, which didn't exist in Arabic and Lana chuckled at the memory of how she'd first read out, "Beter Biber Bicked a Biece of Bickled Bebber."

Because Mrs al-Taj was the only sister of the Imam of the largest mosque in the village, her spinsterhood was tolerated. She'd studied at Haifa University in the days when that was unheard of. The village collective demanded she find a husband, but when one of the village tongues broached this, she said firmly, "I have Allah and my knowledge which I impart to the young. I need no-one else."

One afternoon she invited Lana to her home to see the night sky. "Have you ever seen the stars through a telescope before? They're magical, aren't they?"

Lana recited some of her newly learned constellation names to Ibrahim. "Daddy did you know that all the names come from the shapes groups of stars make?"

Ibrahim feigned surprise. "What are they called?" he asked.

Lana said, "They're called conster...conster... constertations." He corrected her gently, "Almost a hundred percent. It's con… stell… ation. You try it now."

The next time, Lana asked Mrs al-Taj, "Who do the stars belong to?"

"Allah," she said but after a moment added wistfully, "Truthfully? Everyone."

For her next birthday Khadija bought her a beautiful old brass telescope and tripod.

By now the family were moving out of the village and into a house on a hillside overlooking it. It had been Ibrahim's dream to have a house with more space.

"Will it look like a castle?" Lana asked and Ibrahim said, "a bit, something like this," and drew her a sketch, exaggerating the corners into towers and adding Palestinian flags. "Wonderful," Lana said gleefully. He said they weren't permitted to build horizontally. He explained that, "They say it takes too much space", so the new house would be built vertically instead, on four floors, on stilts. Lana knew They meant the Israelis, without knowing why she knew. Most of the people in her world called them Yahud, Jews. Why they could tell her father how their new house would look, she didn't know.

The top floors were to be for Yunis and Yusef her elder brothers, and their brides, whenever they found them; Lana would have the second floor to herself. Her parents had the first floor with the living room and a spacious new kitchen.

Yunis didn't marry and left before the al Batufs moved in. He would make occasional unannounced visits, timed when his father was at work. He was gay and Ibrahim would not have his name mentioned. Yusef went to Dubai. He sent back regular contributions to his family. He didn't visit.

That both his sons were absent was emasculating for Ibrahim. To the village, he packaged Yusef's absence with proud descriptions of his success abroad. But there was no convenient explanation for Yunis. He never referred to him and villagers knew better than to ask.

Lana overheard Ibrahim heatedly telling Khadija that he wanted to disown him and drop the Yunis part of his name, Abu Yunis, the traditional way an Arab father symbolized his first-born son. Khadija urged him not to; it would only draw attention to the situation.

Yunis' top floor became Lana's and the second floor became a guest suite. And when she moved to her new room, she found a gift from her father that made her squeal with joy. He'd had a sliding window cut into the ceiling above her bed. On the first night she set up her telescope over her bed and began stargazing at Sirius the Dog Star. It wasn't hard to find the brightest of stars and she fell asleep with the scope still above her head dreaming she was flying up to touch Sirius's nose.

Chapter 5
1990-1999

One evening five months after their house move, Lana and Khadija sat waiting for Ibrahim. He was late. Khadija kept peeking at the kitchen clock. Then she called Hussein, Ibrahim's field manager. He told her Ibrahim had left at around five, taking a couple of workers home first. He gave her the number for one of them; the other didn't have a phone. Khadija dialed and waited. Lana tried to concentrate on her schoolwork, watching the minutes tick painfully on as Khadija asked Awad's wife patiently after her family, said that hers were all fine thank you and then spoke with Awad.

"What did he say?" Lana blurted out.

"Daddy took Ismail home and then him. That was ages ago. I'm going to call Uncle Rashid."

Lana couldn't concentrate on her work and boiled water for tea. Khadija spoke with her brother-in-law, then put the phone down and sat absently sipping, forgetting to sugar it.

"Mummy, where is he?" Lana asked.

"Rashid'll make some calls," Khadija replied. The food got cold.

The front door slammed loudly, startling mother and daughter. It felt like Khadija had just ended her call to

Rashid, but there he was, exuding calm. He'd driven straight over from his car dealership on the main square. He sat down at the table. "He's at Misgav police station and may be held overnight," he said. Lana burst into tears. Khadija was caught between her shock and Lana's reaction.

"It's something to do with one of his caves, the one off the track going down to the barn in the valley. A box of some sort was found in it and they want to know what Ibrahim knew about it."

"Box? What box?" Lana asked still crying.

"Oh I don't know sweetheart, but I'm sure it's nothing and it'll get sorted out tomorrow when an officer from Jerusalem arrives."

"Why can't he come home now and the officer can speak to him here?"

"It's the way it is, sweetheart," said Rashid.

"It's horrible," she cried and ran up to her room.

A torrent of thoughts flooded Lana's mind. Why at the police station? Had he done something wrong, her Daddy? She'd heard stories; how people were taken and held for days for no reason. In one or two cases they didn't come back, but ended up in a prison in some faraway place. She didn't understand how They could do these things, could it happen to her? It frightened her.

Next day there was a visit to the new big school in the nearby village. Lana didn't want to go and sat uncommunicative in the bus.

After being shown around, the children were taken to a classroom where they sat chatting and looking at everything, so tidy and airy. Mrs al-Taj came in followed by a woman she introduced as Rivka. Rivka smiled warmly and spoke with them in Hebrew, which Mrs al-Taj translated. Rivka's class from a regional school was also visiting and how would it be if they all met up? The village school children looked uncomfortable. Lana wanted to run out of the room.

She sensed a surliness about the Israeli children as if they were looking down on her and her school friends. To break the ice, everyone was asked to draw a picture of their homes. Lana refused.

Mrs al-Taj put that down to Lana's obstinacy and sat her with two Israelis, Ditta and Eran. She didn't move, speak or look up. She could hear Ghazaleh and Rania at another table and knew they were ignoring the Israelis and chatting loudly to themselves.

She had never been this close to Them and at first she was surprised at how like everyone else they were, just better dressed.

As surreptitiously as she could, she glanced at Ditta. She had shoulder length fair hair and wore a black velour top with a wide gold zip down the front. Ginger-haired Eran wore a long sleeved t-shirt with 'Red Sox' on it and wore his ball cap tilted over his right eye. He looked disdainful.

Lana could smell Ditta. It was a fresh clean smell. She wanted to look and smell like that. But then they were Them, and not like her after all. The muttered and not so muttered expressions she heard from her school friends played back in her head, like a chorus of angry whispers getting louder. She thought, "but they look so"…no word came to her at first and then one did, "normal". How do I look to them? My clothes are dowdy, my hair's like a pot-scourer no matter how many times I brush it, and I've got big eyes like saucers, ugly!! Do I smell different?

Eran passed Lana his picture. She still hadn't done one and at first ignored his. But curiosity got the better of her. It was a neatly drawn house with two floors, long and wide with green grass and trees at the edges. "The window over the front door is my room," he said. The sky above the house was black and in it was a large white six-pointed star. It looked familiar.

"What star is that?" Lana asked and when Eran shrugged, she repeated it carefully in English. He smiled a big toothy grin which made him look like a rabbit and Lana managed not to laugh. "Ours," he said.

Lana's self-assurance produced, "Stars are everyone's."

"This one isn't," Eran said firmly.

"It is," Lana said loudly, "They all are."

Eran frowned. Ditta whispered something to him. He grimaced but turned to Lana and said sweetly, "I said it's ours, the way I say that's my house, when obviously it isn't mine; it's my Dad's. I said the star was ours, because it's in the sky above our house most nights this time of year."

"So it's everyone's star, like I said?" Lana asserted.

"Well not really. It is over our house..."

Lana grabbed a black crayon and holding it in her fist she obliterated Eran's white star. Eran and Ditta were shouting. Mrs al-Taj rushed over, Rivka with her, and firmly wrapped her arms around an incandescent Lana and gently led her out of the classroom.

She begged Lana to tell her what was the matter. Lana was silent until her teacher said simply, "either you tell me or we're going home right now to discuss it with your parents."

"Daddy's not there. He's at the police station; he's been there all night. He didn't do anything wrong," Lana whispered and then wept.

Uncle Rashid came to collect her from the school and took her home, where she cried again and used a bad word from the playground about Them that made her mother gasp and Rashid wince.

The phone rang.

Rashid answered, nodded, said, “Many thanks,” in Hebrew and told Khadija Ibrahim was being released. “I’m coming with you,” Lana said and rushed out to the car. Khadija and Rashid followed.

“You’re driving up to the entrance?” Khadija asked, as Rashid drove through the trees that screened the police station. Lana wondered why they hid the place.

“Of course I am,” Rashid replied. He got out of the car. They watched him walk through the well-lit entrance.

“Does he know someone in there, Mummy?” Lana asked uncertainly.

Khadija said, “He’s a businessman. He knows lots of people.”

Five minutes later a stony faced Ibrahim appeared. Behind him another man followed. Lana dashed out of the car, Khadija hurrying after her. Ibrahim admonished Rashid for bringing them, then hugged Lana and mumbled that he was OK. From the car window Lana saw the man standing at the door, watching her. Like Ditta and Eran, he looked normal, more like a teacher than a policeman. Was he the officer from Jerusalem, responsible for keeping her father in there? What had he done to him? She hated him and began to cry again.

At home Ibrahim sat at the table eating soup. Lana started telling him about her day, ignoring Khadija’s signals to stop.

When she finished, he said angrily, “I’ll speak with Mrs al-Taj tomorrow. You shouldn’t have met with the Yahud. They stopped me on my way to my home and took me to be questioned. Someone used my cave without telling me. The officer from Al Quds believed me and let me go, but he didn’t apologize for keeping me over night.”

Up in her bedroom Lana lay watching the stars through the skylight. She wondered if Eran was stargazing.

***

In the middle of that same week they were at a wedding. A debkeh dance began with a fingertip roll on a goblet drum. Ibrahim went straight into a trance, eyes half-lidded, leading a line of men, stamping to the beat of the old wedding song, "Ya Halali, Ya Mali, You are rightfully mine and all I own." It was wholly masculine, powerful, hypnotic and Ibrahim danced masterfully. He whirled his keffiyah as if he was waving a sword. Khadija whispered, "Isn't he magnificent?" Lana nodded uncertainly. Her father's sudden transformation unsettled her. And the title of the song didn't help. Own? The bride is owned by her husband? Like a house or a field or a cow? That couldn't be right, she thought, am I owned?

The men went out into the night air accompanied by shouts and applause from the other guests. Then she asked Khadija, "why have Yunis and Yusef left home?"

What to say, Khadija wondered. She had always tried to shield Lana from the devastating impact of Ibrahim's verbal assaults on her brothers whenever he thought they'd done something wrong.

When the boys were younger, Lana saw them express their respect for their father, as Ibrahim had with his father, by kissing his hand twice and touching their foreheads with it, when he sat down at table for supper. Usually he would return the kiss. Respecting their father extended to how they behaved even when he reprimanded them. They stood still and faced his withering fury, never responding.

Lana would hear her brothers' angry words afterwards, "Silly old fart" and "ass". By their mid teens they were immune to their father's outbursts. For Ibrahim, once he'd spoken, it was over and everyone was expected to continue as if nothing had happened.

So, all Khadija could say to her daughter was, "boys have to find themselves to become men. They can't always do that and live in their father's house and be what their father wants."

"Does Daddy own me?" she asked.

That threw Khadija. "No," she said, "he's your father and you must respect him, but he doesn't own you."

"And what about respect for me, does he have that?"

"Of course he does. He loves you, very, very much."

Lana smiled, but something had changed.

Soon she stopped stargazing. Tarab, the swell of powerful emotion through music which had swept Ibrahim up in the debkeh, began to work its magic on her.

The song that caught her was a folk tale about Zarief's love for Ataba. Only after a king vouched for Zarief did he win his love. George Wassouf, the King of Tarab, sang "They Reminded Me" and Lana became Ataba, a girl in love. Lana played the song endlessly on the tape recorder Yunis had sneaked in for her birthday. She loved her 'sometimes brother' as she called him. For him, seeing her was a high point of his fleeting visits.

Khadija knew her daughter's young soul was beginning its search. She also knew the song from long before Wassouf's cover version. On summer nights when the windows were open and the crooning voice glided out of Lana's room, she would mouth the words in secret duet.

Lana and Ghazaleh eventually became friends and sometimes walking back from school there'd be a group of boys who'd smile and politely greet them. They'd giggle and hurry away to discuss which one they liked.

Lana began to nag Khadija for more stylish clothes, "I'm too old for those flowery jumpers." She said nothing about the boys she saw, especially not Hatem, the handsome boy who she knew was Sheikh Adwan's son. He never spoke but she knew he waited for her. She also knew the village rumors that the Sheikh had many girlfriends.

One evening after supper Lana said, "Mummy, I don't want to cover my hair any more and I want it cut short."

"What, not cover your hair and look like a boy?"

Lana said firmly, "I'll always believe in Allah and Mohammad his messenger, blessings upon him. It's just that I'm a girl and wearing my head covering makes me feel less like a girl, and lots of girls at school aren't wearing their head coverings anymore. Ghazaleh certainly isn't."

Khadija asked, "Why do you think I cover my hair?"

"I never thought about it," Lana admitted.

"I made a promise, to myself and to Allah. When I found the right man, I would cover my head as a sign of my faithfulness to my husband, and to Allah, and I would only show myself to the man I married."

"So before that you didn't cover your head?"

"No, not always. But I never dressed in a showy way."

"I won't either," Lana insisted.

Her mother smiled tightly, imagining the clinging tops and short skirts Lana wanted.

"If I make the same promise, can I stop covering my head?"

"If that's what you want..."

Khadija wondered which boy had caught her daughter's eye.

Chapter 6
September 1996 – March 1997

At Dov's promotion ceremony were Commander Shalit, the Police Commissioner, the Public Security Minister and a sprinkling of senior officers and officials. The Commissioner said, "I'm one hundred percent sure that as Commander of TPI, Dov Chizzik will have a significant impact." His reassuring grin made parallel lines of his eyes and mouth. Dov felt he held it a fraction too long, for the benefit of the cameras. He then announced that he would be leaving the police force for a career in politics. Naturally he would wait for his successor to be found. Meanwhile he would continue to work to ensure the nation's safety. Shalit muttered, "I feel safer already."

As the Commissioner pinned Dov's new Commander's rank insignia to his shoulders, Dov spotted Liora chatting with the Minister. She was enjoying her husband's success, amongst precisely the kind of people she'd always imagined they should mix with.

"Liora, come and join us for the photo-op," the Commissioner called out to her. She whispered to Dov, "I told you to wear your war medal. The Minister's wearing his."

"I couldn't find it," he said. A little blue and white lie, he told himself.

After the reception they celebrated at their favorite steak restaurant. "Let's just enjoy the moment, sweetheart." He clinked glasses with her. He liked the expensive red wine so much, he asked where he could buy it.

Weeks of bureaucracy, familiarization, and re-training followed the ceremony. When Liora asked what TPI involved, he said it was tasked to identify and prosecute those behind the porn video industry. She knew inherently what TPI was, but wanted him to admit it. All he said was, "It's not like my murder investigations, I'm isolated in TPI, like a gun commander without a gun."

Liora tried to sound encouraging. "Do a couple of headline busts and move on. Aim for the top. Why not Police Commissioner? You're twice the man of any candidate."

For a moment he ruminated. TPI wasn't what he'd expected and he knew what Liora was getting at. She'd temporarily given up her business degree and career plans for motherhood and was eager to get back to both whilst showing off her high flying husband. If he pursued a career as an investigator, she feared she'd be trapped as a housewife with nothing to flaunt.

"We didn't actually agree anything," he said belligerently.

She was furious. "That's bullshit. OK we didn't sign a contract, but we discussed it. You'd follow a management path in the police force once you'd proved yourself in investigations. You've done that, Super Cop". Sarcasm not flattery.

He ignored "discussed". It was academic. "So now I'm going to be 'Super Commander'."

"You're not Elliot Ness, this isn't the FBI and I thought we had a deal. You're in the cesspit, with…" she took a deep breath and shouted, "Pornography!"

“Don’t shout…”

“It’s human sewage. You won’t be able to wash the stink of it from your career.”

He tried, “You’re exaggerating. It’s all about the sex video industry and who’s running it.”

“I’m not stupid Dov. This is Vice and you know it and you need to get out of it as soon as you can. They like you, the Minister told me.”

“You sure it wasn’t you he liked?”

“He said they have high expectations of you. Make TPI a success in a year and move on. You can turn this to your advantage, and aim higher.”

“Look Liora, I don’t want to be Commissioner. That’s not policing. But you should get on with your MBA. We’ll find the money for a child minder.”

She wouldn’t be deflected. “It’s time you dedicated a little of your precious vocation to us instead of reneging on your promise.” Her eyes probed his. “I don’t want anything to do with TPI in my house, near my children.”

“Reneging? That’s not fair. I didn’t make any promises like that. You had this dream, and now reality comes along and chomps it up. You can still have your business career. You just won’t be able to say “my husband the Commissioner.”

After another long breath she said, “Something’s changed here, with you. I don’t get it yet. Perhaps it’s the pornography. It’s vile, Dov, it’s corrosive.”

“It’s an industry, mixed up with women-trafficking and yes, it is eating Israel up from inside. I have to do something to stop it.”

Liora had exhausted her arsenal. Dov was changing and she didn’t like it.

***

The floor of the ZarMinSum club, Strange Sex Drug, was glass. Under it was a large lit aquarium with Egyptian Moray eels slithering in and out of crevices in the rocks. To Dov they were a bizarre addition to the ambience of the place, supposed to be erotic he assumed. He thought they were threatening and ugly. In the spot light on the glass floor were two men, one short, one tall. Their torsos were hairless and gleamed with sweat and body oil. The short man was dark, in a leather face mask and black leather shorts. The tall figure was blond, light skinned, heavily muscled. He wore a black leather eye mask, and a long chain around his neck. He moved sluggishly, as if he was drugged. They were the feature act at ZarMinSum. A vicious yank on the chain forced the taller man to his knees with his mouth open. The short man began thrusting a black dildo into it. The eels thrashed about, making the grotesque surreal.

"... See that every day!" Aviel bellowed in Dov's ear. Dov felt beleaguered, like a lost explorer trekking across polar ice.

The amplified music appalled him. In it's constant dulling throb, a circle of people moved across the floor collecting and discarding participants. Some swallowed tablets, others licked their palms after a bar person squeezed drops from a plastic flask as he passed. There were leather couches for drinkers lying under spigots above their heads, alcohol streaming into their mouths whenever they swiped their credit cards.

He looked for Aviel. The intermittent lighting made it difficult. Then a strobe beam touched Aviel, shouting at a bar girl with black hair in a mohawk bristle. Dov forced his way through the bodies.

The bar code pattern printed on her white top fascinated him. More than the mohawk. "Flash your badge," he yelled to Aviel, "I want to talk to her outside."

They exited the back of the club and Dov smiled and asked, “Does that bar code mean anything?”

“You mean is it an invitation?” she sneered and he glimpsed a mouth with too many teeth. She looked all of sixteen. “You’re far too old. Now Aviel, him I’ve had a slice of. Tasty.”

They stood in the loading area at the back of ZarMinSum, a sour waft of refuse from overfilled bins, overlaid with something else.

The security light came on and off as Dov paced about. Aviel watched and smoked.

“I’m paid by the hour. You’re costing me money out here,” said the girl in a Russian accent. Her body kept moving to the music inside.

“What’s that dreadful smell?”

“That’s the eel feed.”

“Eel feed?”

“For the eels?”

“So what’s your name?”

“Angel.”

“From?”

“Latvia and Ashdod.”

“How old are you?”

“Twenty three.”

“Where do you live?”

“Here.”

“Did you do army service?”

“Like the rest of those flies on the toilet rim?”

“And ZarMinSum’s the height of civilization?”

“People are real here. Nothing matters. A guy comes in, drinks ten vodka Red Bulls, crashes out on the floor, wakes up and starts again. Akh’lah, wonderful, he’s a repeat customer.”

"What about drugs?"

"What about them? They're here, so what? They give you focus."

"Focus?"

"Yeah. It's in the music. I'm in the music… I've got to get back."

They turned to head for the car.

"What did you put in my drink, you little fuck?" a strangled voice shouted behind them.

"What do you care? We were good tonight," a second voice, smoother intonations in his speech.

Dov was curious. He signaled Aviel to go on to the car and edged into the shadow of the reeking refuse bins out of the security light's range.

"Leave me alone, unless you want me to fuck you here, now!" the first voice said.

"No, listen, tonight we were good enough for a talent spotter to talk to me. She gave me her card, here, Sara Moledet managing director of Lilac, some kind of agency. Maybe she can get us more club slots."

Through a gap between bins Dov saw the short man still in his mask, suddenly pull at the blond's chain and the mouth opened for the kiss. In the security light Dov registered his en minime haircut above torn eyes. He said, "What do you think about this Sara Moledet woman?"

"Not now. Our act always turns me on," came the reply.

"How about here?"

"Too risky. Kiss me again anyway, you prick."

And after it, the masked man said, "Let's go home."

Aviel hooted. Both men looked up. Dov froze. They went back inside. Dov walked to the car, the voices replaying in his head.

In the car, Dov asked, "Why did you hoot?"

"I was getting bored."

"Oh were you. What's that place to you?"

"A bit of everything and nothing."

"You like it?"

Aviel shrugged. "Shakespeare said it," he said. "We're the 'children of an idle brain'".

"Shakespeare, Aviel?"

Six months into TPI, Dov sat in his office in 'the Shop'. Tel Aviv's District Police HQ public entrance had a plate glass frontage on Dizengoff Street, to fit in with the city's main shopping street. The words of a song from his youth bled into his thoughts, about how a man lives shut up inside himself. And like the song, he felt that was him, forced inside himself by the new ugly realities he dealt with.

He had never felt so isolated. What he had seen in the porn video that first day had been just the beginning. What was it about murder that was clean, as compared to sex crimes and the porn industry that had become his field of expertise? Perhaps it was that death was death; once murder was done it was done and over. It didn't matter that it could be grisly and bloody. He knew where he was with it. This was infinite, an epidemic thriving in tiny Israel. It's gross intimacy embarrassed and disturbed him. He couldn't be dispassionate about it. It had brought him up to yet another red line, the one between sex and love, then it blurred. It was like a slow poison quietly but ineffably working its way deep into the heart of what held Liora and him together and it was beginning to create a distance between them.

Murder investigations followed a distinct pattern and as long as he solved a good percentage of them, he would continue his rise up the ranks. He had begun reading foreign forensics textbooks as a way to provide him fresh perspectives on his investigations.

His last murder investigation before TPI had an unexplored Vice link that occasionally flickered on in Dov's brain, like a faulty light bulb. There'd been a murder in the back room of the classy Pigyon beach bar. The bar's logo was an ancient dagger favored by the Sicarii, Jewish assassins who terrorized Roman Jerusalem.

A knife was the weapon used in what the pathologist Dr Cordova had described as "a double smile murder". The old man punctuated his analysis of his cadavers with "so to say", and told Dov, "the murderer used a curved serrated edged blade, a fairly crude one at that, maybe a banana knife, so to say." That had been an essential clue. As a schoolboy Dov had cut his finger with a knife similar to Cordova's description when he'd been helping a Kibbutz with a banana harvest. The gaping wound took forever to heal.

The first obvious wound to the body of the victim Dov had seen was the slash to the neck below the chin; the mouth had been open in a rictus, hence Cordova's double smile. The murderer was a young athletic Ukrainian immigrant, a successful merchant banker from the commercial neighborhood south-east of the beach. Dimi Demidov loved himself and spent a good part of his spare time and cash toning up his muscles. He was a jealous psychopath who had decided that the bar owner's lover, an American tourist, was sleeping with his girlfriend, a bar girl at the Pigyon.

The American had innocently gone with the bar girl to visit her kibbutz because he'd never seen one before. Demidov planned the murder, watched the tourist go into the owner's back room and waited until he was sleeping and got in and pretty well butchered who he thought was his rival. He had taken the victim's genitalia as a trophy.

One book Dov read, by an English forensic psychologist, suggested that 80% of all killers who escape the crime scene by foot, live within 480 metres of the crime. Demidov's apartment was within that radius. Dov and Aviel had searched the place and found the trophy in a jar in his fridge. A clue that MAZAP, the Criminal Identification Unit, had missed, was a footprint trace left under the rug beneath the bed the victim had been murdered in. Dov had 'micro-analyzed' the room, his own meticulous analysis of a crime scene, and found the print outline in blood that had soaked through the rug on double-sided tape used to keep the rug from sliding over floor tiles. MAZAP managed to produce a cast. But to do the match Demidov needed to be in custody. When they tried to arrest him, their prey glared, stamped his feet, thumped his chest and growled like an American football player then charged at them.

He passed them and reached his bedroom, retrieved the murder weapon and attacked like a whirling dervish, the raptor-like blade slashing as he revolved towards them. Dov remembered having a kind of out of body experience in which he observed from above the ludicrous scene of two armed police officers confronted by a big man with a knife whose every action confirmed his guilt.

He saw himself un-holster his police-issue Jericho automatic and shoot Dimitri Demidov in the right lower leg. The close proximity of the shot in a corridor deafened Dov to Demidov's shrieks of, "Fuck Your Mother!" as he collapsed on the floor. The memory of the event embarrassed Dov who had never shot anyone on duty before. The press and media repeated his Super Cop soubriquet, but he still refused interviews.

Dov was invited up to Jerusalem police HQ where Shalit told him he was promoted to Commander, and being reassigned to TPI.

"You'll still be operationally under my command," Shalit growled.

"Sort of 'first amongst equals'," Dov said rather slyly.

Shalit growled. "It's to do with the growing porn industry and its focus is Tel Aviv. We have to stop it." He outlined the restrictions under which TPI would operate, offered Aviel as Dov's full time number two, laughed mirthlessly about TPI being one man and a dog. His attempt to disguise his frustration at Dov's new rank wasn't convincing. They didn't shake hands.

That was how Dov remembered it.

***

Checking Demidov's background revealed a family link to Russian organized crime. Demidov had adamantly refused to confirm it. But Dov's instinct told him it was real.

Now sitting in his office at the Shop, the sounds of the Tel Aviv night subsiding on the street below, Dov reviewed his latest TPI success. He had closed down an extensive human trafficking ring involving twelve brothels and five phone-sex lines in Tel Aviv and its suburbs, rapidly dismantling the pyramid of a ten year old sex business that had eluded previous police investigations. It had been a hi-tech operation using the latest cellphone monitoring techniques developed by the security services, keen to cooperate with a police investigator who was a military hero.

Dov's failing light bulb flickered on. The fact that Israeli criminals were often Sephardi Jews and the men he'd arrested in the pyramid were of Moroccan heritage, didn't convince him that they were all there was to it. They were middle-men. The Russian mafia that had accompanied the wave of Russian immigration in the 1980s, had a lot of skin in the game, but whose skin it was in this context, was still unknown. So he had arranged to see Dimitri Demidov in prison.

"Go fuck yourself," Dimitri told him next morning. His manic red rimmed stare and slurred speech told Dov he was on drugs. They sat facing each other in a white room with no windows. The two guards standing inside the door were immaculate, impervious to their prisoner, the smells and the heat of the facility in the southern Negev desert.

"How's your leg?" Dov asked.

Dimitri laughed bitterly, a hint of instability underlying it. "I won't be doing beach sports anymore you shit."

"You're unlikely to see a beach for a long long time Dimitri, at least not one of ours."

The man, a slack muscled shadow of the once narcissistic body-builder, quietened.

"How does a transfer sound to you? To a nice migrant detention center. Full of Africans. We move them out every few months, first across Sinai, with the help of friendly Egyptian soldiers who loathe them and use them for target practice and keep them in barbed wire pens out in the desert. And when they get fed up with them, they ship them off to Africa. Not all of them survive the voyage."

"I'm a new immigrant, an Israeli citizen. I'm not some foreign crap!"

"Prove it."

"It says it on my ID."

"Its just a bit of paper, in laminated plastic, in a filing cabinet." Dov said. "Easy to lose in a prison office. Without it you're like flotsam washed up on the beach you used to love swimming off, or a floating turd you'd avoid."

Dov got up and left.

He came back a week later. Demidov hadn't asked to see him. But he was clear eyed and quiet.

"There is another transfer option Dimi, to a high security facility without outside access, a kind of solitary confinement prison. It's not even on the map. So what's your choice?"

"What do you want?"

"Any information on your relative who's in the Israeli branch of the Russian mafia."

Demidov laughed again, then turned serious. "Boris Kamien from Perm. He's only distantly related and I've never met him."

Back at the Shop, Dov tasked Aviel with checking police and Interior Ministry records and requesting assistance from the Russian authorities for details on Kamien. He began picking over the prostitution ring bust. Lilac, an escort agency, was a suspected source of women for "live" sex videos, but there hadn't been enough evidence to prosecute. I've heard that name before, he thought, and then it came to him, one of the two gays outside the ZarMinSum had mentioned it. Dov called the agency number. A soft voice said, "Lilac. How may I help you today?" She said Lilac as Lilach, literally Me – You, suggestively.

"I'd like to speak with…" He paused, waiting for the name to come to him. "…Sara Moledet. I'm Commander Dov Chizzik of TPI."

"Just a moment."

"Dov, this is a real honor to get a call from Super Cop." The voice was polite and well spoken with an indefinable trace of something East European. He said, "I need to talk to you about your agency," irritated at her familiarity.

"Of course Dov, whenever you like. I'm here most days." She gave an address on Rothschild Boulevard, part of the smart street of expensive apartments, banks and businesses that intersected with Tel Aviv Village near and around Sheinkin Street, the always-happening neighborhood south of the city center. He gave her the address of the Shop and said he expected to see her at eight the following morning.

Sitting in the interview room Sara Moledet told him, "as you didn't specify why you wanted to see me Dov, I didn't bring a lawyer. I presume I am safe in my assumption?"

She had long chestnut hair in a chignon, wore a black linen trouser suit and white blouse open at the neck, no jewelry, except for a flat gold watch. There was a hint of Arpege in the room. Liora wore the same perfume.

"You own the Lilac Escort Agency?"

"Yes."

"No you don't. It's a consortium, one of whom, Rafi Sabato, has begun serving an eighteen year sentence for human trafficking. We're still looking for the other two consortium members, Dudu Melekh and Avigdor Sefarad. Can you help me with that?"

"Not really. Dudu and Avigdor provided me with start up capital, five years ago. They came via my accountant and I met them once, Rafi Sabato wasn't with them, to thank them after they signed the contract and deposited the money. I've never met them since."

Dov found that unlikely.

"Really? I've seen your accounts and if I'd been you I'd have been tempted to ask them if they'd like to reduce their percentage, high at sixty percent wouldn't you say? Maybe the violence they'd have offered you in reply has kept you paying? How much did they invest?"

"Two hundred thousand."

"Oh my."

"Dollars."

"My oh my Miss Moledet. And you haven't managed to pay it back and cut the ties? A high end agency like yours?"

“The arrangement suits me Dov and there’s nothing illegal about it.”

“There are allegations that Lilac provides women for live sex videos.” He watched her eyes. They remained impassive.

“Allegations Dov? No proof?”

“You deny it?”

“Of course.”

“What’s your interest in the gay act at the ZarMinSum?”

“It’s an act, Dov, like any other,” she said unfazed. “I like the club and the acts there. Anything suspect in that?”

“Why did you give one of those gays your card?”

Her eyes squinted so fast, if he hadn’t expected it he would have missed it.

“Professional interest or personal?”

“I ask the questions.”

“It was a good act. Very real. Very authentic. It interested me.”

“Professional interest or personal?”

“Yes.”

“Yes what?”

“Yes is my answer.”

“Ever heard of Boris Kamien?”

“Who?”

“He’s an immigrant from Perm in Russia.”

“It’s pretty cold up there isn’t it? Doesn’t the word Permafrost come from there?”

“I think that’s inaccurate. You’ve been there?”

“No.”

“How do you know it’s ‘up there’?”

“Isn’t it common knowledge?”

“Only to someone who knows Russia and comes from there. Where are you from Sara?”

“Here.”

"Where?"

"Givatayim." It was a town east of Tel Aviv and within the city's metropolitan area.

"There's something not Israeli in your accent."

"My father was from Moscow, perhaps that's it."

"Not Perm?"

"No."

"I'll be in touch."

"I look forward to it."

"Permafrost, comes from the word permanent."

Her smile was coquettish, "My oh my Dov, the things you learn."

Monitoring her cellphone calls netted nothing. Her accountant confirmed her backers and was "shocked, I tell you shocked," about Sabato. "I had simply no idea. He represented himself to me as a reliable businessman. His bank confirmed his assets."

"Pity no one asked what the source of them was," Dov said.

"Shocking," the accountant agreed.

But Dov had a premonition, about Sara Moledet. And he kept the monitoring on her calls.

A week later Aviel told him that his checks on a Boris Kamien had proved inconclusive. Dov gave his instincts a rest. There was only so much two men and no dog could do.

Chapter 7

Dov sat in his car opposite the old central bus station. Next to him was an intense young woman talking rapidly into two cell phones. She said, "just a minute!" when he spoke, said, "sorry" into the two phones and continued talking with them, but not simultaneously. Nurit Keter knew more about the sex trade than anyone else in the city. She ran a help line for young women stranded or smuggled across Israel's borders. She spoke the languages of the slaves, as she called them and told him, "all they need is how to fake an orgasm and say 'Fuck me harder!' and 'I'm coming' and 'You're so big!' in Hebrew and English."

"Why English?"

"It's the international language of commerce. The onward trade of these women, throughout the Arab world? That's worth millions. Video sex is a part of it, and part of your new speciality, 'Super Cop is new Anti-Porn Czar,' wasn't that the headline?"

He caught a glimpse of himself in the rear-view. His hair was beyond tousled and there were pale shadows under his eyes.

Nurit made more calls. She was nondescript, except for the vigor in her eyes and voice. He recognized her commitment to her work.

The new bus station had opened after twenty-six years of crime wars for control; the old one was occupied by the third world and the dregs of everywhere else. Dov had loved the old place as a boy, rough and ready, prone to flooding in winter, but vibrant and full of contrasts.

Nurit finished her calls and said, “It’s like a drug, this business. Let’s walk.”

“Will the car be safe here?”

“Nothing’s safe here.”

And they began her tour. Under the elevated road that took buses thundering in and out of the monstrosity of a station, walls sported crude arrows in bright paint, pointing at pay-for-sex places, ‘health club’ and ‘massage parlor’. Cheap lights twinkled and flashed, and several of the women trading their bodies were African, unattractive, worn out, dead eyes in empty faces.

“Many are trafficked into Israel,” Nurit announced. “A natural process of selection weeds out the least valuable, and those end up here.”

“I guessed ,” Dov said.

“OK. I’ll introduce you to someone who’s been through it.”

They stopped opposite Club Couscous and Nurit sent a text from one of her cells. Five minutes later a thin woman, nineteen going on forty, emerged and began walking ahead of them. They followed and entered the shopping mall part of the complex.

Nurit said, “They claim it’s the largest bus station in the world. Aren’t we lucky?”

The woman pushed at a service door and went down concrete steps. She and they stopped in the stairwell and waited. No other footsteps echoed. At the end of a rubbish-strewn corridor, rank with piss, Nurit unlocked a door of an abandoned office suite. The place was bare, a couple of fluorescent lights hanging by their wires, taps but no sink and an electric kettle. Nurit locked and bolted the door.

Dov said Shalom to the woman. She said nothing. She looked pale and spent. The neon light revealed dark roots in her blonde hair. She refused eye contact with him.

"She's called Nana, and in English 'Mint Tea', because they say she 'likes to sip men'. She's from a small village in east Romania. We're trying to persuade her to give evidence against three men for trafficking and rape. If she'll talk with you here, it'll be good practice for her court appearance. That she's here at all is encouraging ."

Nana spoke, never looking up, pausing only for Nurit's translation.

"I came here to earn money. Things are very difficult at home. My family is very poor. My father is sick and can't work anymore. An Israeli girl called Rachel came one day and promised me work in an old people's home for Romanian Jews near Jerusalem.

"How did you get here?"

"Rachel got me air-tickets to Tel Aviv. But we arrived in Cairo. I didn't know. I was in a group of other girls. They took away our passports after the airport. Then we went in a small truck, men with guns wearing scarves, into the desert."

"She means Bedouin," Nurit said.

"After several hours we were told to get out. We walked for many hours. It was hot like I never knew. They made us crawl for a long time until we reached a wire fence and we wriggled under it."

"Were you given water or food?"

"Nothing. Then JoJo met us. I learned his name after. He drove us to Tel Aviv and took us to a hotel not far from here. Three other men joined him, big men. They took us into a room and told us to strip in front of them. One girl refused. They beat her. Then they made us walk about naked, like the cattle market in my village. They examined each one of us, touching and looking in every place. Then a man took me away. He had bought me. He took me to a bedroom in a building. There were strong lights and a man with a camera. They made me get on the bed and raped me. The man with the camera filmed. There were different men each day. Sometimes I was hired out for a party. Always what I did was filmed."

Nurit said, "She's on several Internet sites, 'Nana gets it for the first time', 'Nana learns where it goes,' 'Nana gets a double stuffing.' And if she's in pain they keep that in. When she's not in a brothel, she's being wanked over on someone's TV screen. She's valuable."

"Help me please help me." Nana said in halting Hebrew.

"Will you go to court? Will you identify the men?" Dov asked, his mind cold, trying to sound sympathetic, questions tumbling over themselves in his mind: what did Jojo look like, who were the men who raped her, were drugs used?

"Not sure. How can I be safe if I speak in your court?"

Nurit asked him, "Can you help her or is this outside TPI's scope?"

"I can't promise anything. TPI's very small. But I want these people in prison and I'll need a lot more details."

"We're only a couple of weeks into building up her trust in us. The whole thing depends on her. You can see how vulnerable she is. "

"OK. I'll get back to you," said Dov.

He had a breakthrough a few days later. With help from a surveillance team, the distribution centre for the porn videocassettes featuring Nana was tracked to a warehouse in south Tel Aviv.

The TPI full-time staff budget was limited to Dov and Aviel, so Shimon Ben Shimon was on a short term contract as a Technical Communications consultant. He'd begun as a teenage video and computer nerd and then taken a computer studies degree at the Weizmann Institute. He was an ace programmer and confronted with a problem, his philosophy was "Don't be right, be wise." And then he'd write a computer program to solve the problem.

The closest to swearing was his word, 'Plotnik'. "Plotnik police!" "Plotnik hard drive!" "Plotnik programmers!"

He was strange looking. His goatee beard and metal framed spectacles brought Trotsky to mind when Dov first met him. Below the neck Shimon was nothing like the starchy Trotsky. He never sat up straight, just sprawled, legs out, hands in pockets.

On Dov's only visit to Shimon's work place, his Yafo apartment, no furniture or anything like a home was visible. Every meter was occupied with electronics, cables, tower shells, keyboards, motherboards, soldering irons, floppy discs of various sizes and generations, digital video tapes, edit controllers, screens of different dimensions, and even a couple of video cameras, one minus its lens, its guts in a pile on a cluttered work surface. On top of his PC screen was a Linux penguin and in his shirt collar was a Lightworks red shark emblem. Shimon answered Dov's questions in disjointed sentences: "Lightworks errrrrrrrh the best… Avid's for plotniks…Yow! They're at war errrrrrrh… Lightworks is made for editors by editors… Oy, you should see their edit controller… just like a Steenbeck for film editing… No, so, Dov errrrrrh…Have you heard how Linux… errrrrrrh?" Dov barely deciphered the torrent of language.

He resorted to Instant Messaging. “Good morning Shimon,” he began.

Shimon’s, “Shalom Dov” appeared on Dov’s screen.

He typed: “How do I take out a porn video distribution center? What’s the most important bit of kit they wouldn’t want to lose?”

Shimon: “Roller skates.”

Dov thought it was a computer program: “Is that hard to get? Does it come from abroad?”

Shimon: “Toys R Us.”

Dov: “Explain.”

Shimon: “It’ll be a big warehouse somewhere with hundreds of VCRs which need to be manually loaded and emptied. Can’t be done electronically. Guys on roller skates go up and down aisles.”

Dov: “And the kit?”

Shimon: “What’ll be essential…probably the router from the master player and the computer control for the whole system. Best is to burn it all down.”

Aviel came in to the room. “What’s doing, boss?”

Dov filled him in. Aviel went monosyllabic and echoed Nurit’s concern for Nana’s safety. Dov lost patience.

“TPI’s got to prove itself. Taking out that warehouse does that.”

“But Nana’s life’s at risk. They’ll know only a major institution could mount this size of operation. They’re bound to make the link with us. TPI’s not a secret.”

“God Aviel, who knows how long the court case will last? I’ll advise Nurit when we do the warehouse so she can get another safe house for Nana. How’s that?”

Later Aviel was sure Dov didn’t tell him when the warehouse attack was, and he was certain he forgot to warn Nurit.

Dov wanted the physical evidence that TPI had struck its biggest blow. Only when he ordered up the raid and was on the way, did he begin to feel he was winning.

No one in the air-conditioned warehouse in an industrial estate in south Tel Aviv took much notice of the two white vans that halted outside the entrance. In an area closed off by open-plan office screens Dov saw a Lightworks edit suite and a rack of digital Betacam recorders and players, two routers, and two computer towers.

The warehouse interior was as Shimon had described it, aisles of floor-to-ceiling metal racks of VHS VCRs. The six loaders were ordered to remove their skates then were taken away for questioning. Dov rummaged through a box of cassettes. They all had Nana's photo on the covers. It was the same in the next and the next.

The police photographer took the shots Dov set up, Dov wielding a sledgehammer, debris in the background, Dov next to the wrecked Lightworks edit suite, Dov outside the warehouse doors chained and padlocked with police No Entry! stickers plastered over the glass. He had no sense of post-combat elation.

"SUPER COP SMASHES PORN VIDEO FACTORY!" declared one banner headline. And featured under it was the photo of Nana Dov had seen on the cassette box covers.

Two days later, the story was still hot, but another suicide bomb could blast the TPI story off the front pages instantly. He prayed neither would happen. His cell rang.

"Do you know what you've done?" Nurit Keter shouted. "Nana's missing! She stayed overnight at the bus station, but this morning no sign of her."

"Didn't you move her?" he managed.

"When did you tell me to do that? You said there was nothing to worry about! With those headlines? And her photos all over the papers and TV? Photos of Super Cop, smashing away? It was a hammer to crack a nut. You selfish bastard. You've jeopardized everything and probably her life."

"You don't know that," Dov tried. "There are loads of reasons for her disappearance. The headlines? We kept her name out of it. I'll put out an APB. She'll turn up." He wasn't completely convinced himself.

"Her name? What about her photo everywhere? If I haven't found her, you won't."

"Do you have a picture of her as she is normally?"

She snapped, "Don't be an ass. That's the last thing we want."

"So how can I help? No photo, no search."

"It took weeks for her to trust me. I should never have listened to you," she said caustically.

"I'll get my deputy Aviel Weiss on to it. Meanwhile we've got invaluable videocassette evidence for your court case. Nana'll turn up and then you can proceed. It's not just her word anymore is it?" He shut the phone off before Nurit could gouge more out of him.

The warehouse operation was out of business. The team of workers were being quizzed. His phone went again. It was Shalit congratulating him, "but remember Dov, you're only as good as your next arrest."

"She's dead and we'll never find her body," Aviel seethed. "The traffickers won't be nailed, which was the whole point. You didn't give a fuck."

"The raid was crucial, putting down our marker. Nurit could have moved her if she was so concerned," Dov said frostily.

"That girl's death is down to you!"

"How do you know she's dead? Talk to Nurit, see what you can do."

Aviel was speechless. What good would talking to her do? Why didn't Dov care?

Dov said, "I'm going home. I'll see you here in the morning."

He slept well that night.

Chapter 8
October 1995–June 1999

Lana's special place, high above the al Batuf valley where the family's name came from, was like sitting on the edge of the world, on the spine of the furthest of the Ram's Horns Hills. She loved the isolation, her village and her home behind her and everything before her.

She'd once asked Ibrahim, "Where are you from? Where are you going?"

His answer was immediate. "I am a man of the land. I came from the land and I will return to the land."

And she told herself, "I'm not like that."

The village wasn't a village. It was a town by any other name, but They wouldn't allow it that title. "Town" had too many political and economic implications, both for Them and the Arab inhabitants so a generation after the Nakba, they all called it "village".

Cut down the frenzied spider's web of phone and power cables and spread the houses out and it would have been an attractive place. But roaming today's ugly skyline to escape the ugly reality, you lifted your eyes to the hills and hoped to find succor there.

Ibrahim found only the Nakba's ghosts amongst them. They were easily summoned, working, worshipping, chatting.

He tried to imagine how the village would look now if they had lived.

The hills contrasted hard and soft beauty, jagged heights with straight-line descents, silvery olive leaves with wild dun terrain which turned green after the first rains.

Unlike her father Lana knew no ghosts. Mrs al-Taj had told her that if she applied herself she might get a place at university. It wasn't out of the blue. Mrs al-Taj had discussed it with Khadija at the recent parents evening so when she came home and Lana said, "Mummy, I want to go to university," Khadija said, "I agree. I'll speak to Uncle Basil, I'm sure he'd be willing to help prepare you for your entrance tests."

Basil Khoury and his family had been neighbors when the al Batufs lived down in the village. Basil was a politics and philosophy lecturer at Haifa University where Lana wanted to study. He was also a political activist, ambitious to enter politics and become a Member of Knesset, Israel's parliament. Ibrahim didn't approve of him.

"I want to study education," Lana exulted.

"That's good." Khadija said, "too many Muslim women are locked up in child-bearing and housekeeping, you know. But times are hard and one salary isn't enough. Our men don't accept we can earn too. We can learn from the Jews. They have the jobs. Look at your father. He hates them but he uses their farming methods. What goes on beyond the village is not on another planet, it's next door, it's all around us."

Khadija went on, "Basil will need paying and then there are university fees. Shwaya shwaya, slowly, Lana. I'll speak with your father."

"I know Lana's clever," Ibrahim grumbled in bed that night, on his back, eyes closed, finally relaxing after his long day. Khadija propped up on her elbow. "But what about marriage?" he asked. "There's already hints from several fathers."

"Oh?" Khadija said, "you didn't tell me."

"Well they've only just started. I didn't take them seriously. Not yet."

"Habibti, my love, our daughter isn't a crop of watermelons. It's not as it was when we married. Girls with university degrees are prized as brides."

"Prized? You make Lana sound like a fine mare or something. She's only sixteen."

"Don't pretend you don't know how a university degree adds to Lana's marriage prospects. She'll be seventeen by the time she'd start her course. Anyway Mrs al-Taj is very keen."

"That woman! She's filled Lana's head with this. If she's so keen, let her pay for it!" he growled. "I'll tell her myself..." his voice tailed off. "I don't want Lana being influenced by the Yahud. It's not good this, it's not good."

Khadija asked, "Can we send her abroad? Maybe Yusef can help. He got his degree in Dubai."

Ibrahim was quiet. Khadija was sweetly cornering him.

"I won't involve Yusef."

Khadija lay down, her lips inches from Ibrahim's ear. She whispered, "Basil will prepare Lana for the entrance exams at Haifa University."

He sat up, almost shouting, "He's nothing but hot air!"

Khadija shushed him. "He's said he'll do it for nothing, it would be an honor."

Ibrahim looked down at this beautiful woman who knew him so well. "You've decided haven't you?"

"Lana will go to the university."

He kissed her. But he didn't say that if Lana got into university it would be on his terms.

Lana focussed on the work Uncle Basil gave her. The big

man with curly red hair, normally loud and overbearing, was gentle with Lana, pointing out trick questions in the sample test papers he got her, working through her answers to them. She discovered application and discipline she hadn't known she possessed. She was in awe of Basil. She also noticed how he reacted whenever Khadija came in with tea; he'd stop talking and his eyes would follow Khadija's swaying hips. Lana dismissed it, not wanting anything to interfere with her exam preparations.

***

Lana stood at the front of the dingy school assembly hall the morning it was announced that she had gained a university place. She was the second girl in the school's history to go to university. Ghazaleh grinned at her, Rania looked jealous.

Hatem was heart-broken. They'd crossed the grass line into Ibrahim's best olive grove; Lana never told Hatem whose it was, her little secret within this one, the branches screening them. A natural rocky outcrop called the bourj, tower, rose behind them, high above the trees.

"So, I'm leaving," Lana exulted. "My father made it a condition that I'll have to come home each day, but I'll be spending most of every day far away from here and in the end I won't come back".

"I'll bet you hate him for that," Hatem said.

She wasn't going to admit he was right and kissed him.

"You know I think about you all the time," he began, returning the kiss. "I've hardly seen you and now you're going." He began lifting her sweater. She stopped him.

Hatem was infatuated with Lana.

"I want to remain a virgin until I'm with my husband."

He blurted, "I'll marry you!" His eyes begged for a yes.

"Don't be crazy," she admonished. "Our fathers would

never agree in a million years. Why do they hate each other?"

He didn't know, but realization crept into his look and he said, "That's it isn't it, why you like being with me? The risk."

She smiled, more to herself, and kissed him again.

The night before university Lana walked through the village saying silent goodbyes. Men in coffee houses sat and smoked. Women chatted about the inconsequential things in village life. They had been born here and would die here. Fate held them where they were. Faith gave them solace. Yet in their faces, in their eyes, when they smiled at her, Lana saw their uncertainty. They were anxious for her. They had watched her growing up, a child of one of their respected families, people of the land just like them. That's Lana al Batuf. Isn't she pretty, doesn't she look like her mother? She smiles infrequently, just like her father, but those dimples? Now she might be lost to them, gone to be amongst those who'd caused the Nakba, and the loss of their land and honor. Her leaving was a threat to their fragile continuity. Lana saw and heard it all and was more certain than ever she was doing the right thing.

University began on a hot September morning. The campus awed her. The Eshkol Tower skyscraper dominated the long hilltop crammed with faculty complexes. Each structure was different, with donors names boldly displayed, so much steel and glass, such expense. Lana was simultaneously confused and impressed.

Her first lecture was on Globalization and the Politics of Identity. The lecturer was Dr Fouad Assad, one of her mentors. The hall was crammed with girl students, many from other hill villages chatting nervously. Assad saw Lana trying to mentally change gear.

"What don't you get, Miss… what's your name please?"

"Lana al Batuf. I don't see how this links to Education."

"I see. The word globalization is unfamiliar?" Girls giggled.

"No."

"Ah. How about this – who are you?"

She replied impudently, "I just told you."

The laughter was overt. Dr Assad joined in. He was short and round with intelligent close-together eyes magnified by glasses, cropped hair brushed forward.

"Yes you did," he said after the mirth subsided. "You're from around the al Batuf valley yes? An old farming family rooted in the land?"

Lana nodded, impressed.

"OK. But who are you, in relation to the rest of the world?"

The concept flummoxed her.

"Let me help you," he said soothingly. "Here's the north of Israel." A map was projected on the screen behind him. "And here's the university." His pointer made a red dot. He changed the map scale on the projector so that the map got bigger and the dot smaller, until it was lost in the world.

"What happens here affects the world, and vice versa. Globalization can reduce conflicts, promote human rights and democratic values. It can also contribute to complacency and promote violence."

Lana raised her hand. "And how does that work with my degree?"

"Open your mind, and the rest will follow. Widen your focus." She nodded. "Can you study Education, isolated from the rest of the world? Can you honestly ignore how our little corner affects it?" She welcomed the idea. It took her to places from which her father, Hatem, the village, looked very small.

Chapter 9
November 1995

As Yigal Amir fired his last shot into Yitzhak Rabin, Felipe Abuhatzeira was hammering his wife Anya to death. It was Dov Chizzik's first TPI murder investigation.

Among Dov's videos was a recording of the peace rally in Prime Minster Rabin's honor on November 4th 1995 in Kings of Israel Square, Tel Aviv. Rabin has just left the stage. He walks towards some stairs, and the camera jerkily follows and picks up two figures as Rabin has a brief conversation with them.

Rabin: "Efi it's good to see you here. I value your support and I don't only mean your money."

The camera pans back as Efi Livnat laughs: "Thanks Yitzhak. I didn't always believe in what you were doing. But so many young people support you. One of them is my son-in-law here."

Rabin, with his Humphrey Bogart smile, says what Dov will never forget: "I know him Efi, Dov Chizzik, a brave soldier and the youngest high ranking officer in the police. We need you Dov. You set a fine example. It was good tonight wasn't it?" There is no sound of Dov's reply. There wasn't one.

And moments after Rabin left them, Efi asked, “Well, Dov, what do you think of my friend Yitzhak....” Then there were three pops, and Dov mercilessly pushed Efi to the ground shouting “Gun!”

When a people kill their elected leader, something changes. Dov felt that Israel faltered, as if it lost pace with the rest of the world’s gyrations. Something inside him shifted.

That night very late, he lay in bed with Liora. The two children had long ceased setting each other off and were asleep.

In Dov’s mind the identity of the assassin kept churning; he wore a knitted kippa and was a student at Israel’s only religious university. No one in security stopped Rabin’s murderer because they weren’t prepared for such an eventuality.

During Dov’s long shut-down, Liora anguished over whether he was suffering from PTSD, but knew how he’d react at the suggestion. Why would it, the whole nation was where he was. Why not her too, she pondered, because each individual dealt with trauma differently was all she could come up with. She opted for a soft approach, called two close friends, Gershon and Ruhama, and arranged to visit them during Shabbat.

“We’ve had fun with job interviews,” Ruhama chatting about her work, hoping normality would deflect Dov. “It’s hard finding the right candidate for our Beersheva unit director. Only one shone and he was a problem.” They were sitting on the veranda of the Steinman’s summer home, purchased for “almost nothing” a year before, drinking chilled white Golan wine. The Judean hills were changing into their winter green. Dov was monosyllabic.

Gershon Steinman, a senior Justice Ministry advisor, was one of the crowd from Dov’s school days, on the railings in the square on Friday nights, the nervous one when the other boys were ogling the girls, never a hint of his intellect and ambition. He accumulated degrees from the Hebrew University, Oxford, and a PhD in Conflict Resolution from Rutgers before being head-hunted by the Ministry. "I never wanted an academic career," he'd said on his ministerial appointment, "there's too much to do in the real world."

Ruhama was his third wife, an expert on Restorative Justice, and Gershon was feeding her concepts into the Ministry. She ran pilot programs in Victim-Offender Mediation and trained facilitators.

She was in full flow, her eyes flashing. "The khutzpah of it. He'd actually been the Beersheva unit's assessor, then applied for the director's job and demanded double the salary. Talk about insider trading!"

Dov tuned in and out. These were close friends, Ruhama ready to talk, Gershon's Ministry influence there for him, as his 'rabbi'.

There was a pine tree on the edge of the Steinman's garden, Dov's favorite tree in the world. It had two branches that were curved upwards like arms cradling an invisible burden, waiting to catch a falling someone from the sky. Dov wished it was him.

They discussed children. Ruhama described her daughter Rina's latest boyfriend crisis.

Dov surfaced. "What does he do?" he asked.

"Nothing. Left school. Avoided the army, which he hates, like everything else. But he and Rina were there for Rabin that night…"

All eyes were on Dov. He couldn't stay within himself any longer.

"You should try your mediation on the assassin Yigal Amir and the Rabin family."

The tree couldn't cradle him, save him from Ruhama's stunned, "What did you say?" or Gershon's explosive, "What on earth do you mean Dov?"

It was a mistake, he wanted to say. It was thoughtless, but he wasn't really thinking, just hitting out.

"Look at Amir. A religious student at an orthodox university. Which of the commandments he was taught was he following when he shot Rabin? Tell me!" Liora was pulling at Dov who was standing and shouting. He ignored her. "Many rabbis said the land Rabin wanted to negotiate for peace was God-given. So it was a simple equation for them: Land for peace equals treachery. Rabin was a traitor. Kill him. Go mediate your way out of that Ruhama. What in your restorative justice is there, a bullet for a bullet?" Then he noticed Liora's arms around him, tugging him towards his chair and he let her.

The rest of the afternoon they spent batting their distress back and forth; no West Bank rabbi had condemned Amir; opposition leader Netanyahu hadn't denounced the Nazi demonization of Rabin at anti-government rallies.

"Didn't anyone see where this was going?" Dov asked.

Gershon answered, "Didn't you?" And despite Dov's blazing eyes, and Liora shaking her head, he plowed on, "We're not those rabbis and we're not Yigal Amir. Why didn't the media come to us?"

"Who's 'we'? Gershon?"

After a short pause Ruhama said innocently, "We've started going to a Torah study group."

Gershon added, "It's not a secret. Ruhama knew a fair bit of Jewish law, to understand the roots of restorative justice."

"So who's this 'we'?" Dov repeated evenly.

"We modern believing Jews," replied Gershon adamantly.

"This new club of yours?"

"It's not a club like a gym. We're practicing Jews, engaging with modernity."

"No more non-kosher seafood then? No more driving or working on Shabbat? What we ate today, was it cooked yesterday? You're not supposed to cook on Shabbat."

"Yes to all that. And the food was cooked for us." Ruhama said.

It was Liora's turn. "You mean you have a maid?"

"Not a maid exactly. She's a local girl from a village nearby." Ruhama's tone echoed Gershon's.

"You mean you've become 'newly religious'?" Dov suggested helpfully.

"It's very fulfilling," Gershon said relieved at Dov's description.

"You joined the silent modern religious majority, whose silence was deafening when their orthodox friends denounced Rabin as a traitor, right?" Dov's voice rose.

Gershon and Ruhama looked at each other but said nothing.

Dov took in the distant twinkling lights of Tel Aviv and saw where he was, as if for the first time. He said sadly, "I know you both far too well. I'll always love you even if your 'holiday home' is in occupied territory, in the West Bank, on land Rabin wanted to give back for peace, and even if your maid is a Palestinian." He paused. "We're all responsible for what happened. I just don't know how to deal with it, and I'm really scared about what comes next."

Chapter 10
December 1995–January 1996

Dov went for walks alone along the promenade. The Abuhatzeira murder file remained unopened on his desk two weeks after Shalit had passed it to him. Nothing seemed to galvanize him into starting the case. He even shunned his usual oasis of calm, his classical music CDs.

He infuriated Liora. She felt the balance shifting even further in their marriage.

At Gilad's one night, Dov came out of his limbo and started advocating equal pay for women and Liora had caustically asked, "Yes and doesn't that get fucked up when a woman gets pregnant? Then it's back to Le Maze classes and the wild food urges and sleepless nights. Equality? Men should try pregnancy before they mouth off."

But on the way home Dov carried on. "What do you mean 'gets pregnant'? Yael's birth wasn't an immaculate conception. We talked about it."

"Not really," Liora snapped.

"I forced you?"

"No, it's just not the way I imagined it."

"Aren't you looking at crèches?"

"I didn't for Yaniv. I could get a child-minder."

"I'm not so keen on that."

"Why not? You already suggested it!"

"Let's talk about it when neither of us is so pissed off."

Rabin's murder had created the black hole Dov dropped through and the subject of child minders got lost with him.

Dov's watch said 12.31.95 the last day of 1995. November and December had come and gone in swirls of undefined images that left him with a pounding heart.

Aviel called. Dov hadn't taken any calls for days and there was no reason why he took this one.

"Have you seen the photos of the victim?" Aviel asked, instead of the urge to say, "why the fuck haven't you answered all my calls?" He had a hunch that Dov was still in shock. He'd seen the TV footage of Dov and Rabin moments before the fatal shot. Enough already, Rabin was dead and Dov had a TPI related murder case to solve. Murder investigations were his specialty.

Dov leafed through the copy murder file and found a set of photographs of a woman, the victim. Why she looked familiar was another of the myriad of unanswered questions he'd accumulated.

"You still there Dov?"

"Yeah."

"Remember that first porn video you watched? You couldn't stop talking about it?"

The faulty light bulb in his brain suddenly glowed. "Anya Abuhatzeira was the blonde," Dov said. And then the other figure came back to him, her crimson haired partner, in what was called FFM – female, female, male sex. Sara Moledet.

"Fire and Flame," Aviel said. "Their stage names."

"Arrange to bring Sara Moledet in."

"I'm doing that now," Aviel said and ended the call. That's our Dov Chizzik, he smiled to himself, imagining the analytical cogs in Dov's brain starting to mesh again

Dov strained to retain details of the murder. Names and backgrounds of the three main individuals, the suspect, the victim, the witness who found the body, all remained a blur. He finally decided to visit the crime scene.

That evening, the tranquillity of the Kfar Saba street lined with tall eucalyptus trees was punctured by the media and press circus outside the murder scene building.

The entrance was set back in well-groomed gardens and more eucalyptus, lending an air of permanence. When a reporter called out, "Where's the suspect Commander?" Dov was caught in the glare of his ignorance.

The headline and photo the following morning, TV and flash lights bleaching out Dov's features except his open mouth, said it all: "Super Cop Clueless!"

"They'd been arguing almost since they moved in. I called the police twice because of it," Rikki Rishon told Dov as they sat down in his living room.

"What was the argument about, Mr Rishon?" Dov began lightly.

"Rikki, please, everyone calls me Rikki." Dov nodded.

Of Dov's first impressions, Rishon's plump reddened cheeks as if from physical exertion or a fever, stayed with him, that and his unstylish crewcut. He stayed with plump as his overall impression of the man.

"Nothing specific. He'd come home drunk after work, or get drunk half an hour or so later. Then he'd shout, slam doors."

"How long did that go on for?"

"Oh the first two years…"

"No, sorry, I meant each time?"

"Hours, hours."

"Really?"

"Yes, sometimes three hours."

"When did it stop?"

"When I phoned the police."

"Sorry, I meant what time did the noise usually stop?"

"Well, that was odd. If it was week days, it stopped around ten, ten thirty, as if they both knew that they needed to go to sleep in time to get up for work."

Dov surveyed the living room. If Rishon was materialistic it wasn't reflected in the décor. Like most Israeli salons it had whitewashed walls, a tiled floor with a beige rug, comfortable but old furniture. Dov took in splashes of color from fresh cut flowers in vases on the table in the dining corner, and on the glass-topped coffee table. On the walls, a photograph of an Arava desert sunset, and another of antelope in an arid setting. Through the open balcony doors was an array of flourishing greenery in clay pots.

Rishon was still speaking. "She died about five years ago, my wife. Heart attack. The plants and shrubs were hers and I keep the place as neat as she did."

Dov said, "I'm sorry." Rikki mopped his brow with a sodden tissue. The contrast between the room's air-conditioned temperature and Rikki's made Dov wonder what he'd interrupted.

"Tell me Mr ah Rikki, what do you do?"

"I'm a teacher, well really a departmental head now, of IT, at the Kfar Saba boarding school. We've just built a new wing."

"You mean the famous boarding school?" Dov knew the school's national reputation for excellence.

"Yes," Rikki said proudly.

"Are the photographs yours?"

"Yes. It's a hobby. One's in the Arava, but the other's a wildebeest on the veldt in South Africa."

"I thought it was an antelope. You from there? There's nothing in your accent."

“Yes. We came in 1968. With my family. We went to a kibbutz and then I was called up for army service.”

“How did you get into IT?”

“Oh it was sort of natural. I did communications technology in the army and afterwards at university.”

“Tell me more about the noisy neighbors. You called us in?”

“One night he seemed to be very drunk and I heard screams. Then I heard her, Anya, shouting “Stop hitting me!” So I called the police.”

“And what happened?”

“They came and that was that.”

“Do you know what happened when they arrived?”

“I couldn’t help hearing it all. They broke down the door. Then an officer came to tell me they’d issued him a warning.”

“What about the wife?”

“You’re the policeman. You know what happens in these cases. Isn’t it in the file?”

“She didn’t bring any charges against her husband so they didn’t arrest him.” Dov was guessing. He hadn’t read the file, just skimmed it. What else had he overlooked?

“Right.”

Dov sighed inwardly. “And since then?”

“They’d do the door slamming and shouting. During the Purim festival two years ago, he got very drunk, the row was insufferable and I complained and he stopped.”

“You complained? Who to?”

“First to the police, but they didn’t make it this time, and then to them.”

“To the Abuhatzeiras directly?”

“Yes.” Rishon looked embarrassed. “I went down and knocked on the door and wished them a happy holiday and asked if everything was OK. She looked dreadful, peeking from behind the door, controlling her sobs. She said, "we're fine," and then closed the door. I heard them arguing some more then it quietened after that."

"No further incidents?"

"I couldn't tell if he was still knocking her about, but it was nothing like before."

"Then suddenly the noise started up again?"

"Yes. Then it stopped completely. After a while I got used to the peace and quiet. I could go to sleep without the shock of doors banging beneath me. It used to give me palpitations. I thought they'd gone away together, or she'd left him or something."

"So how did you discover the body?"

"It was really a fluke. I'd stored some of my wife's belongings in the bomb shelter in the basement. I went down to retrieve a photograph I missed. There was a smell from one of the air ducts. It was strong and the closer I got to it the more familiar it became. I'd smelled it in the Yom Kippur war, from unburied bodies. You never forget that."

Dov asked Rishon to show him. The man looked momentarily discomfited, then went to get the key.

"The body," Rishon said, "was wrapped in plastic sheeting and pushed into one of the ducts."

They took the elevator down to the basement car park. Rishon unlocked the huge grey steel door marked Shelter, swung it open and switched on the light. The interior was bare concrete, the floor swept clean, one wall taken up with large metal storage cupboards.

Near one corner, three-quarters of the way up on the wall, was a hinged grating. MAZAP had left police tape across it. Dov lifted the tape, peered in, concluded that a duct was a duct, thanked Rishon for his cooperation and went out to his car, ignoring the baying TV and press pack.

Dov was incredulous. "She was murdered here somewhere, her body was sealed up and put into the air duct, and no one saw anything?" They were in the Abuhatzeira's salon. He opened the blinds and windows. The smell of cheap ammonium cleaning product filled the whole place.

Aviel's impatience dissipated as Dov padded about like a lion inspecting his territory, glancing at photocopies of the murder file and crime scene report. He said, "We need more hands here."

"Why do you think we caught this one? Commander Shalit read the file and made the simple equation: a murder victim moonlighting in sex videos equals Dov Chizzik and TPI, and here we are, an extra efficient use of police resources. There are no more hands. We're less than three thousand police for the three million or so people in the whole of the Tel Aviv metropolitan area. What about a micro-analysis, like last time?" He meant the centimeter by centimeter search they'd done on their hands and knees during the Bar Pigyon murder. It had produced that vital clue.

The layout was identical to Rishon's apartment. But it was completely depersonalized. It was sparsely furnished. The fridge was empty. An old pine packing case with a foam mattress was the bed. The TV was ancient and battered. The décor badly needed refreshing. But the floor tiles were spotless. Dov's eyes narrowed. "Look at that," he said. "The tiles look like they've just been laid."

MAZAP's fingerprinting was on all the obvious surfaces, but reading the crime scene report carefully for the first time, Dov learned that no fingerprints had been found. The officer had scribbled in the margin, "No prints on usual surfaces. No blood residues. Suspect wore gloves?" Felipe's prints were on the body, the tape used to seal it up, the grating, the surfaces in the bomb shelter. But there was no Felipe.

And the crime scene had been sanitized, presumably by Felipe.

After looking into every room, Dov said, “It’s as if the Abuhatzeiras were never here.”

He wandered back to the spare room.

“Saving the best for last?” Weiss called out cheekily from the drying room next to the kitchen.

“What?” Dov barked back.

“Where’s the murder weapon? What was it?”

I hadn’t read that yet? Dov riffled through the photocopies again, looking for the autopsy report. It suggested the victim had died from repeated blows to the head, from an object whose indentations resembled an ordinary hammer. But there were no bloodstains to indicate where this had taken place, and absolutely no sign of the murder weapon.

“Bloody hell,” he said.

“Why?” Weiss asked. “There’s no blood and hell’s where the suspect’s gone.”

Dov groaned. “That was levity?”

“Maybe not as literary as you’d have liked”

“We need MAZAP back, to help with the micro-analysis.”

“We’re not going to do it ourselves?” Dov’s face said no. “OK, if they can be spared. What are they looking for?”

“Anything that tells us where the murder was committed and maybe even where the weapon went.”

Aviel called MAZAP.

“What’s known about this couple?”

“You really haven’t read the file have you,” Aviel said. “Anya Abuhatzeira nee Grivsky was thirty-eight, single, from Russia. After marrying, she worked in a boutique in Kfar Saba. They married a year before getting this place. Felipe was an electrical engineer from Bat Yam, born in

Morocco. His family came to Israel in 1958 when he was four. He was a smart kid, good at math and sciences, and was pushed through officers' course and into university, part of our own GI bill in the 70s, which helped create a new Sephardi bourgeoisie," Weiss said.

"Don't like Sephardim?"

"It's not that. It was in my sociology studies at uni. I learned that just like Ashkenazi is a big generalization for all the Jews of Eastern European origins, so Sephardi is another great catchall. It covers all the Jews of the Arab lands, those who had settled there since the Babylonian exile and those who left Spain after the Inquisition. They were largely responsible for putting the right wing into power for the first time in 1977. Menachem Begin courted them. He gave them a leg up out of their minority social status, even though they were the majority of the population, with positive discrimination in the army, university, jobs. He appealed to their natural conservatism. So they voted for him and the Likud. It's been pretty well tribal at each elections ever since."

"OK. So?" Dov nodded.

"Anya was Russian Ashkenazi. Felipe married out. Part of his new found upward mobility. And I'll bet it caused ructions."

"That's just a hunch Aviel. Talk to the families."

"You didn't read the file. There's no family on Anya's side. Felipe's got a sister who isn't very cooperative. Anya's death seemed irrelevant to her. The parents are no longer alive. The father behaved as if Felipe was dead to him when the engagement was announced. The sister followed her father's fatwa."

"Talked to their employers?"

“No in-depth interviews.”

“It’d be useful to know what kind of hours they worked. If Felipe did late hours or travelled for work; if Anya’s day job performance suffered from what she did when Felipe was away. There’s been a murder. The suspect disappears and everyone goes to sleep?”

“Come on Dov. It starts and ends with you.”

“Yes,” he paused and said, “Sorry, I’ll learn the file. You go and see the sister.”

“OK.”

***

“That’s you and the late Mrs Anya Abuhatzeira,” Dov told Sara Moledet. The juddering freeze frame on the elderly VHS VCR held crimson wigged Sara and blonde Anya at work on that phallus.

Sara feigned embarrassment. “That’s from a past I’d rather forget,” she said meekly.

“Were you forced into it?”

“I needed money.”

“How long ago was this?”

“That’s hard to remember.”

It was close in the interview room at the Shop and Dov was tempted to open the window and let whatever passed for a breeze in, but that would have come with the din of Dizengoff traffic.

“How many videos did you star in Sara?” Dov asked.

“A few. There’s little more to say. It was years ago.” She paused looking at the image. “I was leaner then, quite cute... I needed the cash. I wasn’t a friend of Anya’s. We only met in front of the camera. I’ve no idea who killed her or why, sorry.”

"Who made the video?"

"I think the cameraman was a Yossi, the lighting was done by a Hagai, and I can't remember the sound man's name."

"Where was it shot?"

"In a warehouse on a Shabbat, they set up the bedroom scenery, and shot it in a couple of hours."

"Who owns Zayin Productions?"

Sara allowed a moue to shape her lips at the name, Zayin, slang for penis. "Not sure, maybe Mr Sabato did, or one of the others. I just got a call offering me cash for a couple of hours work."

"How would anyone know to call you? Is there a sex video agency? Do you fill in an application form? Tick oral, anal, fetish, leather, under 'professional experience'?"

"No nothing like that. There're clubs and houses down by the old bus station and I went to one and said I was available."

"Which one?"

"I don't remember."

"You must have known. How long were you a prostitute before you entered the porn industry?"

"I was never a prostitute and I don't consider myself as part of any industry. I run a legitimate agency. I did what I did in those sex videos because I was broke and I haven't engaged in anything like that since."

"Legitimate? That's enough 'butter wouldn't melt' answers Sara. We estimate that video was made six maybe seven years ago. You make it sound like it was an aberration in your misspent youth. Your rise through the porn industry has been pretty rapid, from porn star to escort agency owner in that time frame. It means someone likes you. And I want to know who that is. I think he's the same person behind the sex video you and Anya were in. And she's been murdered. To eliminate you from our enquiries means you give me straight answers to my questions. Until then, consider your business under twenty-four hour surveillance, and be ready to come back here whenever we have more questions. That could be in half an hour, this afternoon, late tonight, any time. OK?"

"You have my number Dov. Call me. I look forward to it."

She couldn't be sure if Dov had the manpower to carry out his threats, but Sara urgently needed to contact the person Dov was as interested in finding as he was in solving the murder. She didn't think Anya's murder was linked to the man behind Sabato and his friends, assuming it was a man. She'd never met him, didn't know his name, but she knew that he'd arrange to have someone killed if he thought it expedient and dump unreliable employees for the police to deal with. The reports of how Anya's body was found didn't fit the methods she'd heard his people used. All she knew, and the now incarcerated Sabato had told her, was how to pass messages through a network.

She took a cab from the Shop down to one of the big hotels at the bottom of Herbert Samuel Street and made her way to the ladies toilets, stopping twice to admire jewelry in one boutique window and a silk top in another, checking to see if anyone remotely resembling a police officer was tailing her. The contact tradecraft Sabato had taught her was based on Soviet methods. She sat on the toilet lid and wrote a note in small letters on a note pad, folded it into a tiny square, slid it behind a wall mirror above a sink and left two lipstick smudges on the corner of the mirror.

The note, picked up an hour later by a cleaner, a Russian immigrant, reached its destination twenty minutes after that. It read, 'TPI.'

A week later and Dov was no further on. Felipe's sister Anita lived in Haifa. Her husband, also Moroccan, was a wealthy insurance company owner. He would only allow his wife to be questioned in the presence of his lawyers. He blustered for a day before consenting to the interview in their plush villa with a picture window looking out over the bay. It was breathtaking and as much as Aviel could do to avoid staring at it.

Anita went from expletive to fuming silence. Then she, her husband and the lawyers all blustered again when Aviel produced a search warrant and a local team to search the villa. He came up with nothing but a deep detestation for Felipe's sister, his brother-in-law, the lawyers, and the fact that they could all afford that view.

Another team re-interviewed the Abuhatzeiras' Kfar Saba neighbors. None were much help except Mrs Levinson, a widow living opposite Rishon. "Now, he's a very nice man," and said she'd heard doors slamming and shouting. "Anya was an attractive blonde, wearing very", she repeated very, "showy clothing." Anya must have made her eyes drop out.

The Boutique Xtra owner described Anya as quiet, confident, not especially chatty, pretty, never discussed her home life. The manageress said her hours had been inconsistent, and a sick mother was Anya's excuse. She hadn't queried it. Aviel didn't tell her Anya's mother had died before Anya emigrated.

The Abuhatzeiras were rare in another sense. They didn't own a car; most in their income bracket had at least one. Mrs Levinson was a veritable mine of information about her neighbors. Felipe used a company 4x4 whenever he needed it. Anya's place of work and the shopping centre were a reasonable walk away.

The MD of Felipe's company shed little light on his private life. He'd met Anya once and said she was very pretty. His "very" sounded like Mrs Levinson's, but with an obvious male inference.

Felipe was a senior engineer, conscientious, reliable, aspiring to be top drawer, but unlikely to make it. He didn't socialize with other staff after hours. When told that their apartment had been poorly furnished, the MD was surprised. He confirmed that Felipe's salary was well above average and surmised that without children to provide for, the Abuhatzeiras could afford a good life style.

Both bank accounts were in credit, but showed no withdrawals after the murder, ruling out theft as a motive

Another ten days and TPI was at a dead end. The press was still gnawing away, but the coverage, relegated to inside pages, alternated between snide and bored.

Yigal Shalit summoned them to HQ. Dov was morose during the drive to Jerusalem. Aviel left him alone. From whatever depths he had retreated to, he grumbled, "there's a discrepancy, between Felipe's fingerprints all over the air duct etc and their meticulously cleansed apartment." And said no more. It was one of those curiously warm January days in which there could be snow on the hills from Jerusalem to Hebron. The light blue sky tinged golden the closer they got to the capital.

"Yes!...Yes!..." Shalit bellowed into his phone as they entered his office. He looked through them as they sat down.

Dov gazed beyond his boss at the view of Mount Scopus. Two could play the I'm-ignoring-you game.

Shalit shouted angrily, "Hebron's such a fucking mess!" He listened, his Hungarian accent thicker than usual, "No of course it's not our fault!" He waited, said, "OK," ended the call, looked up, shrugged. "Problems with those fucking settlers in Hebron again. And of course the Palestinians.

They deserve each other, they really do. Anyway Dov how are you? How's Liora? And the children?" He didn't wait for a reply. "And you Weiss. Hope Dov's keeping you on your toes. In a bit of a cul de sac, Dov with this case?" He picked up his copy of the murder file. "Cherchez la femme Dov!" he barked.

You're mad, Dov thought. Shalit filled his office with his size and sound. He was in shirtsleeves, leaning forward, the blue tattooed concentration camp numbers evident on his left forearm. Dov searched Shalit's eyes. They told him nothing. What the hell was he talking about?

A large paw reached across the desk, pulled at another file. "What do you know about battered women?" Dov stayed silent, he knew a rhetorical question when he heard one.

Shalit read out, "'Women who are being abused do not see themselves as victims. Their abusers, often their husbands, do not see themselves as being abusive. Abuse takes different forms - psychological, emotional, sexual...' Blah blah. Where was that bit?" Shalit's forefinger scoured lines. "Ah yes, this made me think of you Dov, 'If a partner repeatedly uses one or more of the following to control the other partner: hitting, slapping, threatening, and keeping them from friends, family…then they have been or are being abused.'" Shalit looked up, saw Dov's puzzled expression and laughed with a boom that threatened to shake the windows. "Your case! Not you!" Shalit, still chuckling, motored on, "We've got three abuse elements here: the couple didn't mix socially and were rarely seen together; Anya'd been absent from work; two people reported them shouting."

"None of the rest of the neighbors said they'd heard threats though," Dov offered bravely.

"Did you ask? Well did you?" Shalit yelled. "Go back and ask!" His voice dropped to a calmer level, "When I said

Cherchez la Femme, I meant it. We need to know more about Anya. Was the abuse sudden? Did she hide any bruising?"

Weiss couldn't help himself. "Never mind that. It's her moonlighting in sex videos we should be focussed on. Otherwise why is TPI doing this case?"

Shalit yelled, "Shut the fuck up!" Weiss's face turned the color of his name. "Dov, tell your staff to have some respect for their superiors. My guts tell me this is more to do with the couple's internal dynamic. I don't think this was a porn industry related hit. Your famous instinct tell you the same Dov?"

Dov gave a maybe shrug. If Shalit was right, so was Aviel; why was TPI involved? He didn't want a row with Shalit. "Aviel's right Yigal. Her porn video appearances may have given her husband a motive, if he found out about them, but there's nothing linking her murder to the porn industry. So why us?"

Shalit looked like a big cat about to extend its claws. "Because! I! Say! So! And for fuck sake do the background work you should have done when I first sent you the case file. Talk to the absorption centre Anya was in," Shalit demanded, "her Hebrew teacher and classmates, everything from her arrival to their first fuck, Felipe and she, and anyone else in between. Find it all out!"

Shalit enjoyed their silence. In it he continued, "A woman wrote this research paper. It got me thinking. We need a shrink, someone expert on behavior. Profiling's not new. The army's been doing it for ages, on terrorists." Shalit removed his glasses and put them on the desk. The sun shone across his forearm highlighting the numbers. "Dr Irit Sasson will meet you in the cafeteria in five minutes. She's from the Hebrew University. I've contracted her for three months with an option for three more." Dov was beginning to shake his head, wanting to ask where's the extra budget for this? "Take the help Dov. You need it."

As they left Shalit's office, Weiss said, "the Commander's right. We need a fresh mind."

Dov couldn't disagree, though he was surprised. Shalit didn't approve of people with degrees.

Chapter 11
January–February 1996

Dov didn't like her. She was clever, and unconcerned about how her looks affected men. Irit Sasson intimidated him.

As they sat opposite each other waiting for Aviel to bring over their coffees, Dov sensed an impending clash. He was surprised at how protective he felt about the case, having taken so long to get into it.

Irit Sasson was taller than Dov by half a head in her heels. "You know anything about forensic methodologies?" she asked. Combat had commenced. Her gold hoop earrings jangled whenever she tossed her head, as she had just done.

"Yes. I don't know if they fit this case," Dov said, arms folded.

"Why not?" she asked, "the 480-meter radius theory in the Bar Pigyon murder worked."

"That was hard graft." Dov snapped. Aviel guessed what was coming. "Careful analysis of clues, and a down-in-the-dirt investigation."

She stabbed back. "I am surprised. Where's the cerebral Dov Chizzik? You can't ignore that theory." She'd scored two hits.

Dov almost winced. “Yes, but it was after graft, it wasn’t a guiding light,” unwilling to make any concessions so early in this duel.

“OK,” she said. “If we’re going to partner on this, we need to interview Rishon again and the old lady next door. What’s her name?” Dov couldn’t remember. He was still reeling from her punch to his mental solar plexus with ‘partner’.

She’s sharper than Dov, Aviel thought, but rescued him with, “I forgot to add it to the file notes boss. Elisha Levinson.”

“We’ll call her, back at Kfar Saba,” Dov said rising to leave, before Irit had moved.

“I’ll call her from my cell. You have the number?” she said brightly, looking up expectantly.

“That’s an operational matter Dr Sasson and…”

“Oh Irit please, Dov.”

“I’ll think about it,” he said.

They were heading for their cars in the car park.

Irit said, “OK, OK. Let’s stop this now Dov.”

Both men did a double take.

“You’re nothing like your profile and I don’t know why.”

“What?”

“You’re defensive, proprietorial, rude, none of which is you. I’m not a police officer, I’m a behavioral psychologist. This will be a partnership Dov or it won’t be anything at all. Right now I’d suggest you revert to the uncontaminated Dov that’s in the file.”

“Uncontaminated?” Dov ripped at her.

“The Israel Police force? Not a job for a smart Jewish boy. Unless you’re too dumb for anything else, or on the take,” she parried.

Weiss recoiled.

Dov barked, “Attack therapy? On me? How dare you!”

Irit dipped her head. “You reject, I strike. OK, you’re not dirty. But why is someone with your brains in the force?”

“It’s simple.” Dov said. “Duty.”

“I see. ‘A man’s got to do etc’ and you decided to do it in the police.” She held her steely stare another moment, then said, “What you’ve got with Anya is abuse twice over. From her roots in Russia and from her husband. It’s in the genes. I know about it. I came from a similar background to Felipe. Doing army service was hard enough. Me going to university was such a no-no, my father beat me for even suggesting it. Israel has many quirks, paradoxes even, beneath its hi-tech veneer. Women and men working on a par is a no-no. But I’m a Sephardia and you’re an Ashkenazi.”

“All irrelevant,” Dov said firmly.

“I’ll believe that when you start being the real Dov Chizzik. Something happened to you. Maybe it’s you being there when Rabin was assassinated. We can talk about that. But this case is stuck and I’m offering to unstick it. I need this to progress. There’s no fast track for me Dov. Give me a hand here. I’ve shown you mine.”

She walked to her car.

Dov watched her.

“She’s a real piece, huh?” Aviel said.

“Shut up Aviel,” Dov grunted, thinking, something happened to me? I’m already a suitable subject for her treatment? I don’t think so.

He called Kfar Saba and requested a check of the domestic complaints log, then told Aviel to get down to the old Tel Aviv bus station red light area with photos of Anya. “You never know,” he said.

“This is just to satisfy Shalit isn’t it?”

"He's right. My staff should learn respect for their superiors."

Aviel sat up as straight as he could while driving, said "Commander!" and gave a salute.

Irit sat outside the Kfar Saba police station listening to music. Dov recognized a Mozart string quartet. He walked past her and into the police station, emerging a few minutes later and got into her car.

"Let's go," he said. She was smoking a cigarette and Weiss was stunned to see Dov lean across and take one from her pack. Dov didn't smoke.

Aviel vaulted into the back seat saying, "Shall I guide you Irit?"

Dov waved OK with his cigarette hand. "That's the Hoffmeister isn't it?" he asked Irit.

"Yes. It's brilliant, but I think the Prussian's better."

"So do I," Dov said blowing out smoke. "Was my preference for Mozart in my file?"

She replied by gunning the engine and they took off.

"Sorry to arrive un-announced Mrs Levinson."

"'Friends' is finishing," she said. "Can I offer you tea? I don't have coffee."

"Let me come and help you Mrs Levinson," Irit offered.

Weiss glanced at Dov who said without acrimony, "She's good." He stood by the door listening to the chatter. It sounded innocuous, so he interrupted. "Mind if I look around Mrs Levinson? Just to get a fresh perspective from another apartment in this building?" She consented.

Weiss followed. "You're right to let Irit get on."

Dov breathed out slowly and said, "I need help."

Aviel sought to mollify. "Whatever. What are we looking for?"

Dov snapped, “How should I know? Doctor-high-heels probably already worked out Mrs Levinson’s profile, a nymphomaniac with vampire tendencies. What are we looking for? The answer to life? For God’s sake!”

Irit and Mrs Levinson were in the living room. Dov went into the utility drying room, narrow but wide enough for a normal person to stretch their arms out. It had slatted blinds and a drying line. In one corner was a common domestic waste pipe and a white metal hatch next to it on the floor, Dov presumed for maintenance, and as he looked, he heard water swishing through the pipe.

As they came back, Irit was saying, “That’s really very helpful Mrs Levinson. Mrs Abuhatzeira wore long sleeved tops, even in summer.” She made notes.

“You’re smart Dr Sasson,” said Mrs Levinson. “I may be old but I’m not stupid. I worked as a PA to the Foreign Minister. Powerful man. I know people. That young woman was quite beautiful, sexy. She was hiding something. She was frightened. I could hear it. After the shouting and the doors slamming, there were muffled yelps, like a dog being beaten. Now she’s dead and he’s disappeared.”

Dov and Aviel glanced at each other.

“How often did this occur?” Irit asked.

“The yelps? Often. Around ten at night, two or three times a week. I don’t sleep too well. Arthritis.”

“You’re being very helpful.”

“I hope he’s dead.”

“Who Mrs Levinson?”

“That bastard Abuhatzeira.”

“Are you sure you should say that in front of two police officers, Mrs Levinson?” Irit asked with a little smile.

Mrs Levinson said, “I don’t care why he did it. I just hope he’s dead.”

Outside the apartment, Irit said, "Tough old lady. I'd like to come back. Maybe there's more I can help her recollect? "

"Just handle her sensitively." They started down the stairs.

She nodded, earrings jangling, then she stopped and asked, "Shall we go and do Mr Rishon?"

Dov said, "We're here already, why not?"

Irit lead the way back up the stairs. Neither man could avoid studying her legs, and Dov said, "I need a distraction at some point, OK?" Aviel in mid leer, grinned at the double-entendre.

"What?" Dov said.

Opening his door, Rishon looked disheveled, rumpled shirt, half tucked in, unshaven, ragged look in his eyes. Dov introduced Irit. Newspapers were scattered on the floor, a plate of half finished food sat on the arm of the sofa, plants wilted on the patio, definite contrasts to Dov's previous visit.

Irit sat him down and produced her notebook. "I'd like you to tell me everything you can about Mrs Abuhatzeira. Any detail."

Rishon looked like a squirrel frozen at an unexpected noise. He managed, "Anya…" then looked down at his lap and finding nothing there said, "I heard him. Beating her. In the end she..." He looked down again. Dov wanted to tell him there wasn't anything in his lap but when Rishon looked up, his eyes shone with tears.

"Did it sound like a dog yelping?" Irit asked.

Rishon nodded.

"I'll get you some water," Aviel offered.

Irit unnerved Rishon with, "Did you ever try to speak to Mrs Abuhatzeira about the abuse? I know it's hard," Irit said soothingly, "What do you do? Knock on the door and say, 'I know your husband's beating you, can I help?'"

Rishon found a word. "No."

The sound of glasses clinking emanated from the kitchen, followed by a tap turned full on, then slowed.

Dov stood up. "I'll just be a moment. The toilet's down the corridor?" Moments later a door could be heard opening and closing. The tap poured and glasses clinked again.

As Rishon's head darted in their direction, Irit spoke, insistently. Rishon turned back to her.

"It's another man's wife, isn't it? Not your business. But those sounds stopped you sleeping."

Rishon discovered another word. "Yes".

The toilet flushed.

"Here's the water," announced Aviel, bearing a tray with glasses and a water jug, Dov behind him. Aviel handed one glass to Rishon and then filled the other three. He sipped from one. Dov sipped from his.

"Rikki, why have you changed your story?" Dov asked.

The squirrel blinked.

"You said you'd called us, been down there to complain, it was Pesakh, Passover, I think you said?"

Rishon recovered, from their surprise visit, from his inner thoughts, from his speechlessness. "I said Pesakh? No it was Purim…"

Dov looked quizzical. "Well think about which month it was, that should help."

Rishon looked blankly at him. Irit allowed him a couple of seconds for that.

"Your sleepless nights…" she began, and Weiss interrupted. "Can I use your toilet Rikki, too much water on an empty stomach?" Rishon looked back and forth, confused as he was meant to be.

"Well Rikki?" Dov persisted.

"I couldn't sleep…I…"

"Which festival?" Dov threw at him.

"I…the sound…it was…I'm not sure which festival now. I couldn't sleep. I did go down there. But all those things you said doctor. So accurate. It was very difficult. She was such a lovely person …" Rishon's voice trailed off.

The toilet flushed again. Then there was a pause as another door was opened and the bathroom sink tap ran. Then it stopped. Another pause, the toilet flushed again. Rishon's head moved like a sudden nervous tick towards the noise, away from Irit.

"Lovely, Rikki? What gave you that impression?"

Rishon's head turned back unwillingly, disconcerted by the sounds, wanting to know what was going on. "Oh you know. We all have an aura."

"Really? Fascinating. You knew Mrs Abuhatzeira well enough to detect her aura?" Irit, sweetly.

"Only in passing," Rishon said nodding to reassure himself and his audience, "at the entrance to the building, on the street, that sort of thing. You get a sense of a person after a while."

Weiss came back. "Sorry about that," he said, aware of Rishon's scrutiny.

"And yet you never asked her about the abuse, just asked if she was OK?" Dov asked, bringing Rishon back to him.

"It was difficult."

Irit suggested helpfully, "it's the unstated 'it' between you and Mrs Abuhatzeira…"

"Anya? Wasn't that her name?" Dov interjected. Rishon's head swiveled from Irit to Dov and back, his eyes blinking rapidly.

"An-ya", Irit enunciated the two syllables carefully, "would know that if you could, you'd help her."

Rishon nodded emphatically, "Absolutely."

Dov said, “Rikki, there was no log of a second complaint by you to the Kfar Saba police. You said you’d called them but they never came.”

“I know I called.” Rishon protested.

“And which festival was it?” Dov asked.

“I can’t remember for sure ,” Rishon muttered.

“Think about it OK? You need to remember.”

Rishon blinked and nodded.

They drove away from the building. “What did you find?” Dov asked Weiss.

“You first boss.”

They were in the railway station car park. The first train for the end of the working day was due. A clutch of wives waited for their husbands.

“Just like in Mrs Levinson’s place,” Dov said, “there’s a maintenance hatch in the ceiling of Rishon’s utility room, another hatch in the floor. Below it is the Abuhatzeira’s utility room.”

“Interesting,” Irit said.

“Aviel?”

“Mr Rishon’s toilet flushes fine.” The others didn’t laugh. “He’s quite a photographer. His shots of Anya are all over his study walls. Naked, bruises and lacerations on her back and front, in big color close-ups.”

In the sudden electric atmosphere in the car, Dov said, “Irit, you talk with Elisha Levinson again. I’ll update Shalit. Aviel, get a search warrant for the Rishon flat and 24-hour surveillance on him, to start immediately.”

“Before I do those things,” Aviel said, “remember the Fire and Flame video? There was one in a box of photographic paper in Rikki’s studio.”

“OK. Get me some stills of Sara Moledet from our office copy and take them with you when you go out with Anya’s photos.”

"How am I supposed to do that?"

"Get Sara's shots from the video? You're supposed to be in TPI Aviel, that's Techno Porn as in Techno? Use your initiative." Aviel didn't salute this time.

"Good distraction Dov," Irit said. "More like unnerving him."

"Huh?" asked Aviel.

"While you were in the kitchen, Dov said the last call Rikki made to the police about the Abuhatzeira's noise was Pesakh, not Purim."

"Which was it boss?"

"It's not in the call log at all, but I wanted to shake him up a bit." Dov actually smiled.

The following morning surveillance reported nothing unusual. Just after lunch, Mrs Levinson phoned asking to meet Dov as soon as possible. It gave Dov the excuse to check on the MAZAP micro-analysis of the Abuhatzeiras' flat.

She sat down opposite him in her immaculate living area and placed a small tape recorder on the table. "Dr Sasson came to see me," she said and pushed the playback button.

"Now Elisha I just want to help you relax a little." It was Irit. "Get comfortable and close your eyes and concentrate on my voice. That's good, that's very good," Irit soothed, "as I count to three, let all the other sounds gently fade away, you'll hear outside sounds but I want you to focus on my voice. One. Two. Three. Eyes closed. Good. In a moment I'm going to ask you to take three very slow deep breaths and hold each one to the count of five, release each one slowly and as you do just relaaaax..."

In ten minutes Elisha Levinson detailed Anya Abuhatzeira's layers of make-up, the scarves she'd wrapped high around her neck, and her long sleeve tops, and how on the rare occasions she'd seen Felipe, on the stairs, or at the building's entrance, he'd always avoided her. Irit's voice brought Elisha out of what she said was a nice doze. After Irit thanked her and departed, Dov was astonished to hear Elisha saying, "Fucking khutzpah! 'Help me relax'? That's hypnotism, an invasion of privacy!"

"Did she know you were recording the session?"

"Don't be ridiculous!"

"What made you tape it?"

"Habit."

"Habit?"

"I learned it from the Foreign Minister. Whenever a journalist produced a tape recorder 'just for accuracy', he would do the same. I didn't trust Dr Sasson."

"Can I keep the tape? I'll give it back."

"No need. That's a copy."

Before leaving for Jerusalem to discuss what he'd told Shalit was a critical development, he called Gershon Steinman at the Justice Ministry.

Aviel came in as he was saying, "Thanks Gershon, love to Ruhama."

"Nothing new on Anya down at the old bus station," he said.

"OK. I've got to go to Jerusalem."

"Oh?"

"Yes. Anything else?"

"There's a lot of illegals down there, at the bus station, you can hardly find an Israeli face."

"You didn't need to say at the bus station. I knew where you were..."

"It's like an illegal immigrant center, very unhygienic place to be, like I said they didn't know Anya, but one or two did recognize Sara's photo."

"How did you get the images?"

"Shimon Ben Shimon."

"Good. And…?"

"A couple of Madams said she's there every few months looking for new talent for her agency."

"Not a crime. No solid connections to sex videos?"

"Nothing concrete."

"Well Shalit wants us to solve the murder, so let's get on with it."

"What do you want me to do next?"

"Do another micro-analysis of the Abuhatzeira apartment. And I mean micro. MAZAP may have missed something."

"By myself? Oh come on!"

"Aviel, you can do it. Take a magnifying glass. Make sure the glass doesn't fall out of its holder."

"I'm not Clouseau."

"No but you might be Holmes."

"Dov, this feels like make-work. I've get plenty of stuff to..." Dov was at the door, giving a dismissive wave.

At the Jerusalem HQ Dov found Irit Sasson.

"Hello Dov," she said confidently. "I'm just finishing the Elisha Levinson…"

"We can't use it. Any of it. You got information by false pretenses. If I were you I'd delete the report and quit this assignment voluntarily. If you want to climb, climb. But don't use illegal methods to do it."

"I don't understand Dov..."

"Mrs Levinson taped you. I've got the cassette. The Justice Ministry has been made aware of what you did. You might as well pack up and leave. I'm on my way to see the Commander." Her silence followed him out of the room.

Sitting listening to the tape again with Shalit, Dov smiled to himself at feisty Mrs Levinson. "Well?" he shot at Shalit.

"Well what?" Shalit snarled back.

"We can't use any of this."

Shalit glared. Dov knew he was right and that glare rankled.

"It's tainted Yigal. I've checked with Justice. They concur. We can't use anything from that interview. Sasson should be removed from the case immediately."

Shalit appeared to digest what Dov had said, his mouth silently repeating his last words, avoiding Dov's eyes. "Should she? I don't think so. I'm still your line manager, your superior in years of service if not in rank."

Dov said nothing.

"She'll interview Rishon tomorrow in his apartment after you've supervised the search. I agree, her Levinson examination's out. But, she will interview the chief suspect." Shalit repeated then waved Dov away.

On his way out of HQ Aviel called. "I think I've found some minute deposits MAZAP and the 'sanitizer' of the Abuhatzeira apartment missed."

"Magnifying glass still in one piece?"

Aviel sighed.

"OK, I'll get on to MAZAP. Who was the team leader?"

"Yuval Natanson."

At home that night Yuval called Dov back. "There's a variety of ways of detecting blood residue at a crime scene," he began professorially.

"That's if there's any blood to find."

"Right."

"Kastle-Meyer 1903 is one of the oldest tests, isn't it?"

"Yes indeed."

"And I'll bet Meyer was a good old German Jewish scientist?"

"I'll have to get back to you on that, Dov. But there was an even earlier reagent for hemoglobin, in 1887. We call it Scarlet Holmes after Sherlock Holmes' discovery of it in a Study in Scarlet."

"The intrepid scientist turned detective. Well done Holmes! Anyway, I've read that the Americans are using Ultra Violet light to pick out wiped away blood spatters, even if a bleach was used, by spraying them with luminal which fluoresces under UV."

"It isn't available to us here yet," Natanson said. "Budgetary constraints etc. Anyway as you know none of these tests are simple. They all demand time and effort and constant checking and re-checking. Kastle-Meyer uses a chemical indicator to detect possible hemoglobin residues. You take a swab of what you think might be blood, add the reagent…"

"Phenolphthalein," Dov interrupted, "and then a drop of hydrogen peroxide, and if the swab turns pink quickly, miracle of miracles, it's presumed to be blood."

"Well yes, well done again, that is the essence of it, though there are necessary modifications, a drop of ethanol on the swab first of all to ensure it's as uncontaminated as possible. Anyway after your call we went down to Kfar Saba. Despite the various limitations to the Kastle-Meyer test, and there are many, we came up with two areas of hemoglobin residue, thanks to your number two, Weiss. Whoever sanitized these did an almost perfect job, but what you called a micro-analysis gave us minute residue in tile grouting in the living room floor tiles and in the bathroom tiles. The latter were denser. That suggests an event in or around the shower. Of course murderers rarely contemplate serology patterns and when blood spatters it goes everywhere, depending on the type of weapon, the force used for it and the area of the body targeted."

"So an 'event' happened, a murder was committed in the bathroom."

"The murder was more than likely perpetrated while the victim was standing in the shower. The perpetrator probably thought they'd cover the noise with the shower running and have the shower to clean up afterwards. They were right for nearly one hundred percent of the blood. Problem was the shower had a fixed shower head so they thought the shower water would remove the blood under its stream. They didn't imagine, why would they, that splatter could reach above the shower head. It did and we found it. All easy to miss, in our initial examination."

"Hitchcock's Psycho, without the knife? Well that's excellent. Was this the first or second 'event'?"

"The first."

Dov paused. "I suppose you can't identify whose blood it was?"

"Not yet, but we're working on that."

"And the second?"

"More recent, in floor tile grouting in the kitchen. Two months old. Harder to detect, because of the bleach but, well, Dov Chizzik requests a micro-anlysis and his will is done."

"Go on."

"The perpetrator was really thorough. Bleached the whole place, as you probably guessed. But he was in a little bit of a hurry and left traces around his escape route. I'll send the specimens to the lab at HQ for ID."

Liora called out, "Dov, the children want to say goodnight now."

"OK, just a minute," he said and wrote the last details on his pad, said, "That's brilliant Yuval, thank the team for me," and went to kiss Yaniv and Yael.

They arrived early at Rikki Rishon's flat the following morning, Dov, Aviel and Irit, with four uniformed policemen.

The surveillance team confirmed that Rishon was still at home. Dov delayed the start of the operation.

He buzzed Elisha Levinson on the entry-phone. "Come up ," she said loudly.

She was waiting at her door and was about to speak when he shushed her. She beckoned him in and closed the door as gently as possible. The apartment was dark, curtains still drawn.

She offered him some tea. He said there wasn't time.

"Look," he began, "I've come to apologize. I know I can trust you. We're about to question Mr Rishon, your neighbor. The apology is about Dr Sasson. That was about trust too. Trusting her with you. I'm sorry she broke that trust."

He told her what Shalit had decided. "That means that your evidence can't be used. I really am sorry."

Her small hands became fists silently beating a couple of times on the arms of her chair. He reached over and held them. She said, "I don't want it to end."

"It?" he asked.

"This," she whispered. "Being involved. Being relevant again, the center of your attention… any attention."

Dov could find no apt response. He gently squeezed her hands in gratitude and left.

Rikki Rishon sat at the table in his dining corner, eating and watching the TV news. The top story was the release of an amateur video of the Rabin assassination. Rishon stopped, mesmerized, his spoonful of cottage cheese suspended in mid air, as the revelation of how easily the murderer had reached the Prime Minister was reinforced. Then his spoon filled his mouth. The door buzzer went.

He sat still.

The buzzer buzzed again.

The shock of it translated into palpitations. He glanced at the clock in the corner of the TV screen. It said 07.08. Perhaps if I keep absolutely still, he thought, they'll go away.

The buzzer went again. The palpitations quickened.

They continued, frighteningly, as he went to the door, and Dov Chizzik came in holding up the search warrant, followed by Irit and Aviel, and three faceless policemen. A fourth remained by the door. Dov described the warrant details, and went off down the corridor, the policemen following him.

Rishon watched, hugging himself, his right hand absently rubbing his left forearm for comfort.

They all pulled on white nylon gloves and the search began. Dov entered the study.

Rishon stood stock-still.

When Dov closed the white study door, the door to his sanctuary, in his apartment, Rikki Rishon refused to absorb the enormity of it. He convinced himself that this was all irrelevant to him, but his heart threatened to leap from his chest.

Irit guided him to his sofa and pulled a chair over to sit opposite him. She motioned to Aviel to get a glass of water.

"Rikki? There's nothing to be worried about. Really. Get comfortable won't you?"

Rishon slowly sat down, concentrating on Irit's legs. His heartbeat subsided.

"They are nice, aren't they?" Irit began, crossing her legs slowly. "As good as Anya's?"

Rishon gazed a little longer at them, then his head snapped up to her face.

"What?"

"Worth photographing?" Apparently self-absorbed she uncrossed her legs again in an act that was overtly sensual. "Like some of your photographs," she paused. "Of Anya."

"What?" Rishon said again.

"I'll bet you're good with a camera. Its lens always sees the truth."

Rishon was sitting up, tense.

"She was a victim. You could hear her being beaten. You couldn't stop it. You wanted to help her. She was very pretty. And you were very lonely. So you offered to catalogue her injuries. When her husband was away. She'd come up here. Through the trap door in the utility room. So no one in the building would know. And you'd set up your study like a mini studio. To help her. Collect evidence. Against her husband. That's what you told yourself. That's what you told her."

In the study Dov inspected the display of photographs. They were detailed to the point of obsessive, and pornographic. He pulled at the blind to let the morning light into the room and opened the window. He looked out onto an enclosed square with trees, in the center was a children's play area, birds flittering amongst the branches. Pleasant. Safe. Who could guess what went on in this room?

In the salon Aviel put the glass on the table by Rishon's knees and sat down at the dining table.

Dov closed the window and then the blind, took some of the photographs off the walls, left the study. He told the policeman to list the contents and get them packed for delivery to HQ. He'd return the photographs shortly. He took them to Irit. Then he sat down at the other end of the sofa.

"Oh yes Rikki. You're really very good," Irit said leafing through the photographs. "You definitely have the eye. What did Anya think of them?"

He began to speak, but in the end only shook his head.

"Come on. You never showed them to her?"

His head shook again.

Irit looked at the photographs then at Rishon. "All over the walls of your study? When did you put them up? After she left each time? You'd print them off, then you'd sit all alone and look and look. And imagine her. Her naked lacerated back. Her cigarette burned breasts. Her buttocks and thighs striped with the lash of her husband's belt. Such beauty. So damaged."

Rishon's heart pounded savagely.

"And you wanted to be a salve to her. But you couldn't. Not with the real live Anya. You wouldn't allow yourself. You never asked. She was a married woman and her husband was a brute. You would never suggest anything improper. Not in reality." Rishon's breathing came faster. "All alone, you could let your imagination run riot." Irit's voice was silky. "And then you got hold of the Fire and Flame video. So now you could imagine much more than kissing her better, taking the pain away, her pain and yours, at your loss and your loneliness, releasing her and you from it all. Was that the way of it Rikki?" she whispered, "therapeutic masturbation while watching Anya on that video and her photos all around you?"

Rishon exhaled a long sighing breath and sagged back into his sofa cushions.

"Was that a yes?" Dov asked.

"Yes." Rishon murmured.

Dov said, "The maintenance hatch Rikki. Anya could come up through it, and you could go down through it, right? The folding ladder behind your washing machine in your utility room?" Aviel and Irit exchanged surprised looks. They hadn't known about the ladder.

Rishon grinned. "With a bit of a squeeze…if I turned sideways." He confided, "He was an electrical engineer, Abuhatzeira. His company was working on the site of my new wing, at the school. Away long hours. Then he discovered what Anya was doing when he wasn't here, perhaps he found the video like I did. Perhaps she wanted him to see it. I don't know."

"All she said was it was something she'd done once or twice before she came to Israel, she was from a poor family and needed money. She swore she'd only done a couple of those videos since she married Felipe. She never knew what he did with his money, he had lots of it, but never gave her any but expected her to buy food, cook and so on, so she needed her own money. He didn't like her working in that boutique. Anyway he began abusing her, punishing her. The last time he attacked her, I couldn't stand it. I decided to confront him. But then the beatings stopped. Anya just disappeared. I went down through the trap door one night after I heard him come home. I showed him a selection of the photographs and told him I'd mailed copies of them to the police. I hadn't. But he was shocked. He told me what he'd done. It was all about the video. It ate away at him for months. He got drunk, started beating her one night, lost control and couldn't stop. And killed her. Animal. And hid her in the bomb shelter in a duct. There was a skillet on the cooker, one of those cast iron ones, heavy, perfect. I began hitting him with it. He hardly defended himself. I put a stop to him. Permanently. It wasn't difficult. I'm overweight I know, but I'm still strong. I worked for hours afterwards cleaning up, ah anything incriminating? Yes," this last to himself, "anything." And before Dov could ask, he said triumphantly, "He's in one of the cement pillars of the new wing of my IT block. So's the hammer he used on Anya, can you believe he kept it, hadn't washed it off? My gloves are there too. The skillet's in my kitchen."

"There's blood residue on the rim of the hatch, yours." Dov confirmed.

"A loose screw head on the hatch handle. It split one of my gloves, cut my thumb. Thought I'd wiped it clean."

Dov could see Shalit's head thrown back with his fiery "Hah!" when he called to say they'd cracked the case. "Come tomorrow. Bring Dr Sasson. And Weiss."

They sat opposite him. On his desk were some of Rishon's photographs and a spread of newspapers. The headlines were as lurid as they were flattering. "Super Commander Triumphs!" "Super Cop Solves K. Saba Sex Murder." "Clean Cop Chizzik Clears Up Dirty Case". Shalit asked questions. The trio answered. He complained about the cost of drilling out Abuhatzeira's remains from the concrete pillar and then said. "Bit of a psycho this Rishon? Ah well. He confessed."

Irit said, "Yes Commander. He did. To Dov."

Dov said evenly, "But only after Irit's stress tactics."

"Good team work then," Shalit said. "Weiss?"

"Yes sir." Aviel said. He waited for Shalit to ask about the video and any links to the real work of TPI.

All the Commander said was, "Well done," and turned to Irit. "I'll call you later Irit. We'll need you in court. Now I want to talk to Dov." The other two left.

"OK Dov. Nothing succeeds like success, and we all earn from it. This was a big case and it went well, once I kick-started you. I'll see what to do about Sasson's little, what'll we call it, over-zealousness?" Then he looked gleeful, "Justice thinks it's a straight forward conviction for Rishon."

Dov allowed a quick smile. Shalit thought he was trouncing him with that. He was entitled to be sure, Dov thought, no more surprises.

"No more suggestions of firing Sasson?"

"If Justice thinks the conviction is assured, they must have weighed up how Rishon's defense attorney would handle how Irit did her interview with Mrs Levinson," Dov answered. "If I were you I'd avoid even letting that into the prosecution file. Mrs Levinson is sure to complain if you don't."

Shalit acquiesced, "all right," and after a pause, "so, now what?"

Dov told him about the as yet un-identified figure he was sure Sara Moledet was linked to. "This isn't your feverish imagination working over time, Dov? Getting obsessed?"

Dov wouldn't rise to the bait. His reputation was based on his ability to coldly analyze facts, people and contexts. Imagination played its part, but it was never fevered.

"There's an organization behind this industry. We need to dismantle it and destroy it. That's what's now for TPI." Dov knew he sounded lofty. He didn't care, he'd spent enough time inside himself.

Shalit began thinking of how to let him run with that and what contingency he needed if, as he hoped, Dov failed, like a replacement who was just a cop, someone who did as he was told.

Chapter 12
February 1997

"Answer me! Have you gone deaf?" Yunis shouted. Khadija sat impassively, refusing to look at him. Yunis' rage was shocking. "Mummy look at me! Why won't you look at me?"

Lana was up in her room reading for the next day's lecture, unaware her brother was in the house. She ran downstairs to the living room. Why was Yunis here so late? Wasn't Ibrahim at home?

Yunis was more muscular than Ibrahim, identical height, clean-shaven. He was blind with anger and as Lana appeared he was grabbing Khadija's shoulders. Lana called out, "Don't!" Yunis didn't hear.

He yelled in pain as Ibrahim's fist hit the back of his head. No one had seen Ibrahim enter. Yunis staggered forward. "… LAY A FINGER ON YOUR MOTHER?" Ibrahim yelled and punched Yunis again. Yunis shook his head to clear it. His mother remained still. He appealed to her, calling her Umm Yunis.

Ibrahim hit him again. Yunis retreated into a corner.

"Stop it! Stop it!" Lana shouted. "Yunis, go!"

Yunis shouted, "I am what I am and I'm still your son!" This time Ibrahim came at him, his eyes flashing, curses pouring out. Yunis dashed for the stairs.

The only sounds were Ibrahim's heavy breathing and Yunis' shoes clattering down the steps. The front door banged.

Moments later, instead of a car engine, from behind the house came the crash of glass being smashed. It continued, echoing across the valley, making dogs bark. Only then did Khadija move, trying to stop her husband. He rushed out, Lana after him. The land behind the house was a vegetable garden, Ibrahim grew a selection of them for pickles and used his shed to prepare them. Al Batuf pickles were known across the Galilee .

"I'm your son!" Yunis bellowed, punctuating his shrieks with yet another jar of pickles hurled at the wall of the shed, "The son of a shut-minded," Smash! "Pickle farmer." Smash! "Still your son." Smash! "And she's still my mother." Smash! "You're such a shit head!"

Ibrahim had grabbed a fence stave from a stack by one of the concrete stilts and now he brought it down across Yunis' raised left arm bellowing, "ALLAH DAMN YOU! YOU HOMO!"

Yunis collapsed with pain. As Ibrahim stumbled back up stairs he managed, "I don't ever want to see him again. He's not my son."

Lana got Yunis to remove his jacket. She found a cloth in the wreckage and wet it. "I'm sorry," she kept repeating through tears, dabbing Yunis' arm. Her lightest touch brought grunts of pain from him. He looked grey in the light from the stairway.

"Is it broken?" she asked. "Do you need to go to hospital?"

"Don't fuss. My jacket sleeves are quite thick," he mumbled. "If it's still bad later, I'll get it treated in Tel Aviv. Can you help me make a sling? My keffiyah's in the car. I've also got painkillers somewhere in there, for headaches."

After she found them she said, "You can't come back here Yunis, not after this."

Yunis sobbed, "I haven't seen him for ages. I thought it'd be OK." Anguish obvious in his whisper, he asked, "I'm still your brother aren't I?"

"Yes, yes, you'll always be, but you must go, Yunis, now." She helped him to get up.

The pain made him unsteady. "He let you go to university? Amazing."

"But he insists I come home each night."

"Typical," Yunis grunted. "Giving with one hand and taking with the other. Still, he let you go." He grimaced and Lana knew his jacket sleeve wasn't that thick. "Just be careful," he said. "There's a file on you now for sure."

"A file? What do you mean?"

"Oh for God's sake Lana," he said through gritted teeth, "It's the Shin Bet, their security service. Heard of them? You're at their university, they'll know about you.

Despite the cold evening air Lana felt warm. She hugged herself, Ibrahim's violence, Yunis banished, the security services watching her, too much to take in.

Then he took her finger and pressed it to his head, "It's in here. They call it a mental scratch; Israelis who've done things during army service that damaged them inside their heads. I've done things too. Mine's very deep and all I want is that you'll never get one."

She tried to help him with the car door.

He brushed her hand aside, "I'm all right," but she persisted and helped ease him into the driver's seat. "Please be careful. Promise?"

She nodded involuntarily. "You too." She was already thinking, who could be watching? Places and people reeled through her mind: the Haifa bus station, her university interview, Israeli students she sat with, the woman serving her coffee in the cafeteria. Were they...?

The sound of Yunis' car revving up stopped her. "You can't possibly drive."

"It's an automatic, I'll just need to steer and I can do that one handed."

She wasn't convinced. "Do they know you?"

"Don't worry about me. I love you." He jerked the wheel round and called out of his window. "You've got my cell number?"

She nodded and promised, "I'll be your secret al Batuf contact."

He smiled weakly and said, "Y'Allah bye."

She tried to smile through welling tears. It was their little joke about Israelis, they were so confused about who they were, they said goodbye in Arabic and English.

As she got to bed, her cell beeped. It was a text from Yunis, "Thanks & Love". She fell asleep, the phone still in her hand.

Her father entered the kitchen the following morning to find Lana preparing his breakfast. She heated water for tea and warmed pita bread. She took labneh, yogurt cheese, from the fridge and put some in a shallow bowl and added fresh olive oil made from Ibrahim's olives. She was silent and avoided eye contact with him.

"I've never discussed this with you before," he murmured when she handed him his tea. He made it sound like this was the only thing he'd never discussed with her. Daylight was just making itself known through the windows. She yearned for some sign that the tears in the fabric of her life weren't permanent. And that he might mend them.

He took a deep breath, "Sheikh Adwan. Since his father's time they've worked with the Yahud." Lana thought, Hatem's father and grandfather? Collaborators?

"They're always looking for ways to control us, and that man and his family help them."

She understood almost without thinking who 'Them' were. "Just us?"

"No." He stopped again, thinking how to frame his next words.

"Adwan succeeded his father Sheikh Umar as Mukhtar with his wealth and influence, and helped by deals with the Yahud. This is how they control us."

Then he decided to tell Lana something no one else knew. Perhaps it was his way of telling her he trusted her. "When my mother was dying, she told me she'd had a moment of passion with Sheikh Umar and Adwan was the result. What could I say? It choked me but my mother was near death. She told me she was leaving a piece of land to us, me and Adwan her son by Sheikh Umar. She hoped it would bring us together. It had the opposite effect."

Lana gasped, "Sheikh Adwan is your brother?"

"Half brother."

She couldn't take it in, her grandmother's 'moment of passion' with someone not her husband? But another thought emerged, one directly related to her and Hatem. The secret of the olive grove where they'd met, that she never told Hatem it was Ibrahim's. Now there was a bigger secret about it.

Ibrahim spoke firmly, "You remember that time you and your mother and Rashid came to the police station?" Lana nodded. "Adwan's driver Mohammad used a cave that I own for something criminal. I don't know whether Adwan ordered him or whether he did it by himself and thought he'd be rewarded afterwards. Whatever, the police suspected me. That was bad but what happened last night was worse."

Lana saw deep sadness in his eyes. He went on, "What people do behind their own doors is their business. But others will talk about their suspicions. Worst of all the Yahud will get to know about it. When people get found out, they're like a gap in our fence. Who knows who can get in, even if it's thanks to my son?" He said bitterly, "I had no choice last night. He shamed me. I hope the village heard it. Now they can't claim I did nothing."

Lana stood at a point just above her special place. It was an unusually temperate winter day with a deepening blue sky, the air sharp. In a panoramic sweep she saw such splendid diversity, a distant white peaked mountain, sharp-toothed hilltops, majestic valleys, and on this morning a vague sparkling sliver she was sure was the sea. One day she'd go and walk along the water's edge.

She sat and concentrated on the valley below. On its borders were scatterings of trees, the remnants of once lush rolling forests, striations of crops, in greens, beiges and mauves, like a cloak of stripy tints; the national water carrier, white and aquamarine snaking away below to a reservoir. All these were only scratches on the surface, hardly obscuring the natural contours and shapes she knew were eternal. She needed continuity where nothing she thought she knew felt certain. Her gaze drifted to the sky, then slowly down and onward along the beautiful valley. And when she saw the land meet the blue sky, an idea came to her.

Chapter 13
March 1997

Lana and Yehudit had met at a lecture in the first weeks of Lana's first term. The agitated blonde had arrived late, brushed past Lana without apology, sat down, swore, rummaged in her bag for a pen. Lana handed her a spare, hoping to end the distraction. Afterwards in the afternoon sunshine she introduced herself as Yehudit and offered Lana her pen back. "It's OK. Keep it," Lana said and walked away. She sat in a grassy area overlooking Haifa Bay. She imagined the distant point where the coastline turned outwards was what she'd seen from her special place, where the valley and the sky merged and her idea came back to her.

Yehudit interrupted her and sat down and asked if Lana was voting in the Arab students' union elections. Lana remained composed and replied, "I come from a family that keeps away from politics. And anyway I don't have time. I go home every night."

"You travel there and back every day? How long's it take?"

"Nearly two hours sometimes, two buses."

"So, not much time for socializing on campus."

"Not really. My father's quite strict about the time I spend here."

Yehudit was two years older than Lana, born on a Galilee kibbutz and educated at the regional school. She'd done army service, visited the USA and Europe, and Lana envied her.

Yehudit admired Lana's composure, the care she took with her words. The dynamic of liking and wanting to know more, overtook them, but some items of personal baggage remained unopened.

"You said your parents were refugees?" Lana asked.

"They were sent to the kibbutz on the day they arrived," she pointed north-west, "and adapted quickly to kibbutz life, but we left five years ago and moved here to Haifa." Lana thought it sounded a little like her family, which after outgrowing the village home, had moved.

Yehudit quickly detailed the wrench of leaving her childhood environment, that her parents were Holocaust survivors, and that they'd left the kibbutz because its finances, like many others, had nose-dived.

Lana chatted on, "We have two kibbutzim near our village. My father's visited one, to share advice on crops and cultivation." Ibrahim had called the kibbutzim, "thieves of our land". She kept that back. "So, both our families have links with the land."

"Yeah," Yehudit sighed, "I miss the countryside. I go home every night too. I'd have preferred dorms."

"But you can be yourself," Lana said envy more overt, "grow more, without parents telling you what to do."

"I suppose. Anyway, we're here now," Yehudit proclaimed, "So let's enjoy it together." There were no what ifs, just a simple offer to share.

The sea distracted Lana. Yehudit watched how it held her and looked closely at Lana's profile. "Where did you go to school, did you say?"

Lana told her the name of the village school.

"Who do the stars belong to?" Yehudit asked.

An odd frisson of emotion flared in Lana. "No, it's impossible," she replied staring hard at Yehudit, seeing her with long fair hair instead of her close to the scalp bleached crop.

"Ditta? That black top with the gold zip. I wanted one!"

Yehudit reddened, "Ditta was my nickname. The top wasn't so special, but nu, answer the question."

Lana said, "The stars are everyone's," just as she had when Eran claimed the white six-pointed star. "What did you think after I crayoned over Eran's picture?"

Yehudit, her head to one side, said, "Nothing worth repeating."

"What happened to him?"

"We were kids, you know, 'I love you, will you marry me when we grow up?' He's decided to stay in the army full time. We've both changed," she shrugged, "that's the way it goes."

The coincidence strengthened their friendship.

In the Arab students' union office, Lana didn't see the wolfish smile Nabil, the general secretary, gave as she outlined her Sky Blue Sky sit-in proposal. He was checking an expenses sheet. He said, "Who knows?" so quietly Lana had to lean forward to hear him, "maybe some of the Jews will join in."

Arab students got into the hall at dawn and painted the ceiling a symbolic sky blue. Jewish students helped them.

Lana had rehearsed her speech many times but couldn't gauge the reaction. The smell of fresh paint was strong but the place was crammed. She stood up.

"What difference whether it's roasted, marinated and barbecued, or bread-crumbed and fried? It's still chicken and we all have a favorite recipe and it's usually Mama's.

"We have so much in common. Time and history have played cruelly with us all, but this land is where we all come from.

"Redemption is a huge word for simple people like us and we didn't know that was what you wanted. We were the majority before you came, and we never imagined we'd exchange roles with you.

"So here we are, you and we, us and them. There's something we all share, the sky. There's enough of it for everyone. Most of the time it's blue. Sometimes there're clouds in it and at night it's covered in stars, and they're everyone's too. It's our sky.

"I'm calling today Sky Blue Sky day. If it works for today, maybe we can go on sharing tomorrow and maybe we can find ways to live together."

She spotted Dr Assad and Yehudit as she finished. Assad looked inscrutable and he left moments later. Yehudit hugged her. "God Lana, that was really something else."

"Was it my Hebrew, or what I said?"

Yehudit frowned, and Lana giggled when Yehudit said, "No. The contents were rubbish, but the Hebrew…great accent. You've really mastered it…for a Palestinian."

An Israeli spoke first. "Sky Blue Sky? Sharing it? I'm not giving up anything to any fucking Arabs!" This earned equal shouts of approval and disapproval.

Another Israeli said, "Anything is better than war. The way we're going, it's like Alabama in the 50s and 60s. The civil rights struggle, the racial violence? Diaspora Jews won't support such an Israel. Under the sky we're all the same."

That earned, "Go home Yank!" which got sniggers and laughter in equal measure.

The first Palestinian said, “Don’t tell me about war. Half of my father’s family was wiped out in an Israeli air raid on their refugee camp in Lebanon.”

Another suggested, “We do live under the same sky. We’re citizens of Israel, and we want to live equally with our fellow Jewish citizens. I support Sky Blue Sky.”

Lana’s emotions swirled and yes suddenly she had an ego to feed, telling her say some more! Sky Blue Sky’s your idea!

Nabil appeared and to Lana he underwent a chameleon-like change. His voice was strong and he spoke impeccable Hebrew. He looked attractively heroic. He didn’t mention her. A journalist for the Nazareth based A-Sinara daily asked, “You’ve managed to avoid violence today. How?”

“There’s no place for violence. We’re law abiding citizens, we want the same rights Jewish citizens enjoy.”

Lana focused on him as a brunette Israeli TV reporter jabbed at him with her microphone, “you’ve often talked about Zionism’s hijack of the Shoah. Do you still think that?”

His reply was full on. “Zionism appropriated the Shoah for political profit, as an excuse to steal our land and victimize us. We were its victims too. It was a terrible thing.”

Back came the microphone with a jab: “What was?”

Nabil said icily, “They both were .”

Lana followed his quick glance to the doorway to see Uncle Basil silently applauding.

An Israeli with a heavy Russian accent magicked himself in front of Nabil. He yelled, “You dare to mention the Shoah? Fucking Araboosh! You want equal rights in the Jewish homeland? Never!” And he punched Nabil. Blood spurted on impact of fist with nasal cartilage over Nabil’s mouth and onto the aggressor’s shirt. Two large young men shielded Nabil and shoved the bloodstained Israeli away. More punches were thrown. Mayhem ensued. Campus security forced their way in.

Nabil sat, head tilted far back in a chair. From behind a bloody wad of tissues he said, “I’m OK.”

“Thank heavens,” Lana said, her anger at his scene stealing temporarily on hold.

The head of campus security flanked by four security men entered and announced, “this protest is over.”

Nabil invited Lana back to his office. “It’s only a nose bleed,” he said “It’ll be all over the news. They always say Jews are news. Arabs are too and if a punch on camera is the only way we’ll get their attention, OK.”

She was bewildered. He had behaved like any male, just like at home, weighing in, ignoring her because she was a woman. How stupid am I? Why had she assumed an Arab man would behave differently because he was on an Israeli campus? She wouldn’t be so trusting ever again, she promised herself.

Nabil smiled at her and she was dazzled despite her thoughts. “You are an al Batuf, no? Related to Ibrahim al Batuf?”

“Yes. He’s my father.”

“Your father? He’s a hero.”

She was embarrassed. But time, or lack of it, intervened before she could ask what he meant. Her watch said she was going to miss her bus home. Thoughts and feelings crunched together. “Thanks, sorry,” was all she managed hurriedly, “I have to go,” and dashed for the stairs and her bus.

The day’s events remained a jumble in her mind all the way home.

As she climbed the stairs she could hear the TV. The brunette reporter was saying, “So Haifa University witnessed yet another violent disturbance." Over Nabil being punched, the reporter went on, "the sit-in started peacefully then deteriorated as a Palestinian student leader made inflammatory comments," and there was Lana dashing to help Nabil, "about Zionism and the Shoah."

His eyes still on the TV, Ibrahim's words were simple. "If I ever hear that you were involved in anything like this again, I'll stop your fees."

He could imagine Adwan chortling and the village cackling after Lana's public involvement in the very politics they knew Ibrahim despised.

Lana said, "Somebody told me you're a hero. What did you do?"

He sighed. She'd dipped her toes into politics, precisely as he'd feared she would. "It was before you were born, March 1976. They came and took thousands of dunams of our land. They put us all under curfew," he explained what that was, "and erected barbed wire around a section of the Rams Horns Hills, our land. We heard that Sheikh Adwan had received compensation for his land taken up there. No one else got any."

"What did you do?"

"What do you think? We protested and it spread through the villages and the police lost their nerve. The army came in with tanks! Tanks would you believe? Six villagers were killed, three of them women, one right in front of me. I managed to rescue another. She'd tripped on a rock and fell in front of a tank. I grabbed her and pulled her out of the way. It was the first Youm al Ard."

He didn't tell her that after that he made Khadija promise to keep Lana away during future Youm al Ard, Land Day, anniversaries. Now he saw that in creating a politics free zone around her, he'd only created curiosity.

“Politics are for fools and traitors,” he said, “and I saw people get killed because of them.” Biting words accompanied his sweeping hand, “I don’t want to have to bury you.”

“Oh stop threatening me! I’m not one of your sons. I’m Lana. We compromised right? You pay my fees and I come home every day. I’m your daughter, Lana al Batuf, and I’m not about to turn my back on who I am. But let me experience as much as I can, even if you won’t let me enjoy it!” She left Ibrahim speechless.

Chapter 14
March 1997

A week after the exams, Dr Assad invited Lana for her first year assessment.

Assad confirmed what Lana hoped, that she was doing well, in fact better than that. "At this rate," he said, "you'll graduate with honors. What plans after graduating?"

"That's still two years away," she said.

"Have you made new friends?"

"I go home each night, so there's little time for that. But I've got one good friend."

"From the villages?"

"No, from Haifa"

"An Israeli?"

"Yes."

"Look I'm not being judgmental, and I'm not your father."

"Obviously. So?"

He said, "Just like many others from our towns and villages, you came with high hopes. Being here is a form of liberation, from your parents?"

She sort of agreed but was unsure where this was going.

"It's like a tabula rasa process."

"Tabula rasa? I know terra rossa, for our red earth. It sounds Latin."

"Sorry, educational jargon." He gave his toothy grin. "Yes it's Latin, the Romans used tabula rasa, a wax tablet that could be written on and wiped off. I see students with empty minds on which nothing has registered yet."

"We're not empty. I mean we all have ideas."

"Of course. Ideas? About the other, the Israelis? And they have ideas about you."

This was too elliptical for Lana. "What do you mean?"

"They weren't thinking about coping with diversity or coexistence when they built this place. They'll have noticed Sky Blue Sky."

Shades of Yunis' warning but no admonition, he was carefully cautioning her. Am I that naïve, she wondered? He continued. "You're living with the elephant, and it's his room. You hope if you get a degree, somehow a magic wand will change the way the elephant sees you. Right?"

"Yes, that's pretty close."

He said, "Don't turn your back on your roots."

"You think I would?"

"You wouldn't be the first. You came here because you want change, right?"

"Of course."

"And what do you want to change?"

"I want a new direction, to take my own steps. But now…"

"Hold that thought. You said 'new direction'? Somewhere else in the Arab world, or America, the land of opportunity?" He laughed, she giggled breaking the tension.

"I hadn't thought that far."

"Did you ever think about changing them, the Israelis?"

"They're the majority, how does one girl change them?"

"They're the elephant. But I believe it's our moral responsibility to change them."

"Moral responsibility?"

"Yes. Because as long as they think they control us, they continue to abuse us. That's immoral."

"You still haven't said how."

"Have you heard of Martin Luther King Junior?"

"Yes, he was a supporter of black rights in America, and he was shot."

"That's right." He gave her a potted history and included the story of Rosa Parks and her refusal to sit at the back of the bus when a white driver ordered her to.

"Dr King said, 'As long as you sit in the back, you have a false sense of inferiority, and so long as you let the white man push you back there, he has a false sense of superiority.' It's the same for us, for you. First thing is to shed our victims' clothes. Getting your degree is one step. You won't look quite like their victim, but as long they still think we're their victims, there's no equality and our nightmare goes on."

She looked overwhelmed.

"Yes I know, it's a big concept. So start with the basics, the Nakba. Ask our people for their stories of 1948. Challenge their accuracy; people often repeat what others told them. Commemorating the Nakba is about us before it is anything to do with what the Israelis did. We haven't learned its lessons. We have to progress, and not be shackled by being losers in a war we couldn't fight. Think about it." Sounds from the corridor outside intruded. After several seconds Lana stood up. "I will."

In the weeks and months into her second year, Lana began to sketch ideas for her 'project' in a notebook. She saw herself as an investigator of her people's history.

Sitting outside on a campus lawn, she reprised this with Yehudit. "It's very strange, because I don't know where this journey leads to, I am frightened, but only when I think about the not knowing. It's not a conscious fear, and the fact of being on the journey will take the fear away, do you know what I mean?"

"No, not really," Yehudit said. "I pretty much know what I want to do. I'm not as sure as you that your journey will take you as far as you think or hope. I think its great you're ready to go on studying, and learn about the past, but Lana, there's reality around you all the time, and you can't avoid it."

"Why? Am I being naïve?"

"No and it's not a criticism."

"OK so I haven't done what you've done, served in the army, seen the world…"

"Had sex."

"Sex? What's that got to do with anything?"

"Well have you?"

"That's none of your business!"

"I can't figure you out. You're really stunning and you act like such a prude."

"I'm not stunning. But if prude means I don't talk about this the way you do, then OK I am."

"Are you saving your virginity for the wedding night?"

Lana thought how to manage Yehudit's impetuosity; it wasn't simple so she made it easy on herself and answered candidly, "I made a promise to myself, yes."

"You know there's the operation?"

"What operation?"

"I've heard lot's of girls from the villages have had it… had sex and then had the repair operation so their husbands'll never know."

It took a few moments before Lana reacted. "That's disgusting! Ugh!" She felt nauseous, then after a few deep breaths said, "It's like a licence to have as much sex as they want and then cheat their husbands."

"And condoms and taking the pill are not the same?"

"I wouldn't know. I've never experienced either, but cheating?"

"There's a lot of it about."

"I've never cheated about anything. If those girls are doing that, what does it say about everything else they do, friendships especially, married life?"

"I thought most Muslim marriages were arranged and love didn't come into it," Yehudit said.

"Now who's being naïve?"

"Are you Lana al Batuf, Sky Blue Sky?" Lana looked up to see the brunette TV reporter, pointing her microphone at her, a cameraman, his camera's red light on, waiting.

"Hello Lana!" Lana turned startled, to see Basil Khoury standing over her.

"Hi there Uncle…Dr Khoury," she stuttered.

"Do you have permission to be on this campus?" Khoury almost shouted at the reporter, waving his cell phone. "I'm going to call campus security and have you chucked out, OK?" The reporter glared at him, then lowered her mic and signaled to the cameraman that they were leaving.

Khoury glowered some more and when he was sure they were heading for the main gates, said, "It's OK to call me Uncle still. But you've grown so, and you're into campus politics. Sky Blue Sky was your idea?"

"Yes, well, but I'm not sure…"

"It was brave. But you have to get used to the public gaze. How are your studies?"

"Good, yes going well thanks."

"Pleased to hear it. If you ever need any help or advice, you know I'm here for you." He nodded to Yehudit and walked on.

"Uncle? He's your uncle? Wow Lana you didn't say."

Lana explained.

"He's a presence, Lana. But there've been rumors you know?"

"Rumors?"

"He's an attractive man…to some females."

Lana knew about his reputation but felt the need to defend him. "He's married with young children."

"What was that about naivety?" Yehudit jibed.

Chapter 15
March 1997–August 1998

There was a studied ruthlessness to Baruch Hareven. Conventional business practices didn't create quick fortunes. In his home town, he'd begun as a teenager working for a local pimp, collecting money from whores, keeping accounts, delivering bribes to policemen. He surveyed the sex, drug and club scene after his arrival in Israel and when he'd finished his military service he planned to hive off a part of it for himself. He handpicked men, some he'd met in the army, all of them Russians or from former Soviet states like him, and took over a club, a drug ring and a sex-trade ring.

Hareven's business firewalls were impenetrable and made him consistently anonymous. It was his strength. He was not known to the police. Anonymity meant surprise. Boris Kamien from Perm was the new identity he had invested in months before beginning the process of making Aliyah, going up to the land of Israel, as any Jew's decision to live there was described. But no one knew that name; he'd had any record of it expunged, and only used it when absolutely essential, which so far had been twice, and both people who'd used it were no longer in the world.

Violence was his trademark, never prefaced or half-hearted and always successful.

His business decisions were like any other. Sex was the commodity and he exploited it and the girls he traded. There were always new markets and porn video was very profitable. He disdained sex-trash, like the sex cards scattered on pavements and in phone booths around hotels.

He intuited that more TPI activity represented long term deficits. The message from Sara Moledet confirmed this. Dov Chizzik had to be removed; it was a simple business calculation. As in everything Hareven did he was patient. He had a tentacular network of contacts and clients, especially amongst a number of oligarchs, who didn't know they knew him.

Sara had never met Hareven. Like him she had changed her name; she wanted to leave Sophia Gulkowitsch behind in Valga, south-eastern Estonia. She didn't know she was part of Hareven's empire, though she had been almost from her first steps into the sex industry. She became a 'secretary' in an anonymous run down apartment near Tel Aviv's old central bus station, managing a bunch of quick-trick prostitutes for a pimp who also didn't know he worked for Hareven.

A cell phone in a jiffy-bag materialized. It rang that night. The voice was electronically disguised. She accepted the proposal the voice made and destroyed the SIM card as instructed. Over the next weeks she put a team of Lilac girls to work, watching Dov Chizzik and his family.

Liora announced she'd hired a child-minder. She'd posted leaflets in neighborhood shops and a BA student at Tel Aviv University applied. Liora had grilled her; in business mode, Dov knew she could be scary.

He'd showered, eaten and was watching the nine pm news show. TPI wasn't amongst the headlines. He called out, "what's her name? When does she start?"

"Not until Sunday. I've checked her references. I think she'll be all right. Her name's Fania Ostrovsky." Liora pronounced it properly, Astravskeh.

"Russian?"

"Her parents were senior academics in St Petersburg."

"Remind me and I'll run a check tomorrow. I'm going to bed soon. Are you coming in too?" He didn't expect a yes. Sex was now a distant memory.

"No, not yet." Liora replied. "I've got to finish my re-application to the School of Management. They've invited me for interview."

"That was fast."

"Yes, but I had a word with someone in the Faculty who happened to know my father."

"I thought you didn't like using your father's name."

"Come on Dov. It's not like I asked Daddy to call them. It was a happy coincidence. He's a member of Daddy's Rotary Club. He's in Admissions. "

Dov yawned. "How convenient."

He switched to Channel 2, a current affairs show discussing Israel's Arabs. There were archive clips of the annual Land Day demonstrations and then a sit-in at Haifa University which had deteriorated into violence, an Arab student leader being punched and a strikingly pretty girl rushing to his aid. Dov resisted whooping but couldn't control, "Oh shut your stupid mouth!" as Basil Khoury, the Arab politician and academic, mouthed off about Israeli discrimination against Arab citizens. Dov shouted, "You're better off here than you'd be anywhere else!"

"Be quiet. You'll wake the kids." Liora called out.

"It's this bloody Arab!"

The presenter asked, "Will you swear allegiance to the State of Israel?"

"If it's a state of all its people and there's compromises on the oath and the flag."

"What compromises?…" Dov snarled.

The other guest was a Law Professor, expert on relations with Israeli Arabs. "I used to believe you deserved our sympathy…"

"Your sympathy's no good!" Khoury snapped.

The professor continued, "You're right. You want everything from us but you won't participate in our state. What you really want is revenge. Compromise? You've created a huge gap between us, and it's unbridgeable."

Dov cheered and Liora came in to shut him up.

In bed as Dov began the quick drift down into sleep, he imagined Liora's body, her lips, the curve of her breasts. He smiled at what he could see. But it was only a memory.

All Liora's notices were collected and destroyed as fast as she'd displayed them. Fania Ostrovsky provided Sara hard data on the Chizzik's domestic life. Dov never did get round to checking Fania out, had he, her legend would have stood up to scrutiny, Sara had seen to that via her anonymous client; a new SIM arrived every week. To be sure, Liora followed up Fania's references, knowing Dov would forget; they stood up.

Fania was instructed to discover if the Chizzik's marriage was under pressure. The best evidence she got was from overhearing parts of heated exchanges, like this one, which she noted:

Dov: "It's not going to happen. Why go on about it?"

Liora: "Because I'm your wife and I thought we shared our dreams…"

Dov: "At last. Sharing. 'Super Commissioner' is a dream I don't share. I don't fantasize about a corner office at H.Q with a car and driver, state occasions …"

Liora: "No, your job is about people watching fucking on a TV screen."

Dov: "You saw the headlines after we took out that warehouse and me solving the Abuhatzeira case. I don't bring any of it home with me. I…"

Liora: "Yes, everyone saw them, just what I needed, family and friends knowing what you do now. And talking of fucking, you haven't touched me for weeks." Nor you me, Dov thought.

With Fania embedded in the Chizzik's lives, Sara accumulated more details, on Liora's clothes, perfume, Arpege like hers, make-up, underwear and shoes, and the Chizzik's tastes in culture, food and drink. Meanwhile she began the process of acquiring an apartment. It had to be a mirror of the Chizzik's home in every respect, down to the floor tiles. It didn't take as long as normal, because her anonymous client helped. Then work began on redecoration using the details Fania provided.

Two months in, Hareven sent Sara his last instruction: "Do it." It was left to her to finesse the how and where. Fania was crucial to this final phase.

Dov and Liora went to a restaurant in the Yemenite quarter in south Tel Aviv. Sara timed her entry twenty minutes after the Chizziks arrived. She went alone and wore a dress that was elegant and revealing. She pretended not to see Dov at first and then when she did, she left her table to say hello, like old friends. "What a lovely coincidence Dov. Good to see you again. And is this the lovely Mrs Chizzik or another of those Chizzik groupies? Introduce me?"

Dov remained sitting. “Would you mind? We’re having a meal and you’re disturbing us.”

“Oh, I’m so sorry, please forgive me. Enjoy your meal Liora, those kibbeh here are excellent aren’t they? And that red from the boutique winery in the Galilee, velvet on the palate, excellent choice Dov. No need to get up.”

She moved away slowly enough to let Dov, and every other man in the place, admire her and to hear Liora ask, “Who was that Dov?” She wasn’t convinced by his explanation.

Three days later Sara happened to be walking past the Shop entrance on Dizengoff, laden with shopping bags as Dov was entering, and she played the same game again. This time colleagues saw a very sexy woman chatting intimately with Dov, and because they couldn’t keep their eyes off her, they didn’t see or hear Dov trying to get rid of her.

On Shabbat the Chizziks went to the beach. And so did she. The bikini she nearly wasn’t wearing reminded Dov of how she looked in the porn video and for a long moment he couldn’t take his eyes off her. Then he did, ordering Liora and the children home at once. Sara smiled in triumph as she heard Liora say, “why are you letting her harass you like this. You’re a police officer, stop her.”

Next morning Aviel was at her Lilac office. “Dov wants to see you,” he told her. “Lovely,” she said.

“You’re harassing me,” Dov started as she sat down in the interview room.

“Me harass you Dov? You’re crazy. We’ve bumped into each other a few times. Each time you’ve been extremely rude to me. I’ve done nothing to you and as far as I’m aware I’ve committed no crime, have I? If I have, charge me. If not release me now. You’re the one harassing, if you ask me. What reason did you have for ordering Aviel to bring me here? Well, what was it?”

"You're part of an ongoing investigation," Dov managed.

"How lame is that? Who are you investigating?"

"We have evidence that you use illegal migrants for sex."

"What evidence?"

"We think they're for your escort agency. We suspect you channel them into porn videos.

"You think? You suspect? You've no facts have you? Why don't you request my employment records. All my escorts are legitimate. Some would say you brought me here to get another eyeful of what you got at the beach yesterday. If that's what you want…" She started lifting off her top. Her breasts were naked as Dov rushed out, shouting, "get her out of here Aviel!" The whole Shop buzzed with it, Dov and the ever so sexy Sara Moledet, owner of an escort agency, so-called suspect in a TPI investigation, flashing her tits at him.

To Dov there was an unpleasant familiarity to it all, from a film or one of those slick US TV dramas Liora loved to watch, where the innocent cop gets trapped by his naivety, there was no such thing as an unsuspecting cop, and some little detail those setting the trap overlooked, saves him. If Dov wasn't careful he could be accused of gross misconduct. That scene in the interview room... Sara's breasts…

He told Liora about it. He felt as if he'd crossed out of reality into his own drama, with everyone thinking "if only you'd told your wife", like the Punch and Judy moment when the children shout "behind you!"

"Why are you telling me?" Liora asked. "What's really going on here? Something I need to know?"

Is there such a thing as double déjà vue, past and future at the same time, Dov asked himself, as he said, "There's nothing Liora, nothing. Believe me."

And the answer to his question came with Liora's, "How can I?"

And so it went, escalating from challenge to defense, from shout to whisper, until the tap of normal accumulated frustrations in any couple's life was well and truly opened and out flowed anger and accusations, denials and demands. Words never spoken were now hurled with the same deadly result as David's stone at Goliath, turning a marriage into a field of outrageous misfortunes. From which, seeing all of this in shock and amazement, Dov predictably fled, muttering that they were out of his best wine, couldn't Liora at least have managed to get that right, at home all day?

Fania had removed the last bottle of the boutique red. She sent Sara a one-word text, 'Coming', when Dov left his apartment. Everything had been ready for days. Sara checked that the Veuve Clicquot was nicely chilled, and a 10-milligram capsule of Ketamine Hydrochloride was in a twist of kitchen roll. All she had to do was be at the supermarket where Dov usually went.

Sara paused next to Dov as he knelt to find the right bottle in the supermarket wine rack and allowed him to see her slim ankles and follow her legs. She bent down low enough for him to see her breasts again as she chose the same wine and walked away, trailing Arpege. He followed.

At the checkout she couldn't find her purse. Dov found himself offering her shekel notes, warm from his pocket. The tips of her long fingers grazed the pad of his palm. He thought, those elegant fingers, he'd already seen what they could…No. This is the supermarket. What are you thinking?

But the current had started to pulse. Just as it was supposed to.

His hand involuntarily began to close around hers as she took his money and gave it to Dorit the cashier who had been serving Dov and Liora ever since they first moved to the locale. How could Dov drool so openly at this, this piece, and she gave Dov a disgusted look.

Sara said, “Really Dov, thanks, but you must come back to my place…” so that Dorit and anyone else would hear, and in a lower tone finished with, “so I can repay you.” He smiled and stared at her. As he should.

She waited for him outside on Ben Yehuda Street. “My purse’s at my place. I’m just over there.”

Which Dov was this who publicly and willingly accepted an invitation from this porn performer, this escort agency owner, to go to her apartment? The faithful husband? The clean cop? Perhaps he was tired of the hypocrisy of seeing and wanting and not doing. He couldn’t tell anymore where Liora’s Dov ended and this other Dov began. With this enticing woman responding, he believed, to his good looks and obvious sexual signals, he crossed the line into his imagination and left behind past, loyalty, integrity.

Sara took his hand and guided him right across the line of her silk thong. Across the line of Liora’s trust in him. “Why’s it taken you so long?” hypocrisy asked him, welcoming him in, as Sara did.

Both breathless after their first encounter, Sara said, “thirsty”. In the kitchen she poured orange juice over ice over half the Ketamine and added the champagne. He was where she’d left him, his zipper still undone. He drank as swiftly as she did. The stereo played the stealthy opening movement of the Rite of Spring. On the sofa they overtook Stravinsky.

She sprinkled the rest of the Ketamine capsule in the next Bucks Fizz and stayed close to him because the drug could induce a bit of a trip ending with melancholia and she needed to supervise Dov’s mood changes.

She needed him to be obsessed with her.

Naked, Dov admired her sleek body, those ankles, those full breasts, the trimmed chestnut thatch between her legs. She was more erotic in real life than her on-screen Fire persona. Her eyes were emerald green and she crinkled them knowing he would smile back. Then she turned coyly away, her eyes shut, squealing in mock ecstasy. It made him want her again.

In the room's shadows, as the early morning sunlight lanced the gaps in the curtains across their naked bodies, Sara was following her script to the letter, from the next move to the next. Her fingertips traced the battle scar on his neck, a long solid ridge of hard skin. "My trophy from Lebanon," he said.

"You must have been very brave," she replied, her fingers moving down.

He told her, "You make love like a mouzhik, a beautiful Russian peasant."

She almost answered in Russian, but instead asked, "And how many mouzhiks have you fucked?"

He laughed out loud.

He woke to familiar sounds. Children in the kindergarten playground. Gulls in the sky. Morning traffic. He hadn't opened his eyes, but could smell coffee brewing. He felt luxurious but very muzzy. He wondered what the time was. He stayed there. After a long while, he began to map out his next moves. He'd go to the balcony, watch the world as he did each morning, look between the hotel towers at his slice of sea, observe joggers, sunbathers, then pan down to the green of the park in the little square below.

Dov could still remember their first night in the apartment, when he'd carried Liora all the way from the front door to the bedroom with a king-size bed and that view through the glass doors.

He opened his eyes. There were speckles in the sky, something shimmering, mysterious.

He couldn't interpret what he saw, left the bed, loosely wrapped the top sheet around him and made for the balcony.

In the sky, grey still from a bank of unlikely clouds across the city, were the gulls he'd heard, an uneven spiral of them, the sun glancing off their feathers, as they dipped and dived.

He watched, captivated by the effect of light and shadow they created. Then he began his usual pan to the park. Something else, someone else caught his attention. On a balcony in his direct line of sight was a woman, looking out. His eyes sought the park.

Then stopped. The woman intrigued him. He looked again at her, in brief profile as she turned towards the sea, then her head pivoted back to him.

He gripped the cream balcony railing, his knuckles matching the paintwork, standing on his balcony, looking down at his feet, on his mocha tiles. His arms pushed his torso back from the railing. He sought the gulls. The sky was empty. The sea stretched away from the gap between the hotels. The white with gold lettering of the one on the right, the brash red letters of the other on the left , and …

No. The white and gold sign was usually on the right.

Liora stood looking over at him from their balcony.

He looked back at her...Was he delirious?

TPI's work slowed after that as Dov did. He made little attempt to unravel Nana's disappearance. The press became impatient, spending it's fury like howling wolves yearning to sink their denunciations into him.

He ignored them and eventually they found other stories. He wanted to be with Sara Moledet.

Police bureaucracy moved on past Dov. Shalit met with the Commissioner. "He spends all his time with that Moledet woman, a suspect in a TPI case," Shalit said. "It's a scandal and he's corrupt. He should be suspended."

"Not yet. We have to keep it out of the headlines," the Commissioner told him. "We don't want it eclipsing the launch of our case against the Prime Minister."

"What about Chizzik's suspicions of a Porn King and Moledet's links to whoever that is?"

"You tell me. Chizzik came up empty handed, and the file on this is one sheet of his notes, there's no evidence, nothing. Shelve it. And Yigal, you run TPI for the time being, but get ready to shut it down."

Some days, Dov didn't go in to the Shop at all. Sara consumed him.

In late April he was on the beach with her, drunk and swaying. She told him to sit down before he fell down. The beach snitch happened on him. Dov had used him off and on for years, a skinny man in tattered long shorts and t-shirt, his Saluki dog, a desert hunter, always better groomed and fed than him. The snitch regularly had morsels of information useful enough for Dov to pay him. As usual the Saluki arrived first. It was unsure about Dov and didn't nuzzle him as it usually did.

"Cool to see you," Dov slurred, sipping double strength Pina Colada straight from a cocktail shaker. He was momentarily piqued when the snitch told him he was an apology for a policeman, and then jogged away after the dog.

"Just a useless informer," he told Sara, shaking his head, not watching dog and man disappearing up to the marina.

The beach snitch told the Saluki, "Pussy whipped? Dov Chizzik? Who'd have believed it?"

Dov saw a pretty curly-haired girl walk past on her way to the water's edge, trying not to stare.

"And you can piss off too," he mumbled. He had Sara. Who else did he need?

It was decided not to indict the Prime Minister. In an act of cronyism he'd appointed an old friend as Attorney General to get the Interior Minister, a crucial coalition ally, a plea bargain for bribery charges. But prosecutors had not translated 'tangible suspicions' into facts. The old friend lasted one day in post before police announced an investigation of him for corruption, taking cash from a couple of oligarchs, the same shady businessmen who were suspected of bribing the Interior Minister. Dov was oblivious to how all this kept him from being fired.

That evening was the first night of Passover. Dov and Liora usually hosted the large family celebration. This year Dov wouldn't be reading the Hagaddah, the telling of the Exodus from Egypt.

Two months later Dov sat in his office in the half empty Dizengoff Shop. The departments on the top two floors had already moved out to the new HQ building near Yafo. The noise of traffic below on Dizengoff echoed through the place.

So it was, on another day of drift, that Dov bumped into Aviel as he was leaving.

"So how's it going?" Weiss asked, not bothered about the answer.

"Oh you know," Dov replied vaguely.

"Yeah."

Dov halted. "What do you know?"

"That you don't care."

"Why does it bother you?"

"It doesn't."

"But?"

"It's that word – respect. It's what I had for you. Now I don't."

"The 'idle brain's' set in?"

"As long as my salary check's paid, do I give a fuck? You don't. Why should I?"

Dov looked at his watch as if he had a meeting he couldn't miss. "Gotta go," he said.

"Yeah" said Aviel, "haven't we all."

By high summer the Attorney General had been replaced. The Interior Minister was in jail. The Prime Minister had survived and the letter finalizing Dov's gardening leave awaited the Commissioner's signature. Then the Commissioner's successor was announced and he left to begin his political career. The letter went into his successor's miscellaneous file.

Chapter 16
April 1997

Two friends took a day off in the big city. They'd talked about it and planned it, and now like truanting schoolgirls, Lana and Yehudit sat in a bus, watching the world go by.

The coastal highway passed through a series of towns which Yehudit named as Lana had never seen them before.

The bus eventually climbed the ramp to the top of the Tel Aviv bus station. Below Lana saw crumbling poverty, shabby buildings, not at all what she'd imagined. It reminded her of some of the back streets of old Arab Haifa.

Once off the bus they went down through two floors of shops whose cheap goods spilled onto the walkways. The floors below those were disused, with dark stairways, entrances boarded up, strewn with garbage. This is supposed to be such a prosperous nation, Lana thought.

The Israelis she saw were well dressed and fed, noisy, talking loudly amongst themselves. Mixed in were other faces, from Africa and Asia, and she guessed Eastern Europe, and amongst them, a sprinkling of her own people who behaved as if they were on sufferance.

"Where are we going now?" Lana asked.

Yehudit said, "Dizengoff." Twenty minutes later they were in Dizengoff Square, on a raised plaza above the main road in the heart of downtown Tel Aviv.

"Well what do you think?" Yehudit asked.

Lana looked around at the garish fountain, at the tramp lying flat out on a bench. Such people didn't exist in her village. Amongst palms and geraniums in flower boxes bordering the square, were cigarette butts and empty drinks cans. She disguised her dismay with, "I've never seen anything quite like it."

"Let's window shop and then walk by the sea to Yaffa and eat lunch there." Yehudit said, using the Arabic name instead of the Hebrew Yafo.

They made their way to where the light of the sky promised ocean beneath.

The sea enticed Lana. She looked around. Tel Aviv's hotel row stretched south towards Yaffa. In between the hotels were apartment buildings of different styles and periods. New towers were rising and near Yaffa a whole glade climbed inexorably, nurtured by swinging cranes and the clanging of infinite construction. The dilapidated sat crumbling next to the brash new, poor and forgotten eclipsed by rich and now.

Ugly hotel sterns dominated the promenade; sun and salt air had faded and flaked their facades. The beaches were swept but refuse dotted the tide line. A large helicopter thumped the sky heading south.

The sea was choppy, smashing against the rock breakwaters, which created calm lagoons for swimmers. Of the few people on the beach, two caught Lana's eye, an underdressed woman dozing on a sun lounger, and a man standing next to her in a silver thong, sipping from a thermos. The woman said, "For God's sake Dov, sit down before you fall down." He did as he was told. Lana watched as a beautiful dog followed by an emaciated man in tatty clothes approached the man named 'Dov'. The tableau looked so bizarre, Lana wanted to watch it unfold.

Instead the sea lured her. She removed her trainers and socks, rolled up her jeans, and passed Dov in his silver thong, who told her to piss off. She ignored him and paddled in the water for the first time, enchanted by the way her feet were slowly swallowed up in the wet sand. Yehudit joined her. Lana stared out then turned back.

Yehudit saw the look on Lana's face. "Wha-at?"

"This is the Tel Aviv we talk about at home, the biggest city of the people who took so much from us. What did you do with it? It's as if having got it, you don't care about it."

Yehudit said defensively, "It is what it is, messy and vibrant and always on the move, like most big cities. This one's mine, warts and all."

To Yehudit, Lana was brave and clever, beautiful and vulnerable. Some day, she thought, with that caramel skin and those cinnamon eyes, some great guy will fall in love with you and you'll settle down and have a family. But, she told herself, surveying the scene, I haven't seen any Arabs here. Why do I care? What would Tel Aviv be like if it was an Arab city? Thank God it isn't.

"I'm hungry," she said to Lana's back, "let's get some lunch."

They washed the sand from their feet and walked along the promenade.

The closer they got to Yaffa, the tattier the beach. It was like there was an invisible line separating the younger and older of the reluctant Tel Aviv-Yaffa sisters.

"There's a great fish place up the hill there beyond the clock tower. What do you think?"

"Can't wait," Lana said, "I'm starving."

Five minutes later Yehudit said "Shalom," to the waiter just inside the restaurant.

And Lana said, "Marhaba, Hello."

"Welcome," the man addressed Yehudit.

The place was bedlam, Arab waiters bustling with impossibly loaded trays they never dropped, Israeli diners chatting, laughing, arguing, children milling about between tables, babies crying. The fish was excellent.

As Yehudit went to pay, there was shouting outside.

On the street was a white van with slogans in red Hebrew and Arabic letters on the sides saying '$2400', and below 'To Any Arab mother ready to leave,' and below that 'Take The Money And Go!' A scuffle broke out between men waving leaflets and local Arabs. More Arabs joined in, including one of the waiters, raising fists and shouting.

A bearded man was punched, his leaflets flung in the air. He barreled into Yehudit, standing in the doorway. He yelled, "What's a Jewish girl doing in an Arab restaurant? You lefty traitor!"

Lana was next to Yehudit when there was a violent crump of an explosion and they were knocked to the ground as the fighting crowd fled. Yehudit got up and helped Lana to stand. "It's OK, it was only a stun grenade," she said.

Lana heard nothing. She saw the bearded man, hate filled eyes, arms flailing, yelling at the waiter who'd joined the fight. Police finally weighed in with riot sticks and the waiter went down, blood pouring from his head. Another waiter rushed to bring him back inside. Lana crawled over to help, but the injured waiter spat in her face. The ringing in Lana's ears subsided.

She managed in Arabic, "You spit at me?"

"It's only a spot of rain," he said slyly.

"It's not rain, it's spit. I'm a Palestinian."

She was lifted carefully to her feet and lead to a corner chair by a bear of a man. His name was Fadi, the restaurant owner. He wiped her face with a towel and gave her water. "They do this every few weeks those racists, the guy with a beard is a Knesset Member. Feeling better?"

She nodded.

"Where are you from?" She told him.

"Students?" indicating her and Yehudit.

"Yes at Haifa."

"And friends?" Another nod.

"Good," he said, "It's the only way. Forgive Abed," he indicated the waiter, being tended by a paramedic. "He's like many around here, little schooling, work he thinks is demeaning, a family living on handouts and stories of a Yaffa long gone."

Lana could still feel the spit on her face.

"Where you live, in the Galilee, there's still a big community. Here we're like an island, cut off. At least he works," he meant Abed. "Many others like him get involved with drugs and crime. I see it all the time. Wasted lives. We have no choice. We have to live with them, the Jews. Most of them are OK. They come, eat our food, buy stuff from our market."

Yehudit came over. "What a mess. It could have been a proper grenade. You OK?"

"Yes, I think so, I can almost hear again. We should go," Lana said struggling to look and feel calm. "Did you get the bill?"

"No, the fight kicked off."

"Forget about it," Fadi insisted as both girls began to remonstrate. "Just come back soon. You're always welcome. The food was good, no?"

They took a cab to the bus station. Lana thought she knew who she was, a Palestinian, an Israeli citizen, a Muslim, just like the waiter Abed. But in his eyes she was a traitor. Her fun day out was ending in a feeling of ugly fragility.

They drank cappuccinos at a coffee bar and started for the escalator.

“Little sister?” Yunis said from somewhere behind her, “going home? I’ll give you a lift.”

Lana turned apprehensively. She hadn’t seen Yunis since the row. She didn’t need another reminder of violence. Just before her eyes found him, they caught another face. A man lingered behind Yunis. Lana registered slit-like eyes with long lashes, wheat colored hair, before he turned rapidly away, but as she focussed on Yunis, she flicked back to the figure, not knowing why she was sure that he knew her brother.

“This is great,” Lana said smiling at Yunis. She could still see the other man, tall, broad physique, cutting through the mass of passengers even as Yunis hugged her and whirled her around.

To Yunis she’d suddenly grown up. Her village child innocence was evaporating. Then he wondered whether any man had kissed her yet.

Lana said, “How are you? How’s your arm?” He flexed it to show it was fine.

“I came down for the day with Yehudit, my friend from university,” Lana said, as if she needed to justify herself.

“Shalom,” said Yehudit. “I didn’t know you had a big brother Lana. What are you doing in Tel Aviv?”

“I live and work here,” he said, switching to Hebrew, smiling sweetly.

“Really? Cool,” Yehudit said.

“So, skiving off, huh?”

"No, really Yunis. I needed the break." He looked so like their father, the same caved-in cheeks but without the weathered complexion.

"Don't forget to invite me to your graduation."

"Of course," she said, wondering how that would work with their parents.

"Come on, I'll drive you home." He began guiding her to the down escalators. In Arabic she said urgently "No, honestly Yunis, it's OK, we've got return tickets."

"You'll be home a lot quicker with me. Don't worry, I'll drop you at the bottom of the hill. He won't know I was there. By bus you'll be home late."

"It's all right, we'll take the bus."

"OK, OK, but stay in touch. You've got my number?"

"Yes, of course I do."

"Well, you never call me."

"Sorry, busy with studies. Today really was a free day."

"No time for campus politics, sit-ins, anything like that? Remember what I said? Call me." He gave her another big hug. "See you. Bye Yehudit."

On the bus, Lana was quiet. Yunis had obviously heard about Sky Blue Sky.

"He's a real hunk, your brother," Yehudit said to break her mood.

Lana surprised herself with, "Yes, he's a gorgeous gay."

"Lah!" Yehudit gasped. Inexplicably she'd used the Arabic for no. "Sorry, sorry," she added quickly, "I keep shoving my foot in my mouth…but you're serious?" She paused, "I've never screwed a gay guy."

Lana didn't laugh. She shouldn't have said anything. She looked out of the window, and shook her head at Yehudit's reflection.

Chapter 17
May–July 1997

Weeks later, Lana was caught in a late spring shower in Haifa. Hatem saw her and offered her a lift. Seeing her jolted him.

He'd occasionally been to Tel Aviv to deliver and collect rental vehicles for the company he worked for in Haifa, and began visiting the city's club scene. He discovered that being an Arab made him exotic. He met a couple of divorcees at the ZarMinSum club who enjoyed him. One night, Hatem made for the rear exit for some air. Yunis had just finished the stage act and was also there with his partner. Hatem recognized Yunis. The voracious divorcees were suddenly irresistible, but he tripped over a crate and Yunis saw him. His partner grabbed Hatem and demanded his ID, said, "photographic memory," and swore he'd kill Hatem if he ever saw him again. Hatem never went back to ZarMinSum.

As the traffic crawled, she said, "Look Hatem, I'd like us to stay friends, but…" He spun the wheel sharply, driving fast, saying nothing. "Where are we going?" Lana asked alarmed. He turned into an unlit road by the docks, braked, killed the engine. He said, "I love you Lana. I can't forget you," and started to kiss her.

"Hatem!" she pushed him away and got out.

"Lana, please," he called as she ran through the rain. He backed up fast alongside her. "I'm sorry, but I haven't seen you for so long and...you're getting soaked again." She got back in, wet and shivering. Hatem gave her his jacket. "Marry me Lana. Please say yes," he begged her.

Lana imagined married life with him. It would be traditional. She'd have at least three kids in as many years and he'd be off with some compliant girl or other, just like Sheikh Adwan, his notorious father. It all made her shudder. Hatem thought she was still cold and switched the car heater on. She smiled, shook her head, "No Hatem, I won't marry you." The sound of the rain drowned out his sigh of disappointment.

***

"How did you do in the exams?"

"Fuck! When were they?"

"You forgot? They finished last week."

"Shit. It's just that music's kind of taken over my life, know what I mean?"

Lana sat on a wicker stool in the T-House in Haifa, waiting for Nabil. The two students were Israelis, chilling with the local ethnic vibe.

"Are you doing any gigs?"

"Not right now. Too busy developing the sound, you know?"

"Oh right. What sound?"

"Jazz-Arab-cross-over, you know?"

Lana tuned out.

"Great you could make it," Nabil said as he sat down on another stool opposite Lana. "You look well."

She smiled, politely. He'd asked her out a few times before but she'd always said no. She'd been so busy with exam preparations. He was gently persistent and she was sure she would be OK with him, not like Hatem.

Nabil asked, “Are you into music?”

Still thinking of Hatem, she refocused.

“Am I into music? Oh yes, all sorts, Michael Jackson ever since I don’t know when, probably ‘Dangerous’, and before him George Wassouf, he knows about Tarab.”

“So if a passion suddenly overcame you, you’d follow it?”

“What do you mean, passion?” She tried not to sound suspicious.

“You said Tarab. That creates a passion doesn’t it?”

“Yes, I suppose it does. I hadn’t thought of it like that. Anyway I don’t get into it much, I’ve got so much work for my degree.”

“No more activism? Not like your hero father?”

“That was once and he didn’t approve of Sky Blue Sky.”

“Ah, a doer not a talker.”

“Something like that.”

“There have to be both. If we’d had both during the Nakba …”

“Oh please don’t.”

“Sky Blue Sky?”

“You got the TV coverage and the headlines.”

“And you ducked the chance for an interview all to yourself.” How did he know about the TV reporter?

“How did you know about that?”

“Basil Khoury told me.”

“Are you that close?”

“We share ideas. He sometimes advises me.”

Lana said tightly, “Frankly I don’t like being used.”

“That’s politics. Sky Blue Sky was a perfect opportunity…”

"Why did you invite me out? To see if I had any new ideas to steal?"

"That's a little harsh. But yes you certainly have an activist's imagination."

"Nabil, I told you. I just want to get my degree."

"No time for relaxation then?"

She sat back, releasing some of her tension. An apology or a thank you for Sky Blue Sky would have helped. But he'd paid her a compliment hadn't he? It was a bit mean, maybe that's how men were; she gave him a shy smile.

He walked her to the bus stop and waited until her bus arrived. Something in his eyes made her say yes when he asked if he could see her again, "but," she said, "not yet."

Her second year exam results bore out Fouad Assad's optimism, and she'd filled three notebooks on MA project ideas.

She wanted to spend more time away from home. It was delicious serendipity that came to her aid, baklawa. Both Khadija and Auntie Ahlam, Khadija's sister-in-law, were experts at making the sweet walnut and pistachio leaf pastries.

The T-House in Haifa's Wadi Nis Nas quarter was a café owned by the Kaplans, a Jewish couple. It was popular with Jews and Arabs alike and the Kaplans employed Palestinians as managers and staff. She'd tried their baklawa. It was too dry. Out of nowhere came her idea to sell them 'al Batuf baklawa', offer herself as a waitress and split any profits with Khadija and Ahlam. Convincing the Kaplans was easier than getting Ibrahim's permission to work at the T-House during vacations. But the women united behind her.

"You don't need to do this," her father insisted. "If it's extra pocket money, I'll give it to you."

"It's not about pocket money Daddy," Lana countered. "I'm almost nineteen. I want to get a part time job."

"I'll find something for you in the village," he said.

"I've found work."

Khadija came in with Ahlam. They'd been discussing which baklawa recipe to make.

"Really Ibrahim, the difference between how you earn your living from Them and how Lana will do the same with our baklawa is only a matter of product and quantity, isn't it?" Lana smiled.

"She's not a child anymore you know," added Ahlam. "She needs a little room to grow. She'll only be working during the vacation. What's the problem?"

"This is not a good time to be in a city," said Ibrahim.

He meant the security situation. In the two years Lana had been at university, urban centers had become targets for Hamas and Islamic Jihad suicide bombers. Jews and Arabs had been victims. Like many others, the Kaplans employed private security at the T-House. Lana added that to the mix and Ibrahim unhappily agreed.

When students learned that Sky Blue Sky's Lana was working there and al Batuf baklawa was being served, the T-House became packed. One afternoon two Jewish students from the Sky Blue Sky sit-in were arguing about who was responsible for the bombings.

Basil Khoury and Nabil at an adjoining table adopted a plague on both your houses attitude. Nabil asked Lana to meet him after work. "I thought it would be good to walk and talk," he said outside. "Let's go to the sea."

She hesitated. But his eyes had a sincerity that her rejection would hurt. "OK," she smiled.

"I suppose I'm not the first girl you've brought here," Lana said watching the waves at a beach just south of the city.

"I've never brought anyone here."

"So why did you bring me?"

"Because I thought you'd like it."

Dusk was on its way, but the sky was still clear and beautiful from the sun's deepening orange as it magically descended. A warm wind came up as they watched and with it the surf rose.

"That looks exciting," Lana indicated wind surfers dotting the sea, hunting for the right wave and angling always for the right wind.

"Do you want to kiss me?"

Her question surprised them both.

"You think that's why I brought you here? I'm a Muslim. I'd never take advantage of you."

"You've looked at me in a certain way."

His lips pursed, "It's difficult not to. But I meant what I said."

Lana said, "You haven't answered me," and mangled his thoughts and words repeating, "Do you want to kiss me?"

So he kissed her. It was a real kiss. It broadcast messages about love and desire and uncertainty, and first time, and real and imagined, and quick and slow and start and stop and are the wind surfers watching and is anyone else and it doesn't matter and stop asking me if I want to and this is right and this is wrong and you taste wonderful.

It lasted eons and it was over in seconds.

Nabil came a few times more to the T-House where they communicated by look, as if by tacit agreement that one kiss was far beyond anything they'd expected, and they were not ready for anything more.

Chapter 18
September 1997

"Lana," Basil Khoury called out, "how are you? I haven't seen you at the T-House for a while."

Lana was headed from the library to the bus stop, her college shoulder bag worn across her chest, a light jacket with a hood over her shoulders. The air was cool, up on the campus hill in the evening. It was just before five pm and she was early for once. "It was a vacation job. Now I'm concentrating on my finals."

"No more al Batuf baklawa? It really is the best."

"Only when I'm there."

"I'm glad I spotted you." He saw her quizzical expression and said, "no, no, it's you I wanted to talk about, not politics, well maybe a little, but don't worry."

Before she could respond, he said, "have you seen the museum in the basement of the main building? If you haven't it's a must. It'll teach you what they really think of us ." He'd spoken in Arabic but his 'they' made her look up nervously.

"No," she said glancing at her watch, "I don't have a lot of time."

"Oh come on Lana. Take a break. I haven't had a chance to chat with you since that TV journalist tried to pry."

She owed him for that and he was Uncle Basil. They descended to the museum and Basil tapped loudly on the door. He tapped again even though they could hear someone approaching inside.

A prim young man unlocked the doors and stood back as Basil ushered Lana in and down the stairs. "I'm not the public," Basil brayed, "I'm faculty. I'm Professor Basil Khoury, Philosophy Department, with a pupil. Report me if you want!" His professorship had been announced a month before.

"But…" the young man tried. Basil said, "I'm in now, with my student. Don't worry. I won't bite." The young man looked unsure and stood well back as they entered.

The museum was impressive, well lit and laid out, wood floors and white display daises. Basil climbed onto a platform above a recreated ancient Phoenician boat. A plaque read 'Ma'agan Mikhael Ship.'

"They've given a Phoenician ship an Israeli name and hey presto, they've purloined its history. It's the way they are. Look at this place."

"OK." She put her bag down next to him. He hadn't meant it literally and when she walked off to tour the exhibits, she'd seen irritation on his face. Now, everywhere she looked there was a political under-current.

She came back and said, "There's one obvious omission, us. Is it because we lost?" "Naturally," he said stepping closer. This close she could smell different scents from him, a vague perfume, after-shave Yunis had called it, and the same tobacco tang from his clothes, like Ibrahim's.

"Winning or losing? There's a saying, 'It doesn't matter whether you win or lose, as long as you play the game,'" and he laughed, and she knew it was at her.

So far not so very illuminating, she thought. "What really happened in the Nakba?" she asked, stressing the really.

"What do you mean 'really'?" he snapped at her and she resented it, feeling an inner tightening, blushing. It reminded her of school, of being found out, because she wasn't concentrating or because she'd been naughty. But she told herself not to flinch.

"Have we really been deprived and dominated?" His sharp sarcasm was unexpected. "Their Declaration of Independence invited us, 'the sons of the Arab people', to join them in building the state with full equality. Instead they 'encouraged' us to leave. After 1948 we were like a nation of laboratory rats, conditioned to do as we were told, forced to swear a loyalty oath, under military occupation for eighteen years until 1966. It was a dress rehearsal for the occupation of the Gaza Strip and the West Bank after '67."

It was a very accessible summary but he still hadn't answered her. She repeated her question.

His eyes were fixed somewhere ahead. "They came, they conquered." His theatricality made Lana think he craved an audience to impress. She tried again. "What did the Nakba mean?"

"There are many words – justice, equality, freedom," he said still soliloquizing, not looking at her. "We've never enjoyed any of them. That's what Nakba means." Then he looked at her and said, "your lovely eyes tell me that you don't quite get it."

My lovely eyes? She couldn't stop them from blinking under his stare. Is that all I am, a girl who should applaud everything you say?

"Should I say it like this?" he continued, his voice pitched up, like a silly girl's, hers she assumed, "We're all peasants, following the herd. We should have surrendered at the first shots. We were beaten before we began?" He ended reproachfully, "thinking all that, saying it, is true betrayal!"

The intensity of the implied accusation alarmed her. He looked like an angry bear up on its hind legs, roaring.

She nodded nervously. That calmed him. And Lana knew she was right to acquiesce. It had to be all one way on Basil Khoury Street.

He continued, "We need a leader to unite us. But until one appears we must fight. We must rise up against our oppressor."

"That's a call to revolt," she said.

"Don't you dare misinterpret me!"

You mean how dare I question you, she thought.

"We must employ the force of ideas."

"Ideas? Rise up is a call to arms."

"It is an idea." He stamped his foot. "To gain our equality we must create a state for all its citizens. Let democracy decide."

"And the aim would be?"

"There would be a new majority, ours. That would end Zionist Jewish exclusivity, through the ballot box, and we…"

"We'd win. It's all about revenge."

"It would be more just," he said and his jaw clenched.

"Do you really think the Israelis will say goodbye to their country?"

He squinted hard at her. "Ahhh," he let the sound out slowly and smiled. "You haven't a clue have you?" He glanced at his watch. "I'm sorry but I have to go. You know your way out of here?"

"Of course I do." Her contempt startled him, but she didn't take it back. Then it was her turn to look at her watch. Hell, she'd missed her bus. That meant a quizzing from Ibrahim.

"Off to a party?" he asked nonchalantly.

"No, I've got to get home and I've missed the bus."

"I'm so sorry," the sneer was barely disguised. Then he said breezily, "I'm going home myself, so I could give you a lift door to door."

She sat immersed in the buttery leather upholstery of his Mercedes, her bag at her feet. Basil turned up the heater and she instantly felt warmer and took of her jacket.

"This is very comfortable," she said.

"I enjoy driving it," Basil answered as he wove expertly down the winding route behind the campus. He glanced across at her.

He didn't really see Lana. He had impressions, thighs revealed as her skirt hem had risen, firm breasts pushing against her t-shirt, little beads of perspiration on her top lip as the temperature rose around her. His was a practiced look that didn't disturb his concentration on the road but did arouse him.

She was no longer the girl-child he'd coached, she was challenging and brazen.

Lana felt his eyes and she pulled her skirt down. The steep angle of the car's descent and the glossy leather seat kept her slipping forward and the skirt rising back above her knees. And when almost absently, Basil allowed his hand to rest gently on her knee and began ever so softly to caress, Lana laughed absurdly, the way any young woman unused to such intimacy might have done, saying "Oh! Don't do that!"

To Basil it said the opposite. He drove fast through their village and out towards the bourj, the tower, the natural outcrop overlooking Ibrahim and Adwan's olive groves.

Lana asked nervously, "Aren't we going home?"

"Soon," he said thickly. He turned off the main road onto the perimeter of the bourj, parked and got out. Lana was aware of the pine trees, eerily soaring in the dark. She opened the door gingerly, leaving her bag in the foot well.

The pine scent mixed with the peculiar fragrance of the olive trees below, where she and Hatem used to go. Basil stood, a dark shape, by a tree with his back to her, waiting.

He pulled her to him and held her in arms, crushing her against his body, and at once she could feel the size of his phallus, huge, pressed against her. Lana's disbelief became terror as he growled something incomprehensible and she tried to wriggle away but in doing so, her body slid down his erection and he responded as if she'd meant to do that, locking her more fiercely to him, one of his large paws reaching behind, beneath her buttocks, lifting her up. She was sweating profusely, squirming but unable to break free from his bearlike grip.

And then his fingers pulled at her underwear and were probing her brutally and she screamed out. He turned still gripping her, pushed her against the tree and muffling her cry in his shoulder, lifted her up and dropped her all the way onto him. The initial pain she felt as he tore in to her was unimaginable. The shocking violence of it, the rending of her hymen doubling her agony, the revulsion at what was being done to her by this ravening ursine creature, thrusting at her, the trauma rippling each time, excruciatingly, through her body, searing the core of her being, and she could not stop it, any and every sound or movement she tried, encouraged him. His grunts increased in tempo with his invasion of her, insensible to what he inflicted, wanting only to sate himself, on and on until finally his head went back and his mouth opened with a howl of ecstasy.

Afterwards, he lowered her to the ground. She was paralyzed with the absolute abuse he'd inflicted on her, while he smiled broadly at her. "Lana, Lana," he purred breathlessly, "That was so good, wasn't it? And look," he flourished the full condom, "I protected you. You won't get pregnant. You're safe." The lights of a car climbing the road illuminated the trees and in their passing glow, Basil saw Lana's vacant eyes, but misinterpreted them, instead sure she was still lost in the passion they had shared. She clasped her arms tightly and squeezed as if she could expel the last minutes.

Whatever and whoever she had been was no more, vanished, not flying up there to the stars she'd once loved, but falling somewhere deep and murky, down beneath her feet, into the earth, at first cold and slippery, then hot and scorching, where thoughts were not thought and emotions unknown.

In the stillness as the headlight shadows faded, Basil had a sudden premonition of being pushed over an edge. He waited. Nothing happened and he laughed at the absurdity of that and walked to the car, throwing the condom casually away. He left the passenger door open and got in, switched on the engine and sat waiting for Lana. He put a packet of tissues on her seat.

Another Lana, looking but not seeing any details around her, knew that she did not want to get into the car. But she saw it was night and she did not think she could walk alone back to her home.

Yet another Lana with no knowledge of what she was doing, approached the car, pulled at her bag, managed to open the rear passenger door, got in and huddled in the corner, as Basil, still smiling at her, got out, closed the doors, got back in and reversed the car and drove back to the main road. He grinned a couple of times in the mirror and said,

"We must do this again very soon." He tuned the radio to a music station.

This Lana neither saw Basil's expression in the rear view nor heard his words or the music. All she could feel was the unwanted channel Basil had driven through her.

As they neared the village, a fourth Lana came back to reality and panicked. She didn't want her parents to see her. Who could she go to?

She managed, "stop here" at the intersection near the house, and Basil said "of course", conspiratorially, as all the Lanas concertinaed together and she feebly held her bag and staggered out and found the strength to close the door. Basil drove off.

Lana stood wavering, unable to straighten up, running her hand through her tangled curls, dislodging bits of pine bark, shuddering as she did so. She felt chilled and pulled the hood of her jacket over her head, bringing it as low over her face as she could, and was suddenly aware of the deep grazes in her back. She walked unsteadily to the front door. She found her key, and managed the stairs, the chafing inside her at every step making her want to cry through sealed lips. She kept going on and up. There was no sound from the lounge. Her parents were already in their bedroom. She paused, praying that her father's snores would continue. She made it on to the last steps leading to her room, two floors up, relief beginning to nibble at desperation.

Khadija called out, "Lana? Is that you? We tried to phone but you didn't answer. Lana?"

The new amalgamated Lana swallowed, summoning a normal voice, said, "Sorry. I'm all right. The bus broke down and my battery went. I'm very tired. I'll be working here tomorrow. Good night."

“Don’t you want something to eat?”

“No Mummy, honestly, I’m just tired. It’s been a …” Her “honestly” made her cringe. A what? A long day? One of those days? “…It’s been a hard day…I’m worn out… Good night…Kiss Daddy.” The sob stayed behind her teeth. She curled up still dressed on the floor of her shower, losing her tears in its warm cascade.

Chapter 19
August 1998

During Dov's summer of Sara, there were moments of near lucidity between his infatuation and the object of his obsession. They had discovered that they both liked English literature. So in one sober interlude Dov asked in English, "why do I tell you everything about me? Why am I more comfortable with you than any other woman?"

And Sara answered grandly, "because I am the consummate courtesan you never knew and it's my job to put you at your permanent ease."

Dov ogled her boyishly.

It was funny, Liora mused, how the unlikely became normal. There was so much going on, and if one element in a busy twenty-four hours didn't fit the pattern, Liora would work to ensure the rest of the day was not disrupted.

At first, she cried in bed at night for weeks. Until she found another home help, her mother came to look after the children.

Each morning she would see a haggard face with puffy eyes in the mirror. That couldn't be Liora Chizzik, wife of Super Cop Dov. But it was. Anyone asking after Dov, would get an angry, “I bloody well don’t know!” Dov’s friends stopped phoning. Only Gilad kept in touch, maintaining a neutrality that Liora both loved and hated. She calculated that they had all been friends for nearly a quarter of a century, so sometimes she’d just phone to ask how he and his family were and listened, envying the mundane.

The Chizzik and Livnat parents met to discuss ‘this awful crisis’, agreed to make greater efforts with their grandchildren, and promised to stay in touch. They absorbed the ‘predicament’ as Hava Chizzik called it, their contact reduced to bumping into each other taking Yaniv and Yael in or out, exchanging ever more curt pleasantries at the door. Vikki Livnat told Efi, rancorously, “Investigator? Which woman is he investigating now? I never liked the way he looked at me.”

Liora stopped the tears, kept her mourning for the end of her love for Dov to herself, and became aggressively pragmatic.

She got used to not speaking to him whenever he appeared. He slept in the study. The children took their cue from Liora, ignoring his footsteps as he came down the corridor, past their room at night and in the morning. He became a lodger, paying the mortgage and leaving housekeeping money each month.

She called Aviel a couple of times at the Shop and discovered that there too the unusual had become the norm. Aviel’s voice echoed, reminding her that the building was almost empty, and the last time he said he would be gone within a week.

She concentrated on her MBA studies and tried to put her marriage out of her mind.

Until this evening.

Liora was sitting at her laptop working when the envelope symbol announced an e-mail. She had a paper to finish. Her problem was being unable to ignore e-mail traffic and the disruption to her concentration. Liora had turned off the sound so that the 'ding' did not distract her. She carried on, but the symbol summoned. She saved what she was writing and opened the message.

At the Shop, Aviel was packing. There were only a couple of officers doing security duty. Every sound was exaggerated and Aviel heard someone coming up from the ground floor. He stood in his doorway waiting to see who it was. When Dov's head appeared, Aviel turned back. Dov started saying, "just came in to check the last e-mails," but Aviel slammed his door, the bang making pigeons on the windowsill take wing.

He sat at his desk fuming, trying to find the appropriate valedictory words to a man who had for so many weeks returned his approaches with static. He turned to close his computer. A new e-mail had arrived. It told him that a videocassette "containing information crucial to an ongoing TPI investigation" was awaiting his collection at the reception desk.

Liora, the Commissioner, Commander Shalit, a selection of other senior police officers at Jerusalem Police HQ and the new Tel Aviv District complex, and police press and media reporters, all received copies of the cassette. It was titled "Super Dick's Dipstick". Sara's lithe body, but never her face, was featured with a clearly identified Dov in full length and flow with her.

Dov was imagining her stroking fingers as he went down to reception. The desk Sergeant, Tawfik, told him, "I was about to call up to you. A courier just delivered this." Back in his office Dov loaded the cassette into the VCR. It was in a plain white unlabelled glossy slipcover. Why was it familiar? It took only seconds to recognize Sara and then himself. He ejected the cassette and tore and ripped at the tape, then threw the black plastic rectangle to the floor and stamped on it. It wasn't enough. He grabbed the VCR, and hurled it out of the door and was careering down the stairs and out of the building as his desk phone and then Aviel's started ringing along the empty corridor.

The apartment was bare. There were little holes in the ceilings and walls where the miniature camera lenses and microphones had been removed. Dov curled up in a corner on the balcony floor, waiting for sunrise.

With it he stood and looked out as he'd done on the first morning after the first night with Sara. He saw nothing.

Contrition. Depression. Escape. These all came later.

Now, no guilt. No selfless pursuit of vocation. Just the dregs of memory, of selfish obsession turning to self-pity and bitter loathing, suffused by loneliness that became grieving. For his loss of himself.

Shalit called Liora and ordered her not to answer the phone or the door. She disconnected the VCR in the apartment and locked the cassette in her desk drawer.

She barely slept and got up and stood on the balcony, her balcony, her feet on the tiles, her hands gripping the cream railing, looking out across the park and the trees, thinking of Dov, who she'd loved for so long, not seeing him staring back.

Chapter 20
May–August 1998

All the Lanas who emerged after her rape were joined by one more. This Lana was an exam machine, a recluse who rarely slept, ate little and stayed in her room trying to cram a brain that seemed unwilling to retain any data for her finals. But she knew that her only truth was to find the means not only to prepare for but also to pass those essential exams. She would deal with afterwards, afterwards. Sometimes she'd go out and be away for hours and she couldn't have said where she'd been. But the exam machine Lana could not stop what happened when she tried to close her eyes to sleep. Then the concertina of Lanas opened backwards, from the Lana sitting under the shower to the Lana in the abyss far beneath the bourj amongst the roots of the pine trees, after something so indescribable had happened and she could not know what that was, except it had happened to her and one of those Lanas inhabited that abyss still.

She had no recollection of sitting in the exam hall answering the questions.

Her hollow eyes and prolonged silences when she did eat with her parents worried Ibrahim enough to talk with Mrs al-Taj. "It's normal," she told him. "Girls tend to work with greater intensity than boys, especially when the pressure is on. There's so much at stake. When it's over they need time to regain their strength, perhaps even rediscover why they'd invested so much of themselves in the effort."

Those were too many clever sounding words for him. "She looks ill. Is that what you were like?" he asked.

"You'd have to ask my brother. I moped around for ages afterwards. It was such an anti-climax and I just felt empty." She knew who Ibrahim was, and that he would cherry pick from what she'd said in the way he'd choose the best fruits from his crops, on the land that meant everything to him. "If you're still worried in a week or two, tell me and I'll talk with her," she offered.

***

Khadija and Ibrahim attended Lana's graduation. She had achieved a First, but her dread of seeing Basil Khoury eclipsed her triumph.

Khadija looked serene in surroundings that were alien; she'd never been amongst Israelis before. Ibrahim in a dark suit, white shirt and keffiyah looked stiff. He was thrilled when Lana's name was announced. Khadija squeezed his arm in delight and he gave his daughter a little nod of pride as she went up to receive her certificate. She nodded unsmiling at someone else and when Ibrahim followed her eyes, he saw Yunis in a rear seat and quickly looked away. Lana showed no reaction to the Vice Chancellor's words of praise.

Basil Khoury came to congratulate them. "It could have been 'with honors'", he told them, giving Ibrahim a hug which wasn't reciprocated. "She missed it by this much. But getting a First is marvelous. And I'm delighted that I contributed in some small way. It was worth it, no? Congratulations." Yunis watched Basil's smile at Khadija. What he saw in it, the extra seconds of gaze, made his stomach churn. He muttered, "Ass."

They all looked around for Lana, wanting to share the moment with her.

"Mr and Mrs al Batuf?" It was Fouad Assad. "I just wanted to say how pleased we all are of Lana's achievement. I told her she could do great things and here we are. You must be delighted."

Khadija smiled, "Lana's spoken of you." She didn't introduce Yunis. But his resemblance to his mother was obvious.

"You're Lana's brother?" Assad congratulated him too. "I'd have liked to have told Lana herself, but I can't find her." He panned across the crowd. "Could I have a word?" he asked Ibrahim.

Left alone with Khadija, Yunis said, "You banned me from the house, not the world outside." She looked away.

Assad found an empty lecture room. "It's an honor to meet you," Fouad began. "You must be so proud today."

"My wife had more to do with it than me," Ibrahim said.

Fouad smiled. "Of course. I wanted to talk about Lana. I've been worried about her. Is everything OK with her at home? Has she been ill?"

Ibrahim stiffened. "She was in her room. I go to my fields and come back at night and she's there. Then she was here. Her studies finished. She works in Haifa."

"I see. Well I saw a marked deterioration, uncommunicative, and I'm not sure that was pressure of exams. She was always vibrant, contributing to class discussions. Then she stopped."

"Oh?" Ibrahim said.

"No, no," Fouad said, "she didn't stop coming to classes. She stopped engaging. When other students approached her, she ignored them and once she even shouted at them. I tried to speak with her but she avoided me. That's not pre-exam nerves."

Ibrahim tried, "What do you think it might be?"

Fouad hesitated. "I think something's happened, but I don't know what."

"Thank you for telling me. I will talk to her."

"Yes, I think one of you should. Do you know what she wants to do next?"

"No."

"I can help if she wants to do a post-graduate course. I already suggested some ideas to her."

At the other end of the corridor Lana and Yehudit were huddled, watching as other students and their families exited into the warm summer afternoon.

"OK Lana. It's over. You got the best results of our year. I just got a second. But we're done. Lighten up."

Ibrahim nodded quickly and went to find the others.

Like Lana, Yehudit had been cloistered away preparing for the exams and they hadn't seen each other for weeks. But her, "Are you ok?" got, "Leave me alone!"

"Come on Lana, let's go and celebrate," she tried.

Nothing.

"Lana!" Basil's voice boomed out along the corridor. "Lana, my girl, well done. Let me give you a hug."

Yehudit felt Lana recoil then she scurried into the crush of students and parents going out through the double doors.

Basil looked bemused, shrugged and left.

"Lana? Lana?" Yunis called. She darted away. He saw Yehudit and congratulated her warmly.

"Thanks, and Mazal Tov to you and the family – a First, great no? I didn't do as well as Lana, but…" Even with the crowd milling passed them, she sensed the awkwardness between mother and son. He introduced Khadija whose expression suggested that Lana hadn't mentioned their friendship. Khadija kept searching the crowd for her daughter.

Ibrahim appeared and Yehudit shook his hand vigorously as if she'd known him all her life. "Nice to meet you at last. Isn't it great she got a First?" Ibrahim gruffly agreed, but didn't avoid her. It helped that Yehudit was both genuine and pretty. Khadija smiled at that.

"Where is she?" He asked in uncertain Hebrew.

"She was here just a second ago; she seems to have vanished. I can call her if you'd like."

"Thank you."

"I'll wait for her too," Yunis added. "Would anyone like a coffee or a cold drink?" His parents said nothing. "Yehudit?" She asked for a coke and dialed Lana's cell number.

Lana answered on the third ring. "Tell them I'll be home later," was all she said and rang off. Yehudit continued talking to the silent phone, "sure, sure, I'll let them know. You're joining some of the others for a party and you'll be home later on? Yes of course. Y'Allah bye." She looked up to find neither Khadija nor Ibrahim looking convinced. "Well, I'd best be getting along to the party too. Mazal Tov again. Good seeing you."

Yunis came back with the coke, irritated when he saw Yehudit walking away.

When she'd gone far enough not to be seen by them, she turned and watched. Yunis and his parents headed for different parts of the car park.

Her cell rang. "Can I stay over at your place just for tonight?" Lana asked.

Their cab turned off a main road and descended along a street that ended in a quiet cul de sac. Yehudit stopped the cab, paid and got out. Lana's first impression was of tall trees shading white balconies.

Yehudit unlocked the front door. At the end of a corridor was a metal spiral stairway. Had she been feeling frivolous Lana would have run up and down it. At the top of the stairs she found a huge open oval space with four rooms leading off it.

"This is all yours?" she asked. To have a place all of her own was a dream she'd never dreamt, until now.

Yehudit pointed to a white beanbag. "Try that," she said, "it's unusual but comfortable."

Lana sank uncertainly into it and enjoyed the sensation. Yehudit made tea as Lana stared around her. Everything seemed very neat. "Its camomile," Yehudit handed her a mug. "They say it calms you. For that I'd rather smoke a joint or drink vodka. Either for you?"

Lana said no.

Yehudit smiled, "I thought not."

"I'm sorry to take you away from the parties," Lana said gruffly, sipping her tea.

"Don't worry," Yehudit said soothingly, "there'll be others. We could talk, if you want to, but you look like you should sleep." She showed her to a bedroom and Lana fell asleep fully clothed.

She forced herself awake after the nightmare, got up and went into the oval room. It was early morning and she guessed Yehudit was still asleep.

She wandered around looking at the books on shelves covering the walls. She took a glass of water back to the bedroom, and sat up on the bed sipping, hopeless.

Tears began and she lay down and in the end fell asleep as the first birds sang.

Yehudit woke her gently, proffering a cup of coffee. She sat on the bed as Lana took the cup in both hands. “How’d you sleep?”

“I had a nightmare.”

“Do you want to talk about it?”

Lana shook her head.

“OK. Let’s have breakfast. You stay here and rest up. I’ll do some shopping and come back and we can chat or go for a walk. It’s an easy day.”

Over breakfast she told Lana how she’d got the apartment. Uncle Rudi, her mother’s brother, had built this house but didn’t live in it anymore. He’d offered Yehudit the upper self-contained floor. He kept one room on the ground floor as an occasional office. He was a retired civil engineer and lived in a penthouse in a smart Haifa suburb.

“You said he built it, your uncle?” Lana asked welcoming the distraction.

“Yes, he did.”

“You mean with his own money?”

“Yes. No. I mean he built it with his own hands. It was really hard especially up here on a hillside; it took him three years, bit by bit every day, in all weathers. His own money paid for the materials but friends helped when he ran out. It was like a test project. He made a few mistakes but the place is still standing.”

The trees framed the view of Haifa Bay, captivating as ever. After a while her mind wandered to another place with pine trees and she went back to bed.

Yehudit knocked on the bedroom door. No answer. She gently opened it to find Lana sitting on the bed motionless. “I bought a cake. Would you like more tea or coffee?” Lana shrugged her shoulders.

Minutes later she called out, “Come on Lana. The coffee’s getting cold.”

Lana came in and sat sullenly on the beanbag. Her coffee and cake remained untouched. She said, “Stop nagging me.” She looked away and said no more, pursued by Yehudit’s long, anxious silence.

Then she asked, “Your uncle was a Shoah survivor?”

“Yes, that’s right.” Yehudit said quietly. “He and my mother, out of six, four children and their parents. They both say that when they were liberated they were Musselmen.”

“What?”

“Submissive. Apathetic. It’s German, for how Jews in the camps behaved. Like zombies. Close to death.”

“You know what Musselmen means?”

“I just said. They used it to describe the…”

“Yes but what does the word mean?”

“I don’t …”

“It’s the word for Muslim in several languages.”

Her rage produced abuse in Arabic and then Lana rasped in Hebrew, “It’s all lies! You’re thieves and murderers!” She tore blindly at the beanbag until a seam burst and the contents exploded. Sitting partly covered in the synthetic snowdrift, she picked vacantly at the white polystyrene beans.

Yehudit put her arm around Lana and murmured, “It was Basil Khoury wasn’t it?”

***

Lana’s nightmare mixed fact and the wildest fantasy, rooted in unabated fears.

It opened on a bus, this macabre play in her mind. A daughter and a mother sit behind Lana and a second daughter sits next to her talking at them without turning round. Her mother, who Lana can't see, has a long almost melodic smoker's cough. "He tape it?" she asks her daughter between coughing bouts.

"Minute," the daughter next to Lana says and produces a beeping cell phone. "Look at that. He's only gone and sent a text whilst you were asking. It was the best show ever, he says, the Arabooshim were kicked out."

And then Lana is in the same TV show. It's an adult version of the playground tag game. A clock ticks as fifteen contestants have to reach the safe square. Whoever is out when the clock chimes is thrown through a window. At the end Lana is out and runs to the window. Outside is the show's presenter Uncle Basil, standing amidst bodies of dead women. He smiles up at her and says, "You see Lana, we're safe," as a voice announces, "and Lana al Batuf wins tonight's star prize, this big beautiful condom. A big hand for Lana, everybody!"

***

After she'd whispered yes to Yehudit's question, she had given her a phone number for this place, the counseling centre on a quiet street in Haifa's Carmel suburb. Once through the security entry cell, she was on a softly lit passageway with dark wood flooring.

It had taken days for her to summon the courage to make the call. Her greatest fear was of her family finding out. At school there'd been rumors about a single girl from the big village nearby who had become pregnant. Her father found out and he and her brothers murdered her.

Liz Menkin, her counselor, was not surprised when Lana admitted that the assault on her had been a whole five months before. The admission alone, in the first hour of the first session was, she told Lana, very significant.

Lana was dressed in a long shapeless black abaya with a white scarf wrapped around her neck, one end of which she sometimes chewed. She sat with her legs firmly together, eyes downcast, her right thumb pressed deep into the palm of her left hand as she spoke, hesitantly and so softly, Liz had to ask her to repeat her words.

Lana didn't want to be there, to answer any questions, to relive what had happened. She could see, as if the dark robed figure of herself had become transparent, how contorted with rage she was inside, and how the anger kept burning her soul.

Liz noted how this shell of a girl would keep staring at the pattern of the rug under her feet. It was Persian, in reds and greens and golds. Lana's eyes traced the intricate pattern back and forth.

When Liz had first met Lana and began in Hebrew, Lana had asked, "Do you speak English?"

That suited Liz, Scottish born and one of the center's senior staff psychologists. Lana assumed she was Jewish. "No," Liz said simply, "my parents were proud Christians, but I don't have a strong faith. Does that help?"

It did. Losing herself in the carpet pattern was even more therapeutic.

Three months after her graduation, Ibrahim told Khadija that more village fathers had asked him about Lana, but they'd said that when she'd been in the village she looked miserable. "They're obviously thinking about marriage prospects for their sons," he said. "I wouldn't accept their offers. Lana could do better than any village son now she's got a university degree."

Khadija smiled at the ways of men. Asking Lana about her future hadn't happened yet. But the marriage inquiries gave her a new impetus.

She knew her daughter well enough to avoid a mother-to-daughter quizzing.

Lana listened as Khadija told her about the recent 'suitors' for marriage. "With your father and I, our families knew each other," she said. "My father wanted me married as soon as I was eligible and in those days the fathers met and agreed. Love wasn't part of it, it was all to do with tradition. I'd seen your father in the village many times and then at a wedding. He danced that debkeh, you remember? And I secretly fell for him. Why the surprised look? Because I already loved him? I still love him and I've never made that a secret. But traditional marriages don't usually begin like that."

"I know," Lana said.

"So now you've won your degree, do you want to teach?"

"I didn't win anything, I just worked as hard as I could. I'm not sure what to do next. Perhaps research into the Nakba, you know, how and why it happened "

Khadija's brow furrowed.

Lana said acerbically, "Well your generation goes on about it all the time. We're expected to simply feel your pain and identify with the loss of our homeland. I want to know more about it."

Her cynicism, its underlying anger, told Khadija that whatever had happened to her daughter must have shaken her profoundly. Asking outright what it was wouldn't work.

She suggested Lana might talk to family members who went through it all, starting with Ibrahim.

Slowly and surely Liz helped her to put pieces of herself back in place, all the time getting closer to the rape itself.

After her eighth session, Liz told her, "You're making remarkable progress Lana."

Lana was unconvinced. "The nightmare hasn't stopped yet."

"It will. You suppressed what happened to you. Seeking help after the trauma was an enormous step."

Lana looked anxious. "Sometimes I'm so depressed, often I feel really scared, especially if I'm alone. Then I don't want to leave my room, it can be for days."

"We can prescribe medication for depression, it's up to you. I think it would help if you had something else to concentrate on, something with structure."

Fouad Assad was delighted to help her. He and the head of the university's Jewish-Arab Center were close friends. He discussed what Lana wanted to do in her research, edited the proposal and added his written support for what was a Palestinian oral history project on the Nakba.

Yehudit knew her way around university administration and gave Lana some final pointers. Then Lana was called to interview by the Center's head. How she got to the interview was a small miracle.

She didn't want to go. She might see Basil. The anxiety attack that followed made her perspire and she was trembling and mute.

"Rajib's cab's here," Khadija called out and after a few minutes went up to Lana's room. She took one look at her, drenched in sweat and pale and rushed to get a clean towel and some tea, telling Rajib to wait. As she helped Lana change she tried to calm her. "You'll do fine. Didn't you say that the grant has been agreed and thanks to Dr Assad the A-Sinara newspaper is sponsoring you too? It's wonderful. Come on, let's brush out your hair." But she had to hold Lana's arm as they went downstairs.

The radio in the cab reported on a demonstration and Knesset Member Basil Khoury was interviewed. He sounded breathless. Lana froze at the sound. "We're protesting the slum conditions of Arab residents. They can't get building permits for new homes but the government finds millions for new housing for Russian immigrants. Police tried to stop us. They know me, but they shot me."

The announcer said, "That was Basil Khoury, injured after police shot him. His party spokesman is demanding a police inquiry."

Rajib said, "Bastards!" but was confused by Lana's face in his rear-view, smiling as tears coursed down her cheeks.

***

The Haifa promenade seafood restaurant was lively for a week-day lunchtime. The two friends ate and chatted. Lana's first month of MA research was over.

Lana's gaze shifted to the sea. Then she said, "That number you gave me? It really helped." She watched for reassurance on Yehudit's face. "But there's these moments…"

Yehudit said gently, "I'm so pleased I could help. I guessed you were doing something, talking to someone. Anyway, I've got an idea, so let's go back to the flat."

Ten minutes later as they climbed the spiral stairs Yehudit burst out, "Would you be my flat mate?'

It was so sudden and Lana wasn't impetuous. But it would give her space to breath and it would be convenient both for her counseling sessions and university.

Yehudit said, "Nu? I know you love it here and I could use the company."

Lana nodded at the balcony. "Just give me a minute, out there."

Yehudit smiled. "I'll get the key."

She waited a few minutes and then joined Lana, bringing glasses of juice.

"You can get so lost in that ocean," Lana said smiling.

She looked out to sea. A cruise ship was bisecting the panorama. As it headed majestically towards the southern edge, she saw herself on board on the way to some other place.

Yehudit smiled back. “So?”

Lana described her depression and her constant guilt.

“Why do you feel guilty?”

“I…”

“Did you rape him?”

Lana shrank at the word, then gave a quick toss of her head as if avoiding a fly, “He wasn’t my type.” An unconscious smile came and went across her lips. Yehudit saw it.

“Joking’s good,” she said.

After a moment Lana reached a hand out to Yehudit. “You’re brilliant. Thank you.” She took a deep breath, “So, I’ve got to go home and collect my things and bring them back here. Just one condition, I buy a new bean bag?”

Yehudit laughed. “What’ll you tell your parents?” she asked, delighted.

“I’ll speak with my mother.”

Chapter 21
March 1998

Ibrahim said nothing when Khadija told him Lana was going to flat share with Yehudit. His daughter was leaving home. Not with a husband, so no grandchildren soon, his solution to Lana's girlish instability. And now Adwan would gloat once he heard about it and there was little Ibrahim could do.

But Lana hadn't left home in the true sense and came back every few weeks. Khadija saw a change in her. She no longer wore the black abaya and was more communicative.

Lana's cell rang. The voice with its offer-you-can't-refuse tone said, "Hello little sister from the hills, can I buy you an ice cream?"

"Are you here in Haifa? Can Yehudit come too?"

Half an hour later they were spooning ice cream, watching the world go by. "This mint and cinnamon 'Old Yaffa' is outrageous", Lana proclaimed.

"God yes," Yehudit agreed.

"It was better when I was a kid." Yunis said after a mouthful.

"Did they have ice cream then?" Lana asked cheekily.

"So," Yunis smiled, "you're doing research. I'd have loved to do that."

"Why didn't you?" Yehudit asked.

"Our teachers were Jews and they weren't interested in Arabs getting degrees."

"What?" was all Yehudit could ask, still licking at her spoon.

"No Arab teachers?" Lana couldn't believe it.

"Those who stayed after 1948 didn't want to teach in an Israeli system. So the shortage was made up by Jews from Arab countries, mostly Iraqis, Wawis the Ashkenazim call them. It was like a magic act each day, suddenly they were there and at the end of school they were gone. We never figured out how they did that."

"Hmmm…" Lana looked from Yunis to Yehudit.

Yehudit nodded. "We had a Wawi sergeant. God! He was tough."

"What did you do in the army? Play around with boy soldiers?"

"I wish. There wasn't anyone worth it, certainly no one as cute as you," she flirted and reached across to leave a fingertip of ice cream on his nose.

He played along. "Is that the best you can do?" And smeared an ice cream question mark on her cheek. "Come on you two," Lana urged, shyly.

"Why?" Yunis queried loudly, "This is a mixed city where Jews and Arabs live together in harmony."

Yehudit moved to sit next to him, smiling at his sarcasm. It unsettled Lana.

She scraped the bottom of her glass, desperate to stay serious. "With all Mrs al-Taj's efforts, there were times we didn't have enough school books to go round and what we had were out of date. "

"Shortage of books?' Yunis scoffed. "We spent days copying in pairs from one of the few textbooks, passed around the class. One was full of Zionist slogans. What I understand of Palestinian nationalism I owe to the Zionist poets we had to read at school. There were plenty of copies of their works."

Yehudit looked shocked.

Lana smiled again, "at least you had teachers."

"Yeah, but their Arabic pronunciation was different than ours, and I still speak Hebrew like a Wawi. Wallah!" He and Yehudit laughed together.

Lana held up her glass, looked through it, everything distorted. "What happened when you finished school?"

"That's a long story, not for now. Are either of you hungry, for real food? I am. Let's go eat," Yunis said getting up. They walked to the car, Yehudit's hand on Yunis' shoulder, Lana more irritated. Yehudit sat next to Yunis as he drove. Lana knew she was behaving like a jealous child. Yehudit was toying with Yunis and he didn't seem to mind.

They parked near Shlomo's Place in the Hadar neighborhood. Yunis and Yehudit looked like a couple out for the night, Lana trailed behind as the unwanted little sister. The person behind the bar, heavy eye shadow, deep voice, blew kisses at Yunis. "Hey hunky one! Who's this lovely?" and then looking quickly at Lana, said, "Is this your sister?"

"I'm Yehudit, a family friend, and neither of us girls are gay," Yehudit interrupted, "and you?"

"Speak for yourself, Ditti. I'm Shlomo," he answered fluttering his eyebrows.

"Love the hair Shlomileh, where'd you get it done?"

He gave Yehudit an up and down gaze, "Did it myself. Perhaps when yours grows out we can have a little hair party, bring along some friends, you know…"

Yehudit made a "Meow" noise.

"Don't go there, Shlomo." Yunis growled. Shlomo visibly shrank back. "Is the hummus fresh today?"

Shlomo gave him an 'as if' scowl. "And I serve only al Batuf pickles."

"Your Dad's?" Yehudit inquired, the siblings nodded. "Yum, can't wait to try them."

Shlomo asked, "Who wants what in their pita?"

"Be authentic Shlomo, like I taught you," Yunis insisted, "but no pita stuffed with hummus and felafel, that's the Jewish version. Serve it all separately. Don't forget the salad."

"OK, OK."

"It's our national dish, Yunis!" Yehudit taunted.

Yunis came back with, "As with so much else, you stole it from us, but you still don't know how to serve it."

Shlomo whispered loudly, "what's with you and Ditti? Trying a bit of straight?"

Yunis' sharp tut of the teeth was like a slap and Shlomo got on with the food.

"Don't worry Shlomileh, I'll give him back to you later," Yehudit promised.

And for the first time, Yunis looked at her seriously. Her unassuming behavior was familiar. He was comfortable with it, but he hadn't considered Lana's reaction, and he sensed his sister's anxiety from across the table. "Look Lana, the fact that our parents can't accept who and what I am isn't my problem. I knew from school that I was different."

Yehudit flirting with Yunis unnerved her. She was the only person other than Liz who knew about…

Yunis saw Lana's face. "Lana...?"

They ate quickly, and went back to the apartment in the trees.

Yunis watched Lana walk to the front door. "What's wrong?"

"She's fine, I'll look after her," Yehudit assured him adding, "do you want to come in, coffee or something? Wait, you live in Tel Aviv don't you and it's late. Why don't you stay over, there's a spare room?"

"No, but thanks, I have to get back."

There was just a glint of something in his look, so she tried, "Let's get together again, when you're next here," and was pleased when Yunis said, "yeah, I'd like that."

Lana was dispirited.

"What's this about?" Yehudit asked when they were up in the oval room. "Is it about Yunis? We're just having fun."

"That's not it." She tried to find the right words and what came out was, "He doesn't know what happened and he mustn't ever know. Do you understand?"

"Don't you trust me? I would never tell a soul."

Chapter 22
1999

In a rare café meal Dov did what he would never have done before, ignore his host and gawp at women. The young red-head a table away ignored him. The cafe, in a dilapidated Yafo street did good cheap cooking and was a hang out for prostitutes.

Sergeant Tawfik fumed at Dov. After all he was paying for Dov's meal.

He'd been walking home from the new police HQ. Work there was settling into its routine, unevenly because 'we always did it this way' didn't work anymore. The tower and its communications antenna "inspired by nearby church spires" as the publicity blurb had suggested, dwarfed the district. That communications were still disrupted, irritated every officer in the building. The ineptitude reminded Tawfik of the old police story:

Duty officer to Tel Aviv HQ: "There's a dead horse in Tchernikovsky Street."

HQ: "How do you spell that?"

Officer: "Not sure."

HQ: "Can't you move the horse to Yafo Street?"

Tawfik had watched a sun bleached red VW Beetle, its exhaust popping, turn into a one-way street the wrong way and park on no-parking lines. He prepared to cite the driver. He knew Dov, beneath his unkempt appearance, a look in his eyes that he'd seen in many vagrants, desperation born of hunger. Yet Dov signaled something that said he might be down but he wasn't totally out.

Tawfik took pity on him. Now Dov would have to acknowledge him, or so Tawfik had hoped. As the Shop's oldest desk sergeant, Tawfik had seen Dov every day, greeted him politely and rarely got a response. His impatience began its climb towards exasperation.

Dov watched as the red-head wiped her fork on a paper napkin, blood red nails, shades of Sara…

He suddenly left the table. Tawfik stared after him, his eyes firing large calibre bullets into Dov's back.

The creature staring at Dov in the toilet mirror made him laugh. The dispassionate investigator was gone, crashing on the rocky shores of his own destruction, drawn there by the siren of infatuation.

The creature said, "I was not always as you see me now."

Dov muttered, "Oh really? Then when is the old you coming back?"

Back upstairs, Tawfik had left in disgust and thc waiter handed Dov the bill.

He tried and failed to bluff his way out. The waiter blocked him and called out over his shoulder "Bentzi! We gotta runner!" Bentzi dwarfed his puny brother with his sloping shoulders and bulging muscles. Dov protested as Bentzi frogmarched him through the packed cafe back down to the toilet. The other diners ignored the scene.

Bentzi pinned him to the toilet wall and his younger brother searched Dov's pockets. He found almost enough change in one pocket and his out of date police ID in another.

"Oh you're that fuckin' cop'!" Ribald laughter. Derision was more painful than any physical injury. Then Bentzi did the inconceivable, he reached into Dov's tatty jeans for his prick and asked, "You're not one of the abominations as well, a homo, are you, you prick?" Dov could only shake his head at this punk's grab of his genitals.

***

Dov learned of his legal separation from Liora by chance. He went to a cash-point a week after the sex-video revelations and the screen said no withdrawal could be authorized and he should contact his bank. After a shouting match with the manager, an old family friend, he discovered that Liora had put a lien on his bank account and his savings, and that this was one of the final steps in the separation process. Later, his lawyer confirmed that he was legally separated. By then he was living in his car.

There were periods of black. At one point he woke on a beach to a dog sniffing at him and when he opened one glued eye he saw the beach snitch, who mumbled, "man you really fell a long way out of your tree." The Saluki cursorily marked Dov's leg and trotted away, its master trying as ever to keep up.

He had cashed in a life insurance policy to buy the VW and to have something to live on. For some reason he thought Shimon Ben Shimon's computer wizardry included acquiring motor vehicles. It didn't, but he helped Dov anyway. He had been unusually coherent when Dov called.

"The Plotnik department terminated my contract!" He added, "I've been diagnosed with diabetes. It's from stress. When I try to apply for new work, it's like my file's got a red question mark on it. I'm running out of money to pay for my medications."

Experiencing momentary guilt, Dov slipped a few notes in an envelope under Shimon's front door. Then he was angry with himself, worrying how he would replace the money.

Though it had been a tiny short lived operation, TPI had earned a disproportionate reputation, largely thanks to Dov. In his heyday the force benefited from it, in his fall it was severely damaged, so TPI was sliced off without a trace.

Commander Shalit was given early retirement. Reading the official letter, Shalit remembered how he'd hoped TPI would impede Dov's career. This was definitely not what he'd planned.

Aviel was next, transferred to a prison service unit, lost behind tall grey cement walls.

Dov blanked out his feelings for Liora. In his obfuscation, he believed there was nothing to say or do. The legal separation only strengthened his conviction. Blame, responsibility, neither seeped into his conscience. What had happened was someone else's fault, perhaps even someone named Dov Chizzik, but though he and that person shared the name, now they were definitely not one and the same. Super Cop was no more.

During his student days, Dov had come across the Socratic philosophy that the unexamined life is a life not worth living. There seemed little after life with Sara. Misery ensued. Not seeing Yaniv and Yael every day was unbearable. They haunted him when he tried to fall asleep in the back of the Beetle. Introspection was unhealthy, he concluded, so Socrates may have been wrong.

Dov contacted Gilad. His old friend had never said anything about the Sara catastrophe.

Gilad knew everyone. He owned a security systems installation company. He never hired friends or family. He made some calls and called Dov back.

To his surprise Gilad said, “You’re still in the force, suspended from duty indefinitely. Human Resources confirms your past excellent service record and your regular shooting range attendance. So call Yonni at this number. It’s just a matter of procedure, familiarization and special weapons. It’ll be work in air security, like a street cop but on a plane. You were a street cop once, weren’t you?” Dov thanked Gilad profusely and that surprised his old friend.

***

“You have three point thirty seconds for two rounds to target from concealed holster; eight seconds for four rounds in double tap time from low ready position; three seconds thirty total for one round each at two targets two shots per from low ready; eight seconds total for two rounds from slide lock reload fire for four shots from low ready.”

Dov was at a private shooting range in the final stage of the air marshal’s training course. It gave his life some of its former discipline.

He’d cleaned up, used spare clothes kept in a kit bag, and went to the course. A hollow man needed no emotion for action. The physical exercise put him in reasonable shape and weaned him off his irregular fattening diet. He learned the basics of aircraft security, ground control systems, processes at major airports, recognition skills, key codes in in-flight communication. At his qualifying shoot his grouping was almost perfect. His monosyllabic instructor reviewed his results and said, “OK.”

By the time he’d had enough of being an air marshal, he was halfway to being Dov again. His penultimate flight was what determined him to quit.

He’d been seconded to a charter company at the last minute, more for crowd control than terror alert. There were technical problems with a late afternoon outbound flight. Three hours and forty-two minutes after the scheduled take-off came the announcement, “ISRA-WINGS flight IW 542 to London Gatwick will be boarding in twenty minutes. We apologize for the delay.”

Eighty per cent of the passengers were orthodox Jewish families going home after the Feast of Tabernacles festival. The men were immersed in a world of study and prayer. They spoke Yiddish together. Dov sympathized with their wives, young childbearing machines, prematurely aged.

The plane now docking was from a Czech charter company and he groaned. The crew would be unfamiliar with these passengers and their idiosyncrasies, and he understood why he’d been called in.

A young, fresh-faced naïf sat next to him and asked, “Are you feeling all right?” He had a loud friendly voice, wore a black suit, and a frayed sweater.

Dov’s reply was a curt, “Yes.”

The fellow nodded and continued, “Pre-flight nerves? I find reading Psalms helps,” and offered him a miniature print copy. “Reciting them walking is also good.”

Dov managed, “No thanks.”

Boarding began.

The Czech cabin crew’s reaction to their orthodox passengers’ demands bordered on the anti-Semitic and a riot seemed imminent.

It was his first crowd-control experience. He reviewed in his mind the procedures for “individuals endangering the safety and security of passengers and crew.” Who of those categories were the likely suspects? Dov walked the aisle, deciding on the former. Maybe there’d be one smoking in one of the rest rooms. No, he checked. But, wait, there he was. Ideal. A black-coated individual wearing earphones, open mouthed at the latest Bond film, whilst his pregnant wife struggled with their three crying children.

Would "on suspicion of gross hypocrisy" qualify as a reason for apprehending him? Dov was past the point of caring. He walked down the aisle to the galley, alerted the chief steward, then went back and stood over the rabbi.

"Which community are you from?" Dov asked pleasantly, as he flashed his ID card and neatly slipped flex-cuffs around the man's wrists. The man's face went from incredulity to silence.

Dov tugged him to his feet and marched him to the front of the plane, waving his ID before him, and sat him in a spare seat next to the cockpit door.

Moments later the naïf appeared and offered to read Psalms to the man. Dov gestured at him with more flex-cuffs. He retreated. The rest of the flight was incident free.

After the return flight, Dov called the company. The money was good but he didn't see this as an alternative career. He needed a daily distraction from his demons. This wasn't it. What it was, he couldn't say.

Two months later, Dov had little money left. Most of it had gone on a one-room rental near the old bus station, and basic necessities. Having the air marshal salary had created a renewed desire for normality and that excluded living in his car. But normality had a cost. The elderly Beetle needed serious maintenance, eating away at his dwindling capital.

Why keep it?

Pride and seclusion.

Pride because living in infested rooms was bad enough but better than calling a car his home.

Seclusion, just because.

Chapter 23
December 1998–January 1999

It was a Saturday afternoon in December, one of those days that couldn't decide to be winter or some other season, not cold, not warm, but clear.

Lana was home for a visit and she and Khadija were walking back from the village and lunch with Auntie Ahlam and Uncle Ahmad. They were on the final climb to the house. They could see its profile. From here as from most other angles, it looked as if it had grown out of the hillside.

Khadija stood stock-still. On the nearest wall, spray-painted in tall red letters were "Khadija", an equals sign and the word "Traitor".

Ibrahim was on his way home from his watermelon fields in the valley. He was imagining a competition between his field hands and an Israeli robot watermelon harvester he'd heard about, as his pick-up reached the Rams Horns Hills road and the last stretch to his house. His team of pickers would win on an average row, but he guessed it was whole crop quantity the robot was devised for. It was still an investment he wasn't planning on, but he enjoyed imagining the looks on the faces of his fellow villagers if he did.

As he neared his home, he saw Khadija and Lana on ladders whitewashing the side of the house. He was impressed. They were painting furiously and he smiled, thinking this was a surprise for him.

But on the bend, Ibrahim saw the pink trace of what they were painting over through the whitewash. They hadn't got to "Khadija" yet.

Ibrahim parked, surveyed the two women, hands and arms spattered white, stopping when they heard his brakes, turning to see him. He put the column shift into reverse, backed up, and drove off.

He returned twenty minutes later and maneuvered a paint drum onto the ground, carefully poured some into a can, took a large brush, climbed the ladder and began painting thick white matt paint.

As he worked, he decided that this public humiliation was to be the last battle with Adwan.

The land their mother left them was the sputtering fuse. For Ibrahim it was a constant symbol of his blood tie to Adwan and how that occurred. To make something of his portion and sweeten the bitterness his mother had left, he'd planted olive trees and worked to produce the best crop he could. Your mother leaves you land; land is what defines you. Disposing of it is like cutting off a limb. The terms of their mother's gift were that if either wanted to sell their plot, both had to agree. Ibrahim the farmer would never sell his. But Adwan the businessman needed cash flow. No sale, no cash. Ibrahim had let natural grass grow as a dividing line with Adwan's plot.

One day, Adwan drove past the olive grove. He stopped to talk with one of Ibrahim's fieldworkers. He asked, "If I want to profit from my land, which olive variety do you recommend?" Perhaps passing traffic drowned the answer, but Adwan missed the "Not" before Muhasan, an unsuitable type of olive for lower Galilee soil conditions. Adwan planted Muhasan olive trees thinking he would be smarter than Ibrahim. The fuse burned on.

Adwan, Adwan, always there, watching, scheming. It was enough. Ibrahim put down his brush and stepped back. Khadija and Lana came and stood next to him. The paint completely covered their whitewash. "You haven't finished." Khadija said.

"That's your name isn't it? I'm leaving it there."

Of course, that wasn't the end of it.

Ibrahim called his brothers for an urgent meeting.

In bed that night Khadija pulled him to her and held him tightly.

"You know Lana is researching our history. I suggested she might talk with you. This might be a good time to tell her some of your story."

"I've told her a little, Adwan and his father, doing business with the Yahud."

"Did you ever tell her how she got her name, where she was born?"

Next day Ibrahim didn't go to work. Instead he woke Lana at sunrise, and told her they were going to spend time together.

They drove out along the Rams Horns Hills road. After quarter of an hour the terrain flattened out onto a plateau. The road surface was uneven, but Ibrahim picked up speed. Five minutes later Lana saw the beginning of a high barbed-wire fence on the left. It was several meters high. Another five minutes and the fence was still there. They shot past a gateway with a guard post, the Israeli flag on its pole.

After two more kilometers Ibrahim pulled off the road, got out and Lana followed. They clambered up a steep yellow crag. From the top, the countryside they'd driven through was still in the early morning light. In a break between clouds, two birds with long flat wings thermaled together. “Bowaz,” Lana said.

Ibrahim nodded. The honey buzzards soared lazily apart and then back. He watched them. “They can see the place where you were born. In there, where our village once was.” He pointed to the fenced off area they’d passed.

“I thought I came from the village where I grew up.”

“No, you were born up here,” so Ibrahim began. “In the Nakba, food was running out and I went into Haifa. I was young, about sixteen. The Arab Liberation Army had occupied our village, with ‘liberators’, mostly Iraqi irregulars. They were bandits in uniform,” he said bitterly.

“I somehow got into Haifa without being wounded.” He described his journey along streets of the war torn city, doorway to doorway, gunfire and explosions ripping the air. Where he would find food he didn’t know. “I told myself, Allah will provide, over and over.”

“Why didn’t we fight? It was our land.” Lana asked desperately.

“Nothing is straightforward in war. There’s a difference between shouting for the militias and forming one. We didn’t really have a fighting force. Local leaders wanted to avoid bloodshed. I wanted to fight. It never happened. Most thought they would survive and preserve the life and the place they’d always known by not fighting.”

She’d heard this before, but it didn’t satisfy her. “So we didn’t fight? People say that we fought and we lost the war in 1948, that the Jews caused the Nakba, when we didn’t fight at all!”

“How we lost doesn’t matter anymore. It was our land, our dignity, our history.”

That didn’t explain it, but she wanted to hear the rest of his story.

"I passed a Muslim cemetery with fresh bodies piled up by the gates," Ibrahim said, "no time for burial. I reached the main square where the Arab buses and wagons used to come. Empty. Shops were shuttered. No food, nothing."

He'd had to get off the street when gunfire intensified. "It was like winter hail storms, only it was hot shards of metal showering the street and me. There was a hole in a big placard on the street, for a cinema film, you must have seen them? One of those great big pictures on a wooden frame. The hole was big enough for me to dive through just as the next explosion happened. I would have been right in the middle of it."

Lana was captivated.

"Behind the picture was an old empty building. I went through a door and down into the cellar and waited for the gunfire to stop. The rats there were as frightened as me, scuttling about at each bang. Then the shooting stopped and when I got out I saw a funny name on the picture, Moose-Ka-Teers, and the name of an actress called Lana Turner," he said, "Toornair."

"I liked the name Lana, so I gave it to you when you were born. When I came back, about where we are now, I couldn't see the houses. The 'liberators' were nowhere in sight but neither was anyone else.

"Imagine you go away from our house, just for a day. Then you come back and," Ibrahim blew softly on his fingers, then opened them, "it's not there. Everything you knew has gone."

From above, one of the buzzards cried "peee-lu"- and the "lu" echoed.

His family had lived in their small village house for centuries. Ibrahim was born in it, so were his brothers and his father, grandfather and great grandfather. "It was a traditional

Palestinian house, solidly built, square with a domed top. The house had an upper floor divided into a living space and a food store. Under that we kept animals. It didn't have running water or electricity and there was no privacy. It was a hard life but it was what we'd always known. And when I came back from Haifa I found just broken stones scattered over the ground. All the houses had been blown up."

"My family went to stay with relatives in the village. But this is where we came from."

She asked, "Where was the house?"

Ibrahim pointed in the direction of the Israeli industrial buildings whose flat roofs were just visible. His voice was a monotone. "It disappeared slowly. First, it was blown up. Then bushes and weeds grew over the remains. A little time after you were born the land was finally taken and fenced off."

"How could I have been born in a house that no longer existed?" Lana asked the obvious question. She was enjoying every word Ibrahim spoke, more than she'd ever heard him speak.

"That's easy. They couldn't be everywhere all the time. Up here, there were no roads then, just tracks. We knew the way and when each of our children was due, we came here, your mother and I and the village midwife and you were all born amongst the stones of our family home. Each time no one disturbed us. They thought that we'd forget. If they'd really wanted to do the job properly they should have taken all the stones away."

The honey-buzzards were gone and the sun was climbing. Wild sage scented the warm dry air.

"The land behind the fence is what they stole from us in 1976."

After a moment Lana asked, "What about the graffiti?"

"I'll take care of him," her father said simply.

"What will you do?" She asked

"People gossip," Ibrahim said obscurely, as they drove back. "They always will. So I'll give them something to gossip about for years."

"What are you going to do?" she urged. He ignored her and kept the truck near to its top speed as they sped back along the fence. He continued when he was ready. "You remember I told you about Sheikh Adwan?"

"Yes, and Mummy told me about his father Sheikh Umar."

"They're collaborators," he spat out of the window. "They accuse your mother, my wife, Khadija, of being a traitor."

"Daddy!"

Ibrahim stared ahead.

"I'm not a child. What do you mean to do?"

"That is enough!"

"Tell me."

"Tell you?"

"Yes."

"Don't ask me any more questions."

"What are you going to do?"

"Whatever I do, I do," was all he said, reverting to his usual taciturnity.

Another month and Lana came home again. The deputy mayor was holding a party for his son Asif. No villager had ever been to the White House. Asif, a member of an American sponsored peace organization, had met the President there. He'd been to the USA three times, the White House visit the week before. The whole village was talking about him. He always wore a green t-shirt with the movement's white hand-in-hand logo.

They were aware of each other. Asif was four years younger with a smile that lit Lana's heart. He was athletic in build, taller than her, wore his hair very short and had eyes that were almost sea blue with little flecks of green. He was very attractive.

"What was the White House like? What did the President say to you?"

"I'll tell you if you tell me about Sky Blue Sky."

"How do you know about that?"

"It's not a secret. I'll show you." His study walls were covered with photos, posters, sketches, paintings. He sat at a keyboard and a page came up on his computer screen with a freeze frame of Lana at the Sky Blue Sky day followed by text.

"I've never seen that," she exclaimed, then saw the text was in Hebrew.

"It's from Amos, an Internet friend. It went all over the place. You really had an effect."

"Crazy things happen when you're naïve."

"But …"

"Asif, really, I'm embarrassed about it now."

"OK. So the White House." He described Washington and meeting the President. "He was doughy looking, with gleaming teeth, very tall, but he made me feel like the only Palestinian he'd ever met. He asked me about my family and my life; he knew everyone's name and where this village is located "

"No," she was overawed.

Asif smiled his blinding smile. "Even though I'm younger than you, we're at the same place. Sky Blue Sky was an inspiration. The anger gets passed on through the generations."

"But it's justified anger isn't it?"

"Of course. We shouldn't ever forget what caused it, but we must learn how to handle it differently."

"How do you do that?"

"Look, two more of my Israeli friends, Shmuel and Yoav, will be going to the army very soon. They are both in my heart and I'm in theirs. Will they still be if they're called to 'protect' and do their duty on another Youm al Ard? And will I?"

"Well will they? What you all say on neutral territory is one thing. Being back in this reality is something else."

"I told Yoav there's no such thing as an enemy. I want to change this to a better place where there's no need for that word."

Lana thought, how naïve he is, but what a decent human being, someone I could love and respect.

"I've a present for you," he said. "Something I saw surfing Internet sites. I'm printing it off. It's a poem by Azza El Wakeel, an Egyptian poetess."

She read the poem:

"The oriental woman has been promised
To be the puppet of a man
Her existence can only be achieved
By being someone's spouse…"

And when she got to:

"Girls in the orient are
Confiscated from fiction
Dreams exacted from their minds… "

She touched her finger to her lips and pressed it briefly to his.

Chapter 24
February 1999

The two-act farce Lana and her father played out that Saturday was peculiarly childish. For the prelude, Ibrahim had been popping in and out of his pickling shed, saying he was checking on his stock. She knew he didn't do that on a Saturday and kept an eye on him. She mentioned it to Khadija who just shrugged. Father and daughter were cats on the prowl, watching each other and pretending they weren't.

Ever since the red graffiti episode, Ibrahim had been going down into the village at odd hours. When Khadija asked him where he'd been, he'd say, "to see Rashid", or "I popped over to Ahmad's".

In the first act, Ibrahim said, "I'm meeting up with my brothers tonight". Something in the way he said it alerted Lana. She went up to her room and up on to the roof with her telescope.

In his shed Ibrahim broke down his shotgun and packed its parts and cartridges into a holdall. He sensed Lana's eyes on him, as he got into the truck and drove off down the hill.

Lana raced down to the shed. There were boxes of jars and sheets of al Batuf pickles' labels on shelves. She pulled open a drawer under the work surface. Inside was a box for shotgun shells. It was empty. The shotgun was not in its usual place under the worktop.

She called Yunis. “Something’s wrong,” she said and told him about the graffiti and the missing gun. “OK,” was all Yunis said and ended the call.

She trained her telescope onto the village, searching for Sheikh Adwan’s house. She found it, lit up as usual on the square, lights from side windows illuminating the alleyways on either side. She checked the square every few minutes. Khadija called up to her to say that supper would be ready soon. Lana kept looking at the house on the square. Just as Khadija announced that the food was on the table, Lana saw Ibrahim and his brothers emerge into the square and approach the house. Ibrahim was carrying his holdall. She managed to call Yunis again, her fingers trembling. His voice message came on.

The second act began when Lana grabbed a jacket and rushed past Khadija promising breathlessly, “I’ll be back soon,” and began running down the hill to the village.

At Sheikh Adwan’s house there was a knock at the door. Hatem went to answer it.

Adwan sat in a high back chair, watching television, drinking coffee, nibbling pastries from a box. His large frame filled his chair. Even relaxing he looked dapper.

He glanced up, a half eaten pastry in his hand. Three men had pushed his son back across the front door’s threshold into the room.

“Ya Adwan how are things?” Ibrahim inquired.

“Ya Ibrahim, I’ve been expecting you for a while,” the crumbs around his mouth undermining his attempt to look unruffled. He wiped them away and picked up a large silver automatic with a black handle from the table and placed it in his lap. "I'll bet you didn't come to gloat about your olives," he said wiping his mouth.

Ibrahim's mouth tightened, seeing Adwan's gun. He signaled to his brothers and Hatem was ordered to kneel before his father. Ibrahim rested his shotgun on Hatem's shoulder, the barrels pointing at Adwan's chest.

Ahmad and Rashid stood either side of Ibrahim, both displaying handguns.

Adwan gave a suave grin, annoying his visitors. He made it worse with, "For someone with a daughter as bright as yours, you're quite stupid."

Ibrahim tilted his gun up at Adwan's head.

"You always talked too much. Your collaboration days are over. What you painted on my house was the end. "

Adwan raised his hands. "Do you see any red paint on these?"

"Others did it for you. You've tried to undermine my family and me for years, implicating me in a murder, publicly dishonoring my wife. Now it stops." He pointed to Rashid who exited.

"You can't prove anything..."

"The guilty always do that, demand proof. I have it."

Rashid returned with a tall youngster called Zaed.

"Ya Zaed. Tell us what you know."

Zaed stared at the floor, intimidated by the weapons.

"Go on, it's OK," Rashid said.

Zaed avoided Adwan's stare and addressed Ibrahim. "I was in the mosque near my home, when Mohammad came and said Sheikh Adwan wanted to speak to me. I came out and the Sheikh's car was there."

He gulped audibly and continued. "I got in and the Sheikh gave me money and told me, 'Go and buy red spray paint and go to Mr Ibrahim's house and when no one is around, paint these words on the wall so the whole village can see them.' He wrote the words down. He didn't need to. I did it. I'm very sorry Mr Ibrahim."

Ibrahim held up a slip of paper. "Zaed gave me this. I'm sure it's your handwriting Adwan. Thank you Zaed."

Sounds of a commotion, and someone shouting, "You prick!" reached the room.

Adwan waved his hand dismissively, his automatic in his lap. "People will say and do anything for enough threats, or money, or both."

"You'd know about such things."

Rashid reappeared with Mohammad the driver, hands tied, blood trickling from a wound above his right eye.

"Thought he could curse me," Rashid grumbled.

Ibrahim said, "M'hammad, were you in the car when your boss told Zaed what to do?"

Mohammad grunted, "Yes. Sorry boss, but I was there."

Ibrahim waved typed sheets at Adwan. "These are statements by Zaed and M'hammad, confirming what happened. And Imam Al-Taj of the mosque signed them as a witness."

Mohammad was released and went away with Zaed.

"And that business with my cave?" Ibrahim said.

"I didn't tell him to do that," Adwan said.

"You didn't reprimand him either, did you?"

It wasn't clear what Ibrahim wanted. Adwan thought, if he's got all this, will he still kill me? We're of the same blood, the same mother.

Ibrahim as if he'd read Adwan's thoughts said, "Perhaps I'll shoot your son?" He moved the shotgun barrels to Hatem's neck.

Adwan showed fear, his automatic forgotten in his lap. He murmured, "Can we talk as brothers?"

"There's no deal here."

"Take my share of mother's gift."

Ahmad muttered, "Mother's gift? What's he talking about?"

"Forget it, he's trying to divert us."

Adwan pleaded, "Mother wanted…"

"What's he saying?" Rashid demanded.

"Mother?" Ahmad almost shouting, "what's our mother to do with this?"

Ibrahim ignored them and reminded Ahmad, "You know what to do."

"But if there's something that can stop…" His brother began.

"He's had years to do everything to avoid this. Do it now."

Ahmad shoved Hatem into a corner with his revolver firmly pressed against the back of the young man's head. He pulled back the hammer.

Ibrahim took Adwan's hand, put his silver automatic into it and brought it up, the barrel tip indenting the carefully arranged hair at Adwan's temple. Utter resignation came over Adwan's face.

Ibrahim said softly, "I'm going to count three. At the end, either you pull the trigger or Ahmad does."

He began to count.

The room became suddenly still, as the fullness of his last moments flooded Adwan's consciousness and he closed his eyes.

After a beat, six other figures appeared into the room.

A voice, cool, commanding and in Arabic said, "Put all your weapons on the floor."

Adwan's eyes opened, seeing but not comprehending. The three brothers obeyed. Adwan let his automatic go. A tall man surveyed the scene. He and the other five wore black face masks and the combat gear of the YAMAM-Police Special Unit. One of them unloaded each downed weapon and took them outside.

"You," the speaker prodded Ibrahim's shoulder, "take your brothers and leave now. Give me those," he pointed at the witness documents. Ibrahim shook his head, disgusted, resigned, and mechanically handed the statements over.

On the square in the night cool were black SUVs and more YAMAM men who maneuvered the brothers up against one of the vehicles, next to Zaed and Mohammad. The brothers were body searched.

Back in the house, the Israeli pointed a black-gloved finger at Adwan, "You're finished here. Your wife's in an SUV outside. Join her."

Adwan rose slowly and the finger followed him, as if it was moving him through space, all the way out of the door.

Hatem turned from his corner. The Israeli removed his mask and gloves; his torn eyes stayed on Hatem as he sat down in Adwan's empty chair. After a long pause he beckoned to a terrified Hatem.

The Israeli said, "I told you at the club…."

Hatem tried to speak.

"Don't ignore my orders again. Leave. Find somewhere else. We'll know where you are."

He focused on the documents, reading them while Hatem ran up to his room.

Lana was on the other side of the square, catching her breath, trying to decide what to do, when the SUVs, big black rectangles on wheels with no lights on, arrived. Her heart began pounding all over again at the shadows of six black-garbed figures, silently entering the house. Lana moved slowly round the other side of the square, not knowing that her father and uncles were being escorted out. She reached the alleyway and moved towards the window. It was open and she stood on tiptoe to look inside. A tall figure in black was sitting in profile reading some documents. He did not look up when Hatem struggled past with a heavy sports bag and out of the front door.

Her toes began to ache and she was about to relax them when the figure stood, folded the sheets, buttoned them into a patch pocket, hesitated over the chair as if he'd contemplated taking it with him, pulled his face mask back on, then left.

She'd seen those eyes before.

Moments later Lana heard a series of loud cracks. She inched back to the corner, terrified at what those sounds meant, to see men using nail-guns to fix sheets of metal across windows and the front door and knew they'd be coming to do the side windows next. She ran to the end of the alleyway and made her way out to the road leading home.

The officer spoke to Ibrahim.

"Adwan and his wife are being removed, for their own safety. You won't see them again. We'll keep the documents. You'll get your weapons back later."

The convoy of SUVs, one carrying Adwan and his wife, took off at high speed. Hatem watched from a dark corner of the square then walked away. The work on sealing up the Sheikh's home was finished. Posters were pinned up, declaring the building a public hazard, structurally unsafe, citizens warned not to enter. The posters up, the men departed in the remaining vehicle.

The three brothers walked to Ahmad's home nearby in dazed silence. In Ibrahim's head the thought "Adwan's gone," kept repeating itself. Ahlam greeted them but their faces told her not to fuss. They walked, their feet almost dragging, to the lounge.

"How the hell did they find out?" Rashid muttered, lowering himself into the soft cushions of a deep dark sofa.

"Someone snitched," Ahmad complained from his armchair.

Ibrahim stood in the centre of the room. "It wasn't any of us," he said. He was about to say, "I can't work it out," but a thought began to take shape.

For many moments no one spoke.

Then Rashid said, "In the time it took us to walk here, the village will have heard all about it. Adwan's as good as dead. His son's gone, their house is shut up. And it's all because of us. And who did the job? They'll think we got the Israelis to remove Adwan."

"I'm no collaborator!" Ibrahim yelled.

"Everyone knows that," Ahmad insisted.

Rashid reassured his elder brother. "Absolutely."

"Think about it. You haven't got anyone's blood on your hands this way," Ahmad pleaded with Ibrahim.

Ibrahim stomped towards the door. "Blood was the only way to end this," he said.

Out in the night, Ibrahim breathed the air. It tasted sweet. He decided to let the dogs of anxiety rest. But they wouldn't sleep and neither could he.

He exploded into Lana's bedroom, every day of the defeat of his generation, every minute of his frustration at the lack of justice for it all, all the years of the feud with Adwan, consuming the residue of his pride and him.

Lana, sitting up in her bed, saw Ibrahim's terrible anger. Her cell under her pillow had a text from Yunis, with one word, "Done." She read it and closed the cell down.

"You had something to do with what happened didn't you?" His question scorched her.

"What else could I do?" Lana implored. "You were going to kill Adwan ," she said.

"What other way was there?"

"I'm right. You were going to murder him. There's no justification…"

He yelled, "Justification? A big word you learned that at their university? You don't know what it means. What Adwan was doing for years, a collaborator, was wrong. That falsehood about your mother, that was the end," Ibrahim fumed, "and Adwan should have been cut down long ago, like a diseased tree. Sometimes that's the only way."

"It's choking you isn't it?" she said pulling her quilt around her for reassurance more than from the early morning chill.

He roared. "WHAT DO YOU KNOW? ABOUT ANYTHING?"

"You believe we can survive by keeping to the ways of the past. That's OK if we're like crops we plant or animals we herd. But it stops us from thinking, from questioning, if we think, from challenging what we know."

"Challenging? Challenging me you mean!" He turned to the door. "Khadija come here! Come and listen to this!"

Khadija came in. "Stop shouting Ibrahim," she said. "You can't stop Lana from questioning."

"She thinks I'm some kind of monster, without a brain! That's what she thinks."

Lana summoned up all her love for him. "No. I don't," she said.

She lay awake long after her parents left her room The Israeli officer knew Arabic well enough to read the documents he'd pocketed. Yes, it was his eyes, those she'd seen walking away from Yunis at the bus station.

Her next thought kept her awake, what her father might do if he ever knew what had happened with Basil.

Sitting on the edge of his bed, Ibrahim admitted that Lana might be right. Whatever she had done, it had saved him from spending the rest of his life in prison.

He praised her in his heart.

In the morning Lana went in search of Ibrahim. She'd smelled the unmistakable scent of freekah, smoked cracked green wheat. It came from Ibrahim's furnace in the barn next to the dairy, down in the valley. Khadija's freekah soup was the best.

She passed the olive press building and entered the barn. At the back Ibrahim was adding wood to the furnace. She kissed his cheek and he gave her one of his brief smiles and carried on working.

"In the village they're twittering like birds, about last night," he said.

"They would," she said after a while. Ibrahim nodded.

Chapter 25
September 1999

"It was in November 1948. They bombed our village," Hanna said quietly. "Our Mukhtar refused to surrender to them. He was loyal to our leader, the freedom fighter Qawuqji, so the whole village faced destruction. Many in the village supported the freedom fighters, but none of us wanted to lose our homes."

Lana sat in the two-room apartment above a women's clothing shop in a poor part of Nazareth on a noisy road. It was tiny and sparsely furnished, so small Lana was sure the refrigerator on the landing was Hanna's. Her son Faiz managed the shop.

She was an ageless diminutive woman with a linnet-like face and movements, perched on the edge of her chair, as if she would take flight any moment. Lana hoped the tape recorder microphone caught Hanna's soft voice. Faiz sat next to Hanna. The room was stuffy and in the shadows Lana thought they looked like sister and brother. Faiz watched his mother tensely. They were dressed smartly, he in a grey suit and wide tie, she in an embroidered abaya.

Hanna described her village. It was only ten kilometers north of Lana's, adding familiarity to what she heard.

An A-Sinara reporter had taught Lana to concentrate on interviewees' faces and say nothing as they answered.

"Those who fought the army of the Yahud set our fate and cost the lives of many innocent people," she raised her hands momentously. "We had a group of irregulars, who came to save us, from Morocco, Tunisia, Syria and Iraq. But the Yahud bombed us and then attacked. They brought the whole village, those still alive, into the square and divided us into groups, the irregulars, the local young men, the old men and the women and children." Hanna paused, her eyes darting around. "Then they tied the hands of a number of men and shot them all before our eyes and threw their bodies into a well."

"And after that you fled to Lebanon?"

"No. It didn't end with the murder of the men. They also murdered women."

"Why did they do that? The women didn't fight did they?"

"They did it after they'd raped them, behind the mosque where they couldn't be seen. They didn't want witnesses. One girl was fifteen." Her eyes roamed again.

Lana's mouth had dried and she couldn't speak.

Faiz snapped, "Don't you want to know what happened to the murderers?"

She tried to say yes, but could only rasp, "Some water please."

He got sullenly to his feet. "Where's the water bottle mother?"

"In the fridge," Hanna said, "behind the milk."

Her head followed Faiz as he went out. Then she fluttered and stood over Lana. Her hand covering the microphone, she whispered, "the fifteen year old girl? Was me. They thought they'd shot me dead but I wasn't. I survived. I became pregnant. Faiz is the result. He doesn't know."

She was back on the sofa when Faiz returned and poured Lana a glass of icy water.

"Did she tell you?" He demanded.

Lana struggled not to choke on the water, got what Faiz meant and managed, "Not yet."

"I will. None of them were ever punished."

She nodded, then asked Hanna. "How did you come to be here?"

She smiled for the first time. "My mother's uncle lived here and he looked after us."

The bus back from Nazareth took its time. Lana replayed the tape of Hanna's story. The woman's hand had partially muffled the microphone but in her mind she could hear Hanna's quick words. How she had kept her secret all these years, she hadn't asked.

It was after six and the flower stall by the bus stop near Yehudit's apartment was closing. She was looking forward to a shower and some food before transcribing the Hanna interview. In the cul-de-sac she spotted an Audi that looked like Yunis'. Surely he'd have called her.

She busied herself in the kitchen. A door handle clicked, and Lana turned to see Yunis emerge from Yehudit's bedroom, wearing only a T-shirt, going to the bathroom. Moments later an unkempt pink looking Yehudit followed in her bathrobe. She leaned against the counter, arms folded, saying nothing. Yunis came back and was about to speak when a cell phone rang in the bedroom. He took the call then came out, fully clothed, gave Yehudit a hug, Lana a kiss on the cheek, said, "Late for a thing in Tel Aviv."

Lana shook her head, trying to clear the confusing collage of images, Hanna and her son, Yunis and Yehudit.

Yehudit's voice cut through them. "How was your day?"

"It was… it … what's going on?"

"What do you mean?"

"You and Yunis?"

"What?"

"Making love?"

"Having sex."

"Ah…"

"Say it Lana."

Lana said nothing.

Yehudit hadn't moved or uncrossed her arms. "Did I fuck him? Did he fuck me? Is that what you want to know?

"No, no. I don't …Oh this sounds so wrong," apology in her voice.

"It's not wrong Lana. Yunis and I are just two human beings."

"Yes you are, but…

"But what Lana? It's no concern of yours."

"Not my concern? He's my brother and you're my best friend."

"So? I'm Jewish and he's an Arab, and that's wrong? And who's your best friend?"

"No that's not what I meant at all, and I know this sounds like me being paranoid…"

"Look Lana, this isn't some research interview you're doing. This is about Yunis and me. Maybe we fucked and maybe we didn't, but, don't look like that Lana, the word is sex, S.E.X. and I won't say this again but," she shouted the next words with gaps in between, "I did not tell your brother that you were raped by Basil Khoury, OK?"

Lana waved at her to quieten down, "Shhhhh, don't shout."

"Maybe you should shout it then, maybe it's time for you to stop hiding from it for God's sake Lana." Yehudit went to the fridge for a bottle of sparkling white wine. She poured some and offered it to Lana who shook her head.

"Just drink some. The earth won't open up under you."

Lana hesitated then sipped. The effect was new, a tingling in her mouth and throat and a warmth that crept through her.

"We should eat something," she said starting to make a salad.

"Sex always gives me the munchies." Lana shrugged.

Yehudit boiled eggs, opened a tin of tuna and added them to the salad Lana prepared and they ate, Lana thawing but still not ready to trust Yehudit or Yunis.

She didn't answer when Yehudit asked, "How did the interview go?"

Instead she asked, "So did you call him or…?"

"He called and said he wanted to see me and I said yes. What did you expect, that he'd call you and ask if it was OK?"

Lana felt empty. "No of course not," she sighed, and persisted, "what did you talk about?"

"All sorts of stuff. Remember when we went out together, he asked about my army service? So he wanted to know more."

Was that before or after, Lana quelled the urge to ask. Her brother's query sounded innocent enough but Yehudit had never discussed it with Lana before. She said she'd told him that after basic training she'd been assigned to a border control unit, "Nothing special."

"Like passport control?"

"Something like that."

"OK." The quiet between them stretched until Yehudit said, "Look, army is army and you do what you're told."

Lana had an uneasy premonition but said nothing.

"OK. I served at the Allenby Bridge terminus, checking passengers coming across the river Jordan. You know Jordan's population is mostly Palestinian. We have to search people entering from there. Who knows what they might be carrying? It's the same for women as for men." Yehudit focussed on Lana whose eyes didn't waver. "So, that was my job, to do those searches."

The most private of parts of any Palestinian female, invaded by Yehudit's militarily ordained finger.

"What did Yunis say to that?"

"Nothing. Then you were here."

Trust. The word had never meant so much to Lana as it did then. It was such a small word, yet massive in what it stood for. Perhaps in her naivety Lana had taken it for granted. She had set unattainable standards for friendship. But with the man who had been 'Uncle' and had coached her for her entry exams, trust had never been a conscious matter. She had assumed it, and accepted his offer of a lift, and then, and then…he had grabbed her and forced himself into her, raped her, R.A.P.E.D. She said it to herself.

How could she trust Yehudit? Lana loved her spontaneity, yet now it unnerved her. Why judge Yehudit so harshly? Why judge her at all? Because she still couldn't be certain she hadn't let slip to Yunis that his little sister had been raped. And if she had?

Trust and the fundamental purity she had endowed it with, would not let her alone and when she held it up to the light of her especial measure, it was flawed.

Lana went to her room and with a self-control she wanted absolutely to abandon, packed all her belongings, and walked to the spiral staircase, Yehudit standing there. She was deconstructed, head, shoulders, waist, thighs, feet, as each step took Lana down and round. The white incredulous face stayed with Lana.

Outside, she called the local cab company and asked to be met by the flower stall.

The stall's shutters were padlocked, the hosed down pavement glimmered in the streetlight, and the cab waited, its diesel engine idling noisily. The driver was an Arab, and said OK when she told him to take her to the village.

"Going home?" he asked.

Chapter 26
October 1999

Lana could never have predicted her leaflet's impact. It was Basil's nonchalant wave and cheerful grin that compelled her to write it.

She had been walking to the bus, past a faculty parking lot after a meeting with her supervisor at the Jewish-Arab Center. She was checking off new research ideas in her head as she walked.

Basil saw her.

Something in the way she moved attracted him like no other, as he'd been getting into his car.

In his mind, what had happened between them at the bourj was just a quickie. What heightened his wish for a longer night with her, like the memory of a spice in a good dish, was Khadija. He couldn't forget how she had looked at the graduation; he'd always desired her. He believed that you could often tell how a girl will turn out, by seeing her mother. And here was Lana every bit as desirable as Khadija. He'd wanted to be a Knesset Member and now he was. He liked getting what he wanted and he wanted Lana again.

He drove swiftly from the lot and up to Lana. She was lost in thought, when he hooted and when she looked up startled, he'd grinned and waved.

Lana ignored him, and had moved on quickly, fuming, cutting across a grassy space to avoid him, needing to remedy the sense of abysmal injustice that still surfaced within her. Why should she skulk around scared of seeing Basil? He was the rapist. And he's free to carry on as usual, making her jump, grinning and waving at her, as if it what he'd done to her was just a prank?

She had to be exceptionally cautious. That Muslim men traditionally enjoyed preference over women had lead her to ask Khadija, "Why don't men and women pray together in the mosque?"

Khadija told her what the Quran said of leadership, that women have similar rights to men but that men are a degree above them. "Muhammad, blessings upon him, was asked why men and women are separated in the mosque, and he replied, 'Because men shouldn't be tempted away from their devotions to Allah.'" She had added cynically, "our enticing behinds in front of men during prostration at prayer."

The words of Azza al-Wakeel the poetess came back to Lana about women being puppets of men.

She hand wrote her leaflet in Arabic and Hebrew and then photocopied it at the Jewish-Arab Center whilst making copies of her latest interview transcripts.

And so it came to pass.

"What was that on the corridor?" a cleaner might have asked. A night breeze blowing from an open window? The ghost of a past student, perhaps a little drunk or high, tiptoeing along in search of a forgotten bag, book, bottle?

No. It was the specter of Lana's innocence vanishing, replaced by cold calculation as she pinned her testament to notice boards across the campus.

By the third day, five other girls had produced copies of Lana's leaflet, anonymous as hers was, but in different colors.

“People gossip,” Ibrahim had told her.

Basil Khoury addressed a crowd from a stage outside the Independence Mosque on Haifa’s Feisal Square. It was a hot afternoon and he was pleased with the turn-out.

“There’s a conference planned at Camp David to discuss the future of our people. They’ll demand that in return for a Palestinian state whose borders they’ll dictate, we’ll accept their settlements, and Yahud control of al-Quds and no right of return for our refugees.” He paused dramatically, “And will the Palestinians of Israel be represented at Camp David?”

There were approving murmurs. He went on, “Hezbollah, our brothers in resistance, has rendered manifest losses to Israel, and caused Israel’s unconditional withdrawal from Lebanon after all these years, an ignominious defeat.”

More murmurs, different, not of approval. Something had distracted them. Undeterred, his eyes on the customary fixed distant point, Basil’s voice rose with conviction.

“We have to find a new model of leadership for our community, and we needn’t look further than north across the border.”

He sensed growing unease, then a voice he knew shouted, “That’s very dangerous talk.” Nabil climbed onto the stage and grabbed the microphone. “Hezbollah is a Shiite movement. We are Sunni Muslims.” The crowd applauded. “But, we’re all Muslims, moral people, and Islam forbids Zulm, cruelty and abuse. Such crimes cannot go unpunished and young women accuse you of that crime.” He waved a leaflet and passed more copies down to the crowd. “These are shocking accusations and you cannot speak for us until you answer them.” Anger erupted and fists thumped thunderously at the edge of the stage.

Basil grabbed a copy and his eyes bulged:

Basil Khoury Raped Me
He Relies On My Silence To Avoid Punishment
Not Any More

Then he bellowed, “Empty words!”

“Lah, Lah! The voices punched at him. “Get him!”

One screamed, “Hang him!”

It became a chant. “Hang him! Hang the dog! Hang him!”

Basil Khoury ran.

The university suspended him. The Knesset Speaker demanded an investigation. Basil slipped out of the country.

Arabic and Hebrew press and media screamed for his blood. One or two in the Arab world said it was all another Shin Bet plot.

Chapter 27
November 1999

Dov's battered cell phone showed battery close to empty when Gilad called him. Maybe the VW's cigarette lighter charger didn't work. Nothing else was right, why not that too?

Life viewed from the back seat of a VW Beetle in a multilevel parking garage in a scruffy Tel Aviv neighborhood, was grim and not just because the windows were filthy. Dov had been up there in the headlines, happily married, the media's darling Super Cop and now he was down, here. As if to reinforce his misery, the garage was near the new bus station.

He pulled at the blanket, not sure if he wanted the sweaty comfort of its darkness, for his phantoms resided there. As soon as he closed his eyes at night, Yaniv and Yael were playing in the Shabbat sun, calling Daddy; Liora was kissing him on a beach; the headless bodies in the microbus in Lebanon turned towards him.

He sat up, blind to the Beetle's interior, accumulated rubbish of a homeless existence, his eyes sore from endless wakeful nights. He yearned for an omelette and chips or felafel in pita and salad. He would have to find somewhere he hadn't begged from before; most local café and felafel stand owners had long run out of charity for him.

The parking attendant would pretend not to see Dov walking to his early morning shower on the beach. In warm weather he'd sometimes find a few drops of shower gel in a discarded bottle.

As a police investigator Dov knew what occurred in the cavities of parking garages. His remaining guile produced a deal with the attendant; he would not report what he suspected, if he could remain undisturbed on his 'deep cover' assignment.

"Dov, it's me," Gilad repeated. "Professor Steinman wants to meet you in Jerusalem at ten tomorrow morning."

Gilad lent him laundered clothes, gave him enough money for bus fares and ran him to the bus station. "At least going by bus will save the hassle of parking the Beetle in Jerusalem," he said, "It's murder." Gilad nodded, wished him good luck and drove away.

Dov sat on one of three plastic seats on a busy corridor in the Prime Minister's Office building. The atmosphere reminded him of hospital visits with Liora during her pregnancies, controlled tension, resolve in the face of impending crises in the fixed looks of staffers.

The building was one of three identical structures of the government complex, brick sentinels protecting the Knesset, Israel's parliament, on the hill behind and above them. Waiting, Dov brooded over Gershon Steinman's climb from Justice to the PMO. That gave way to the apartment with the little holes in the ceiling, proof that Sara had been part of a plan and that whoever was behind it was still out there. Why didn't I ever try to find out who set the honey trap that destroyed me, he asked himself. Some Super Cop!

Ruhama Steinman's voice said, "Dov, how are you? It's been too long." She stood over him, her arms held out for a hug.

"What are you doing here?" he asked, standing.

She took him into an office and they settled into armchairs by the window. Regaling the table were flowers in a glass bowl. Had they come from the Steinman's West Bank garden?

Ruhama wore a charcoal power suit. She looked gaunt where she'd been almost plump when he'd seen her last, after Rabin. Was her blonde highlighted coiffure her own hair or a sheitel, the orthodox woman's wig? The wall clock showed ten fifteen, and he said, "Gershon's usually more punctual."

"Gershon?" Ruhama said, laughing, "there are two Professor Steinmans now. Didn't they tell you?"

"No. Gilad called out of the blue asking me to meet Professor Steinman. I presumed…"

"I gave my inaugural a year ago, and then they asked me if I wanted to work here, and of course I couldn't refuse." Not if you're as ambitious as Gershon, he thought, and then could not recall a year ago.

"No, of course not," he said, "So from Restorative Justice to the Prime Minister's Office. Impressive."

"Thank you," Ruhama smiled, "someone appreciated the work I did. The Prime Minister scrapped the Minority Affairs Ministry, but he can't ignore the issues and that's what I advise on."

If the Prime Minister had cared that much about the issues, he'd have kept the Ministry, Dov thought.

"Basil Khoury," she said, "has left the country."

"Oh? On another Israel haters' trip?'

"No, this is permanent. He's in Lebanon, escaping a major scandal involving accusations of raping a number of female Arab students. The Arab sector's outraged and we have to show that we'll investigate the crime or crimes the way we would for any citizen. Frankly we need evidence we can publish to keep Khoury away indefinitely. This has to be informal, swift and quiet."

"Maybe you need a rape counselor too," said Dov.

"Well, we have one who's a specialist in honor killings ready to brief you, though you know about that, don't you, from The Woman And The Baby In The Box? "

She hadn't made this a formal request yet, and he sensed there wouldn't be one. He said, "not even our salacious tabloids could have invented this story."

Ruhama nodded, "As long as he's still a Knesset Member, he draws a state pension. That's embarrassing. We can shut the door on him for good if we can say that he did what is alleged."

"Trial by government and public opinion?"

Ruhama's lips narrowed and she produced a copy of Lana's leaflet.

"Anyone could have made this," Dov said.

"Five 'anyones'?" Ruhama insisted. "They used different color paper. All female, late teens. Graphology analysis confirmed it."

"Mmm. But the writers can't be identified can they? Not if time is short."

"You were one of our best investigators."

"I was," he agreed. "Not now. There must be dozens of others you can ask."

"I don't know any others. I mean I can't trust anyone else with this. It's kind of a favor Dov."

And here come the politics, he thought.

She told him nothing new. The Prime Minister had ignored the Arab sector's support in the general election. Now with this Khoury affair, he wanted to be seen acting even-handedly. Yes there'd be headlines and, "of course there'll have to be a police investigation, though with you having done the spade work..." Ruhama said with a quick conspiratorial wink; it suited her somehow he thought. But timing was everything. Behind the media glare someone had to find a version the Prime Minister could use.

Dov couldn't get why the Arab minority deserved any of this. They were just Arabs. The real motive he suspected, for Ruhama using him, was deniability. This was a political inquiry. Khoury was a Knesset Member. Ruhama had been assiduously elliptical, about the evidence she wanted and the kind of investigation to produce it. His results would be buried in the Prime Minister's announcement, "Our careful study of the facts …" or "After an in-depth investigation by our top officials..."

He hadn't lost his acuity. First, they didn't want Khoury back because he'd have to be arrested, charged and tried and that risked Khoury becoming a martyr, or equally as bad, that the whole thing would be bungled, by the 'human elephant' as Dov called human ineptitude. Second, he asked, "Who do I work to? How much will I get for it?"

Ruhama's grin exuded manufactured sincerity. "Me, and how much does it cost for a week's work?"

They haggled and agreed on a month's work at a figure he invented. She did that act Israelis in authority relish, picked up her phone theatrically and got straight through to the President of Haifa University, an old friend, who understood the need for confidentiality, and didn't need reminding that as long as questions about Khoury remained unanswered, so did questions about the University's reputation.

Politics, Dov thought, dirty games. But not sleeping in the back of the Beetle for a few nights was too tempting. Walking to the bus stop, he gave Ruhama top marks for professionalism. She hadn't referred to Liora once.

After another of Ruhama's power calls, this one organizing a cash advance, Dov paid the garage attendant to have the Beetle serviced, valeted and stored until he came back. He went to the Hamashbir department store and bought two complete new changes of clothes and a smart cabin case. On the way to the hotel overlooking Bar Pigyon, where he'd booked a room, he stopped off at a music shop. He asked for something recent and got three CDs. He ate a proper meal at Mike's Place and went to sleep in a real bed.

Early next morning before breakfast, Dov decided to go down to the swimming pool. After ten lengths he went to shower. The Old Memories Club members, elderly lane swimmers, were also there chatting away.

"Baruch, was it the dentist from Budapest who used to shtup his female patients under anesthetic? What do they call it today?"

"Rape."

"No, a shtup's a fuck, it's not rape. Isn't there a drug they use today, 'date drug' something; it was on the TV."

"Dates? They make drugs from dates now?"

"No, no, now you're confusing me."

"They'd have a sweet after taste."

"What?"

"Drugs from dates."

"Oy shut up from dates. I've got it, date-rape drug."

"It's still rape."

"What is?"

"What that dentist got up to."

"The date-rape drug they call it, it's got a name, Ro something."

"A shtup under the influence is what it is."

"What's it called?"

"I told you, rape."

"No, the drug."

"He was a rapist, not a dentist."

"Who?"

"Oy Baruch!"

As Dov breakfasted, the old men's joke reminded him of the counselor Ruhama had offered. He hadn't taken that up. The Woman And The Baby In The Box had indeed given him enough insights.

He paid the bill, collected a rental car, and listened to one of the CDs, enjoying his temporary lightness of being, not quite in tune with the latest music.

He tired of the music and switched to radio news. The Prime Minister, the man he was unofficially working for, had met Yasser Arafat in Tel Aviv. Dov knew he should be wowed, but the two leaders had already met at the Israel leader's home, so meeting in Tel Aviv wasn't big news. Peace was unlikely what with the continued violence of the last months. And it was the fifth anniversary of Rabin. Depressed? Ready to be. Wallow away then. No, he thought, the sun's shining and I have purpose. Leave the past alone for a while.

He tried. And thought only of future possibilities, which took him half way to Haifa on the coastal road, passing Netanya's urban sprawl burrowing out of the dunes. They gave way to wild scrub on both sides of the road and the tip of an incisor of guilt produced again the pinched features of the disappeared sex-trade girl Nana Mint Tea. Maybe they'd find her body out here one day. Maybe not. His negligence was the seminal act that had begun his decline. No! It was Sara. No it wasn't. It was you. He played the CD again loudly to drown the bleating voices of his conscience.

He aimed for the Eshkol Tower, the symbolic heart of the university, and found the head of campus security, a gruff non-descript man named Benny Gryn. He gave Dov files on Basil Khoury and showed him some CCTV footage. Dov watched and read the files. Then Gryn took him to the cafeteria. Yehudit Aaronson, a young woman with spiky blonde hair was having lunch with some other students, chatting. Gryn introduced Dov. The table quietened.

"I'm sorry to interrupt your meal," he said, ignoring the other individuals. "Benny here suggested you might be able to help me."

Her eyes assessed him. "I'm just about to eat lunch," she said.

"I'll be in the first floor conference room," Dov replied.

She arrived five minutes later. Dov said, "I'm gathering information on Basil Khoury, about the allegations against him?"

"I'm not one of his students."

"I know, but you might be able to help with female Palestinian students he might have been friendly with." The thought train was simple enough and Dov watched as Yehudit caught it.

"You're asking me because my file shows what I did in the army and you assume I know about these rumors."

"Yes, and I'm short of time."

"I can't help you."

"Can't or won't?"

"I really don't know anything about this." She was nervous.

"OK. I understand."

"You could try his departmental colleagues."

He said, "I've seen CCTV footage of you and a Palestinian friend, together with Khoury," and waited. The camera angle hadn't shown any detail of the other girl apart from the back of her head and at one point a quick profile.

"That was just a chance thing," she said. "I know her from classes we shared."

"What's her name?"

"Is that really necessary?"

"Yes."

"It's Lana al Batuf."

"Thanks. What can you tell me about her?"

"I've given you her name, that's enough." Her foot tapped insistently on the floor.

"Look, Khoury's a Knesset Member and a senior academic here, and he's been accused of rape. We have to investigate it. The CCTV material tells me he knew your friend. How did she know him?"

She spoke softly and quickly. "They come from the same village. That's it, no more ." She got up, anxious to warn Lana, erstwhile friend or not, paranoid about the safest way to do it.

"Thank you."

A little nag low down in his memory started up, something about that name.

Benny Gryn came in as Dov was reviewing his interview notes.

"If this Lana girl is still on campus, we'll find her."

"Do it carefully Gryn, I don't want anyone upset."

Twenty minutes passed and a young woman entered the conference room and sat opposite him. Gryn came back and gave Dov a file. It was Lana al Batuf's. He scanned it quickly, pausing only at the still frame from a sit-in she'd been involved in.

Lana al Batuf sat at the table, a graceful young woman, calm cinnamon eyes, full lips, and caramel skin that suggested velvet to the touch.

Was that a lightning flash? Dov found himself searching through the window at the cloudless sky for another.

Focus, Dov told himself

"Thank you for agreeing to answer some questions, Lana."

Lana inclined her head briefly, composure maintained, no emotion legible.

"What are you studying?"

"It's an MA on Nakba narratives, investigating what happened to my people in 1948."

"That's interesting. That makes us both investigators." He smiled. She didn't. "To save time let me ask you a simple question. How long have you known Professor Basil Khoury?"

He wanted to applaud her, just a quick blink at Khoury.

"His family and mine have known each other a long time."

"That wasn't what I asked you."

There was a slight flaring of nostrils, but her eyes didn't waver. "He helped prepare me for my entrance exams."

"Where did that take place?"

"In my parents home."

"Did you like him?"

He saw something new flicker in those almond shaped eyes. Another investigator used to criminals with limited repertoires of reactions would have missed it. Lana was too poised, but he sensed rather than saw shades of guilt and shame in her eyes, and yes, he was sure, pain too. Whoever or whatever was the cause, sympathy and then anger ignited in Dov, and not only that. Inexplicably, he wanted to discover what had happened to this beautiful young woman so he could erase any shred of her unhappiness.

Her eyes said, 'I can't talk about this.'

She said, "I've nothing to add."

Dov's heart missed a beat. For scary seconds he couldn't breath then forced a cough and said, "Sorry, must be the air conditioning." His thread was forgotten and there was a growing hush between them. What was my next question? What was my last? What did she say? What did it matter?

No one had ever looked at Lana like this before. And just as Dov had glimpsed something in her, so, shockingly, Lana saw an unexpected comprehension in him, that he did not need to be told anything of what had happened to her, he already knew, and then she tried to still her heart, because that could not possibly be.

He saw her lips narrow and her chin rise as she said, accusingly, "I've seen you before, years ago. You interrogated my father about his cave. He was innocent."

He sat back, his mind racing. The girl with the curly hair in the car window? Dov filled the silence with, "That was you?" and knew instantly that his smile at the memory was wrong for this moment. "I remember now, Ibrahim al Batuf. You ran to hug him..."

Lana looked away for the first time, embarrassment on the heels of her shock, that this man could recall such an intimate moment. She stood up. "Do you have anything more to ask me?"

"Oh no, no," Dov said, his smile evaporating, conscious that he wasn't thinking coherently, unable to produce more questions, so she could leave, which he really didn't want, and then Lana was no longer in the room.

Dov saw two other female students, Walaa and Hadeel before calling it a day. Both had been in Khoury's classes but their files revealed nothing relevant. Walaa the younger, taller and slimmer, was deep voiced, and Hadeel large, plain and garrulous. Both wore scarf head coverings. Walaa wore jeans with a short caftan while Hadeel wore a dark full-length abaya. Dov didn't like being ignorant, despite his prejudices. He'd asked Ruhama for a complete run down of all the clothing Muslim women in their region wore.

Dov guessed that these two had compared and tuned their stories. They both said, "He was just a teacher," to the first question about Basil Khoury. The interview with Walaa would follow a graph with no big spikes, a few highs but mostly lows. But one early spike intrigued him. "Dr Khoury used rhetoric a lot," she said.

He laughed. "He liked making speeches?"

"No. You don't understand," she said. "He lectured in Hebrew, but used the Arabic rhetorical style, we call it ta'rid, it's an old way of making a formal presentation. It's supposed to be very impressive, but instead his lectures were really boring. He didn't care what we thought."

"There was little interaction in his classes?"

Walaa held back, regretting she'd said anything. "Ta'rid doesn't work in Hebrew."

"Despite that, he must have had a class favorite? Teachers do."

She murmured, "No", her eyes avoiding his.

"Look, this isn't official. These interviews are for background, not evidence. I'm trying to find out anything to confirm the allegations against Professor Khoury."

She said no more.

Walaa with a little make-up could have been quite pretty, Dov thought, and that deep voice, well, who knew what turned men on?

He put her on his possible list.

Hadeel was irritable. When he asked about girl students and teacher's pets, she replied, "I am going to be married in six months time," as if that precluded any suggestions of impropriety and any further questions. In his mind her interview graph stayed flat.

"Do you know any of the girls Professor Khoury may have assaulted?"

"No. I'm not a collaborator."

At the Haifa hotel that night luxuriating in bed, he reviewed what he'd gleaned. He was no investigator in this case, more a blend of soothsayer and jester for Ruhama and the her boss, telling them what they wanted to hear, juggling with the truth. So far he 'liked' Lana as one of Khoury's victims, and thought Walaa was a likely one too. This was not a criminal investigation; it was political and much depended on perception.

He saw Lana's eyes and wanted to know more about her and fell asleep in the process. When he woke up next morning she was his first thought.

That day he interviewed another five Arab female students. Of them one was a possible possible, and the rest were like Hadeel, unable to hide their discomfort, honest enough not to be rape victim suspects.

His emotions seesawed when he thought of Lana, between childlike elation, and a pit in his stomach at how she thought he'd treated her father.

At lunch at the cafeteria, he saw two of the girls from that morning's sessions talking with Hadeel, who looked over at him a couple of times. Benny Gryn appeared. "The smartass head of the Arab student union wants to meet."

Dov said he'd meet him at the end of the afternoon. Gryn gave Dov Nabil's file. He also handed him a translation of

Basil's speech and details of Nabil's intervention at Feisal Square.

Nabil was a smooth operator, Dov decided, and very sharp. So were all the girl students he'd interviewed, he was surprised at how they were articulate and intelligent, but hey we're not prejudiced are we? The large white knitted skullcap and bookish demeanor masked a skillful activist; the file showed he coordinated a network across other universities.

"This is a confidential inquiry?" Nabil asked sitting down and added, derisively, "Not quite the usual territory for the ex-Super Cop."

"It's confidential, yes," Dov answered, neither rising to the taunt nor ruffled by not asking the first question.

"We want to know what you plan to do about Khoury."

"What can you give me to support the allegations?"

"No hard evidence, that's for sure."

Dov said, "I know what you did at Khoury's last public appearance. Where did you get the leaflets?

"They were on every campus notice-board. We made copies and took them to the square. Khoury's ego got too big and he became a liability to our movement. Rape is a crime. Islam absolutely forbids it, and five accusations?"

"'Liability'. You said that before talking about his crime. Interesting priorities."

Nabil shrugged.

"If I tell you what's planned for Khoury, what do I get?" It's all perception, Dov reminded himself.

"What do you want?"

In the end Nabil gave Dov four names rumored to have been Khoury's victims. Lana's wasn't one of them. Walaa was one of the other victims. Dov said he needed one corroboration for each victim, for credibility.

"No one will tell you," Nabil.

"OK," he said, "how about a friend of a victim."

"They won't speak to you. I'll see what I can do."

Dov gave him his cell number. As Nabil turned to leave, Dov asked, "do you know a Lana al Batuf?"

Nabil paused mid-stride, half turned, "she came and went as an activist," he said quickly.

Hadeel was as irritated as before and Dov asked why she'd agreed to meet him again. She sat with her hands on the table's edge, as if holding on for safety.

"Nabil said I should."

"Why did that persuade you?"

"He's the General Secretary…"

"I know who he is, but still…"

"He's very influential."

"I see. So what can you tell me?"

She shook her head emphatically from side to side.

His questions masked his impatience. "You said you were getting married soon?"

"Yes in six months."

"Where's your fiancé from? What's his name?"

"Why do you need to know?"

"You have to be smart to study here, and you are. So it's either help me with my investigation or we'll find out who your fiancé is, we can do that, and we'll interrogate him, and who knows what'll happen, you might be asked to leave the campus..."

She hesitated, then said, "He offers them lifts in his big car and they go somewhere quiet, and that's where he does it."

"Does it?"

She hissed, "He forces himself on them!"

"That's what happened to Walaa?"

Her fingers left sweat marks on the table when she moved her hands to her face. She nodded once.

"How many times?"

Her head shook back and forth. "Only once, then he tried again, with the lift I mean, but she refused."

"When?"

"The first time was five months ago, and the second a couple of weeks ago."

Dov let her calm down. "Only one more question. Did she get pregnant?"

Her head shook again, vigorously.

"How do you know?"

"He told her he used…he said he was…protected."

He said, "I see. Thank you for helping," and hoped it sounded genuine. She was a very astute player he thought, she gave me nothing about her fiancé but came up with crucial details instead, neutralizing my threats.

He called Nabil and agreed to meet the following morning.

He ate an evening meal and then strolled along the hilltop promenade. Haifa port, the Bahai temple and the bay were all lit up below. Loneliness, his companion for too long, returned. He loved the view and thought how much more beautiful it would be if he had someone to share it with.

Next morning he outlined to Nabil what was intended for Basil Khoury. He was carefully nuanced, surprising himself at how easily that came to him. He stressed he could guarantee nothing and could never be attributed. Nabil understood implicitly.

Then Dov said, "I might need to talk with Lana al Batuf again. Do you know where I can find her?" and Nabil told him to try the T-house.

Dov sat at a corner table near the entrance, watching customers, undecided about what to eat or drink. He looked around to order and saw Lana crossing the room. She saw him. He smiled. She walked on. His heart raced.

A month later, the Prime Minister announced that following a careful and intensive investigation, Basil Khoury would face charges of rape of several students on his return to Israel. He added that a special Knesset bill was planned, rescinding all Khoury's rights and privileges as a Knesset Member and he expected it to be passed with an overwhelming majority.

Chapter 28
2000

Lana hadn't avoided Yehudit but neither had she signaled a desire to reconnect. Then Yehudit had called her and they agreed to meet. She didn't like feeling guilty about Yunis and she was seriously discomfited by the session with that investigator, re-inforced by his appearance at the T-house.

"I'll keep this brief," Yehudit said. "First off I'm glad Khoury's gone. I tried to reach you after I saw that investigator."

"Yes." Lana said. She'd seen the calls on her cell phone but didn't pick up.

Yehudit said, "Second, you're my best friend, I love you."

Lana felt defensive. "Have you seen my brother again?"

"That's got nothing to do with you."

Lana struggled with that. "Maybe I was too tough on you," was what came out.

"Maybe you're too tough on yourself?" Yehudit said. "You need to give us both a chance."

"Yes, you're right…" it was Lana's turn to feel uncomfortable.

"Anyway," Yehudit said, "Uncle Rudi asked after you and when I told him what you were researching he came up with this."

Yehudit gave her a plastic folder and they parted. But Lana followed her. “It’s no good. You were…are my first best friend. Friendship isn’t automatic is it? It takes work, building up trust. I didn’t stop loving you as my friend.”

Yehudit asked tentatively, “Coffee at the flat?”

“With some of your favorite cake?” Lana asked playfully.

A week later, after research at the A-Sinara newspaper archive, Lana knocked on the thick wooden door of a house on a hill between her village and Sakhnin, the nearest town. A short wizened man opened the door and she peeked in. She saw an old large one-room structure under a domed roof. It reminded her of Ibrahim’s description of his family home.

“Can I come in?” she asked.

The man stared at her then apologized.

Inside, dominating one wall was a photograph of a small uniformed man with a mustache, standing to attention next to a horse that dwarfed him.

The uniform, black fez, white gauntlets, gleaming boots with shiny spurs, would have been comical had the man wearing it not looked so proud. A plaque on the frame read, “To Sergeant Badr Tawfik from his grateful colleagues of the Palestine Police.”

“That was me in 1935,” he said. “We’ve been policemen for four generations, my grandfather and father served under the Ottomans and then the British. I served with the British and the Jews, and my son follows our tradition, he’s also a sergeant, serves in Tel Aviv.”

Next to the portrait hung a pistol in a holster. “Yes that’s mine. I used it only twice, once in the line of duty and once in self-defense. The first time I shot a Jewish terrorist. The British gave me a medal. The second time, my attackers were Palestinians.”

“How terrible,” Lana said, trying to calculate his age and getting to around eighty. “Was that when nationalists attacked Arab policemen?”

His glance told her he was impressed at her knowledge.

“Yes it was,” he said. “Al-Qassam, the Imam of the Independence Mosque, lead the Black Hand terrorist band. The British killed him, with help from local Arab villagers. He became a legend, a symbol of resistance to our people.”

“Yes he was certainly that and very controversial. I’m learning that there’s new thinking about him.”

Badr smiled at her. “Time allows for that. So, in 1936 his supporters issued a declaration listing their enemies.” He was about to get up, “I’ve kept a copy somewhere…”

Lana interrupted, “don’t worry, I think I’ve got a copy,” and produced one of the documents Yehudit had given her.

“Yes, that’s it,” he said. “It included informers, land speculators, civil servants, the British and of course the Jews. Policemen were civil servants.”

“And that meant shooting them?”

“First, policemen were ostracized and attacks against them increased. The nationalists published another list, naming officers they saw as traitors to be killed. One, who had helped catch al-Qassam, a fellow Muslim, was shot dead.

“When I wanted a burial service for the dead officer, a mob attacked me. That’s when I used my pistol. A year later they created the ‘purge unit’ to assassinate all traitors. They killed him.” His eyes burned.

Lana had no idea who ‘he’ was.

“He was a gifted writer. He didn’t care what people thought of his words. Producing them was all that mattered to him.” He went to a wooden chest under the portrait and came back with a ring binder.

"I'm sure you don't have these. They're his originals."

She read the first handwritten lines:

"How can you youth be so ignorant? How is it that you know so many suras from the Holy Quran but have no words to say against our leaders and the sins they commit in our name. Ask them where's the money they collected from you for our cause. Ask them why the Jews progress and we are being taken backwards. And because you don't speak out and stop them, you aid them in their crimes against our people. We will carry the burden of this forever if we do not speak and act now."

"I've seen this in an old newspaper, but I didn't understand the context," Lana said.

"It was in a book, "The True Path" by Badr al Ansar, his pen name. He took the Badr from me. He was one of many who criticized the nationalists. The Jews paid some of them. Others just wrote anyway. In those days writers were highly respected."

"What did you think of what he wrote?"

"He was my best friend. I was in a difficult position. But I chose it. Without law and order there's nothing but chaos and we'd had enough of that. Could I stand up and say, 'Badr is right'? It would have meant resigning."

"You said Badr was killed?"

"He was murdered because he spoke out against the leadership."

"How did it happen?"

"It took place on the main street of the village."

"Which village?"

"Your village of course."

Lana was too surprised to respond.

"It was very public. He was sitting outside a coffee house, with a couple of friends. A boy who sold cigarettes from a tray around his neck offered him a pack. Instead of giving him the cigarettes, the boy produced a pistol and shot him."

"Was the boy caught?"

"I chased him…"

"You were there?"

"I was one of the two friends sitting with him. We never found the boy."

"How did the village react?

"They admired him. He was a writer and knew the risks he took. He didn't care."

"So he was from my village?" Lana mused.

"You really don't know about him? You're so much like him."

"I…?"

"He was your grandfather. When I opened the door I thought you were Khadija, his daughter."

And there they were, the two words in red on the side of the house "Khadija=Traitor."

Chapter 29
October 2000

Ariel Sharon was seeking election as Prime Minister. He wanted headlines.

He chose the Old City of Jerusalem as the place to challenge the incumbent Prime Minister. The Wailing Wall, the historic remnant of the Jewish Temple stood below the Golden Dome of the Rock plateau, where the third holiest place in Islam was located. It had become a regular scene of violent confrontation between Israeli police and Palestinian Muslim worshippers. Jews rarely visited the plateau in any numbers.

Sharon, without police or government permission, decided on a walk-about on the plateau. He went with a large press pack and a police presence. He was Arik. It was an act of sheer political provocation, mocking his competitor and the Palestinians. It ignited the second Intifada, another Palestinian 'shaking off' of Israeli occupation; riots spread out of the occupied territories into the Palestinian community inside Israel.

Seven Palestinians were killed on the Dome plateau and Israeli police were deployed across the Galilee. Clamor in the village to react intensified.

According to the Commission of Inquiry Report into the events of October 2000, a mixed police force was sent 'to secure access' to the kibbutz opposite the bourj, drawn from units of Northern Region Center, Special Patrol, Village Border Police and regular police. One of the senior commanders was Gil Reiss former deputy chief at Misgav police station, promoted regional commander. He ordered his force to line up along the crash barrier from the bourj down to the junction of the main and dirt roads. He was in his element. This was war.

It brought village protestors onto the dirt road near the junction. Some crossed onto the main road and stopped three Jewish vehicles, by rolling lighted tires onto the road, shouting slogans, and throwing stones at the police. Police forced protestors back across the junction and into the olive groves beneath the bourj, specifically the grove still owned by the absent Sheikh Adwan. Some ventured through the trees towards the police lines and were repulsed by tear gas.

A honey buzzard watched, wheeling in the sky above. A scavenging fox flinched at the sounds of violence.

After the YAMAM officer's second warning, at his father's house, Hatem had moved to Haifa. He'd become transport manager of a car rental company branch. He wasn't an 'Ashkenazi', as Palestinians described 'Israelified' Arabs. But he was judicious about expressing his views.

Hatem's Jewish staff avoided politics but Jerusalem was headline news. One staffer told another, "the Basil Khoury scandal tells you what kind of men lead the Arabs of Israel. Sharon's right. Ehud Barak shouldn't give any part of Jerusalem to the fucking Arabs."

Hatem's office door was open and he said loudly, "Jerusalem's divided. You don't go to East Jerusalem and we don't go to the West." He came to the doorway and asked,

"Can you see me?" Several pairs of eyes stared at him. "Then stop pretending I don't exist." He closed his door.

At daybreak on the second day of October, Lana sat in her father's best olive grove. Ibrahim was very proud of his daughter. She had pursued her own path and succeeded. He felt justified in trusting her with his greatest secret and with his land. But he thought one degree was enough and hoped the new responsibilities he was giving her would keep her on the land and she'd forget her Masters. His inheritance and her first degree would make her a very attractive wife for the right man.

Khadija applauded his pragmatism. "Excellent," Khadija had said, when he told her he'd sought advice from a local attorney rather than from the Sharia court. She added, "Don't take anything for granted Ibrahim, particularly her Masters studies. Have you told her any of this?"

"Not yet, but I will."

So they sat in the grove an hour or so after dawn, the sun not yet risen enough to add its warmth to the air. He wanted family continuity. He believed in the land. It was his guiding spirit and to ensure its continuity he had taken surprisingly progressive steps.

They had been unaware that a demonstration was brewing.

What color is our truth, Lana asked herself? Neutral? Pastel? If truth's colors are national, then truth was more than the colors of the Palestinian flag. Black was an Arab symbol of wars since before Islam. White was the first flag color chosen by the Prophet, and adopted by his four successors. Green was the choice of the Fatimid dynasty. The red triangle symbolized the Arab tribes which conquered North Africa and Andalusia. They were all encapsulated in an old poem Lana knew by heart:

"White are our deeds,
"Black are our battles,
"Green are our fields,
"Red are our swords."

"What is the color of anger?" she asked Ibrahim sitting with his back against an olive tree trunk.

Lana had given no reason for her return home, but Ibrahim's heart sang. Without saying that he wanted to keep her from leaving again, he told her what he'd done so far. He'd drawn up a will making her the main beneficiary after Khadija, on condition she assumed a managerial role in his estates, and carried on after he died. Yusef would receive a proper share. Yunis wasn't mentioned. When Lana married and bore a son, he would be next in line. Ibrahim felt good about it.

"Red is the color of anger," he answered Lana. "This land has seen too much anger and bloodshed," he leaned down, ran his hand over the ground, pausing as if to feel its heartbeat and picked some earth up. "They say that's why the earth is red. It is," he rolled some of it through his fingers, "an angry land."

Lana looked up at the bourj. Its trees had been speechless witnesses to something which had almost deprived her of reason. She believed she had regained her balance, and Ibrahim's resilience and Khadija's calm were amongst her sources of endurance.

She listened intently as Ibrahim spoke reverentially of the other love of his life. He opened his fingers and sieved the earth from his other hand through them. "The olive tree is me. These trees will be here long after you and I are forgotten." He plucked an olive, his fingers finding one without looking away from her eyes and pressed it softly between his thumb and fingers. “The wind may have carried seeds here from wild olive plants. Who knows? Only Allah. Some of the trees in our other groves are over five hundred years old.”

He showed her that the olive flesh was, at that crucial point, still firm but most importantly, at its maximum ripened size and not yet black. “The darker the olive the better the oil, but too dark, the more acid its oil.”

From the top of the bourj, the plot of land their mother had left to Ibrahim and Adwan looked like a long arrowhead whose tip formed a junction between the lower dirt road and the upper main road. The dirt road ran back along the lower edge of the arrowhead. The upper edge followed the main road, bordered by a crash barrier as it climbed up past the bourj and ran north. Opposite the bourj was a hill, like a finger, covered with scrub and more pines. Beyond the knuckle of the finger was a kibbutz. There were pathways through the olive groves, wide enough for two people to walk shoulder to shoulder. With their leaves fully grown, Ibrahim estimated each tree averaged twice the height of a man, plus a head.

“You remember the secret I told you about my mother and Adwan’s father? The old village way for a pregnant widow to prove that the dead man was her husband, was to walk under his body as it was being carried to the cemetery. My mother could never have walked under Sheikh Umar’s body to prove to the village tongues that the dead Sheikh was the father of her child...” he inhaled slowly. “That would have been her end. She kept her secret. To this day I have no idea how she passed off her pregnancy and who brought Adwan up. Someone must have.”

There were two shots from the direction of the junction. They both looked towards the source. Minutes later the unfamiliar smell of tear-gas carried to them. The trees and the grass line shielded father and daughter. The sound of chanting protesters reached them through the groves. Lana's pleading eyes told Ibrahim she wanted to see what was happening.

"That's all about politics,' Ibrahim said with a dismissive nod. "What we're talking about is much more important," he carried on as if his words would somehow protect them both. Not long after, they heard the sound of someone running through Adwan's grove in their direction. Ibrahim motioned Lana to get down by the base of the trunk.

It had become impossible for Hatem to ignore the tension as the Palestinian community across Israel reacted to events. News of the demonstration at his home village drew him to the dirt road close to Ibrahim's grass line. He crossed the trees to the junction to see what was happening, then returned and chatted with a protest organizer. A youth with a slingshot stood by.

A black SUV carrying a three man YAMAM unit had come slowly along the dirt road towards the junction. It stopped before the olive groves, and parked pointing back the way it had come. The unit exited the vehicle and advanced on the protesters.

The few slingshot throwers were masters of the ancient but deadly weapon. Reiss up at the bourj radioed down to the YAMAM unit commander with the location of the sling shot thrower near Hatem. The commander issued a shoot order to one of his men.

The sling began to twirl, then suddenly the thrower found himself spinning round, yelling in pain, clutching at his upper arm, his sling hurtling off into the trees behind him, blood pouring through clawed fingers.

Neither the protest leader nor the thrower had heard the gunshot, the din swallowed its crack. Calling for help for the wounded man, the organizer shouted for everyone to scatter.

The YAMAM commander recognized Hatem in his binoculars. He signaled his two men to follow him.

Something made Hatem look up to see three men in black combats and face masks streaking towards him down the dirt road. He was terrified for his life.

He understood he was their prey and ran into the groves. He crouched low and zigzagged towards the grass line. He remembered the olive trees whose leaves had once sheltered him and Lana and made for them. Thump. Something rammed into his back and he sprawled onto the earth, struggling for breath. "I told you to go away," said the calm voice, "now try."

Hatem knew that voice. He scrabbled forward. They let him go some twenty meters. Then something zapped at his left thigh and the leg wouldn't work. He kept on, numb with pain, dragging his wounded limb. His right knee exploded, from a shot from the second YAMAM man, and he couldn't stay upright.

The commander told his men, "They'll say this was a stray shot".

Hatem didn't hear or feel the third and final zap, milliseconds after the red laser dot from the commander's assault rifle found his forehead. The commander ordered the two men to lift Hatem's body and dump it.

Reiss radioed another order, "Take out the guy in the green t-shirt."

Asif was with a huddle of protestors, sitting under an olive tree on the edge of the dirt road near the tip of the arrowhead, oblivious to Hatem's fate. Once again the unit dashed up along the dirt road, frightening the group with their ferocity, converging on Asif.

Terrified and dumbstruck by what they'd seen, Ibrahim and Lana were about to start crawling towards the dirt road, when Lana pulled roughly at Ibrahim's ankle. Running towards the grass was another figure. Lana saw Asif.

They witnessed an almost carbon copy of the previous murder. Asif desperately jinked further into the grove, only to be brought down with a rifle butt to the back of his head. His pursuers were silent. His overwhelming will to escape gave Asif an energy boost, and he got up. He was dazed from the blow to his head and was outflanked and tackled to the ground. In smooth and precise movements, the commander un-holstered his automatic pistol and fired into Asif's head. "That's a confirmed kill," said one of his unit. The other said, "Yeah that's one the boss can add to the score on his 'You Can't Hide' t-shirt."

The arrogance of brute force in men of arms is a failing that creates carelessness. Instead of sweeping the whole area for anyone else, Asif's body was dragged out of the olive trees towards the dirt road and dumped. He was still breathing, though the unit members didn't check. Moments later the SUV's engine started up and it disappeared back up the dirt road.

The sudden discovery of two bodies, Hatem dead, Asif almost, caused panic amongst the protesters. The organizer detected Asif's faint pulse and yelled for help.

Paralysis, physical and mental, generated by the fear and shock from what she'd witnessed, battled with guilt that Lana couldn't save Hatem or Asif. Fear won. Later, she imagined that she and her father had merged into the grove, as still as the trees themselves. The sounds from the main road subsided.

Lana seemed to rise above the trees, watching Ibrahim crawl through the tall grass towards where Asif's body had fallen. He reached out to the bloodied earth.

The fox scented it. The buzzard spotted its glisten.

Ibrahim showed his blood-tinged fingers to Lana. "Al Daam al Ard – Blood on the ground," he murmured.

Chapter 30
March 2003

His mobile woke him. Bleary eyes said it was close to six. He'd had about an hour's sleep.

"Gershon Steinman," said the voice.

Who? Then as he surfaced he cleared his throat and asked, "Hihowareyou?"

Gershon decoded that deftly. "I'm well thanks Dov. What are you up to these days?" There was no pause between statement and question; Gershon didn't care about the answer.

Dov's one room apartment was on the top floor of an old building at the crummier end of Hayarkon Street, the road that more or less followed the sea front. The building was hidden from the sight but not the noise of traffic by a jungle that was once a garden. It all threatened Dov's seclusion and matched the precarious nature of his life. The landlords had propped up one wall of the building with timbers, hoping that developers would take the plot off their hands. But tall weeds had long obscured the For Sale sign. Hope was on hold.

He'd canvassed private security companies and discovered he was a valuable commodity. It seemed that the whole world was a terror target. 9/11 and an endless wave of suicide bombings had become facts of life. His suspension from the force and his interrupted air marshal's stint were overlooked because of his shooting skills, his age and relatively good physical shape. His medal helped, though he was oddly comforted that his name meant nothing to his interviewers, low echelon men and women younger than Aviel.

Restaurants, supermarkets, shopping malls, all had private security men checking everyone on entry. And that's what Dov did. Sometimes it was night duty in office blocks, for extra cash, like last night's shift that had finished at 0.500.

He had rescued his stereo and his CDs from the family apartment and the music fended off some of his loneliness. Beethoven and Mozart infrequently filled the void and sometimes so did thoughts of Lana.

Gershon Steinman? Was it really him? It had been nearly three years since he'd worked for Ruhama.

"Not much, Gershon," he said dolefully, "I'm doing security work." It was 06.02. Sleep deprivation was an understatement.

"Aha. Excellent. Keeping busy. That's good to hear," said Steinman. "Well, I wondered if you'd find some time to come and see me at the house? What was once our holiday home? I feel we owe you for helping Ruhama. We're here permanently now, ah not on holiday of course. Ha ha. Shall we say eight?"

All those questions, implied commands. No we shan't say that. I for sure won't. Less than two hours from now? "Can't. Tomorrow'd be better."

Steinman. His old friend. So what? Why the hell call at this hour? Leave me the fuck alone. "Mid-morning tomorrow. OK?"

"Yes all right." Steinman petulantly. If judges, lawyers and other government officials complied with his summonses, why not a tainted ex-police officer?

The Beetle's exhausts whistled Dov sweetly into the West Bank.

He sat sipping good coffee. Gershon's kippa looked like it was glued to his pate. He'd gone bald since they last met. Ministerial anxiety?

"What do you recall of the October 2000 incidents?" Steinman asked.

"There were riots in the Galilee," he began. "They dovetailed with the Second Intifada in the territories." He didn't know how he knew that.

Steinman nodded. "Yes. Good. This is official, not like the work you did for Ruhama. Who knows what might come out of it, you know what I mean? I can probably get you a salary on a par with what you'd have got if you hadn't ah... short term of course, but, you know, once you're in, you're in."

Dov still didn't know what was being offered.

Steinman became imperious. "It's giving something back Dov. You still have a duty to us, to this country. You shouldn't need reminding, you're a war hero after all. I'm offering you another chance. I'm doing it for Liora. Don't give me that look. She still feels something for you. Yes she does. She asked me a while back if there was ever anything I could do to help, please would I. This came up. If you want it, I'll set it up. But I need to know now. It's not very complicated. Just review a draft report by the Ministry's Police Investigations Department about those riots in the Galilee. The Commission of Inquiry requested that the PID investigate them. Your review will set the seal on it. Clear so far?"

Dov nodded.

"Well?" He didn't want to beg. Say yes, Dov, for heaven's sake man say the word. I need you to get to work ASAP and I'll get credit for giving a fallen hero a second chance. Of course if you screw up you'll be burned alive and it'll be me who lights the match.

"Yes," Dov said.

No word of gratitude, Steinman wanted to say, but instead mentally marked Dov's card with that too.

Steinman told him to be at the Justice Ministry in Jerusalem at 08.00 sharp the following Sunday to sign the paperwork and be issued with a temporary Justice Ministry ID. Steinman made the power call, and with the cash it generated, Dov found a place in Ein Karem in southwest Jerusalem to rent. He told the security company he had other work and his Tel Aviv landlords that the room would be vacant next day. He packed everything into the Beetle and drove to the capital.

Dov knew Police HQ intimately but had never ventured south of it. During his first lunch break he walked along the street bordering the lower end of the Ministry compound. It was a rat-run, always choked. It featured a 1960s style hotel, a few unattractive shops, a coffee shop and a barber. At the entrance to a building on the corner with the teeming Salah Ad Din street, plaques in Arabic, English and Hebrew announced the Oral and Dental services of a doctor qualified at Cairo University.

Dov smirked at the idea that anyone he knew would ever have their teeth treated there. Cairo University? Get my haircut there? Eat in there? Sleep in that hotel? You must be kidding.

There were twenty five pages of the PID report he found on the desk in the office given over to him.

The front page read:

DRAFT ONLY. NOT FOR PUBLICATION!
Ministry of Justice
Police Investigations Department
Conclusions On The Matter
Of Incidents of Clashes
Between Security Forces
And Israeli Citizens
In October 2000

The first five words were more than a warning to him, they said we don't trust you with the full document. OK, OK, I'm on parole here. He banished that thought and instead was immediately struck by 'Israeli citizens.' Arabs? "Hardly," he said aloud to the room.

A secretary opened the frosted glass panel to her outer office. "Did you want something?" she asked. There was no 'Sir'. Perhaps she didn't know who he was, who he'd been, Commander Chizzik no less.

"No. Sorry." he said, "Just talking to myself." She gave him a look that said 'you're weird,' and closed the panel.

He'd have to try to be more affable. There was no computer but he found some notepaper. Was he supposed to write his own notes?

He read the report's five-page preface then re-read the first paragraph: "The confrontations in which hundreds of thousands of demonstrators took part, included roadblocks on main highways throughout Israel, damage to public and private property; Molotov cocktails, stones and metal objects were thrown; sling shots (very dangerous) were used. As a consequence of the stone throwing, an Israeli citizen was killed, and citizens and police were injured."

The word 'citizen' caught him again. What kind of citizens were these Arabs who threw Molotov cocktails at Jews? Molotov cocktails for fuck's sake!

He needed a timeline of events and went out to the secretary's desk. She wasn't there. He switched her computer screen on, pleased he'd accomplished that. The Government seven-branch menorah emblem came on screen and 'Ministry of Justice' below, then 'Please enter your security code.'

"Excuse me!" the secretary called out, hurrying in.

"I was just trying to…" he said embarrassed.

"You shouldn't do that," she replied, officiously.

"Sorry. It's just that..." I'll try a smile. He smiled. No reaction.

"Ask me and I'll get you whatever you need," she said disgruntled.

"Sorry." I have to stop saying that. "I don't know your name. Could you help me?" then added, "Please." And waited.

She looked up at him, a blank face, once pretty perhaps, dressed in beige, almost women's army service issue, no make-up, no jewelry, no name.

He went on, "I could use some newspaper articles for the period," he tapped at the report, "of the 'October Incidents'?"

"Don't touch my computer again," she began.

"Yes. I'm sorry", he really wasn't, "but I'm a bit short of time." He smiled again. And lied, "Professor Steinman's urgently waiting for my first evaluation, so press clippings of the period would speed things up."

She nodded at Steinman's name.

Back in his room, he noted on his pad as he re-read the report, "<u>PID believed investigation impossible</u>". Then he added bullet points:

- PID began preps for investigation while incidents ongoing
- Violence too serious to risk investigators in the field
- Non co-op of Arab sector leaders
- PID halts work during Comm of Inq sessions

- Comm of Inq requests PID investigation into 13 deaths after publishing own findings. Comm of Inq unable to identify shooters
- Forensic IDs "unlikely after passage of time", some families reject exhumation/autopsy. Match between bullet fragments and shooters still possible

The language of the report was eloquently opaque, stressing the difference between the Commission of Inquiry's investigation into possible crimes and police handling of the incidents, and the PID investigation into police criminality.

He was reading the first 'incident' when the secretary came in, placed some pages on his desk, a departmental newspaper digest, and said, "the articles you asked for." The "Sir" was implied, he imagined.

Dov was horrified because the details of the whole thing had passed him by somehow, down and out, air-marshaling, private security nobody: violent riots in main Jewish cities; huge demonstrations in Arab towns he'd never heard of inside Israel; dozens injured; property damaged; roads obstructed; Jewish villages besieged. What the hell was this? The 1948 War of Independence all over again?

It was in their blood, wasn't it, those Arabs? What the hell did they want? More land? Kill more Jews?

Chapter 31

He awoke to something softly scratching at his nose. He sneezed. The scratching stopped, but mewing began and a black and white kitten appeared in front of his face. He sneezed again, the kitten vanished and sunlight broke through the morning mists, leaving the treetops on the ridge opposite his window exposed to the warmth of the sun.

It was Friday morning, the end of his first week at the Ministry. His landlady greeted him with a mug of coffee at the foot of the stairs. Dov gulped it, garbled, "one of your cats got into my room. I'm allergic," politely refused breakfast and drove to work.

"The Professor wants to see you," Ms Blank-face proclaimed as he arrived.

"Good," Dov said. He collected his notes and went down.

As a special Ministerial advisor to the Justice Minister, Steinman had an airy corner suite at the end of a pale blue corridor. Steinman's secretary said, "He's here," into her intercom. "Well knock then," she told Dov.

There was a stentorian "Enter!" Dov did. "Just a moment," Steinman said not looking up. He was immersed in the contents of a thick pink file.

"Gaza disengagement," he said.

It was an invitation to a mental waltz, but at least this one wasn't foreign to him, he'd read the papers and watched TV news. "Right," Dov said.

"Don't be evasive. What do you think?"

Dov said, "Sharon needs public support to evacuate our settlers from the Gaza Strip and if he gets that, the whole thing'll have to be handled with kid gloves." He paused, and then plunged on. "Put yourself in the settlers' shoes, imagine you're forced to evacuate your West Bank home."

No come-back on the inference that he was a settler, Dov noted when Steinman said, "Precisely. We have to be as sensitive as possible. The Attorney General wants the Gaza Strip settlers to know that their right to public protest is untrammeled, as long as they don't cross any red lines. If I was a settler I'd want to protest about the State that told me I could go to Gaza and is now ordering me to leave. I'll tell the Minister we can't afford to be ambivalent. How's the review going?"

"I've read about a third. Shall I go through my notes?"

"No, no. Take your time. This disengagement business'll take precedence. First impressions for now'd be useful." Come on Dov, Steinman urged silently. It's just a one-act play with one soliloquy, 'we did the best in difficult circumstances; it's three years ago; who can be blamed?' But you have to write it.

"It looks pretty thorough so far," said Dov. "The police tried their best at containment; there were unfortunate incidents; lives were regrettably lost. The passage of time and the victims' families refusal on autopsies has reduced the chance of conclusive forensic evidence."

Almost there, Steinman thought. He said, "Excellent. If you need further information, just ask, OK?" He thought, don't get your feet under the table my friend.

"Fine," said Dov and left.

Steinman called the secretary assigned to Dov. "Make absolutely sure he doesn't see any of the Commission of Inquiry's draft reports. Get him the briefest summary if he asks for one." He wanted to be sure that Dov remained ignorant of the glaring differences between the PID's conclusions and the Commission's.

The awed female voice said, "Yes Professor. As you instructed, he has no computer access, and when he needs any documentation he has to ask for it and I filter that." Her tone suggested she'd do anything for him, murder, arson, take off her pants, name it.

Fridays were half work days for most Israelis, but Dov worked until close to two. He left the empty building and drove back to Ein Karem, stopping off at a pharmacy to get anti-histamine. He'd talk to the landlady about making his room 'feline-frei'.

Next morning Dov broached the cat issue. She'd invited him to join the family breakfast but the smell of cats in the kitchen and the sight of her slicing bread next to open cat-food tins had nauseated him.

He'd said it was so nice outside he'd prefer to eat there. She joined him.

He began obliquely, intent on confusing her with an out field approach. "Where's the line between normality and socio-psychopathy? I've dealt with many psychopaths as an investigator. How do we discover why an individual 'went over the edge'? There are many warning signs before psychopathic outbursts, increased aggressive language, wild gesticulating etc etc." He ignored his own gesticulations and the anxiety on the woman's face. He went on. "Can a nation be socio-psychopathic? If the people were revolted by the smell of cats and their food, would there be a cull of all its cats?"

"Umm. Yes, I see. Well spoken," she said uncertainly, generosity in her look and a mouth that smiled easily. "Is this to do with our cats? You've got an allergy and the way to sort that out is by, um, destroying them?"

Just for a minute Dov wasn't in a forgiving mood. "Hang them up dead by their tails," he indicated the drying line behind them.

With a half smile, she said, "No, I don't think we'd do that. I was a little unsure about what you said before, especially about us as a people. I got lost in the words, us Jerusalemites, you know? Up in the hills, small-minded."

He warmed to her. "It's simple really. Where's the line for us between normal behavior and stepping over it? I mean we do have a propensity for overreacting, don't we?"

"What's that got to do with your cat allergy?"

"Just thinking aloud. We're used to reacting aggressively, but how will we react in normal situations, when, let's imagine, there aren't any real threats? Or are we so immune to normal, we don't know any other way of being; we must do overkill, it's like a national addiction." Then he said, "So we keep creating situations to which we can react disproportionately. Is that normal?"

She looked perplexed. He liked this place and her; it gave him a new sense of ease. Quickly he said, "Sorry. Forget all that. I'm taking anti-histamine and honestly? No dead cats hanging on the line or anything."

"Fine, fine," she said mollified. As she went off up to the kitchen, Dov knew that something in the PID report had wormed its way into him and produced this crazy thought process. It was absurd wasn't it? Did Israelis overreact? Ridiculous. So the police had resorted to live fire. Over the top? Hardly. Hadn't riots spread into Israeli towns and cities? And in live fire, someone's bound to get hurt. Fucking

Arabs. No, there was nothing to suggest that any policeman had crossed the line from normal to psychopathy.

He climbed the stairs to his room, and dozed. When he awoke, the sun had begun to set. He stood outside on the domed roof to watch.

The white orb slid down a gold-to-ochre sky above the trees lining the periphery of Yad Vashem, the national Holocaust memorial center, at the start of the ridge opposite. He saw the outline of the solitary freight wagon, symbolizing the last journeys for Holocaust victims, sculpturally perched on a precipice. He considered how frequently the Holocaust was the justification for his people's persistent abreactions, part of the national DNA.

"Fucking Arabs" he muttered again and went to have supper.

A week later at the Ministry, Dov reached two conclusions. The first concerned his reaction to the report. He wrote of the Arab riots, 'October incidents' was too euphemistic, "They're Arabs, doing what Arabs do."

The second conclusion was as simple.

Here he was 'investigating' a report by the PID, who policed the police. As an investigator he'd had to find proof of guilt, and often individuals emerged who were more than suspects. But this was different. Steinman made his instincts twitch like primitive antennae. He had to redeem himself without compromising what shreds of his integrity remained. Naïve? What choice did he have?

This was a rubber stamp job, that's what it was. The public would remember his successes as a Super Cop, if as he imagined, Gershon would spin the presentation of the report with his name attached, his past mistakes would be forgiven and the report's credibility would be boosted.

When he'd asked the secretary, he received a two-page summary of the Commission of Inquiry's earlier draft reports. He requested a more detailed draft. She told him, "That's got restricted access." Meaning I won't see anything more than this summary.

Her peremptory tone reminded him of the summary for each of the thirteen cases in the PID report, "No alternative but to shelve this file for lack of evidence."

So he noted on his pad: Must visit a scene of crime. Get Steinman's ok, expenses etc.

Where to go? There'd been something about a siege of a Jewish settlement in the Galilee.

When he called Steinman's number he was put straight through. Steinman agreed. "Of course. I'll authorize your expenses, you probably want them in advance? Go down to finance at lunchtime. Do you want a Ministry car and a driver?" Dov said he'd prefer his own VW. "I'll get you contact details for our people in the north. I think there's a regional office not too far from where you'll be. Oh and one other thing Dov, you'll need a weapon. You can never be too sure."

Chapter 33

As soon as he was in Arab Galilee, Dov pulled over, loaded the automatic he'd signed for, clicked on the safety, and put it back inside his shoulder bag in easy reach. He had had a long Lana moment seeing that the settlement he wanted to visit was close to her village.

At a traffic island Dov saw a dirty-faced boy in grubby clothes staring pleadingly at each vehicle. He wasn't selling flowers or cleaning windshields. From the vehicle in front, a late model white Mercedes, a hand emerged at the end of a white shirted arm; a gold cufflink winked momentarily in the sun. The hand held a white plastic bag of pita bread. The boy took the bag. The hand then produced another bag full of apples, and then two water bottles. Too much white, Dov thought, car, sleeve, bag; there was nothing perfect about what he'd seen. Cars hooting behind Dov pulled him out of his next conflicting thoughts of 'Fucking Arabs!' and 'below the poverty line'.

The Beetle sturdily climbed onto the Rams Horns Hills. He experienced the same feeling of being in alien territory when he'd last been there investigating the cave. But the view was still enchanting, and when he'd parked and walked to see it, he filled his lungs with clean pure air.

The valley below stretched away to his right. The hills bordering it were painted in the subtle silvery greens of olive trees, against a red earth backdrop.

"It's something isn't it?" A strong male voice said behind him. "There's rosemary and lavender and sage in the breeze. If you like birds, we've honey buzzards, swallows, and falcons."

"How many families?" Dov indicated the houses of the settlement planted along the hill's contours.

"Sixty and we'll double that in the next five years."

The man pointed to an area partially terraced and cleared, awaiting foundations. Dov nodded and returned to the view. "How are the neighbors?"

"They're as numerous as olives," the man beamed quickly, "and outnumber us, roughly two hundred thirty thousand to our fifteen thousand here in lower Galilee."

Grey hair, sun tanned, a look of confidence, comfortable with himself and his milieu, the kind of man Dov had once been.

"Everyone calls me Sprinz." Then he frowned at Dov. "I've seen you before somewhere."

Dov said, "I'm Dov Chizzik, with the Police Investigations Department," and waited.

"Chizzik the former Super Cop?" Dov nodded. "What brings you here Commander?"

Dov warmed to him and told him.

"We get along somehow with the Arabs. Most of the olive groves you can see are theirs. We know how to mass market and they have years of cultivation experience. It's a good partnership. But they'd rather we weren't here."

"They hate us?" Dov guessed the answer.

"Many do, yes. Resentment's too nice a word. It's a combination of past defeat and present success, theirs first, ours second."

"I'd like to hear more about the siege in 2000."

"Not every detail was reported to official Israel. We were confronted by a mob refusing to let anyone in or out. I'll tell you the rest over lunch."

They sat outside at wooden tables and ate from a spread of cheeses and olives, fresh bread, vegetables and olive oil.

"The village down there?" Sprinz pointed to the large splash of houses across two hillsides. "In the main square there's a huge banner of a young man, Asif, one of the two, they call them Shuhada, martyrs, who died on one day in the riots."

Dov nodded.

Sprinz continued, "So the two deaths inflamed the villagers and they came up here, blocked the gateway and threatened us with Molotov cocktails for two days."

"No one rescued you?"

"No. There's a kibbutz just north of the village on the hill by the junction." He indicated what he called the finger of the kibbutz, white buildings located near the knuckle. "The police protected them." He turned back, "It's not like the West Bank. We're not fanatic religious settlers. We've lived here since the twelve tribes, lived, not came and went." He was in profile as he spoke, and Dov experienced pangs of envy of a man so committed. "Did you know there's a rabbi and his wife from the time of Jesus, buried in the village? During the riots they tried to set fire to their tomb."

"Terrible," Dov said. He studied the man again. Then it came to him, the early Zionists he'd loved at school, their dedication. Sprinz had it too.

Driving through the village, Dov saw a chaotic layout of streets and houses, no urban planning, a clutter of styles and shapes, phone and power cables wildly criss-crossing the sky.

On a square, he passed a modern house. The place was sealed up, with warning signs in faded Hebrew and Arabic.

Within ten minutes he reached the turning for the kibbutz, and parked under trees. He pulled out his copy of the draft PID report and turned to Chapter Five. It was titled THE INCIDENT OF THE DEATH OF and named one of the deceased.

He read the description of the layout of where the action had occurred, and walked back down to the junction with the olive grove to begin matching the words with reality. Then he crossed over to the crash barrier and walked up a few meters alongside it. On his left was a rocky outcrop overlooking the olive groves near the turning for the kibbutz. It was like a castle turret with a glade of pine trees on top. He carried on up the incline to the top of the outcrop, went through the glade and out to survey the groves from above. He saw a line of tall grass, stretching away from the base of the turret. The olive trees right of the line were four or five meters high. The trees on the left of the grass line were shorter with gaps between rows and individual trees, as the report had described them. He walked back down to the junction.

Dov tried to picture: "Demonstrators threw stones and advanced towards the main road." How many demonstrators? Which part of the main road? Maybe Steinman could get him some TV archive footage. He understood the decision to 'force the demonstrators back towards the dirt road and the olive groves.' Free access to the kibbutz was the security priority.

He had underlined 'An order was given to arrest the deceased who was hiding in amongst the groves. Following this a unit went in the deceased's direction, and chased him towards olive groves on the edge of the road.'

The description continued: ‘At a certain point, the deceased was shot and fatally wounded and later died from his wound. On the matter of the shooting and specifically the identity of the shooter, there is no complete clarification. Several testimonies suggest that the shooting was preceded by the deceased receiving a blow from a rifle butt from one of the pursuing police officers. As a result of this blow, the deceased fell, got up, kept going and was shot.’

There was a sentence about an Arab doctor’s evidence which he ignored, looking for something he’d seen from an Israeli forensics source. But what he found was a one sentence comment from an expert at the Abu Kabir national forensic medicine center; maybe it was Cordova, he smiled, but it didn’t have his characteristic ‘so to say’: ‘The deceased’s body should be exhumed for autopsy to reach possible conclusive findings as to the identity of the shooter and the cause of death.’

There was conflicting evidence about the officers at the scene. Several not involved in the pursuit of the deceased, admitted firing rubber bullets and live rounds at the demonstrators. The precise distance of these officers from the ‘incident’ was not provided. To Dov this raised the possibility that the deceased’s fatal wound may have resulted from a stray round. But hadn’t someone described a, ‘bullet fired at close range?’ He searched and found that that was from the Arab doctor. Dov dismissed it as speculation, unsupported by any factual evidence.

Of the three officers implicated in the deceased’s shooting, which they denied, two were polygraphed and passed the test. The third refused to take it. The report stressed the stray round theory, odd as it had come from the Arab doctor. It wasn’t that that worried Dov. The PID had revealed the conflicting findings, which was creditably honest. Lacking was any follow up on the officer who had refused the polygraph or clarity on the source of the bullet that killed the deceased.

From the junction Dov turned onto the dirt road, stopped, and looked up at the crash barrier and then down across at the groves, trying to visualize the police positions from the demonstrators' point of view. What had the police faced here? 'Violence including stone and metal objects thrown… burning tires rolled onto the road to block it.'

God! What was the time? Nearly six forty-five? He'd forgotten to call the regional PID office to arrange for somewhere to stay. There were no signal bars, the hills probably interfering with the signal. Dusk was near. He went back up to the Beetle and decided to head for Carmiel, the nearest Israeli town, hoping for a better signal on the way.

He turned onto the main road signposted Carmiel heading towards a steep sided wadi. Still no signal bars. His was the only vehicle on the road. There had been no one in the fields he'd past.

Then he knew why. It was Friday. He'd been so engrossed, he'd lost track. Shabbat was almost in and wasn't Friday a non-work day for Muslims too? He floored the accelerator, hoping to exit the wadi, and get signal bars.

The accelerator pedal was almost to the floor, but the speedometer needle lazily turned back to zero. The car slowed and he guided it off the road as it rolled to a halt. Dov switched the engine off. Darkness had begun to reach out from the west. There was occasional bird song, and the clink of metal contracting in the car's cooling exhaust, and a growing and perfect silence.

At first he sat still. No signal bars.

He turned on the ignition. The fuel gauge showed he had plenty. This was obviously a mechanical fault.

He switched on his hazard lights and took out the red warning triangle and set it up on the road.

Could thoughts make sounds? Were they mechanical, like cogs meshing? Or were they more like a bird's breath, a feather falling? Did the cortex crackle, even minutely, as a thought passed through it? Did thoughts have colors?

His strongest thought was a crimson red of anxiety, then emerald green for someone will be along soon, bright orange for maybe, turquoise blue for loneliness - and there it was again, the red, glowing urgently.

Barkbarkbark!

Three descending cries. Pause.

Barkbarkbark!

Pause. Those cries! Piercing him. Not an echo. Very close.

Dov reached in, and lit the headlights.

A movement ahead. There. Eyes large, nose long and narrow…what was that? A smile?

The fox, its paws in forward motion, was frozen in the lights.

Dov mused: I've never seen a fox before. The fox is staring at me. His thoughts addressed the fox. If I whisper will you answer? You're still staring. What do you see?

The dog fox stared back coolly. In the beams, his tawny yellow coat was washed out, but his ears were dark and his brush splendidly thick. He moved nonchalantly on down the center of the road, stopping twice to look back over his haunches and his look said: I know you. You're frightened. I'm frightened. You won't harm me. I can't harm you.

'How do I know?' Dov whispered.

The fox stopped. Sat up. Stared again.

They exchanged colors in equal silence.

Dov blinked. The fox was gone.

Better turn off the lights to conserve the battery.

He examined the gun and listened.

Wait! Was that movement? Where? There?

Both hands cradling the gun. Three shots. Carefully spaced. He felt invincible. It passed.

After the echo of the shots faded he sent out this flaming red thought: I'm warning you. Anyone. I'm armed.

And then: Is there someone out there? Someone coming to help?

Not too long after that, came the familiar droning of a jeep engine. He stood still by the Beetle, wearing a sheepish smile, the automatic quickly shoved into his waistband.

His smile froze as the jeep came and went, his hopes lost in its slipstream, the driver ignoring him, the officer next to him looking at Dov and then away. The two Border Policemen sitting opposite each other in the rear continued chatting. How many Arabs had Sprinz said, two hundred and thirty thousand?

The jeep mollified him even if it hadn't rescued him. Israel was in control here. What am I really frightened of? I have my gun. If there's one jeep patrol there'll be others.

Is that it? The jeep and my gun against all those Arabs?

Is that enough?

Look what happened in October 2000. They were many and we were too few. Our control over them was stretched to breaking point.

It snapped didn't it? That's what the PID report was trying to hide.

The image of the fox in his lights returned. Who was more scared? The biblical Samson and the foxes of Timna came to him, a saga of revenge and control, control and revenge.

He stood outside again. The air was soft, an occasional breeze cooled his brow.

Another engine sound, also familiar, another Beetle? He stood still, his hand on the butt of the automatic in his waistband.

The vehicle was a vision of '50s panache, a two seat Karmann Ghia VW convertible, its top down. It was pink and immaculate. It stopped almost nose to nose with the Beetle. The driver was good-looking, an Arab with a pair of bikers' goggles pushed to the back of his head. He turned on his hazards, and got out.

Dov's hand tightened around the butt.

"Having trouble? Can I help?" asked Rashid.

Rashid's house was in the village, which he insisted on calling town – "I'm just near the town centre", "I do good business in this town".

As they got out of the car, Rashid said, "We've met before, at Misgav police station over that stupid accusation about my brother's cave."

"Yes, that's right," Dov said recognizing him without the goggles. He wondered whether he could or should ask about Lana.

Once inside the spacious living room, Rashid said, "you'll have some coffee and refreshments," a statement not an inquiry, and returned a few minutes later with coffees, iced water, and slices of cake. "My wife's away at her parents. She'd have loved to meet you. Help yourself," he said. "My tow-truck will bring your Beetle to our garage. We'll do the repair within the hour. Can I have your car keys?"

As Dov handed them over, Rashid explained, "It's the washer on the fuel pump rocker. They don't do individual parts anymore, it'll be a new pump, but I've got them in stock, there's still a few Beetles about."

"Thanks very much," Dov said genuinely. "What do I owe you for all this?"

"Nothing at all, it's on the house. But do me one small favor? Put your gun in your bag. No one here's going to harm you, I promise."

Dov was embarrassed and Rashid said, "The butt poked out as you dumped your bag in my car."

Dov put the still loaded automatic into the bag. He sipped at the coffee. It was fine.

Rashid asked, "What's a former Tel Aviv police investigator doing up here in the Galilee?"

Dov replied bluntly, "Why are you being so helpful?"

"I'm no detective, but you must have been out there a while, a stranger in a strange place; I guess you had no phone signal, there was hardly any traffic, it's Friday, you were in hostile territory, for you, hence the gun. In all likelihood another 'local'", he grinned at his self-deprecation, "would've helped you out; it was just your luck that it was me. I love old Beetles. That makes us like brothers under the hood," he laughed. "So what are you doing here?"

What to say, Dov thought, carefully constructed truth or complex lie?

Rashid waited, then quipped, "Oh, it's that serious?"

"I'm doing follow up into the October 2000 incidents, sort of tidying up." He hoped that was bland enough.

"Two of our young people were killed in those so-called incidents." Then he gave Dov a long look. He left the room again, and Dov heard him on the phone.

Dov was impatient to get back to Jerusalem. The Beetle would be ready very soon and he'd be on his way. He would complete his review and with a bit of luck he might be reinstated. Steady salary. Rebuild his reputation.

The PID's conclusions could stand. Yet those words still niggled: …"no alternative but to shelve the file…" Ah well. And Lana? A beautiful fantasy.

"Do you know their names?" Rashid asked evenly, coming back.

"Their names?" Dov asked, jolted by the question; he'd subconsciously kept the deceased anonymous.

"Yes, the two victims."

"Yes. I, yes…ah…"

"They were Hatem and Asif." Rashid gave Dov a quick hard stare. "My niece knows about their deaths. She's on her way over. You should talk with her."

Chapter 33

Stars do not career across the sky. The earth spins past the stars. Lana knew this and from her ultimate special place she'd seen the valley's hues change through the seasons, her father's fields tended, the crops harvested, life in the village following its course through the ages. And she had seen herself grow into a village woman, the traumas slowly healing, the scars forming, the memories bearable. She'd been wrong to want to leave; this was her normal, her familiar, she felt safe with it.

She achieved a distinction for her MA and everyone who could get there came to the graduation ceremony. Yunis and Yehudit were in the hall, with Fuad Assad sitting between them. Lana was brighter and happier. Her parents beamed with pride, though Khadija detected a new reserve in Lana she couldn't explain.

She had plans for a PhD. She continued accumulating stories of her people's survival and knowing that she was not a victim, prepared to tell everyone that she wasn't theirs. In the spare time she carved out of her estate management schedule, she researched on the Internet and read voraciously. She discovered Khirbet Khizeh, the Ruins of Khizeh, a sinister Israeli novel about the forced evacuation of an Arab village in 1948. It had been a bestseller when first published in

1949. For Lana it represented one of many Israeli paradoxes. They could publicly admit to doing terrible things in war and occupation. She knew such catharses could never happen in Arab society.

She and Yehudit spent time together and she made up for the socializing she'd missed. Every offer of marriage Ibrahim presented, she rejected. Nabil asked her to meet again and she refused. Alone she remembered trysting with Hatem, Asif's gift of the poem, bitter memories of dead souls, whose ghosts would stay with her.

She abhorred the martyrdom the village had built around them both. They were not martyrs. They had not sacrificed their lives for the Palestinian cause. They were murdered and she had witnessed it. The lesson of memory overlays convinced her that she had to leave the village and the land for good. But her need to somehow find justice for Hatem and Asif held her back.

Uncle Rashid had called as she was preparing to go out for the evening. She was finishing her make-up. She was dressed simply but with an indefinable chic. She wore a white sleeveless blouse with the collar turned up, her hair was cut short, its raven blackness gleamed.

She listened to Rashid, called one of her friends to say something important had come up and drove straight to her uncle's home.

They both felt a tremor as she entered the room.

Rashid had not told her it was Dov Chizzik he'd rescued. It was essential she lead the conversation before Dov could say, "Oh yes, we met at Haifa university. I was investigating the rape allegations against Basil Khoury…"

She said, "Nice to meet you. I know some people you should see," and shook hands. There was a charge of static between their fingers and they looked up at each other mystified.

Lana gasped. Rashid looked up.

Dov said, “Sorry, I’m always doing that with handshakes, don’t know my own strength.” The change in her since Haifa, impossibly more beautiful, made him lightheaded.

Outside Dov tried, “Ms al Batuf…Lana…” They were crossing a large square, more an intersection, with an electricity pylon in the middle. It was dominated by a banner of a young man’s face strung from a window on the first floor of the house. This must be what Sprinz had referred to. Below it sat a man in a white plastic chair, smoking a cigarette. He stood up. “This is Asif’s father, Hussam, our deputy mayor,” Lana said as the tall man stubbed out his cigarette and shook Dov’s hand firmly. It was a big hand. Hussam was a big man. He said in good Hebrew, “Please come inside for coffee.”

Dov didn’t want to enter another Arab home and the banner was intimidating.

“I’ve drunk a lot of coffee already, so nothing thanks. And it’s cooler out here in the square. ”

Hussam stiffened but said to Lana, “I’ll bring out more chairs.”

“It would have been more polite to accept his hospitality,” Lana said quietly, looking up at the dead boy’s face on the banner.

Dov bridled, “Thanks for pointing that out,” then paused. “Sorry, I didn’t mean it to sound like that.” Another pause. “Look I wanted to tell you that…

Lana turned away from him, her emotions jumbled.

Dov looked at the banner, his thoughts and feelings in chaos.

"He was a good looking boy," Hussam said, returning with two chairs. Dov thanked him. Hussam's wife Leila emerged, carrying a tray with glasses of tea, not coffee. Her look said, I know who you are; I've nothing to fear from you; you can cause me no pain I haven't already felt. He muttered more thanks.

Hussam said, "Asif was shot to death in the olive grove near the junction at the bourj. Lana will tell you what she witnessed yes?"

Lana nodded.

"Bourj?" Asked Dov.

Hussam explained and Dov told him he'd already identified it, then he listened as Hussam gave his version of how his son was murdered. The surrounding homes were hushed, as if the neighbors were listening. The effect was chilling.

"I brought Asif up in the spirit of peace and brotherhood. It's what I told the Commission. During the Gulf War he drew pictures of rifles with flowers sticking out of their barrels. I kept his drawings."

Dov wanted to say how pointless.

Hussam said, "In an essay he wrote, he said that the people of both our nations, "especially youth", need to work for peace."

Dov asked, "What 'both nations'?"

Hussam said, "Why such a naive question?"

"Tell me anyway," Dov said, patronizingly.

Lana stood up. "Mr Chizzik, this isn't easy for Hussam and Leila and me. I won't listen to another Israeli put-down."

"Lana please. He asked about 'both nations'," he turned back to Dov. "Do you want an answer?"

Dov ignored that. "Wasn't the rabbi's tomb here damaged during the riots?"

"We stopped hotheads from setting tires alight at the tomb," Hussam asserted. "They inherited our disillusion with your always broken promises. Either they follow militants like Basil Khoury, before his shame, or the fundamentalists. We've struggled hard against both without any help from you. And then there are louder Israeli voices for Transfer, for simply sending us elsewhere. We won't be refugees again. But instead of helping us, you let the issues we have fall through the cracks."

"It's all our fault?"

"No. But to you we're the enemy when despite how you treat us, we still believe in a future with you.

"The Arab nation wants to destroy us." Dov said.

"Maybe the Arab street says that. But no one really thinks Israel can disappear."

"And what about the suicide bombing at the Passover celebration in Netanya?"

"That was terrorists. They don't want peace. We all condemned that attack. It's against Islam."

"You're always saying that."

"And you think we're all terrorists. If you're genuine about peace, start with us, make peace with us, let us be with you, and we'll become the best ambassadors you have."

Dov gave no response.

It was Saturday morning in the olive grove. Dov had stayed overnight with Rashid. It was close to midnight when Lana had walked him back. His VW was waiting for him. It had been valeted.

Lana had arrived just after seven. They'd breakfasted and then driven in convoy to the junction. She said, "Perhaps it would help if I told you what I saw." They were parked off the junction with the dirt road.

She wore no make-up, but to him she didn't need it. She had on a black t-shirt, a denim skirt and sneakers. He forced himself to focus on what she was saying.

She showed him the tree near which Hatem had been killed and the spot where Asif had been fatally shot. Dov kept his skepticism to himself. The blood on the ground had long soaked into the soil. She walked through the tall grass into her father's grove. "This is where my father and I were," she said.

"What made you choose that morning?" Dov the investigator asked.

"We were talking."

"Were you planning to join the riot?" he asked sharply.

She was riled. "It wasn't a riot, it was a demonstration. Anyway, my father and I weren't involved."

"You didn't know about it in advance?"

"Of course we'd heard talk, but we didn't join in."

"Why not?"

"My father doesn't believe in politics."

"What were you discussing?"

The air between them moved.

"Just answer my question."

"My father owns land. He's asked me to help manage it. Does that surprise you? All Arab women walk ten steps behind their men?"

The shift in the air happened again. They both blinked, Lana first.

"My uncle said it would be helpful for you to hear an eyewitness account of the murders."

"Helpful means I ask and you answer."

"I've told you."

"Why were you here?"

"I've already said."

"This isn't helpful."

"Isn't there going to be any give, from you?"

"What?"

"In the sense of give and take."

"This isn't that. I'm an investigator. I'm just doing my job. I came here to…"

What was that? Both felt something again.

"Why did you come here?"

"To do my job."

"I don't think so. You didn't come here to learn anything. Not details. Not the real story, not the truth. Arabs rioting, you said riot. You've already decided. But we were demonstrating."

"So you were in the riot."

"The 'we' as in my village, my friends. And it wasn't a riot."

"I need you to tell me…"

"What do you really want to know? Tell me and I'll tell you what my father and I talked about, before we saw a YAMAM officer and his men hunt down and kill two innocent young Palestinians right in front of us."

"How do you know they were YAMAM?"

"I know the officer and the uniform."

"You're certain it was a YAMAM officer?"

"No more give until you give."

"How do you know it was this tree?"

"Because I remember my father touching the blood there next to it. How could I forget that?"

Her hand reaches down to that place, her fingers touch the place where a young man's life-blood had begun to drain away.

His fingers meet hers.

The air trembles around them and it is as if the very ground beneath them shakes.

Their fingers pull back, just as they had at Rashid's. What was that in those eyes? Their eyes stare, each imagining how it might be between them.

Dov watched his rear-view mirror.

In it he saw Lana walking to her car. He drove up to the main road.

He waited. After a couple of minutes he drove back towards the village and on to Haifa, and the coast road.

Where's my professional detachment now? He asked himself, the Beetle behaving itself thanks to Rashid.

What on earth was that, back there under those trees?

It was what could have happened with Lana, the girl who had made his heart stop when she'd come for the interview at the university, Lana who kept giving him 'moments'. To be with her, to show her love. But not yet. She had been raped. Being with her as he had imagined it in the olive grove could only happen when she loved him in return and trusted him and trusted herself to be with him.

Meanwhile, crack the case, solve the problem, end the investigation? Nuts. There is no investigation. It's not what Gershon wants.

Right. No investigation then.

Absolutely.

Cherchez la femme?

Ya Allah! What was that? Lana asked herself. She'd turned back from her car and returned to that place, to the tree where only minutes ago…

It.

What was it?

Desire, yes?

You admit it?

Yes.

Love?

It cannot be.

An impulse? You just wanted it.

It?

Him.

Him?

I don't know.

You do.

No.

You want him.

NO. He's that policeman who…

Yes. From the moment you saw him.

Impossible.

No. I…

What happened just now in the olive grove?

I don't know.

And now?

I don't know.

Driving home, she wondered if what she had imagined in the grove counted as a memory overlay.

"So you're signing off on the report?" Steinman asked.

Dov had rehearsed this. "Pretty much. Hardly anything to add."

"Hardly? That implies there's something." As his annoyance began to boil, he wanted to yell, 'just say yes I'm signing off and we can all move on!'

"My car broke down and I didn't get a chance to finish my survey of the..." He was going to say crime scenes, but knew how Gershon would react.

"Perhaps you should have taken up my offer of a Ministry car."

Dov nodded, and then he remembered the Ministry's weapon. Three bullets missing? He'd have to tell the truth. Later.

Steinman saw Dov look at his watch and hissed, "Late for another meeting?"

"Sorry, no. There was a query about YAMAM."

"YAMAM?" Steinman snapped. "I do not recall any reference to YAMAM."

Dov felt the heat in Steinman's words. "No. It's just that one person said they saw a YAMAM unit. There may be someone else to corroborate that. I'd be a lot happier if I could eliminate them from this inquiry." And knew he'd gone too far. And didn't care.

"Eliminate them…? There is no inquiry! It's done. It's over. Sign it off. Now!"

"I don't think I can Gershon. It'll only take a couple of days, then I'll come back and sign off."

Steinman sat back. Why give him another moment's grace? He could live without Dov's signature. Gershon Steinman says it will be this way, and so it will. But he had put himself on the line with the Minister, who'd said it was a good idea using Dov. Everyone trusted Gershon and the Minister was a fan of Dov's, so why not? Because Gershon's credibility could be challenged, and then who knew what else? He decided on tough but fair.

"I've had enough. I've taken a big risk with you and it's backfiring. I needed the report today." He became conciliatory, "I wanted you because you're a professional. If you deem it necessary to see this other witness, OK. One condition. You give me your word that your review will be complete by this time next week."

Dov said. "You have my word".

Before he left the Ministry he called the kibbutz near the groves and rented a chalet.

Chapter 34

She stared at him.

He stared at her.

"Why are you here?" Lana asked. His answer could take her perilously close to her olive grove fantasy.

Looking at her, Dov thought she made the natural beauty of the olive grove look dull.

"I have more questions about what you witnessed," Dov said. "Did you give a full statement to the Commission?"

She had prayed he wouldn't ask. Neither she nor Ibrahim had given evidence. They were frightened that if they mentioned YAMAM they'd be putting their lives in danger. Telling Dov was not the same as standing in front of the Commission. And she admitted to herself that for no logical reason she trusted him.

"Haven't you read the witness statements?" she asked.

"My focus is the Police Investigations Department report," he said tightly, suddenly feeling warm. It wasn't the morning heat. "Access to the Commission's final draft is very limited. I've been given a shortened version." That was skating across the truth, he felt bad at doing it with her. To move on, he read her the sections on Asif's and Hatem's deaths, and the PID's conclusions.

Lana's lips tightened, her eyes closed, "Please read that again."

When he finished, she said, "Incredible. Why was Asif's arrest ordered? No reason is given. Why so little detail about Hatem's death?" The memory of Hatem with her under the trees flared and faded.

She opened her eyes. "They know the outcome don't they? With Hatem it's because they know his parents aren't available to challenge them."

He asked why.

She told him the village gossip version of what had happened to Sheikh Adwan and his wife, that they had been spirited away for their own safety one night and their house had been closed up by the authorities; she nearly said, "by you". Dov recalled the Sheikh's haughty tone when he'd met him those years ago with Gil Reiss.

"Asif was shot here in this grove and not by some stray bullet from the main road or the junction," Lana said, "I saw it."

Dov scanned the paragraphs and read, "…even if an autopsy was carried out, it could not be conclusive because if a bullet hit a bone and disintegrated, it could not be matched to a specific weapon." Wonderful what conjecture can do. He looked up at her.

She said coldly, "So they blind us with science, then they tell us that it can't prove anything. All this is to hide the real killers. Because those the report says chased Asif, were not the ones. I saw who did it."

Dov looked down at the dark red earth. Reading aloud the names of the dead, in the place where they'd died made them more human somehow.

"This is all a smokescreen. The polygraph tests? One refused to take the test?" Her incredulity made Dov flinch.

"It's a joke," she announced. "None of these men had anything to do with it, including the one who refused the test. This is all a smokescreen, isn't it? It's as if neither Hatem and Asif were murdered." She continued, "Hatem was shot in the head with a weapon that placed a red dot on his head, from only a few meters. Asif, was also shot in the head, but with a pistol, and…" Lana clenched her teeth at the truth so easily shredded and tossed away, exonerating everyone responsible.

"We're just objects, we Palestinians, the stings in your eyes and the thorns in your sides."

Every word she fired penetrated to the very Dov-core of him.

Why was she inflicting her pain on him? I love you, he cried out inside. "I don't know about Islam and autopsy," Dov said apologetically. "But bullet fragments can still be identified in a body and who knows what they might reveal." He said, "I want to see Hussam again." His eyes found hers, "and I must speak with your father."

"How many children," Lana asked, "do you have?"

"That's none of your…" then he sat back. It was irrational, but then so was his love for her, and he said, "two, Yair and Yael. He's nearly eight and she's nearly six. And I miss them so much. I have not been a good father to them or a husband to my wife or a friend to my friends."

Her eyes softened, and then he told her about how he had left them and lost Liora, Sara Moledet, everything.

"I…I don't know why I told you all that… I had to." He hadn't said sorry.

Lana tried to cope with his flood of words. She said, "I wanted to see if there was a human being behind those tough questions. Now, I don't know what to say. I'm a complete stranger, and you've told me things I'm not sure I needed to know."

He shook his head. “No, you’re not a complete stranger to me. Don’t you understand Lana? I know. You were one of Khoury’s victims.”

She stood up, her eyes desperate.

“No, Lana don’t do that, don’t go.”

“Who told you?” she demanded.

“You did.”

“I never said a…”

“No, but I was an investigator for a long time and I know people.”

She slumped back onto the earth. “You make me very frightened.”

“Why?”

“Because only two other people know what you know and I think I can trust them.”

His fingers softly stroked her forearm, trying to reassure her. His touch started her skin tingling and his too. “I love you,” he said.

She didn’t move his hand for timeless moments. Then she said, “Is this why you came back?”

Dov’s eyes told her yes.

And then she was running through the grove.

The stone building in the valley was as Lana had described it to him. He’d seen it from the settlement.

“Shalom,” Dov called out, “are you there, Sir?” He’d thought hard about his first words. Salaam would have been pretentious, but he hoped that using the Arabic for Sir wasn’t.

Lana had told Ibrahim it was important he meet this man again, the one who’d released him from the police station all those years before, and Ibrahim decided to put that out of his mind. He agreed to meet Dov, not because Lana had asked, but because he had to. This was not collaboration. It was trying to get justice for Hatem and Asif.

Neither mentioned their last meeting. They stood facing each other.

"I was in my olive grove with my daughter." Ibrahim began. His Hebrew was basic. "We saw three Jayish…army."

Dov nodded.

Ibrahim continued, working hard to find the words, filling in with gestures. What Dov got was: "Hatem they chased like an animal. He ran like a fox, but then the officer caught him. He spoke to him the way you do with a chicken whose neck you're about to ring, and then he let him run again. They shot him in his legs, one after the other. The officer put a red light on the boy's head and shot him with his rifle. They came after Asif, the one who had been in America. Once he was down the officer shot him in the head with his pistol." He glared at Dov. "What had they done wrong? Nothing."

Dov had observed intently as Ibrahim spoke, the coolness of his recollection. "Did you know the officer?"

Ibrahim just stared back.

Dov asked again. "Have you seen the officer before?"

The pause was long. Ibrahim thought, I don't want to lie. But I won't say where I saw this killer. If I lie, this man will know. I can tell by the way he watches me that he knows when people lie. "Once," he said.

"Where?"

"It was in the village."

"Why was he there?"

"I don't know." It was a sort of true answer, Ibrahim thought.

"Would you recognize him if you saw him again?"

"By the sound of his voice, by how he moves. Not by his face. He wore a black mask," then he asked, "why don't you write down what I tell you?" embarrassing Dov.

He said, “To use what you’ve told me, I’ll have to come back and take down a witness statement which you’ll have to sign. Would that be all right Sir?”

“If you come back. Perhaps.”

After the Israeli left, Ibrahim sat down and remembered Hatem’s funeral. Black security vehicles brought the grieving parents back to the square outside their abandoned house. Armed men stayed with them. Ibrahim saw Adwan’s silent agony and smelled the scattered sage leaves from the grave, believed to repel evil spirits, before Hatem’s shrouded body was lowered in. The whole village was there. Only the men were allowed to be at the cemetery just inside the village. The wailing of the women was a chorus of grief for the shrieks from Hatem’s mother, echoing from the square. The Imam at the graveside intoned, “Who are you? What is your faith?” the questions to the deceased the Angel of Death would ask. Ibrahim was the last in the line waiting to console Adwan. He embraced him, kissed his wan cheeks and whispered “my brother” as he recited the traditional words of condolence. Adwan held on to Ibrahim’s hand and then kissed it and touched his forehead with it.

The use of ‘Sir’ surprised Hussam, as Dov sat in the lounge. Leila heard it and her head lifted. Her scrutiny reminded Lana about the village gossip.

They’d arrived at Hussam’s house in their own cars.

“I know this is painful for you Sir,” Dov said after he’d assiduously sipped coffee, taken cake, complimented Leila on both, expressed his thanks.

Then he asked Hussam, “Where were you when the shooting happened?”

“I was standing on the dirt road, near the junction.”

“Had you been there long?”

"No, about ten minutes."

"Where was your son?"

"He was sitting a few meters back, off the dirt road under a tree, talking with some friends."

"How many meters from you, roughly?"

"About a hundred."

"Did you see him join in the demonstration?"

"No. He was there in solidarity, not to demonstrate. Many of his friends were there."

"Were they using sling shots? Throwing metal objects?"

"There were slingshots. The police had automatic weapons. "

"Asif didn't let the excitement of the moment get to him?"

"Young people get excited. But as I told you, he was against violence. If he could have taken everyone's anger away he would have."

"Could he have got into the front of the demonstration without you seeing him?"

"It's possible, through the trees just below the crash barrier, it was far enough away from me. But in the time between, when he was under the tree and when the men came after him, I don't think so. "

"You saw them?"

"Yes. I had this gut feeling about them. But it was all so fast. I couldn't stop them."

"So you couldn't actually see what happened."

"It was like watching one of those old flickering films, you know? The olive trees kept interrupting what I could see, Asif, running; three men in black chasing him; one hitting him in the back with a rifle; the trees got in the way the further they ran. Then a few moments later I heard a shot…Asif's life was ending."

“I’m sorry.” Dov said. He meant it. Terrible this, making a father revisit the murder of his son. “The PID version says your son was hiding in the olive groves.”

“He wasn’t hiding. He was under a tree near the dirt road.”

“… A police unit gave chase …”

“They weren’t regular police, they were Special Forces, YAMAM you call them, dressed in black and they rushed at him; he tried to escape. They scared him and he ran.”

“… At some stage the deceased was shot and mortally wounded.”

“That’s right.”

“… When it comes to the shooting and especially the identity of the shooter, this is incomplete.”

“Lana and Ibrahim saw who it was. I told the Commission of Inquiry what I saw. Why is it so different in that report?”

He looked straight at Hussam and said, “I can’t answer you.” Then he asked, “Did you tell the Commission about the YAMAM men?”

Hussam shook his head.

“Did you see Gil Reiss at all?”

“He was up in the bourj. He was controlling everything that went on that day. Relations with him had never been good and after Asif’s murder I never wanted to see him again. I shouted at him during the Commission of Inquiry. He told me to behave myself. How would he have reacted if it had been his son, and no one is blamed for his death?”

Dov waited as Hussam drank more coffee. After a long pause Dov re-read the paragraphs about the autopsy.

Hussam said quietly, “‘Out of respect for the dead?’ They showed him no respect in life and now they pretend they’ve discovered some for him in death? So much respect that they wanted to dig up his body and cut it up – for what?” He lowered his head to his hands.

Dov reached across and touched Hussam's shoulder.

His eyes opened to Dov's.

"Autopsy is not permitted in Islam, I'm told," Dov said.

"There are exceptions; needing to know the cause of death is one. A man killed my son, a man who believes we are nothing. But why dig up my son's remains to prove that that's what you think of us?"

And once more Dov had no answer, but he said, "Look if I can ever help, please let me know."

On the drive back to the kibbutz chalet, Dov remembered he hadn't given Hussam his cell number, and he decided not to. He'd been more sympathetic than he'd intended. He felt like a man who'd inadvertently seen an intimate moment in a stranger's life, a passionate kiss with his wife, or a letter in a drawer he couldn't stop himself reading. The gesture to Hussam felt hollow, merely a gesture, identical to his parting words to Ibrahim al Batuf, inconsistencies, no Dov, promises that you may never keep. It left a bitter taste.

After a light meal and a review of his notes, he watched television. He couldn't concentrate and got to sleep after a struggle.

The next day, Tuesday, at Misgav police station he interviewed officers who had been present the day of the demonstration.

They were predictably guarded and corroborated too perfectly what the PID report said. There was a nod-and-wink air to their replies.

Lana was on his mind and he called her. He listened to her voice and then to her breathing when he repeated, "I love you." She ended the call.

He went down to the grove and to the place where something had shifted all around him. He sat under the same tree thinking how Lana had looked, and stayed there until darkness began its swift advance over the treetops.

On Wednesday morning Lana woke him. He had had a tortured night, surreal snatches of forgotten people in his life, and at first the cellphone rang in a dream and he answered it so anxiously he was shouting into it and then he wasn't dreaming.

"It's Lana al Batuf,' she said.

All that came out of his mouth was "Aaaghh!" There was silence and then Lana giggled.

"Sorry. Hi," was the next thing he managed.

She said, "Please, don't call me again."

He ignored that.

"I need you …

"It was very embarrassing when you called. I was with my parents."

"…to meet me," he was struggling to think where. "You know the junction with the road to the kibbutz? There's that area with the trees that looks over the groves?"

"I can't."

"Look, for me it's like a bird's eye view of the crime scene. You can show me where everything happened."

Lana said nothing.

"Are you still there?"

"You said crime scene."

"Yes."

"You believe what happened were crimes?"

"Yes."

They stood at the bourj looking down over the groves. He showed her the positions of the various police units according to the report and asked her to recall where the YAMAM had first materialized. There was an aura of tension around her that Dov wanted to draw out, like sucking poison from a snakebite.

He kissed her.

The last time she had had a kiss like this was with Nabil, and she had initiated it. This was different. Did she want it? She didn't know. Did she enjoy it? The taste of him was like no other taste, with hints of coffee and orange, perhaps from his breakfast and there was something else. If sadness and longing and complete love had a taste, they were this. It was warm and tender and it was him, and with this kiss she discovered even more of him. And she found her tongue imitating his, wanting more, and as she did that she felt she was losing herself, everything was moving as her tongue searched further, and she was breathing quickly and so was he and then it wasn't their tongues but their bodies, tight together, beginning to carry them, with a momentum she had no control over, he was swelling and she was wet and …"Lah!" The word came from deep within, urgent. Her lips twisted away from his, leaving a damp trail across his cheek and she wriggled out of their embrace. "LAH!" she shouted.

"What did I do?" he pleaded. She shook her head. There were eyes watching her, she was sure. Perhaps it was the trees who had seen her here before.

"I'm being so careful Lana. I would never do anything you didn't want to do, you must know that. I love you."

"It's not right. Not here. If someone saw me with you…"

"Is that what you're so scared of?"

"I don't know you."

"You do, after that kiss..."

Her arms were crossed and she shook her head again. "You keep saying you love me. I don't understand." Her inner voice said that she didn't recognize herself saying such words

Dov could only smile. "I don't understand it either." He stopped but could not, did not, want to avoid saying what he thought. "Liora is the only woman I ever loved. When I fell for her, I gradually saw her differently to the way I'd seen her before, she emerged as a wonderful woman. With you," he gestured with both hands, "you were in the room, that day at the university, and again at Rashid's house, and that was it. You tell me why. It's irrational. You can't tell me can you? But what I can tell you is that I've thought about you every day since then."

She had no words, just the sudden desire for this to be, but not here, this want for him, irrational just as he had said. Dov rode no white horse. There was the power of his love for her, in his eyes, his touch, his kiss, moving her far beyond Tarab. She began to see him. He was a man, the way no other man had been to her. He was so… was it wrong with this man? And because she couldn't answer herself, she said sadly, "I'm sorry. I can't."

Chapter 35

No more “meet me”, no “I love you”, no “you scare me”. No. There is no future in this, nothing but running away, hiding from prying eyes and wagging tongues, impossible to walk together in love; if they banished Yunis I’d better pack my bags and go now if I let this, let him, that kiss...Where to go? I’ll talk to Yehudit, no that won’t work, she’s…she’s my best friend; I told her she was, so why not? Because of Yunis? Oh grow up Lana! New experiences, Liz had said? This isn’t just that. What is it? He’s… I’m…

It was late Thursday afternoon. She went to Mrs al-Taj.

Her teacher and mentor knew the minute she saw Lana that she needed her help. The diversity of worries parents and children had presented her over the years created a well of understanding. She had missed Lana. “Tell me what it’s about.”

Even in this oasis of trust, Lana wasn’t sure. The version of events she related excluded salient details, Basil Khoury, Dov’s name, which meant not telling the absolute truth. She was getting used to it.

“So my little Lana is in love,” she said, “and so you should be. I see it in your eyes. You’re very beautiful. I’ve been in love three times in my life. It’s hard to believe isn’t it? An old woman like me? What matters only is that the love you give to the man who loves you is true love."

The jagged edges of Lana's uncertainty began to smooth with these words. She had spent all night listing the possible warnings Mrs al-Taj might issue, but there were none.

"Who is this man?" The question scored at her momentary ease, and Mrs al-Taj added, "Is he single or married?"

The name Dov sounded strange in Arabic, and would be a give-away. She said, "He's single." Her heart surged remembering how sad he'd been, telling her; she wanted to comfort him and that was crazy. What comfort could she give him?

"Is he handsome?" His face came to her, those dark chocolate eyes and she smiled that she knew. She wanted to see him and the urgency of that need astonished her. She stood up quickly patting her pockets for her car keys.

"Ah," Mrs al-Taj clapped her hands, "he is." She spoke as Lana grabbed her bag. "Wait just a moment longer, and listen to me. Be careful. The village is very jealous of its children. That's what you wanted to escape. What is your truth? Is this it ? If it is, then go with it."

Would she say that if she knew it was Dov? Outside Mrs al-Taj's house, in the car, Lana called him.

She bowed to love's absurdity, choosing the olive grove and not the bourj, never there, being with Dov where she had witnessed murder, using that as the pretext, praying for a new memory to wipe out those others. She couldn't see how it would be, just that she wanted it to be.

Lana said, "I am obeying something that tells me I willingly want to be with you."

He said, "And I want to be with you."

He was terrified of hurting her, failing her.

He wanted to be gentle.

He couldn't stop her.

She didn't want to be stopped.

She was mad, silent, whirling.

Desperate. Hungry. Iridescent.

All that they imagined might happen after that first time when Dov's fingers met hers on the ground where blood had spilled and everything had shuddered, now took them over.

The vibration after their second ever kiss never seemed to end. The air trembled around them and it was as if the trees and the earth beneath shivered. Oh the need, the urgency for release, the blind demand to challenge, to share, to taste – tongues seeking and flicking, arms engulfing, fingers pulling, wrenching, tearing at clothes that impeded, to touch to feel to know – he her, she him, until they were absolutely together, bone to bone, skin on skin, he was inside her and she cried out and he cried out with her, first her against the tree, then she turned them, and pushed him gently down to the earth smiling and crying and sank slowly down on to him and started to thrust and he answered.

Finally they fell apart, their bodies weakened by the immensity of their collision, he drained, she sated, dizzy after the energy they'd expended, mute in amazement, glimpsing each other, breast and chest, dark tangled hair where he had been and she had engulfed him, he slowly growing limp as she watched fascinated, his love the new sensation she craved, to fill her void with his love.

They held each other as if letting go meant that what they had together would shatter, it was so fragile, precious, new. Dov craned forward to nuzzle the enticing nape of her neck, and Lana let her lips graze gently over his mouth, the taste of each other lingering.

Very slowly everything began to return, all the bits of the place they left came back, the red earth, the grey brown trunks, vehicles on the road, birds calling in the groves, the blue sky darkening as the first stars began to glitter.

"When we first touched, our fingers I mean, here in this place, what did you feel?" Lana asked.

"This," Dov said, with the wide boyish smile.

The next day, Friday, they decided, love already blinding them, to take the risk and meet in the afternoon at the chalet. First, Lana drove to Haifa as Dov combed the PID report again, anger beginning to replace conviction. What could he possibly do with the evidence Lana and Ibrahim had given him? It would not stand up in a court, but on the other hand he was obliged to report what they had told him. He guessed Gershon's reaction and didn't care. He had allowed himself to be used, but that was over and he knew what to do.

Lana was sitting at the kitchen table with wrapping paper and tape, packaging the gift she had bought Dov, when Khadija came in.

"Who's that for?" she asked. Her interrogatory tone made Lana look up.

"Oh just a friend," Lana said lightly.

"What did you get?"

"It's a book, one I read at university and I thought he … they'd like it."

Khadija sat down opposite Lana. "Who's this 'he'?" Her teeth bit her lower lip.

Lana stuck the last piece of tape on the package.

"It's for that policeman," Khadija insisted.

"It's an important story. It's about us."

"Let him buy his own books."

"It's one of theirs."

"Even more reason for him to get it himself."

"I thought I'd …"

"You thought what? That you know which books he should read?"

"Yes. Why not? All I want him to do is learn about us."

"Did you have to buy it? Couldn't you just have told him its name?"

"Look Mummy, I don't see what the fuss is about. I read this book at university and when we got talking..."

"Got talking? About what? Rashid's got you into this and I wish he hadn't. Now we've got this policeman asking about our murdered children. What for?"

"He's not like the other policemen, not like Reiss, the officer at the Misgav police station, who hates us all. He wants to know what really happened."

"They know what happened. They massacred our children and they'll never admit it or pay for it."

"He's different."

"What does that mean?"

"He's more understanding. I'm showing him…"

"Stop. Can't you see how many ways this is dangerous? Your father and you saw a dreadful thing. He should never have taken you to that grove."

"He didn't know what was going to happen."

"But it did happen. You saw a man kill two of our village sons. If that man knows you saw him, he'll come to find you."

"I've been very careful. I don't even know his name …"

"You've seen this policeman before."

Lana's heart skipped a beat. How did she know about the interrogation at the university?

"He questioned your father about his cave," her mother said and Lana's panic subsided.

"He said he'd come back to get your father's signature. He hasn't. The whole village is talking about you and him.

Don't talk to him again. Don't see him. Don't give him gifts. I'm telling you…"

"Why do you care what the village says?"

"Leila called me. She didn't like how the policeman looked at you, the way men do with pretty young women."

"Oh for God's sake! This is absurd. I'm just helping him to find the truth. They've written a report and it's so obviously wrong."

"Enough. You're putting us at risk. I don't want you anywhere near him. I won't tell you again."

"Why? What do you think? That I'm planning to sleep with him?"

Khadija's hand, the hand of a mother who had never raised it to any of her children was caught in the air by her daughter's hands. In that strange silence, their angry eyes searched each other's hearts and souls and found fear in one and hope in the other.

Lana said, "Mummy, I know about your father. Old Sergeant Tawfik told me."

She tried to hold on to Khadija, who slowly pulled her fingers away, leaving Lana's in the air, empty.

"It was long, long ago."

"It was murder."

"Think of the rivalry between Sheikh Adwan and your father. Sometimes nothing can stop it, until death finishes it. Adwan breathes the terrible truth each day that he outlives his son. If that isn't fate repaying him for his past, I don't know what is."

"And what about the boy who killed your father and those who sent him to do it? Are they being repaid? We need to know our truth."

"You're not a detective Lana."

"You encouraged me."

The silence followed Lana out to her car.

Chapter 36

The chalet door was open and Lana walked in.

There was another sudden shiver in the air, just like the first time.

"I have a present for you," she said after they kissed.

"Thank you. Can I look at it later?" He put the wrapped gift on the table. "Let's go back to the olive grove one last time."

"Why can't we stay here?" Lana asked.

"The light's going," Dov said. "I haven't finished examining the crime scenes."

"I don't care."

"I have to finish this Lana. It's still my job and…Ahh... yes..."

They showered together after they made love and dressed. Lana giggled as she watched him pull his underwear on. "You don't wear the silver...?"

Dov looked perplexed, shocked. "How did you…?"

Laughing she said, "I saw you on the beach in Tel Aviv. I just realized that was you!"

His embarrassment gave way to their laughter.

They walked through the trees over the knuckle hill.

Birds called warnings to each other as Lana and Dov crossed their territories. Their footfalls made occasional twigs snap.

They reached the road and crossed it separately to the bourj. “Could you see anyone up here?” He felt her momentary hesitation, enough to ask, “What is it Lana?” And as he had intuited that she had been a Khoury victim, he knew that this was the place. He pulled her to him and she resisted, saying, “let’s get down to the grove.”

When they were in the safety of the overhanging branches, she said, “There were police on the bourj searching the groves with binoculars.” Her cell rang. “Hello? Hello?” She looked at the display. It said YUNIS. She said “Yunis?” Then looked across at Dov. “My brother. Strange, there was just noise.” She listened again. Nothing. “He’ll call again, probably the usual poor reception.”

“Was this grass as tall as now?” Dov asked.

“It’s much taller.”

“Hussam said the demonstrators were closer to the junction and not spread out in the next grove.”

“We never went to see”.

He asked more questions and she told him everything she could. He stood and went through the grass line and Lana followed and showed him with her hands how high the grass had been on that day. They walked further into Ibrahim’s grove.

A vehicle could be heard on the dirt road. They ignored it.

Then there was movement across the grass line. A figure appeared, and then another.

“Hello little sister,” Yunis said. “What’s this?” He waved the still wrapped gift.

Lana looked up, and was shocked to see the man on the other side of the grass. The YAMAM officer.

“Where did you get that?” Dov demanded standing up.

“Stupid question. From your chalet.”

“What are you doing here?” Lana demanded.

"Tribal drums. Mother called. I called my friend here, he called communications-monitoring, then you answered my call and here we are."

Dov inspected Yunis carefully, and saw his likeness to Ibrahim. He sensed something feral about the other man, like a tiger staking out its optimal attack point.

Yunis tore the gift-wrap off the book. "Why this? There's nothing new in it."

"What are you doing here?" Lana disregarded Yunis' sarcasm.

Dov demanded, "Give me that book."

Yunis eyes locked with Dov's. He let the book drop to the ground. As Dov bent to retrieve it, Yunis turned to Lana. "Mother's desperate, so she turned to the gay son she'd disowned. I warned you to be careful. But this, you with this policeman, is so wrong. Can you imagine Daddy's reaction?"

Dov tried to predict the other man's next move.

Yunis continued, "Whatever's going on between you is a big problem. And if there's a child, well... but you'd know all about that wouldn't you, Super Dick?"

Dov glowered at him.

"What about you and him?" Lana pointed across the grass at the YAMAM man. "You love him don't you?

"That's not the same. In Tel Aviv we're accepted. No problem. The rules up here are different."

Then his eyes hardened, "How many times have you had her?"

Lana's hand went to her mouth.

Dov reached for the gun in his bag. It was rage. He wanted to fire at Yunis' face.

"Don't take it out Dov," the other man said impassively, pointing a large automatic at him, and Dov came back to reality.

Lana asked, "Is that the gun you shot Asif with?"

There was no answer. Yunis looked as if Dov had actually shot him.

Lana persevered, "where's the gun you used to shoot Hatem, the one that makes the red dot? I saw you, from here."

"I didn't check beyond this grass," the man said. "How stupid is that?" His voice betrayed exasperation, as if he'd come back from the supermarket with the wrong wine.

"Menachem?" Yunis tremulous.

Lana and Dov shared a look. Finally he has a name.

Yunis spoke trying to expel words and air without choking. "You killed Asif? And Hatem?"

Dov pulled his gun out and pointed it at Menachem.

Menachem said, "I love you Yunis," in the same flat tone as his warning to Dov.

Dov said, "I need to question you about two murders," Dov's gun indicated Menachem. "Menachem, put your weapon on the ground."

To Lana, "This is the YAMAM officer you saw here?"

"Yes." She was terrified.

"Have you seen him anywhere else?" Dov demanded.

"Once at the bus station in Tel Aviv, it was just a glimpse." She added, "and in the house of Sheikh Adwan when they were being taken elsewhere." Dov glanced at her. "I didn't tell you. I should have."

Menachem parted the grass and stood next to Yunis. "I warned that little shit Hatem. He'd recognized Yunis outside the club."

"Which club?" Dov asked.

"The ZarMinSum."

"I know it, and I've seen you both," Dov said. "You two do an act together?"

Yunis closed his eyes affirmatively. "I love you too

Menachem," he said, as if that would take them away from here. "You always helped me, whenever I asked, even with my father at Sheikh Adwan's, and now here. But..."

Dov appraised Menachem. He was tall, fair and with gashes for eyes, and long curling eyelashes.

"I love you Yunis." This time Menachem's words had a pleading note to them.

"You murderer," his lover stated.

"The boy in the t-shirt was on orders."

"Shoot to kill?" Dov said.

"So?"

"Why?"

"We know. They want justice. They want our country. It doesn't work, two peoples in this place. It's either them or us. No more. Either they stay here and die, or go." He pointed at Lana. "That book, Khirbet Khizeh? Crap. What did we do wrong? They were trucked away elsewhere in 1948. It wasn't like that for us. The Nazis mowed us down or gassed us."

"I didn't know what he did," Yunis implored Dov as if Menachem wasn't there. "Take him. Take Lana. You want her, have her. I swear no one will hear about you both from me."

"He's right," Menachem told Dov, "have Lana. She's who you really want. We'll leave. We just wanted to scare you and Lana off."

Dov said, "Don't lie."

Menachem exhaled. "OK. You'd asked about YAMAM. Very problematic. There can't be anything about YAMAM in your review." He waved dismissively at the grove. "And forget about all this."

Yunis rushed at Menachem, punching. Menachem let

him. Yunis yelled, “I’m one of them! Kill me like you killed them!” Menachem appeared to tap Yunis gently on the side of his head with his gun barrel. Yunis collapsed. Lana rushed to her brother, unconscious, bleeding onto the earth.

Dov raised his gun. Menachem slid his into his shoulder holster. “Steinman’ll know how to find you,” Dov said. Menachem snorted, “Yes, but will he bother?” and retreated through the grass line. Minutes later the black SUV sped down the dirt road, dust in its wake.

Chapter 37

The moon's reflection rippled on the sea, never still.

Watching it through the hotel window it comforted Lana.

The room had been her temporary shelter since she and Dov had left her father's olive grove.

After they got Yunis to the ER at the Rambam Hospital in Haifa, they found a shopping mall where Dov bought food and Lana a change of clothes, then went to a seaside hotel.

Dov said, "I'll get us a room." Lana looked shrunken and vulnerable. He was back in five minutes and walked ahead, gave the suite number to the security man and went on through the revolving doors.

"Where are you going?" the man asked Lana. She motioned towards Dov. "With him."

"ID," he demanded.

She produced it. A young Israeli couple entered with a smile from the man. He looked back at Lana's ID and asked, "Where are you from?"

She told him.

"What's your business here?"

"I told you. I'm with him, the man who just went in."

"Really? Which man?"

"The one who just went in."

"I have to check this." He was about to call another security staffer when Dov came back.

"Problem?" he asked.

"She says she's with you. I wasn't sure. I have to check her ID."

"It's an Israeli ID, and she's with me. OK?"

"If you say so."

"I do."

"All I'm doing is…"

"You're obstructing a citizen."

"Her ID says she's from one of their villages. There's been suicide bombings. We have to check."

Dov produced his Justice Ministry ID.

"Any more queries?"

"No."

Dov guided her into the shower of their suite, and then dried her and got into bed with her and held her gently. In the morning he made them breakfast. She washed and dressed and cleared away the breakfast things so he could work at the table.

She stood looking at the sea and then down at the beach where Nabil had kissed another Lana. She called the hospital. Yunis had discharged himself. The duty nurse said, "He insisted, though he has concussion."

Lana tried Yunis' cell. A voice message said the number was no longer in use. In the evening she walked along the front, trying not to think about anything. The murders and the revelations kept crowding in.

Dov finished his review and called Gershon who shouted, "Why aren't you here? You promised." Dov held the phone away from his head until Gershon paused for breath and said, "Sorry. Delayed with last minute issues. See you at eight tomorrow morning." He wanted Lana to read what he'd written but she refused. He insisted on reading the sections containing her evidence and her father's, which would be anonymous. Lana listened but made no comment.

A commuter train rumbled by behind the hotel, its horns suddenly in the room.

"Will Menachem be tried?"

"That depends on the Ministry and the Commission."

"Will you call him in for questioning?"

"It's my first recommendation."

"Who was that you called?"

"Gershon Steinman. He's sort of my boss."

"Menachem knew his name," she said. "Sort of?"

"Yes. It's only a short term assignment." Then Dov asked, "What did you and your father talk about that morning."

"It was wrapped up in a future that won't be."

"Why?"

"Because I love you."

He laughed. "You love me? Really, truly? You love me. She loves me. Lana. Loves. Me."

She grabbed him before he opened the door to shout it out. They reversed roles because she wanted to shout out, "I love Dov Chizzik," laughing and kissing, until ultimately they had to make love.

Afterwards, they talked.

"I can see me through your eyes," Dov said. "Scared, right? That's what we see in the mirror, when we're honest with ourselves, how scared we are that we might be victims again. We were everyone's victims for hundreds of years. It's someone else's turn, and that someone else is you."

Lana took his face in her hands and kissed him. "I had no idea you lived on such a precipice."

"Yes we do. It's always 'Them – Not Us.' 'They're against us.' 'They're Arabs.' 'They want to kill us'." Then he shook his head. “Those are things I’ve said.” He paused. “I’ve been saying I love you in Hebrew. How do you say I love you in Arabic?”

“Ba Hib Ik, that’s what you say to me, and I say Ba Hib Bak to you.”

They walked by the sea. When they came back, the security man didn’t even look up.

In the bedroom he repeated the Arabic words to her and they made love as if it was the first time.

***

“You never got it did you Dov? This isn’t a meritocracy, it’s a war zone, we’re at war and you fight for us in it.”

It was Monday morning. Dov’s review was on the desk in front of Steinman. He continued, “Success isn’t a key you’re given for each door you go through on the way to the top.”

“Gershon, I …” was all Dov could say. Steinman was withering.

“You thought you’d be virtuous? A public servant, something like that, hmmm? Well merit alone isn’t enough. Sorry. No. Not sorry. You’re a fool Dov. And you’re finished.”

He would convince the Minister that Dov had overstepped the limits in his review and to avoid embarrassing the Ministry, Gershon would terminate the agreement with Dov.

“First of all, your recommendation to open an investigation into the role played by the officer commanding local forces during the riots you looked into is ridiculous. Gil Reiss is a decorated officer with an unblemished record, unblemished Dov, not like yours. He did his duty in difficult circumstances and deserves praise for it. Secondly, you want to question a senior YAMAM officer about an alleged double murder, based on statements by two,” he searched for the appropriate word, “anonymous individuals, who can’t positively identify that officer, with one of whom you're intimately, and may I say stupidly involved. And I thought I'd be able to offer you the chance to come back. Forget it. All you had to do was what I told you. This is what your report is worth." Steinman reached down to a paper shredder by his desk, and shredded Dov's ten pages, one after the after.

Then he produced a copy of the original PID report and went to the last page. He tapped a blank signature space. "I'm submitting this as is. Sign and date it as the reviewer. It's legally true. You did review it. Here's your pension release form. You won't be getting the full scale, because you were suspended and now you're never going back to duty. Sign and date that as well."

Dov signed. Gershon sighed with satisfaction. "So, finally, your career is over." He waited for Dov to leave.

Dov said, "You invoked our friendship the first time we met at your home about this assignment. But that's meaningless to you Gershon. All that mattered was how good you looked and how I helped in the whitewash you really wanted from me. Even if I'd done what you wanted, I doubt you'd have got me back into the force."

Gershon, peeved that Dov wasn't more cowed said, "We'll never know will we?"

Dov went on. "You think you fool the Ministry with your knitted kippa and newly religious persona, as if you could buy your way into faith. They know you. Clever. Manipulative. But transparent. And they'll see right through you."

Chapter 38

Four months later the Commission of Inquiry published it's findings, and rejected the PID report. Among its recommendations were that Gil Reiss be suspended from duty indefinitely, pending an inquiry into his command of local forces during one demonstration in the October Incidents. The Police Investigations Department of the Justice Ministry needed a thorough reorganization, the Commission stated.

The day after publication, a Commission member, a Professor, gave a lecture at Tel Aviv University, excoriating the state of relations between Israel's Arab and Jewish citizens. His final remarks were about the PID. He said it was incredible that the PID's report had failed to recommend any police officers for trial. He added that the State Comptroller had condemned various aspects of the PID's work. "I believe that we need a new, efficient and credible Police Investigations Department." The applause was sustained. As the Professor left the dais he saw Dov, shook his hand and said, "Thanks for sending me your review."

The next day the Justice Minister fired Gershon Steinman. Rumors suggested a new PID report was being considered, but no date for submission was set.

Seven weeks later a TV news bulletin reported that a suicide bomber and a YAMAM officer were killed after a confrontation at a shopping mall, whose shoppers had been evacuated. The officer shot the bomber at close range as the bomb-belt was detonated. Yunis went to Menachem's funeral in south Tel Aviv, and after all the mourners had left, he went to the grave side and recited a prayer in Arabic.

The Justice Minister said, "Dov, your original review of the October Incidents was what we should have presented. We need you to help ensure PID will never produce another report a Commission rejects. Steinman said it couldn't be done. He's history. Ben Gurion once said, 'If an expert says it can't be done, get another expert.' You're it."

Dov laughed at the irony of getting Steinman's office as a senior PID investigator. But it meant working in Jerusalem.

The first tests of their relationship were about time together. They had snatched hours here and there. Dov couldn't very well turn up at Ibrahim's front door saying, "Hi Mr al Batuf, just come to make love with your daughter." Lana was uneasy about coming to Tel Aviv. So it was Saturdays at Yehudit's flat. But it wasn't enough. Often his workload meant Dov couldn't make it. Lana would text "Nu?" and get "Tonight" or "Tomorrow night" or "Can't".

Lana did an assessment of Ibrahim's land holdings, applying her conclusions to managing them, computerizing work schedules, crop yields, fertilizer and irrigation programs, market prices. The Jewish-Arab Center had accepted her PhD proposal investigating how her generation coped with the Nakba and as with her MA, she fought for time to work on it.

At odd moments, she smiled, thinking of Dov, their lovemaking, something he said, his smile. For Lana being in love was a revelation. This man loved and cared for her; he had helped her trust herself. She learned to trust him.

Then work spiraled and they couldn't meet for weeks. Lana told him she couldn't stand it another moment and he was feeling the same and said, "let's go abroad," and Lana said, "that's a big place," and he said, "I've never been to Florence."

Chapter 39

A couple walked across the Ponte Vecchio in Florence. It was a day of extraordinary warmth and clarity, for January. Every few minutes, the young woman skipped ahead like a little child to turn and photograph the man, older and as happy. She stopped to gaze at the jewelry stores on the bridge, beckoning to him to share her glee. The streets were empty of the summer throng, and the couple had to wait before a willing tourist photographed them, with the Arno River and the majestic Uffizi gallery behind them.

"Where are we going today?" Lana asked Dov.

He waved his arm across the view. "All Florence awaits you. You choose," he said.

They'd arrived separately late the night before and Lana argued with the desk clerk before settling into a better room with a balcony overlooking the river. Their excitement at being in a place they didn't know and that didn't know them, exploded with a new passion. When eventually Lana woke, she joined Dov to gaze at the famous bridge right opposite their window.

So they toured the Uffizi and whispered in agreement that there was too much of Jesus and the artists should have gotten over themselves, he was dead. The grandeur of the place enchanted them and she promised to imitate

Botticelli's Venus, back in their room. They got stiff necks from the sculptures on the Piazza della Signoria. Dov discovered that the original sculpture of David was at the Galleria dell'Accademia. There they were speechless at the youth's matchless perfection, taut and apprehensive before fighting Goliath.

After walking round the sculpture, Lana said, "Slingshots haven't changed much."

Dov said, "the sculptor is a genius, but he made a mistake."

"What?"

"David's big, but not circumcised," and Lana couldn't stop laughing.

In their hotel, Lana in Dov's arms traced his tendons, veins and muscles and said, "David looked so alive." She stood in her Venus pose before falling onto him. He asked her, "Do you always you keep your eyes open when you kiss me?"

"I try to."

"Why?"

"I love watching you."

They ate enormous Florentine steaks at the Latini restaurant, with the hams hanging from the ceiling. Lana was more amused than offended. The next day they went to the leather goods market and Dov bought her gloves, two handbags, a purse, a belt, and a bag for Yehudit. They ate ice cream and walked and talked and loved.

Sharing the same room for a whole week, they got used to his socks on the floor and her hair in the shower. Florence produced new experiences, whose weight, like an olive press, squeezed out the bitterness of the past. The last morning walking along the Arno, a tall African was selling bronze figurines and Lana bought Dov an elegant horse. "Every prince should have one," she told him.

"Why did you travel abroad?"
"Why did you travel to Florence?"
"Why did you travel alone?"
"How did you reach the hotel"
"Did you meet anybody in the hotel?"
"Do you know anybody in Florence?"
"Did anybody give you anything?"
"Where did you visit in Florence?"
"Did you visit anywhere else other than Florence?"

In the Ben Gurion airport interrogation room Lana was all alone. She wanted Dov to be there, but they'd traveled separately as they had on their outward journey. She took the train to Haifa and went to Yehudit's flat, where she felt miserable. Next morning she drove home.

Their love lived in Yehudit's flat, in Florence, in brief phone calls and voice and text messages. The pain of loving was exacerbated by being apart and wanting each other so much. As Ibrahim passed seventy, Lana undertook even more management, making it harder to stretch her daily schedule.

"You have to make up your mind Lana," Yehudit told her, during another Saturday evening without Dov. He was leading a major fraud case involving a police commander.

"He always wanted this, my father, giving myself to the land just as he has. Then there's my PhD and Dov." Lana said. "This isn't how I wanted it."

"I can't help you decide, but I have some news. My uncle's sold this house and I've got to vacate it in a month."

Where could she and Dov be together?

Driving home, Lana's head was filled with Dov, and what she'd learned from him. She enjoyed Mozart, the depths the music plumbed and the heights they soared. She loved Dov's jokes. The world meat shortage story was the latest.

A researcher goes to Moscow, New York and Tel Aviv to see the effect the shortage was having. In Moscow he asks, “Excuse me, how’s the meat shortage affecting you?” And is asked, “What’s meat?” “Excuse me”, he asks in New York, “what about the meat shortage?”, “What’s a shortage?” In Tel Aviv he asks, “Excuse me, but how’s the world meat shortage affecting you?” And he’s asked, “What’s Excuse me?”

Dov called next day. “I can’t do this. I have to see you. I’m on my way.”

She told him about Yehudit’s flat and they argued about where they could go that night. So they didn’t meet. A week passed and frustration mounted. A car park at ten after midnight was the best they could come up with, and afterwards they promised that however hungry they were for each other, they wouldn’t repeat that.

Chapter 40

"Have you been away again Lana? You look great." Yehudit and she were in the T-House. It was one of Lana's research days and she'd taken a break from the library.

"No, no," she said wistfully, "I'd love to go away with him again. It's been so crazy with work for Daddy. The PhD studies are a break in themselves."

"You haven't sorted out another place since the flat?"

"No. We neither of us seem to find time."

"Perhaps you don't want to." Yehudit was as candid as ever.

Lana smiled weakly, "He suggested we get a place together. He'd pay for it. A weekend apartment. But I couldn't think of anywhere that was close enough to drive to from home and wouldn't risk us being seen together."

"When was the last time you saw him?"

"A month ago." In a long pause, her lips narrowed and her chin came up.

She broke the silence whispering, "I've missed my period."

Yehudit almost leaped to her feet in delight. Lana shushed her, begging her to be quiet. "This is the first month?"

"No, it's the second month I've missed."

The pregnancy test kit Yehudit got her showed positive.

Next morning Lana went to her special place in the world. She sat there sure that this would be the very last time. All night after she'd done the test she'd gone over what to do. Reaching decisions at the dead of night when thinking was frenzied was never healthy, she knew. If she had been paranoid about her parents, her family, anybody from the village knowing about her and Dov and now about their child, another word for what she was that night had yet to be created. Being wise and in love, she understood, did not happen. Being in love, unmarried and pregnant had happened.

Sitting looking at the fields below, Lana knew she had to see Dov. He would be like Yehudit in the first moments, ecstatic. Then his protective and patriarchal nature would take over. He would insist on marrying her, even if it meant going abroad for a civil ceremony. They would find somewhere to live, somewhere in Tel Aviv, somewhere Israeli, she would have the baby, be his wife, have another child. She would join him, join Them. He was her prince, but he was not the man for whom she would cover her head.

There was no chance of bringing the baby up in the village, at home with Khadija and Ibrahim as doting grandparents.

She had to leave.

At last she admitted out loud, to herself, what she had been feeling with the knowledge of the baby inside her. "I don't love him as much as he loves me. I will bring up my child alone. When I'm ready, I'll tell Dov." It wasn't rational, but it felt right to her, to be the child's mother, to give it her identity. That this would have to be somewhere in Israel and not in the village or anywhere near the world she'd grown up in, presented it's own practical problems. She had the conviction that she would survive, and in this land of paradoxes, it was just possible.

After lunch, she told Khadija she was going to Nazareth to pick up some office supplies. She'd packed two bags with some essentials and locked them in her car trunk. She'd called Dov to tell him where she wanted to meet and drove and parked a few streets away from the bus stop she had picked. She couldn't worry about the fate of the car. Dov was reluctant about being so public, worried for both of them, but her tone and the brevity of the call made arguing impossible.

Three buses arrived and departed, collecting and depositing passengers. Then Dov was in the Beetle on the other side of the road. Lana could not cross to him, and stood with her bags next to her. A handful of passengers stood with her. Anguish welled up inside her that she'd be recognized, but it didn't show on her face. Another bus came and she willed all the passengers to climb on board and leave. They did. Except two.

She ignored Dov. Another bus drew up. The two passengers ascended. No one descended. The bus pulled away.

Dov did a U turn and stopped next to her and wound down the window. He leaned forward, frustrated as Lana began loudly giving him directions to the Nazareth District Court building.

"Get in," he insisted. "I'll bring your bags."

She pointed back up the road. "…Then you take a left and you're there. It's a big building. You can't miss it." Tears began and she swallowed before whispering. "I'll miss you." She raised a finger to stop him speaking, and then mustering all her self-control, she said, "After that, getting back to Jerusalem is easy. Follow the signs to Haifa and from there it's straightforward." He was shaking his head but she would not let him speak. She said, "I don't love you enough," and stood back, her hand going to her eyes as if shading them from the sun, quickly wiping away her tears. A horn sounded. A bus had drawn up behind Dov and he had to move the Beetle. Lana got on the bus. It hooted at Dov again.

He didn't move.

The bus pulled out and around him, the driver shouting. Lana watched from the rear window as the bus kept going. Dov was still there, long minutes after the bus and Lana had gone.

***

A year later Lana is in her office when the phone rings. It's Friday mid-morning. "Hello little sister from the hills. Meet me at the bus station?" It's Yunis.

He stands at the point where they'd happened on each other that day when Lana first came to Tel Aviv with Yehudit.

"How did you find me?" she asks as they walk to a café.

"It wasn't that hard."

"That's encouraging."

They sit. She hasn't seen him since leaving him at the ER. He looks ragged somehow. His eyes perplex her. They say 'where I've been you don't want to know, but I'm not going back'.

"I don't need to ask how you are. It's obvious. You're radiant."

"I enjoy what I do."

"It's more than that. Motherhood suits you."

She says, "You guessed."

"What else would make a woman glow like you?"

"You said he could have me."

Yunis murmurs. "You say stupid things when you're in love. You don't think. Neither did Menachem. Now he's dead."

Lana says nothing.

"So, you're a 'Tel Avivit,'" Yunis nods approvingly, "a Palestinian Israeli who's making it. You're not like others who've tried to do the same thing. No. Not my little sister. You found a niche."

"I live in Yaffa and work in Tel Aviv. It began at university, something I was told about shedding my victim's clothes. The Not For Profit I'm with combines everything I wanted to do. We're presenting Palestinian memories of the Nakba to a new generation of Israelis and we're learning how our generation deals with our past."

Yunis looks a little dubious.

"We're holding a Nakba commemoration at Tel Aviv University. Next week. It isn't just for Arab students. A Jewish law student told the press that it's a recognition of the pain and loss the governments caused people in this land."

"Is it being held anywhere near the hill that was once an Arab village and is now a university cafeteria?"

"What do you want Yunis? That Jewish student did my course at our center. Lots of his friends are coming. That's progress. You should come."

Her brother's cold little smile is progress too, she thinks.

Lana says, "I get my doctorate in a couple of months."

It's an invitation to her graduation. He isn't sure about accepting; he is sure their parents won't be there.

She says, "Older Israelis say I'm a liar. Some Palestinians call me traitor."

"Then there's me."

"What do you think?"

He stops and looks everywhere but at her.

"Come on Yunis," she implores him.

"You broke the link."

"No I didn't, I'm still who I am, I…"

"You're all the same you divas, never let anyone finish," his old smile flashes. "You broke my link with home," he says. "I know I wasn't always there. How could I have been? When I first left, you were a child. But I didn't really leave, until he banished me, and then you grew up, my only connection with them."

"But…"

"Let me finish. Yusef's never coming back. To what? To home? He's a Diaspora Palestinian, doing well, sending money. He doesn't despise his roots but doesn't boast about them either. He's in Daddy's will, but he won't bring the grandchildren for a visit to be spoiled, forget that. So it's me and you."

"You never said how much you relied on me."

"Yes. Now look what's happened. You left." He paused. "He won't have your name uttered. Mummy? She's so conflicted. She blames herself."

"And you think this is easy for me?"

"No, but…"

"I am the diva, so let me finish." Yunis opens his hands.

"To live here, fulfilled in my work, a mother, a Palestinian and an Israeli, I edit my day and I have to prepare the next thoroughly each night."

"Was I in your plan for today?" Yunis asks bitingly.

"No. But I always leave a gap, for contingencies."

"Oh, I'm one of those?"

"Everything is like that for me. Mummy and Daddy are edited out. And the 'little sister from the hills' is gone. But not my past, or my people's past.

"And him?"He meant Dov.

"Edited out," she said, with her Khadija face.

"Do you have that mental scratch?"

The question was so unexpected, but the reply was immediate. "No. I have Yakub my son. Any scratch I might have had, he wiped away."

Yunis nods, his eyes softening. "I hoped so. Yakub, good name." He takes a breath and says, "I'm going home."

"Going home…?"

And then she sees it, how so much has changed, but nothing has.

He smiles as he watches her.

"It's so simple," she says, comprehension in her eyes. "All he has to do is remove my name from the will and put yours in its place."

Yunis waits.

"Because it's all about the land."

Yunis' head rises once. "I knew, no matter what, you wouldn't forget that. He drummed it into us enough."

Lana says, "And it's all about the men; a male al Batuf must own the land. I was his glorified 'managing heir', and had my Yakub's father not been Dov, he would have inherited." She rubs her hands together as if washing away everything that had been.

"You're not the only one who edits life. There're always choices. He's made one. I'm not exactly the kind of man he had in mind for male heir. But he's ready to compromise."

"You're the best out of a bad bunch," she grins.

"Thanks."

Lana shrugs, "So all we're doing is reversing roles. I broke the link for you. You're going to be it for me."

"That's it. Think about it Lana. He's getting me back, but I won't father any children. It'll be up to me, when I come to write my will, to find a suitable male heir. But now I think what about appointing Yakub?"

Lana surprises them both with, "I think our father has made all the compromises he can. Khadija? Even for her..."

He squeezes her hand. It's a gesture of love. "The bus'll be leaving soon."

"Bus? You're going now?"

"When else?" he stands and is gone in the crowd.

***

Another year passes. Dov enjoys an evening meal at his favorite restaurant, Batia. It boasts the hottest freshest khrayin, hot horseradish sauce, for the best gefilte-fisch.

"What do you think of that?" Dov asks his guest, sitting back to observe the fissile effect of a forkful of khrayin on top of some warm minced fish, as Tawfik swallows, slowly reaches for the tall glass of borsht and sips and grins at Dov.

"Please don't take what I'm about to ask the wrong way. I'm not being racist," Dov says.

"You Dov, racist? Naïve maybe. Racist? Never," says Tawfik, "Not knowingly."

"It's just that you're so, ah, swarthy, I can't see if you're suffering or enjoying the khrayin."

"I was brought up on hot sauces Dov, chilli pepper sauces. I love them," he grins.

Towards the end of the meal, whilst they eat apple strudel and drink lemon tea, a man, a deformity bending him almost at a right angle, walks slowly into the restaurant. He goes from table to table, selling red roses. He is in his late seventies, with carefully combed silver hair and a pleading expression. "Have I been here before?" he asks. Dov replies, "It doesn't matter", buying a rose. Is it in memory of Love or Loss?

"Next week?" he asks Tawfik.

"Why not." They shake hands and Dov walks up to the promenade. He stops to watch the placid waters. A plane can be seen on its final approach, wing-lights flashing like distant lightening, reflected on the beach bound waters.

He'll put the rose in a thin glass vase on his bedside table, next to the bronze horse.

Shabbat morning. It's Dov's day with Yael and Yaniv. He takes them to the beach. He is jealous of Liora having their children six whole days of the week. They do the things children do at the seaside, even those at the age where they don't do them so eagerly. It's because it's Daddy's day, and they used to love being with him.

The music from the loudspeakers for the Israeli folk dancing aficionados is loud along the promenade. Though the dances are of mixed origins it's the old songs that get the most participants.

Sitting at the water's edge keeping an eye on his children as they wade and splash, Dov sees a familiar figure struggling towards him behind a large loping hound. The elegant Saluki intimately nuzzles Dov's hand. His master bends down to Dov and says breathlessly, "I have something for you. See you at the marina in an hour?" Dov says, "OK." He doesn't say that he works for PID in Jerusalem now. Good snitches are always valuable. The Saluki takes off, his master in tow. Dov watches them, then turns back to his children.

Lana on the promenade pushing Yakub in a baby buggy, passes the dancers. The child is restless. It's hot. Lana leans down, fans him, whispers to him. He drifts off. The dance music grates. The Israelis dance it as if they created it. They didn't; it's a very old Palestinian wedding dance, a debkeh. Lana knows it well.

She passes within a hundred meters of Dov and his children, without knowing it. She carries on walking, the children keep playing.

At the marina the Saluki's nose seeks Dov's hand for a nuzzle and Dov gives it as naturally as any trusted friend would. The beach snitch opens a pouch on his belt and hands him a visiting card. On one side there's tiny writing in English and the other is blank. Dov reads, and asks, "who gave this to you?" The snitch says, "some kid came up to me about half an hour before I found you, gave me a Ben Zvi and said to get that to you as soon as possible." Dov smiles at the slang for the one hundred-shekel note, he secretly misses street life, says "here's an Agnon" and hands him a fifty-shekel note. He gives the Saluki a farewell pat and begins walking slowly back to the beach. The card reads:

"What's in a name?
My first is a land that is mother's or home.
The second is a mountain all made of stone.
Who am I? And who is he?...
'Sorry' the last word should really be.
Sorry too about Mint Tea.
But it isn't. It's goodbye."

The following Saturday on the beach again, with Yaniv and Yael, Dov is wading through the lump of weekend news pulp. A center fold with a screaming red headline catches him, 'Porn Poisons Our Cities.' It is an exposé of the porn industry and provides lurid tales of sex for influence, money and drugs in high places, together with titillating photos that he knows as the litter of calling cards on the streets and in phone booths by the promenade hotels. The exposé suggests that the industry is drenched in the bloody violence of territorial crime wars, and amongst its victims is a former Estonian immigrant Sophia Gulkowitsch, aka Sara Moledet who ran the Lilac escort agency. Her body was found by a group of teenagers one night in scrubland near the coastal hi-way between Netanya and Hadera. She had been shot once in the back of the head, a source at the Abu Kabir forensic center confirms. This gives Dov his first clue. Moledet, he knows, means motherland or homeland. And Sara's death is linked to the disappearance of Nana Mint Tea. Sara must have known of her own imminent death, hence 'goodbye.'

An hour later, as his thoughts power up and down between the solution to Sara's ultimate clue and what he felt about her death and how he loved Lana, Dov's cell rings. At first he doesn't hear it, the surf, noises on the beach. But then he does and reaches for it. The display reads 'Private Number'. Dov answers. "Chizzik," he says.

"This is Hussam, from the village, Dov."

"I remember," Dov says and sees Asif's face on the banner.

"We're going to open a case."

"We?"

"All the parents."

"I see." He wants to ask, maybe you got my number from Lana?

"Will you help us?"

"Yes of course…what can I do?"

"I'll arrange for our lawyer to be in touch for your statement."

"Statement?… OK…"

"Your name's been passed on already."

"Passed on…?"

"Yes, to the court."

"What court?"

"The International Criminal Court in the Hague."

"What?"

AL-NEHIYAH – END - SOF

Turn the page
for a sneak peek
at the next riveting Chizzik Saga
featuring Dov Chizzik
"An Incomplete Silence"

And look out for the third in The Chizzik Sagas
"Just People"
soon to be available

AN INCOMPLETE SILENCE

Paul Usiskin

Chapter 1

Silence is never complete. There is always something to disturb it, a barking fox, a crying baby, a distant plane, a sudden thought.

Australian eucalyptus trees. A line of five. Ignored by everyday traffic. Old. Tall. Surreal in the blazing sun. Skeletal in the moonlit cool. Strange shadows of temporary refuge. To reach them, every footfall risks hidden traps of strewn rocks, alarms of parched twigs and scrub. But he knew how. Time was the secret. Meter by meter, testing the surface, avoiding a rhythm, adopting shapes he encountered, shallow breathing whenever he paused, the first trunk nearer now, beckoning to him.

They want to kill me, flared his thought, badly enough to make mistakes.

The night bus engine started, down at the turning point overlooking the Jerusalem forest.

Curled up by a rock, he heard the diesel motor and counted off the seconds to the moment he would rise, and make for the bus stop.

A woman in a car followed the bus, an ER nurse late for her shift. She lost patience and decided to overtake. She watched for oncoming headlights preparing to pass the bus at its next stop.

Night accentuated sound. He filtered out the oncoming bus and heard a breath to his right. Then a foot scuffed loose stones down there. They were meters away.

From a patch pocket he withdrew a red can. It didn't contain a soft drink. He yanked out the incendiary grenade's safety pin and in a silent liquid move, threw it in a high arc at the branches of the tree above the source of the exhalation. In the four or so seconds of fuse time, he pulled his hood over his face and began to throw himself in the opposite direction. The grenade ignited with a hiss and a sudden brighter-than-sunlight glare. Flames shot up the tree. It burned instantly. So did the dry grass and scrub at its base. So did the figure dancing in the intense conflagration.

His hood flew back as he burst from the wavering shadows to cross the road. The nurse saw his face, his eyes glancing at her, as he ran right in front of her. Another moment and she wouldn't have avoided contact. She didn't have time to hit her horn. She carried on up to the bend, swearing her shock out of her system, unable to see more in her rearview for the glare of bus headlights and the blaze.

Four hours later she saw the face again, part of it. He was in an intensive care unit and she rushed to assist when the crash cart alarm went, leaving the three smoke inhalation victims. The first jolt revived his heart.

Somehow, his eyes, still calm, were unscathed, as if a line had been drawn across his face, from his mouth to his forehead. The rest of him was severely burned. She told him, "You're very brave," and that everything was OK. She didn't know if he heard or understood. As she watched the monitor line showing a weak unsteady wave, he mouthed words. She bent to his lips. It sounded like 'camel' and 'Solomon', but very indistinct and then his heart stopped again. Further jolts didn't bring him back.

***

Reuven Aaronson a dumpy haggard police officer with a kippah on the back of his head showing he was religious, found the nurse in the crowded staff cafeteria at lunchtime. She offered him some of her chicken schnitzel. He said it was tasty and asked who supplied the hospital. She wanted to tell him to piss off, lunch breaks were precious and she enjoyed them best alone.

"I'll never forget his face," she told Aaronson, "I nearly hit him, but he wasn't distracted. That was so strange." The detective remained impassive. She shrugged, "I presumed he'd caught that bus."

Reuven said, "He was found at the bus shelter by the driver of the last bus, the one after the one you overtook. By then the fire trucks had put the fire out, but after it reached nearby houses and that Arab restaurant."

"It's been firebombed before, that place," she mused. "They said it was 'Doss' arson. They don't like Arabs.'

She used the slang word for orthodox Jews.

"What happened after he ran in front of me?" She asked.

"We don't know. We don't even know what his name is. We hope we'll learn more from the post mortem," he said, unable to guess how a man making for a bus stop ended up burned to death, escaping a fire on the other side of the road.

She told him what she'd thought the dead man had said. It made no sense to Reuven, but he scribbled it down, finished eating, thanked her and left.

Printed in Great Britain
by Amazon